VOLUME

SUZIE JOHNSON
LISA KARON RICHARDSON
DINA SLEIMAN
NIKI TURNER

*A*USTEN
~ *in* ~
AUSTIN

WhiteFire

SIMPLY LILA © 2016, Suzie Johnson
FULLY PERSUADED © 2016, Niki Turner
MANSFORD RANCH © 2016, Dina Sleiman
SENSE AND NONSENSE © 2016, Lisa Karon Richardson

Cover image of historical Austin, TX courtesy of AustinPostcard.com
Cover images from Shutterstock.com
Cover Design by Roseanna White Designs

WhiteFire Publishing
13607 Bedford Rd NE
Cumberland, MD 21502

ISBN for Austen in Austin, Volume 2:
        978-1-939023-79-7 (print)
        978-1-939023-80-3 (digital)

Table of Contents

SIMPLY LILA

SUZIE JOHNSON

To Zoey, the new light in my life

To Kirk and Geri for the wonderful gift

ACKNOWLEDGEMENTS

To Pamela Mynatt, thank you for your encouragement every step of the way. It means more than I can say. And thank you for being one of my first readers. I love you!

To Narelle Atkins and Heather Steiner, thank you for your friendship, your writing insight, and helpful critiques. I really appreciate you being with me every step of the way.

To my amazing and fabulous editors, Dina Sleiman, Wendy Chorot, Roseanna White. Thank you for everything you do to make my writing better. I love working with each you.

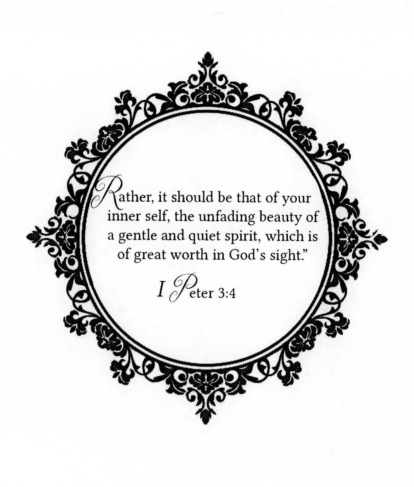

Rather, it should be that of your inner self, the unfading beauty of a gentle and quiet spirit, which is of great worth in God's sight."

I Peter 3:4

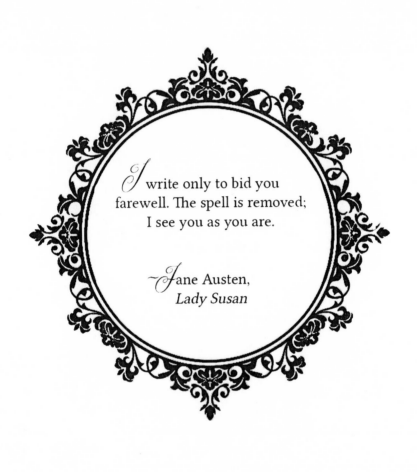

I write only to bid you farewell. The spell is removed; I see you as you are.

~*J*ane Austen,
Lady Susan

One

Austin, Texas 1893

Lila Wentworth watched as the two women sitting across the table from her absorbed the words she'd just spoken.

Rebecca Larson's green eyes seemed to flash behind her eyeglasses as she gasped.

Annie Ellis's hand wobbled as she placed her cup of tea on the round oak table in front of them. The matching saucer, painted with delicate pink flowers, clattered beneath it. A small bit of tea splashed over the brim and onto the saucer. Her soft brown eyes went wide and her mouth dropped open. "Oh no, please tell me she didn't?"

Wishing it didn't hurt so much, Lila confirmed the painful truth with a nod and a rough, choked whisper. "Yes. She really did."

"Oh my. Lila." Annie spoke in a gentle tone and reached across the table to squeeze Lila's hand.

The earnestness in Annie's expression was genuine and Lila's heart warmed, though she felt a slice of guilt over telling her friends about her troubles—especially Annie who was still dealing with the grief of losing her own mother. Besides being fellow teachers at the Jeanette C. Austen Academy for Young Ladies, Annie and Rebecca were also friends. Lila hadn't had many of those in her life.

"Listen to me, Lila. You are not ugly, far from it. And the right man is out there somewhere just waiting for you."

"Not if my mother is to be believed. She's also stated it in several letters to her cousin in Atlanta. I know because Penney, my mother's maid, showed them to me."

Annie's mouth fell open in disbelief. On the other side of the intricately carved oak table, Rebecca gave a cry of outrage. "I can't believe a mother would say such a thing to her own daughter."

"You clearly have not met *Lady* Sarah Wentworth." Lila pressed her lips together, annoyed by the disrespect that spilled from her mouth. As much as her mother couldn't be called *motherly*, she still didn't wish to speak poorly of her. Lila concentrated her gaze on the curved wall and rectangular window behind Rebecca. For a moment, the soft blue of the rosemary blossoms beyond the school's tea room lifted her spirits. This room with its round walls and narrow windows that looked out at the garden was something of a haven, and the three friends often met here at the end of the school day.

"I didn't know your mother was from England," Annie said.

"She's not." Lila sighed, tired of the story her mother oft repeated. "Her grandfather was from England, unable to inherit, so he came to America to seek his fortune. Mother is so in love with the tale, she fancies his fortune equates her with his family in England. Therefore, if her grandfather's brother was a British lord, her grandfather was an American lord. Thus, she *is* Lady Sarah, and I should strive to become Lady Lila."

"Lady Lila." Annie smothered a giggle with the back of her hand. "It doesn't even sound natural."

"You're right, it doesn't. It's quite the sore spot between Mother and me, along with the fact that I prefer to teach French at a girls' finishing school rather than spend my time seeking a rich husband." It had also been a source of contention between her parents before her father died, but Annie didn't need to know that. Lila wished she could forget it herself, but it did seem to be at the root of her mother's animosity.

"It's just like *Lady Susan*."

"Lady Susan?" Lila looked at Annie, then across the table at Rebecca. "Do we know her?"

Like Lila and Annie, Rebecca was an instructor at the girls' academy that had come to be known affectionately as Austen Abbey. The serious expression in Rebecca's green eyes was magnified in the lenses of her round eyeglasses. Just as Annie was a good friend, so was Rebecca. Lila knew she could keep a confidence.

"No. *Lady Susan* is the title of a book. The girls in my literature class are studying it. It was one of Jane Austen's first novels, but never published in her lifetime." Rebecca spooned a tiny bit of sugar into her tea, stirred it twice, and tapped the spoon against the delicate cup. "Actually, *Elinor and Marianne* was written around the same time and later revised and published with a new title. *Lady Susan*, on the other hand, was printed in her nephew's memoir many years after she died."

Rebecca pursed her lips and sipped at her tea. Lila feigned patience, when all she really wanted was to hear more about *Lady Susan*. How did an old Jane Austen novel compare to Lila and her mother?

Finally, Rebecca set the cup down and looked at Lila. "*Lady Susan* is not your average Austen novel. It's about a cruel woman who schemes to find her daughter a wealthy husband. The book is told in letter format with most of Lady Susan's letters filled with cutting remarks about her daughter, Frederica."

Lila released a breath filled with uncertainty. She didn't know why the story should rattle her so.

Rebecca added a second, rather generous spoon of sugar to her tea before speaking again. "Everything will be all right, Lila. Believe me. So forget your mother's words and put that beautiful smile back on your face. What she said was disgraceful and untrue, but I'm also sure she didn't mean it."

Though she didn't dispute Rebecca, Lila knew better.

"Rebecca's right. Just because she said it, Lila, doesn't mean it's true." Annie, the only one of the instructors at Austen Abbey who drank coffee, blew softly across the top of her cup. "Perhaps your mother said it because she's jealous."

"Either that, or she's frustrated that you're twenty-three and not yet married," Rebecca added.

"Rebecca!" Annie's eyes flashed with irritation at the teacher who never failed to speak her mind.

"Not that there's any shame in that," Rebecca rushed to say. "A lot of women our age—"

Annie raised her eyebrows and glared at Rebecca. Though she was often reluctant to admit it, Rebecca was much older than Annie and Lila. Tall, willowy, with fair skin and eyes that sparkled behind her glasses, she was too beautiful to not be married. Lila often wondered if men were put off by her outspoken nature.

"Okay, a lot of women *your* age are unmarr—" Rebecca broke off at the sound of a gentle cough directly behind Lila. A very *masculine* sounding cough, one discreetly intended for the women to notice someone else had entered the room. Eyes wide, Annie stared past Lila's shoulder while Rebecca's mouth gaped open.

Horror crashed through Lila at the thought of their conversation being overheard. After an uncomfortable silence, she shifted in her seat to face a tall man with hair the color of sand on a warm beach. His eyes, the green-gray of the ocean on a stormy day, reflected an empathy that told her he had most definitely heard. She couldn't help but wonder if he shared her mother's opinion.

Lila didn't want to know. "I—I need to go." She stood and pushed back her chair.

"Lila, wait," Annie called.

"Excuse me," she mumbled as she brushed past the man, fled the tea room, and headed for the school's front door.

When Lila finally slowed from an unladylike run to a brisk walk, she realized she wasn't far from the park. Out of breath and out of energy, she leaned back against one of the massive trees and slid down to the hard ground that was knotted with tree roots, bark, and other debris.

"You're useless. No one will ever want to marry you."

Lila could picture her mother in various poses uttering the hateful words. If only she could block them all out.

"You aren't pretty enough. You don't try hard enough."

"You shame me with your so-called career."

The situation bothered her more than she dare admit to Annie and Rebecca. But truthfully, the spoken words didn't hurt nearly as much as the written ones. She'd heard them over and over for years, but the fact that her mother wrote them down in a letter to a cousin....

That made it oh so much worse.

Palms pressed against her forehead, elbows on her knees, Lila squeezed her eyes shut. No need for anyone to notice her crying. If someone were to offer her help, she would undoubtedly fall apart—just like she wanted to do when the man showed up at the Abbey.

Who *was* he, anyway? And why was he at the school—*inside* their private tea room? Was he there to pick up one of the students? Most parents wouldn't normally enter the tea room. As a matter of fact, men rarely entered Austen Abbey. Besides, he certainly didn't appear old enough to have a daughter who attended the school.

Lila stood and brushed the dirt from the back of her skirt. It was so humiliating to have a stranger overhear the details of such a personal conversation. It had been difficult enough to tell Annie and Rebecca. But she'd been in need of comfort. Had she known someone else would overhear, she would never have said anything.

If only she could take back the words.

She could still see the man's eyes, soft with compassion—or maybe pity—at what he'd overheard. Those eyes would have taken Lila's breath away had she not been so upset. Annie, with her artistic eye for color, would probably appreciate their unique blend of gray and green. In fact, he very well could have been there for the pretty art teacher. Or Rebecca, for that matter.

Why hadn't that occurred to her before? Either woman might have a beau Lila didn't know about. She swallowed hard, surprised at how much the thought bothered her—which was plain silly.

Even if he wasn't Annie or Rebecca's beau, a man like that would never take a second look at Lila. She was a plain brown wren always hiding her head, where Annie was a beautiful green hummingbird flitting gracefully about. And Rebecca, in spite of the eyeglasses that made her look more like a teacher than any of the others at Austen Abbey, was a bright red cardinal comfortable in the things that made her different. Cardinals and hummingbirds received second glances, not common little wrens.

The far-off clanging of the trolley reminded Lila she should head back to the school. If she could get to the trolley stop in time, she could ride it back and speak to Mrs. Collins, the headmistress, before the woman sat down to supper. Lila usually went home each evening, but she couldn't face another night of her mother's ridicule and unhappiness. She would ask to stay in one of the guest rooms. Just for tonight. Although, what would change at home in just one night? Perhaps Mrs. Collins would allow her to room-in permanently.

Rushing down the street, Lila's heartbeat echoed the thrum of her shoes on the sidewalk. Not in response to exertion, but rather sadness and disbelief.

The trolley bell pealed again, this time sounding closer. Gathering her skirt in front of her so she wouldn't trip, Lila picked up her pace. Her left heel hit a pebble and her ankle wobbled unsteadily. Righting herself before she fell, she was relieved to see the crowd waiting near the trolley stop. She'd made it. Almost.

Just another few steps.

She barely missed tripping over the small brown and white dog that crossed her path. She didn't miss the boy running after the dog, however. He murmured an apology and kept running. Lila wobbled, then toppled.

Face first.

Directly onto the trolley track.

Women's gasps and men's shouts filled the air and, somewhere in the back of her mind, Lila wondered how fast the trolley could stop.

Somehow she managed to keep from hitting her face on the ground, but the palms of her hands weren't so fortunate. They hit hard and stung like they were scraped raw.

She scrambled to her feet and was about to glance at her hands when a low voice rumbled in her ear, startling her. "Here, let me help you." Strong hands grasped her elbows, pulling her away from the tracks.

"Thank you." Lila wiped her hands on her skirt and looked up. Directly into the very eyes she'd so recently been thinking about. Her heartbeat skittered to a halt along with her thoughts.

"Are you all right?" he asked. "Miss Wentworth?"

"F–fine." Lila nodded. He knew her name?

"Here, I've got you. Let's get you away from these tracks before you get hurt."

As if in response, a cacophony of high-pitched squeals pierced her ears as the trolley's brake-shoes rubbed against the wheels.

The trolley screeched to a halt, right where she'd fallen seconds earlier.

"Say, is she all right?" The driver leaned out his window and pushed his hat up from his forehead.

"She's a little shaken, but she'll be fine."

"Thank the good Lord above," the man said. He pulled out a blue cloth and rubbed it over his face while the trolley's passengers disembarked.

"I appreciate your help." Lila's voice quaked as she whispered her thanks.

"You're welcome, but I'm sure you would have been fine if I hadn't have been here. The driver made a perfect stop."

Lila attempted to smile, but her face wouldn't cooperate.

"Let's get you over to the medical clinic so they can make sure you don't have any serious injuries."

"No. I'm fine. Really." She looked down at the ruffled layers of her skirt. Hopefully Penney would be able to repair the tatted lace and lovely pink rosettes. "I just want to go home. I mean the school. I want to go back to the school."

He looked at her oddly, and then offered his arm. "I'll escort you."

Instead of taking it, she asked, "How did you know my name?"

"Miss Ellis told me. Or maybe it was Miss Larson." He shook his head and smiled. As he did, fine lines accented the corners of his eyes. "I know we weren't properly introduced at the academy. I'm Kirby Ross."

"Abbey," Lila said without thinking.

"Pleased to meet you, Abbey. But I thought your name was—" He shook his head. "Never mind."

In spite of the situation, she couldn't help but smile. "No. I meant the school. We call it the abbey, or Austen Abbey. The school's founder is rumored to have been a relative of Jane's."

"Jane?"

"Austen. The writer."

"Oh, yes. *That* Jane."

Lila wasn't convinced he really knew who she meant, so she did the gracious thing and reached for the arm he still offered and let him set the pace. Perhaps she'd be able to find out which of her two friends he'd come to call upon.

His arm was firm and muscular, and as they walked, she took the opportunity to sneak more than a brief look at him. He was taller than she, but not too tall. Like most men in Texas, his face was tanned by the sun—a golden tan, to match his hair. Unlike most of the men she knew, his eyes weren't hidden in the shadows of a Stetson. Instead, he wore a low-crowned bowler in a dark gray shade that matched his light-weight jacket.

Goodness, being escorted down the street by Mr. Kirby Ross. Her hand trembled on his arm. Had anything ever felt so right? Perhaps she no longer wanted to know which of her two friends he'd been there to call upon.

"You're a teacher at the abbey, is that correct?"

"Yes, Mr. Ross. I teach French."

One corner of his mouth tilted up, and the smile in his eyes was genuine. "It sounds like an interesting subject. Perhaps you can tell me more about it sometime."

Was he flirting with her? Or was he serious?

Lila didn't know what to say. If he meant it, he'd undoubtedly take it all back were he to ever meet her mother. A man as kind as Kirby didn't deserve to be exposed to the likes of Sarah Wentworth. Of course, it would never happen. She blinked rapidly to try dispelling her fanciful musings.

Much to her relief, they'd reached the lovely three-story building of gray stone of Austen Abbey. It had white balconies on each level, and an exquisite looking turret which housed the tea room on the bottom level. She turned to face him. "Well, good night, Mr. Ross. And thank you again."

"You're very welcome." He reached for both her hands, and she winced.

Walking with him, she'd almost forgotten how they stung. He turned her hands over and studied her scraped and bleeding palms, then drew his eyebrows together. "Are you certain you don't need the doctor?"

"Quite. I'll wash up and be perfectly fine tomorrow morning."

"Very well, then." He relaxed his face and slowly let go of her hands. Then he opened the door for her. "Good night, Miss Wentworth. Perhaps we'll meet again sometime."

Lila reluctantly stepped through the door, and just before it closed she heard a whisper. "She's wrong, you know."

Leaning against the door, Lila groaned. But her heart lifted at the same time. He truly had overheard. And yet he offered words of kindness.

She wasn't sure whether to be humiliated or happy.

For the moment, she chose happy.

Two

"It's just like *Lady Susan.*"

"Excuse me?" Kirby glanced at Mary Beth, who sat across from him at the restaurant inside the Driskill Hotel. Just because his sister roomed at the academy didn't mean they couldn't share a meal once in a while. Kirby looked forward to it after a long day of hammering out the logistics for Austin's new electric street lights.

"*Lady Susan.* It's a book by Jane Austen. We're actually reading it in my literature class right now." Mary Beth wiped the corner of her mouth with the fancy linen napkin, and her blue eyes practically danced with delight. A budding writer, his sister loved talking about anything to do with books and literature.

"Right. The mother is cruel to her daughter." For the second time that day, Kirby heard about the cold and unpleasant woman who spent considerable time attempting to marry her daughter off and snag her own rich husband along the way. His sister loved absolutely everything to do with Jane Austen and the stories she wrote. He should have made the immediate connection when Miss Wentworth's friend mentioned her name, but he'd been so struck by the sadness on her delicate face.

"Kirby, are you listening?"

Kirby smiled at his sister and half-listened as she continued with the tale of Lady Susan. He supposed finding this school where the founder herself had loved the author was a blessing from God. After the ice storm that took their parents' lives, he'd feared Mary Beth would never be happy again.

At least, she'd been happy before she overheard some of the girls talking about what happened with Miss Wentworth. In spite of his assurances that her teacher had not been hurt, a puzzled frown creased a deep furrow of worry between her eyes.

How had the girls even heard about it so soon? Had the young girl who'd directed him to the tea room overheard the same thing he'd heard about Miss Wentworth's mother and her unbelievable treatment of her daughter, and then gossiped about it?

He set his jaw, disliking the fact that someone was spreading tales about a woman who held so much pain in her heart.

"I'm just glad you were there to rescue her from the trolley."

Taking a deep breath, he tried to focus on her sister and their conversation. "It wasn't quite like that, Mary Beth. She was already getting to her feet, and the trolley was still several yards away."

"Still, I'm glad you were there for her." She said it like she didn't believe him.

Ah, the ideal romanticism of youth. Mary Beth would try to make this into something it wasn't. Becoming an instant guardian to a young girl had its difficult moments, and Kirby often found himself at a loss as to what he should do or say. His sister had such stars in her eyes right now he didn't have the heart to tell her that even if her teacher happened to be seeking a courtship, he was not.

"She's so sweet and kind to all of her students." Mary Beth sighed in a long, dramatic manner. "I wish there was a way to make her happy."

Kirby put down his soup spoon and gave his sister a measured glance. "Does she seem sad often?"

"Yes. I mean, she smiles all the time. And it's genuine. She's not just smiling because she's at school and feels obligated. I've seen her when she's alone at her desk or talking with the other teachers. She's always smiling. But there's something in her eyes that tells me she doesn't have a very happy life. I'm not sure how else to explain it."

"I think you've explained it very well, Mary Beth. I think your ability to see beyond the smile is a gift from God." Kirby reached across the table and squeezed his sister's hand.

"Really, you think so? Do you think Mama would be proud of me?"

The innocent question tugged at his heart strings. Kirby tried to be mother, father, and brother to Mary Beth. But he worried she wasn't getting what she truly needed. "I know she would."

Mary Beth's smile lit up the room, and Kirby would give anything he owned to see her smile like this for the rest of her life.

"Now tell me about this latest school project of yours."

As his sister talked, Kirby marveled at the change that had come over her since he'd enrolled her in the girls' school. She seemed almost happy—at least a good deal more so than she had in Indiana. At the very least, her grief over the loss of their parents didn't seem to hinder her as much here as it had before. In Indiana she'd withdrawn from all of her friends and had barely even spoken to him. Though he'd been uncertain about the move when his company first made the offer, he was glad he'd agreed to manage the project here in Austin.

After they finished their meal, Kirby walked his sister back to the Abbey then made his way back to the hotel. As he let himself into his room, he thought about Mary Beth's literature project and her plan to write an alternate ending for *Lady Susan*—a happy ending for Lady Susan's daughter. Not only was it brilliant, it spoke of Mary Beth's tender heart. It also made him wonder about Miss Wentworth.

He'd been so caught up in listening to her, he'd almost forgotten the reason he'd stopped in to see the petite, dark-haired French teacher. He'd have to go back and see her. And now he had an excuse to stop back by and talk to her that didn't involve anything school related. After all, a gentleman would call the next day to make sure she hadn't suffered any ill effects from her fall.

For the first time in a long time, Kirby found himself looking forward to the following day.

For the second day in a row, Kirby found himself escorted into the entryway of the Jeanette C. Austen Academy for Young Ladies by one of the students. Much like the girl had yesterday, this girl also pointed him to the room where he'd made his egregious error yesterday.

This time, Kirby knew better than to enter uninvited. He stood in the doorway observing for a moment. He studied the room but didn't see Miss Wentworth among the women who were seated around the oak table sipping tea from tiny flowered cups while they chatted. The cups matched a large flowered pot that he assumed held tea.

The walls of the room were a beautiful work of architecture. They curved gently around the room, with one large window facing the street and a smaller one facing a garden. Obviously designed to appeal to women, the walls were adorned with delicate tapestries depicting ballet dancers in various poses. The effect was such that the pictures appeared to be artfully painted onto the tapestries.

He shook his head to free it of distractions and reminded himself he was here to see Miss Wentworth.

But Miss Wentworth wasn't there.

Surprised at his disappointment, he started to turn away. But stopped and chided himself for his selfishness. He didn't want to disturb these women, but he hadn't come here for himself. It didn't matter if Miss Wentworth wasn't taking tea. He still needed to ask after her. Perhaps the girl who'd let him in would be able to check on her for him. He needed to assure himself that her scraped hands were better today and that she hadn't discovered any other injuries.

What if she had? What then? What if these ladies told him she wasn't here because she was injured?

He would, of course, offer his assistance. And he'd extend an offer to her that when she was better, he would like her company on a stroll through the park. He still wasn't interested in courtship, but he wanted to show her that her mother was wrong. Very wrong.

Just as he was about to turn and look for the girl who'd let him in, a tall woman with red hair and eyeglasses waved her hand at him and walked over to the door.

"May I help you?"

"Yes. Thank you. I'm Kirby Ross. I'd like to speak with Miss Wentworth, please. That is, if she's available."

The woman looked at him so long the moment grew awkward. Kirby had the feeling she already knew his name. As he matched her stare, he realized she'd been at the table when he'd overheard Lila's conversation with her friends. Finally, she nodded.

"I'll be right back."

She walked over to another woman and said something to her. While they were engaged in their conversation, Kirby grew uncomfortable. It didn't take a genius to know they were discussing him. But why? What was so difficult about saying Miss Wentworth was or wasn't available?

Dare he explore the school himself?

He thought again of the girl who'd let him in. But he didn't want to give the impression of being impatient. That wouldn't help his cause at all. Especially if he was being appraised. Which, if the looks of that conversation meant anything, he was.

Didn't they realize he could see them?

Finally, the two women shared a glance and gave each other a slight nod. They'd apparently come to some sort of understanding. The woman with red hair came back to the door.

"I'm sorry, Mr. Ross. But Miss Wentworth isn't able to receive visitors today."

"Visitors? Or just me?" He tried not to show his irritation at the blatant lie.

"Visitors," the woman said firmly.

Had she told her friends to tell him that, anticipating he'd come by to inquire about her? Or had they taken it upon themselves to give him that answer?

Kirby bit his lip. "Well then, will you give her a message and let her know Kirby Ross stopped by to check on her?"

Only then did the woman grant him a smile, although it didn't really seem sincere. "I'll tell her."

He started to ask if Miss Wentworth was doing well after her fall, but the woman turned before he could ask her.

Frustrated, Kirby left. But he wouldn't let it end here. He'd talk to Miss Wentworth one way or another. And after he was certain she was well, he still needed to discuss his initial reason for coming here yesterday—the French class she taught, and the influence she had on his sister.

The only other thing that fascinated his sister more than books was France. She talked non-stop about how her teacher studied there. And now Mary Beth wanted to study there. For a year, she said, or maybe two.

But what she didn't understand was Kirby could barely afford to keep her enrolled at the girl's academy. He definitely couldn't afford to send her to a school in France. His sister had already experienced the loss of her parents. She'd been uprooted from her friends so Kirby could come to Austin and work on the moonlight tower project. He couldn't bear for his sister to have one more disappointment.

Miss Wentworth needed to stop filling Mary Beth's head with ideas. She needed to stop talking about the years she spent in France. But now that Kirby had semi made the acquaintance of the lovely teacher, now that he'd witnessed the hurt she'd experienced, could he really bring himself to have a stern conversation with her? He didn't think he could.

But for his sister's sake, he must.

Three

Still disturbed by her mother's letter and all it entailed, Lila decided to take her mid-morning tea out in the garden instead of sitting in the tea room with all the teachers who were chatting about their morning classes.

Meeting there during the mid-morning and mid-afternoon breaks was something they did each day. And oftentimes Lila met her friends there at the end of the school day. But she felt awkward today, as if she didn't belong.

Though Lila's situation with her mother had been difficult to explain, Mrs. Collins had been kind and understanding. There was a bedroom in the teacher's quarters that wasn't occupied. The headmistress was more than happy to have Lila use it. She'd even summoned the school's driver and accompanied Lila to get her belongings.

Her mother was most unhappy to have Lila move out, but she didn't throw any insults at her with Mrs. Collins standing by. Perhaps there was someone on this earth who intimidated her mother. Instead, she sweetly begged Lila to agree to dine with her on a regular basis. But the ugly words in her mother's letter came flooding back the instant they drove away from the house, and Lila immediately regretted the agreement.

Was her mother right? Was she too stupid for anyone to love? Too ugly? She'd studied her face in the mirror this morning, trying to see what her mother saw, but all she could see was hurt pooling in her eyes.

Suddenly cold despite the warmth of the sun overhead, she cradled the warm cup in her hands. Not wanting to think on it any further, she sat down on a bench among the jasmine and wisteria and breathed in their sweet perfume.

Just as she took her first sip of Earl Grey, Annie and Rebecca stepped outside. As they drew near, Annie's brown eyes practically gleamed.

"May we join you?"

"Of course." Lila scooted to one end, making room for her two friends.

Annie turned to face her, smile wide, and Lila was even more positive about that gleam.

"What are you two up to?"

Annie shrugged, but her smile didn't fade.

"He came back," Rebecca said.

"Who came back?"

"Mr. Tall, Handsome, and Blond." Rebecca's voice held a dreamy quality Lila didn't think she'd ever heard, and instantly knew who she meant.

"The man from yesterday? Kirby Ross?"

Rebecca nodded.

Lila's hand trembled and her tea sloshed toward the brim of the cup. "Not to see me?" Panic rose in her throat. What could he possibly want?

Annie nodded.

"He did ask for you," Rebecca squealed in a somewhat dramatic fashion. "He was here to check on you. Falling in front of the trolley was a brilliant move on your part."

"Rebecca, you make it sound like she did it on purpose." Annie's tone was indignant. Then her voice softened as she turned back to Lila. "We told him you couldn't see him just then."

Rebecca pulled on Annie's arm so she could see Lila. "Actually, I told him you didn't want to see him."

"What?" Lila's heart pounded. She probably wouldn't have seen him had she been available, but to be so blunt? No. Rudeness wasn't a behavior she practiced. "Why would you do that?"

"To build the anticipation, of course. If you're not available, it will only increase his desire to see you."

Shocked, Lila could only stare at her two friends.

"He did say to tell you he'd inquired after you. I'm sure he means to come back," Annie said.

"Oh." A strange feeling rose in her chest. Half dread and half something else. Fear at what to say to him, or eagerness to see him again? Both, or neither? He'd witnessed her shame. He knew what her mother thought about her and saw how it sliced her heart. She wasn't sure she could look him in the eye.

It still plagued her when she bid her friends good-bye and headed back to her classroom.

Lila was sitting at her desk when Mary Beth swept into the room, and a thought struck her. Could it be possible she was related to Kirby Ross? Lila bit her tongue to refrain from asking. The last name could be a coincidence. But she didn't believe that and found herself studying the young teen from time to time, imagining she could see a resemblance between her and Mr. Ross.

The distraction cost her when she mangled a few French phrases. But it elicited some good-natured laughs from her class, and she couldn't help but join in.

"Apparently I taught you ladies well." She looked at the girls and smiled before starting the next phrase. Before she could, a young girl named Franny poked her head inside the classroom door.

"Excuse me, *Mademoiselle* Wentworth." Franny was one of Lila's students and kept with the ambiance of the classroom.

"Franny. *Bonjour. Qu'est-ce que c'est?*" The young girl was usually in this class, but today she was helping Mrs. Collins with office duties. The headmistress often engaged assistance from the girls on the pretense of needing help. But it was really so they could see how an office was run.

"Oh, no, nothing is wrong." Franny held out an envelope. "*Madame* Collins sent me to deliver this to you."

When Lila reached for it she was overwhelmed by the all too familiar scent of perfume that wafted from it.

Her mother.

Dread instantly filled her, but she took the envelope from Franny. "*Merci beaucoup*, Franny."

The girl beamed and waved to the other girls before she turned and went back down the hall.

Lila dropped the envelope into the pocket of her skirt. She waited until class was over and the last student trickled out the door. Then she took her seat behind her desk and slowly opened the envelope, chiding herself for being so afraid. But once she opened it, her fear was validated.

"Your presence is requested for dinner this evening. Wear your newest Worth."

Not ready to face her mother so soon after moving out, she groaned. Her heart still hurt over the hateful letter to her cousin. And really, *hurt* was too mild a word. Her heart didn't just hurt. It ached.

Now she was supposed to summon a cheerful demeanor whether sincere or not, dress in a pretty gown, and smile her way through a meal with her mother as if nothing had happened? Then there was the fact that her mother requested—no, ordered—her to wear her newest Worth gown. Was there a hidden motive?

Lila almost laughed out loud.

Why bother questioning it? She already knew the answer.

"You don't have to go," Annie said a few hours later.

"Of course I do. But I..." Lila felt defeated. Her friends were sweet in their defense of her, but they didn't understand. And truthfully, she didn't either.

"Yes?" Annie raised one eyebrow as if challenging her.

"It was hard enough to tell her I was moving out of the house and into a room here. I can't refuse dinner with her, too."

Rebecca studied her for a moment, which made her uncomfortable. "Perhaps it's time you should, Lila."

Lila blinked. "Say no to my mother?"

Her two friends shared a look, then said in unison, "Yes."

"But I..." She pictured a scene with her mother hurling insults and hatred at her in a shrill voice. She simply couldn't.

"But what?" Rebecca's tone was challenging. "No one's ever said no to your mother before? Or are you afraid she won't love you anymore?"

Lila almost laughed at that, but she was too embarrassed to answer.

"Lila." Annie put a gentle hand on her arm. "I know she treats you otherwise, but I can guarantee you, she'll still love you even if you say no."

But Lila wasn't so sure.

"She's jealous of you," Rebecca said.

That gave Lila pause. There was a new chill in her mother's behavior, the depth of which she'd never seen. She'd always been standoffish and had never put Lila or her father first. Perhaps there was some truth to what Rebecca said. At times it did almost seem as if they were in competition. But she didn't want to think it, let alone say it out loud. Especially not to Rebecca.

"I don't know that I'd say that." Lila noticed both of her friends staring at her. "What? She's beautiful. There's absolutely *nothing* for her to be jealous of."

"Lila, you are so smart, but so naïve."

Annie and Lila shared a look.

Where was Rebecca going with this?

Lila wasn't comfortable with this conversation. "I don't want to gossip." She swallowed hard. "Especially about my mother. It doesn't feel right."

"But Lila," Rebecca protested. "It's not gossiping. We're trying to help solve your problem."

"I'd rather not."

This time it was Rebecca and Annie who shared a look.

"You mean you'd rather your mother degrade you?"

"No, of course not. But I don't want to sit here and ascribe motives to her that may not be true."

"*May* not?" Rebecca clapped her hands together. "You're beginning to believe me?"

"I don't know, Rebecca. You can't take something I've believed my entire life and expect me to believe something totally different in a matter of a few seconds."

"You're right. I can't. But will you consider this? Perhaps she's desperate to keep her home, Swan Castle or Swan Manor or whatever she calls it, and thinks if she can steal your prospects she'll be able to find someone who can support her."

"It's Swan House." Lila flushed as she said it but neither woman appeared to hear her. Swan House was the pretentious name her mother had given the large Victorian house she'd purchased when she'd had to sell the even larger stone mansion she'd called Wentworth Castle which, of course, wasn't a castle but a large manor on a sprawling estate.

Across from her, Annie was nodding as if she agreed with Rebecca about her mother. But Lila didn't. "You think my mother, who was married to my father for twenty-six years and took care of him while he was dying, is a gold digger?"

"She was always upset with your father for sending you to France to study."

Lila shook her head. "You ladies are dear friends, and I know you're trying to make me feel better about myself. And I appreciate it more than words can say. But I'd rather not speculate anymore. I need to get ready for my dinner."

"Lila, we're sorry," Annie said.

"I know you are. Thank you." She gave them a smile that felt weak and pitiful. She hoped it wasn't. She wanted them to know she was sincere and appreciated their friendship. "Now if you'll excuse me, I need to get dressed."

Rebecca pursed her lips. "You're still going?"

"I have no choice."

She walked away, not feeling any better. It warmed her that her friends cared so much. But at the same time, she was still the same pathetic woman her mother was desperately trying to marry off.

As she left the room, she heard Annie mutter, "Yes, you do have a choice."

Four

Even as she dressed for dinner, Lila regretted the conversation with her friends. Annie had enough to worry about, trying to keep her family from losing their ranch while seeking refuge from all the anxiety. And Rebecca, well, she was sweet and tried to understand. But Lila wasn't sure her friends knew what it was like to feel hideous and devoid of a mother's love.

When she arrived in the foyer, she was surprised to see Annie again.

"Annie, hi." Lila drew her friend into a quick hug and, when she glanced through the window over Annie's shoulder, noticed her mother's carriage just pulling up in the drive.

Annie stepped back and gave Lila an appraising look. "My goodness, Lila. Look at you."

Lila felt overdressed and silly in the fancy pink gown of silk and lace. "One must look one's best to dine at Swan House. I can't believe she requested I dress in this." Lila smoothed her hands over the cool silk skirt of her gown. "Listen, Annie, I want to apologize for complaining to you when you have your own problems to deal with."

Annie waved her hand through the air. "Nonsense. You weren't complaining. Besides, you're always there for me when I need it."

Lila reached out and squeezed her friend's hand. "I didn't really want to talk about this in front of Rebecca, even though I'm sure she knows. Goodness, everyone in Austin must know. I'm sure it's a set-up. She'll have someone she wants me to meet, but then she'll pull her usual sabotage by doing what she does best." Lila bit her lip and looked away, too ashamed to look at Annie even though Annie knew the details of her mother's behavior when there were guests.

Everyone knew.

And that's what made it so bad.

Criticizing Lila in letters to her cousins was the least of the horrible things her mother did on a regular basis.

Inviting men to dine under the guise of meeting and hopefully making a match with her daughter was perhaps the worst thing *Lady* Sarah did. Because the *match* wasn't really for Lila. The gentleman was really invited for her mother's entertainment. And a sick entertainment it was.

Her mother would start by flirting, then by fawning, then by drawing physically close to the unsuspecting dinner guest. It wouldn't be long before Lila would flee the house in mortification. She shuddered to think of what went on once she left the house, but she heard the gossip on a regular basis. So did everyone at the school. Annie and Rebecca were just too kind to mention it to her face.

Because her mother didn't limit her behavior to the house, speculation abounded in the Wentworth's social circle. If her father had been alive, he'd be so ashamed.

She tried to think back and recall if her mother had behaved this way before her father had taken ill. But it didn't really matter in the here and now. What mattered was what awaited her in her mother's dining room.

"You know the things she said were lies, don't you?"

Lila couldn't meet her friend's eyes. "We're back to that again, are we?"

"Lila, you're not going anywhere until you look at me."

When Lila raised her head, she saw compassion burning bright in Annie's golden brown eyes.

"You do know she's lying, right?"

A leap of hope fluttered within, but Lila quickly squashed it before she looked away from Annie. If only it were true.

"Lila, think about this, please? She's just trying to make herself feel better."

At this, Lila looked up. "She has nothing to feel bad about. She's a beautiful woman who has everything she could possibly want."

"Yes, I agree, she's beautiful. On the outside. But people who degrade and belittle others usually do so because they're unhappy with themselves. She's getting older, Lila. You've grown prettier by the year. Men look at you before they look at her. That threatens her somehow. She's trying to give herself a boost. And you fall for it every time."

Lila shook her head. How she wanted to believe her friend.

Annie squeezed her arm. "You don't have to agree. But the fact is, no matter the reason, you've been told something for so long you can't see the truth any longer. She's won. You believe her."

Sudden tears misted her eyes, and her throat tightened. She struggled for a response but the words wouldn't come.

"Just do me a favor, Lila, please? As soon as she starts belittling you, please get up and walk out."

"Oh, Annie, I couldn't." Her heart thudded at the very thought.

"Yes, you can. You've taken the first step by moving out. You can do this, too. It will make you stronger inside."

Lila wasn't sure she'd ever be stronger, but she wanted Annie's words to be true. "Do you really think so?"

Annie nodded and drew Lila into another quick hug before pushing her toward the door. "I know so. Now, be on your way. And remember what I said. You're beautiful. Inside and out. Now scoot. George or Charles, or whomever is your mother's newest carriage driver, is waiting."

"Gilford," Lila called over her shoulder. "And she calls him her footman."

Kirby stared at the massive wooden doors of Austen Abbey, debating whether to turn and run. The last time he stopped by to check on Lila, her friends said she wouldn't see him.

Was he wasting his time? He wasn't even sure why he came back to check on her again. Was he eager for rejection?

No. It was something about the vulnerability he'd seen in her eyes. She was hurting in spite of the brave face she'd put on. And that meant he'd try again. This wasn't out of a need to rescue a woman in distress, or to try and make everything better for her.

No.

It was simply Lila who caught his attention and lit a desire for him to try and soothe her pain. And because of that, he would ask to see her. If she refused, he'd just keep trying. He only hoped that tonight she would agree to see him.

The door opened just then and Lila stepped through, a vision in pink fabric and lace. He started to greet her, but before he could, she turned and waved to someone inside just beyond his field of vision. Then, before he could process the fact he should take a step back, she turned and barreled into him.

Surprised, he put one arm behind her waist to steady her and the other on her shoulder. She was light and delicate and she smelled wonderful, too.

Almost immediately, she extracted herself from his arms. "I'm so sorry."

"It's all right, really." Kirby would have been happy to hold her in his arms for more than a split second.

Then she blinked as if just now seeing him. "Mr. Ross?" She looked at him quizzically, opened her mouth, and then closed it again as if trying to comprehend his presence outside the school's front doors. Finally, she spoke. "It seems like you're always seeing me at my clumsiest. Thank you so much for not letting me fall. Are you here to visit someone?"

"I just stopped by to see how you were feeling after your fall."

"I'm well, thank you."

"I'm glad."

Her lips curved upward and her face brightened. "Thank you for coming by to check, though."

"Miss Wentworth, now that we have that out of the way, would you like to take a walk? It's a beautiful evening for a stroll in Hyde Park."

"Please, call me Lila."

"Only if you call me Kirby."

This time her smile was complete, and genuine. "I'd like that."

"Now, about that walk?"

She shook her head, and dark curls spilled beneath the fanciful trim of her hat and brushed her delicate cheek. He was so caught up watching her that he missed her rejection until she spoke. "I'm sorry. I can't."

He could feel his heart sink in his chest and was surprised at the depth of his disappointment. "Is it because of what I overheard yesterday?"

After a moment that felt eternal and awkward, she finally looked up at him with clear blue eyes. "It's because I have to be somewhere in just a few minutes."

Of course. That's why she was dressed the way she was. Some of his disappointment faded to nothingness. "Does that mean I might ask you again another day?"

This time she tossed the answer over her shoulder as she stepped onto the running board of the waiting carriage, without even waiting for assistance from the driver. "Maybe." Was that a hint of a smile he saw in her eyes?

He watched as the carriage made its way down the drive and turn left before it finally disappeared from view. Then he turned to stare up at the massive gray building that housed the school.

Though Lila's answer had lifted his spirits, shame washed through him. While it was true he'd been concerned about her and wanted to see her again, he'd just led her to believe that was the only reason. He still needed to have a serious conversation about his sister and France.

But could he really do that now? His stomach still clenched at the unbelievable things her mother had written about her.

There was no mistaking Lila's hurt and devastation. She didn't seem like some silly insecure girl who'd misconstrued the meaning in the letter. Kirby had no doubt the words she said were true. Lila was a wounded bird—fragile, frightened, and desperate to flee.

Yesterday hadn't been the time to confront her and demand she stop filling his sister's head with foolish ideas. Nor today.

So now he was in a quandary. He still needed to talk about France, but how could he reconcile that with the surprising desire to get to know her and maybe help push that hurt from her eyes?

Which one took precedence, and how did he decide?

Heat flamed Lila's face as Gilford turned the carriage away from Austen Abbey. She'd resisted turning back to wave at Kirby Ross. Who was he, really, and what did he want from her? She couldn't believe the flirtatious way she'd ended their conversation. It was unlike anything she'd ever done. What had come over her?

Had Annie and Rebecca's encouragement given her false bravado? Instead, Lila was beyond embarrassed. So much for being brave.

Rearranging the heavy skirt of her dress, she tried to relax as Gilford turned the carriage toward home. No. Not home. Never again would Swan House be home. It was just a structure where her mother lived with her small cadre of servants.

Home implied a sense of belonging, family, people who loved you unconditionally. Lila would never find those things in the large, cold structure her mother had labeled Swan House. She was glad she moved into the dormitory at the school. Now she would only come here for Sunday dinner, or on days like today when she was summoned. And it wouldn't be because she wanted to. It would be out of the inexplicable sense of obligation that she still felt.

Just because her mother was cruel didn't mean Lila had to return the behavior. In spite of the way her mother treated her, Lila always forced herself to behave respectfully. She imagined by doing so, her father would have been pleased.

By the same measure, she wondered if he would have been appalled by her mother's behavior. Perhaps he'd known and decided to put up with it. Had her mother always been this way? It could have been the reason her father showered Lila with so much love. Maybe he'd been trying to make up for—and cover up—her mother's true self.

Once the carriage turned off Congress, the horse picked up speed and the wind brushed at Lila's face. When they finally turned the corner onto Peach Street where Swan House sat at the end of a long drive, the breeze lifted the hat from Lila's head. It was gone before she could react.

She started to ask Gilford to turn back, but before she could even open her mouth, another carriage headed straight toward it. Cringing, she watched as it disappeared beneath the horse's hooves. The hat wouldn't be worth salvaging...and she'd just given her mother one more thing to criticize.

Standing on the front step of Swan House, Lila smoothed her hair as best she could while waiting for the butler to open the door. This was a formality her mother insisted upon. No one entered the house without the butler greeting them first.

Much to her dismay, once she'd been led inside the house, her mother stood in the foyer.

"There you are." Sarah Wentworth pursed her perfect lips in disapproval. Or was it disappointment? She wore a gown of royal blue, and her dark hair was swept up on her head in a magnificent swirl that would have left even the most glamourous woman in Paris feeling inadequate.

Lila resisted the urge to touch her own hair again.

"You're late. And you look as though you've been running through the fields like a wayward child." As her mother's remarks went, this one was rather tame. And she couldn't be sorry about being late since it was time spent talking to Kirby.

Her mother stared at her as if to say she expected an apology.

Though she wanted to resist, it wasn't worth enduring more of her mother's criticisms. "I'm sorry, mother. My hat flew off when the carriage turned the corner."

"Nevertheless, you might wish to consider pinning it on your head a little more firmly so this doesn't happen again."

Rather than argue, Lila nodded and followed her mother toward the dining room.

As they drew close to the doorway, her mother turned to her with a smile. "Lila, darling. I'm so glad you came." Her voice was loud and her tone artificial as her words gave rise to the suspicion that someone was beyond the door and likely seated at the dining table. "I do wish you would reconsider your decision to move away from home. There's no need for you to live at that dreadful school. And I really don't understand why you insist on working there. Really my dear, it's so embarrassing."

My dear? Anxiety anchored itself in her belly. Her mother was putting on an act. Someone really did await them in the dining room. Because of that, Lila refrained from asking if her teaching at the school was as embarrassing to her mother as her looks. She was more concerned about who lurked behind that door.

Though her mother made a show about finding Lila a match, she fawned over every male she'd invited to this house. But when called on it, her mother would never admit to any interest in the men she lined up as potential matches for Lila.

Swallowing hard, Lila entered the room. She stopped abruptly. Heat balled in the center of her chest and stole her breath.

Two men rose from their seats at the long table. Two men she'd hoped never to see again. Both had been prospective beaus until her mother had entered the picture in one manner or another and ended up caught in compromising positions with both men.

Now her mother looked at them and fluttered her eyelids. "Lila, you remember Robert Bigelow and George Metcalf?"

"Of course I do." She gave them her best *I hope you don't remember my past humiliation* smile. "Mother, may I speak to you in private? There's something I forgot to ask you." She turned to the men. "If you'll excuse us for a moment?"

"Of course." They both spoke simultaneously.

Lila gave them a weak smile before she turned and fled the room without giving her mother a chance to respond. She had no intention of returning.

"Lila, really. What is wrong with you? You're embarrassing me in front of our guests. First you come in looking like a harridan, and now it's as if you've left your manners outside the door."

"I'm sorry, mother." Was her mother trying to boost her own feelings as Annie had said? She drew on the nugget of strength she'd felt during her talk with her friend. But could she really stand up to her mother and say everything that was in her heart?

"No, on second thought, I'm not sorry. I won't be able to stay for dinner after all." It was a start. Albeit a weak one. Still, it gave her a bit of fortitude.

"What?" A look of menace froze her mother's face, and Lila took a step back, relieved she hadn't said more.

"You heard me." Lila hated the way her voice quivered, but she resolved not to back down. Annie would be so disappointed in her for the pitiful response. But Lila remembered something she'd heard Annie say. *"Sometimes we have to take tiny little steps before we get where we want to be."* Maybe her friend wouldn't be disappointed. Maybe she'd be glad for Lila having taken any kind of action at all in standing up to her mother, no matter how small.

If Annie was right, this step forward would not be in vain.

"I'm not going back in. You and your gentlemen friends will just have to dine without me. I don't appreciate being deceived."

Her mother's mouth gaped open, and she simply stared. Lila took advantage of her speechlessness and fled the house.

Just as her feet hit the dirt at the bottom of the steps, she heard her mother screech.

"Lila Wentworth, you get back here this instant."

"Sorry, mother." Lila gathered the front of her dress higher. "Until you start being honest with me about dinner guests, I'm not interested." She ran past the carriage, pebbles skittering under her feet. She ducked under the wisteria that grew on both sides of the wide path and wound together across the top to create an archway. She didn't stop even when the carriage path met the sidewalk.

Two more blocks and she'd reach the park. She didn't care that it was almost dark. The closer she drew to Austen Abbey, the more her initial heart-thumping dread dissipated.

She'd stood up to her mother, and it felt surprisingly freeing. Her heart was light, and the next time Kirby Ross came around—if he came around—and asked if she'd like to take a walk, she would say yes.

Five

But he didn't come back. It had been more than a week since Lila had seen Kirby Ross and a more than a week since she'd run out on her mother and her guests. After that disastrous evening, she hadn't gone for their weekly dinner and thankfully hadn't heard a word from her mother. Not about the skipped meal, and not about moving out of Swan House. Tomorrow was Friday. Would Lila be expected to show up for dinner this weekend?

Just thinking about it made her stomach hurt.

She climbed into bed and reached for the book on her nightstand. *Emma.* Tracing the gold embossed letters that spelled out the title, she hoped to get lost in the pages of Jane Austen's book. But her eyes wouldn't focus on the page, no matter how many times she forced it. Her thoughts kept wandering back and forth between her mother and Kirby Ross.

Finally, after managing to read a few pages, Lila closed the book and sighed. It was not a sigh of satisfaction.

It was time to stop reading these books. Her life was so far removed from a Jane Austen novel she couldn't identify with any of the characters. And right now, she found it hard to believe anyone could.

Although, word of Mrs. Emmeline Whitley's matchmaking attempts were legendary. Certainly Mrs. Whitley could identify with Jane Austen's Emma.

For the briefest of moments, Lila wondered what would happen if she caught Mrs. Whitley's notice. She *was* one of the academy's most generous benefactors, and frequently mentored some of the students. And she'd been known to set her cap on making a match for a teacher or two.

Before Lila could bring a halt to her thoughts, an image of Kirby Ross danced in her mind.

No. Absolutely and more firmly than she'd ever expressed it to herself before, *no*. Not only that, she wouldn't dare approach Mrs. Whitley with such a preposterous idea.

But would she ever meet her match? A match her mother wouldn't swoop in to ruin? Or was she destined to be alone for the rest of her life?

Letting the book drop to the floor beside her bed, Lila reached up to switch off the lamp and then settled back in bed.

Her life was more like Frederica, the unfortunate daughter in *Lady Susan*. After Rebecca had mentioned it, Lila had thumbed through a copy of the book just enough for her stomach to hurt.

The thought only depressed her more, and Lila squeezed her eyes shut, determined to get to sleep. Instead, she thought of Kirby again. It surprised her that he'd come back to ask her for a walk. She couldn't imagine why. Surely he only felt sorry for her. Once more, she wondered if he was related to Mary Beth.

When his face continued to dance in her mind, she raised her head, turned over, and slapped her pillow a few times. Then she settled back down and closed her eyes to no avail. Kirby's smiling face and tender eyes were all she saw behind her lids. She heaved a great sigh and punched her pillow again. It was no wonder she couldn't sleep.

At quarter to two the following Monday, fifteen minutes before her last class was over, there was a knock at the classroom door. The students were taking an exam, and Lila crossed the room hurriedly, hoping the girls wouldn't be disturbed by the interruption. She opened the door quietly, surprised when she saw no one standing there. A quick glance down the hall revealed no one at either end. But she'd heard the knock. Perhaps whomever it was had changed their mind. But they sure disappeared fast. As she started to close the door, her eye caught a flash of pink on the floor.

A perfect pink rose lay just in front of the door. The thorns had been carefully stripped off the long stem. Its delicate petals were fluted and just barely opened. Whoever chose it had taken great care. A small envelope was attached by a thin pink ribbon.

Again, she glanced down the hallway. But it remained empty.

She stooped and picked up the rose.

"What is it, Miss Wentworth?"

Franny sat in the front row studying her curiously, and when Lila turned she sighed dramatically. *"Vous avez un admirateur."*

The other girls, now seriously distracted from their exam, all stared at her with open curiosity.

"No." Lila shook her head. "I couldn't possibly have an admirer."

"Au contraire." Franny beamed, her cheeks as pink as the rose. "A pink rose signifies admiration."

She had an admirer? But who could it be? And when had it started? She wasn't engaged in a courtship. Prior to last week's disaster, the last gentleman she dined with was seen the next day strolling through Hyde Park with her mother on his arm. Without a doubt, *he* hadn't delivered this rose.

"Why Franny, I didn't know you knew so much about flowers."

"I don't." Her smile was wide and filled with delight. "Just roses."

Lila sniffed it delicately, thinking, wondering. Kirby Ross? Her heart stuttered.

All she had to do was untie the note and open it. But she didn't dare do it under the curious gaze of her students. That left her nothing to do but think while they worked on their exams.

"Back to work, *les jeune filles*. Finish your exams and then you may leave early."

As happened more and more frequently, Kirby's smiling face and green eyes persisted in her thoughts. A flower from him was highly unlikely. He'd happened across her awkward conversation, escorted her back from the park, and then stopped by to ask her for a walk. And she'd declined. It had been more than a week. The teasing way she'd ended their conversation would be long vanished from his mind. The rose wasn't from him.

Looking up, she saw Mary Beth studying her. Lila turned from the girl's view and walked to the window and didn't turn around again until she heard footsteps approaching her desk.

Mary Beth. She was the first to finish her exam.

"Bonne journée, Mademoiselle Wentworth."

Was that a gleam of mischief in the girl's eyes? Lila simply nodded and refrained from asking.

Once the last girl left the room, Lila hurried to her desk and untied the envelope. Slipping the note free, her heart thumped as her eyes ran over the words.

"Rather, it should be that of your inner self, the unfading beauty of a gentle and quiet spirit, which is of great worth in God's sight." ~ 1 Peter 3:4

What did it mean? That whoever sent this thought she had a gentle and quiet spirit? That God admired such qualities? Did that mean they did, too? Her hand shook as she tucked the note back in the envelope. She would have to think on the verse. And perhaps she should pray on it, as well.

Sniffing the sweet perfume of the rose, she reaffirmed her previous decision to accept an invitation from Kirby if he decided to once again ask her to take a stroll.

As much as Lila loved her French classes and teaching the girls a little bit about French culture along with the language, she'd spent nearly a week overwhelmed with self-doubt wondering if there would be any word from her mother. The fear of another summons weighed heavily on her mind. When none came by Friday morning, she finally allowed herself to relax.

She'd received two more roses, with no note to decipher and no visitor to accompany them, leaving her to continue wondering who they were from. The girls enjoyed teasing her about it, and when a note was delivered to her classroom that afternoon, they watched expectantly. But she could smell the heavy perfume coming off the paper and knew it was a summons to Swan House.

"Sorry to disappoint you, *mes jeune filles,* but it's only a note from my mother." One she planned to ignore. Her mother could dine alone. Or with whichever bachelor she currently had designs upon. Lila wouldn't be around to be humiliated, or to witness her mother's humiliation— even if her mother were too vain to recognize it.

Though she anticipated hearing from her mother after she didn't show up that evening, an angry note at the very least, she heard nothing.

Annie and Rebecca chose to celebrate her newfound gumption with a late night tea and cookie party in Rebecca's room.

Rebecca took a dainty cookie from the plate and handed it to Lila. "How does it feel to stand up for yourself?"

Lila passed the plate to Annie and took a slow sip of tea before answering. "I think it feels...wonderful." She stretched the word out before smiling at her friends. "Thank you both for being so supportive."

Both ladies drew her into a hug, and as she went back to her room for the night she couldn't help wondering what it meant for her future. Could she really step forward with confidence and forget the awful words written in her mother's correspondence? The terrible things her mother continuously said to her?

The thought of ignoring it all was strange, yet oddly freeing.

But would it last?

Or would thoughts from the biggest question paralyze her? After all, if one's mother didn't love one...then who would?

On Monday, Lila was in the tea room for her mid-morning break and just getting ready to head back to her classroom when she heard a laugh coming from the direction of Mrs. Collins's office. It sent a chill straight to her heart. What was her mother doing here? She found it rather odd that Mrs. Collins would even entertain her mother's presence after everything Lila had told her.

But none of that mattered at the moment. Lila needed to disappear before someone led her mother to the tea room. And she couldn't go out the main door. She placed her cup on the tray and slipped out the door leading to the garden.

Her heart thumped in her ears as she made her way through the garden and down the path along the back side of the abbey. She'd have to go in the door that was furthest from the front entry in order to avoid her mother. But it was also far away from her classroom. She'd be late.

Her students were always prompt so they'd wonder where she was. They were well-behaved though, so she needn't worry about them getting into mischief.

That's why the chaos that greeted her when she entered the classroom took her by surprise.

The girls were all gathered around the corner of the room and the moment they noticed her, they all began speaking at once.

"Miss Wentworth!"

Not *Mademoiselle*. That alone sent alarm skittering up the back of her neck. "What is it, girls?"

"It's Mary Beth. She stood on a chair to try and get a spider off the wall."

Lila hurried across the room, while the girls tried to speak over one another.

"She didn't want to kill it so she put it in a teacup."

"She was trying not to drop it and lost her balance and fell."

"We don't know where the spider is."

Several things went through Lila's mind in a jumble as she reached the huddle. She didn't like spiders. They gave her the shivers. The broken teacup was hers, given to her by her grandmother. But of course, the most important thing was Mary Beth. Mary Beth, whose eyes were closed. An angry red welt was quickly blooming on her forehead.

"Someone go fetch some ice. And who can run for the doctor?"

"I will."

"Thank you, Franny."

Mary Beth's family would need to be informed as soon as the doctor arrived. In the meantime, she shrugged out of her lightweight walking jacket and placed it under Mary Beth's head.

"Mary Beth." She stroked the girl's pale blond hair away from her forehead, careful not to touch the welt, and whispered softly while she knelt at her side. "Can you hear me, sweetheart?"

There was a hushed silence among the young ladies as they gathered around. Even Lila found herself holding her breath, only remembering to breathe when spots swam before her eyes.

Finally, Mary Beth stirred and all of the girls exhaled.

"Mary Beth, can you hear me?"

The girl turned and focused green eyes on Lila. When she nodded, she also winced. She started to sit up, but Lila stopped her with a hand to her shoulder.

"No, dear. Stay where you are. The doctor will be here momentarily."

Mary Beth did as Lila asked, and before long the doctor stepped into the room.

Once she was certain Mary Beth was receiving the best care possible, she raced down to Mrs. Collins's office to find out where Mary Beth's family lived. They needed to be notified at once. It was only as she approached the door that she remembered her mother. It didn't matter. Mary Beth was more important than a family squabble.

Pushing the door open, she was surprised to see Mrs. Collins was alone. Concern pinched the headmistress's face as Lila informed her of the situation. "I'll have a look in my files to find the business address of her guardian."

"What do you mean, her guardian?"

Mrs. Collins gave her a pensive look. "Mary Beth is an orphan."

A wave of tenderness went through her at the thought of the girl losing both parents.

"Who is her guardian?"

As soon as she asked, she knew the answer. Mrs. Collins had finished thumbing through files and held up a small file card. Instead of looking at it, she looked at Lila. They both spoke at the same time.

"A Mr. Kirby Ross."

But Mrs. Collins added the two words that confirmed what she'd already suspected. "Her brother." Then the headmistress peered at Lila. "Do you know him, dear?"

"I met him once, recently. Could you tell me where to find him?"

"Yes, of course." Mrs. Collins held the card at arm's length. "My eyesight, don't you know." She tilted her head, squinting one eye. "Here we go. You can find Mr. Ross at City Hall. That's surprising. One would think I'd have remembered a detail like that."

"I'll leave right away."

"There's no sense in walking, Lila. Why don't you take the school's buggy? I'll send one of the girls for the driver."

Lila shook her head. "There's no need. I can take the trolley. It stops not far from City Hall. By the time the buggy and driver are ready, I'll be at the park and boarding the trolley. But you may want to have him stand by to escort Mary Beth home with her brother so she doesn't have to walk."

Mrs. Collins nodded. "That's a wonderful idea, dear. I'll make sure he's ready. Oh, and someone delivered this for you. I'm sorry I haven't had a chance to bring it to you."

So that explained why her mother was here. Lila reluctantly reached for the envelope Mrs. Collins held out to her, certain it was another summons. But instead of reading it, she hurried out the door and down the drive. In a matter of moments, she was at the corner. She lifted the front hem of her pink cotton skirt and half-ran, half-walked. By the time she reached the trolley stop, she was certain her face was the color of a tomato. She forced herself to slow her breaths lest she attract even more attention by huffing and puffing.

To distract herself from her painful breathing, she glanced down at the envelope she still held. *Odd.* Her name was scrawled across it, but she didn't recognize the writing. Even stranger, it didn't give off the overwhelming scent of her mother's perfume. Could it be from someone else? But who? She glanced around, not sure she wanted to open it here in front of all the people waiting for the trolley.

When the trolley arrived, she stepped past all the passengers and slid into the last seat. When she broke the envelope's seal she had to look twice at the slip of paper to believe what it said.

Your eyes sparkle like the bluebonnets that dot the Texas hills.

That was it, one sentence? It didn't even make sense. Bluebonnets didn't sparkle. Her cheeks burned, and her hands trembled. Although she appreciated the sentiment behind someone taking the time to write niceties, this one was awful. She glanced around to make sure no one was close enough to read it.

Were Annie and Rebecca trying to make her feel better by writing clumsy poetry?

No. They had more pride than this. If her friends had come up with a poem it would have been better crafted. So then was this a joke, or could someone really mean this? The sentiment was sweet, even if the poetry was awful.

As soon as City Hall was in sight, she stood and made her way to the front of the trolley. She stiffened her legs to maintain her balance when it lurched to a stop.

As soon as the trolley pulled away, she crossed the street and walked straight to imposing building. She stood in front of two large oak doors with full-length glass windows and the words CITY HALL painted on them. She took a deep breath and pulled one of the doors open.

It took a while to find someone who knew Kirby Ross. It would have been easier if she'd known his occupation. But she eventually found someone who led her down a long hallway past several offices. When she was finally directed to the last door on the right, she knocked.

"Come in."

She pushed the door open to see Kirby with his head bent over large sheets of cream colored paper that were scattered across his wooden desk. They looked like maps or diagrams of some sort. Suddenly overcome with nerves, Lila hesitated. Had he sent the roses? Had he written down the scripture about inner beauty? It didn't matter at the moment. Mary Beth was the only one who mattered.

"Mr. Ross."

Kirby looked up and immediately rose from his chair. "Miss

Wentworth? Wh—" He tilted his head to one side and narrowed his eyes in a quizzical expression. "How may I help you?"

A slight shadow of pink washed up his neck. Did she make him uncomfortable?

"Mr. Ross, I'm here about Mary Beth. There's been an accident. The doctor is with her, and he says she'll be fine. But he wants you to take her home so she can rest."

"What happened?" He didn't argue with her as he stepped away from the desk.

"She fell. I wasn't in the classroom when it happened." She told him about the spider.

Kirby gave her a half-hearted smile. "My sister is such a sweet soul. She'd never hurt a living creature no matter if it has eight legs or wings and a stinger."

"The doctor said she'll be all right with some rest but shouldn't be alone. If you can't take her home right now, she can rest at the school." Lila tried to stop herself from speaking in such a rush. Embarrassed, she glanced away.

"Hey, it's okay." He spoke softly. "I'll be able to take her home. Let me accompany you back to the school." He grabbed his hat and coat off a rack near the doorway. "I appreciate you coming to let me know." He stood back so Lila could go through the doorway first.

They made it to the trolley stop just as it arrived. Sitting next to Kirby, it was hard not to think about the poem, the Bible verse, and the rose. Had he sent them? Inexplicably, she wanted the answer to be yes. Although it was still difficult to reconcile the Bible verse with the poem. It seemed so peculiar that the same person sent them.

Your eyes sparkle like the bluebonnets that dot the Texas hills.

It was oddly sweet. It may not make sense, but the sentiment behind it was genuine. She wondered if she should get permission from Mrs. Collins for him to sit in on a few of the school's poetry classes. The thought made her force back a smile.

"Are you all right?"

"Oh. Yes, I am. My apologies, Mr. Ross. I was thinking of something else. I shouldn't let my mind wander at such a serious time as this."

"No apologies necessary, Miss Wentworth. I wish, however, that you would share whatever it is that put the smile on your face."

The trolley slowed toward their stop, saving her the need to reply.

Once they arrived at the school, Mary Beth was sitting up and talking to the girls who had remained by her side instead of heading to their next class.

Kirby quickly bundled her to his side and steered her toward the door. His loving concern for his sister warmed Lila's heart. He lingered for just a moment, his green gaze settling on Lila's face. "Thank you, Lila, for everything."

"Will you send word to let me know how she's doing? I don't think I could possibly wait until Monday."

When he smiled, fine lines feathered the corners of his eyes. "I'll be certain to do that."

It sounded like a promise, and Lila watched as he disappeared through the door. She whispered two prayers. One for Mary Beth and, though it made her ashamed, one for herself—because what kind of person looked forward more to a visit from a gentleman than she looked forward to learning the well-being of an injured girl?

Seven

Late Saturday afternoon Lila was sitting in the garden, still struggling to read *Emma* while thoughts of Kirby kept invading her mind. So when Annie came outside, brown eyes sparkling and lips curved into a grin, Lila was happy to see her.

"You have company," Annie announced.

"Company?"

"Yes."

"My mother?" Lila tensed.

But Annie, bless her, shook her head. "No. Don't worry. It's not even her messenger."

Lila wanted to wilt from relief.

"It's Kirby Ross."

A moment of panic seized her, and she smoothed down her skirt. She was wearing her oldest but most comfortable blue cotton skirt with a white blouse. Not the best thing to wear when receiving visitors. Although, she reminded herself, he wasn't here *for* her. He was here to let her know how his sister was feeling after the fall. She would do well to remember it.

"Shall I show him back?"

"He's here about his sister, so this might be a little too informal." Lila stood. "I think the tea room would be better."

"Sure. I'll give you a minute and then show him in."

"Thank you." Lila smiled at Annie, grateful for her friendship—for someone who understood her.

48

When she entered the tea room, she instantly thought of the roses and the verse attached to that first one. Her heart skipped a beat. Maybe even two beats. Then she remembered the single line of poetry. Her ears burned.

He's just here to tell you about Mary Beth's condition. She needed to calm herself before he came in and she said something foolish.

When Annie appeared in the doorway, Lila took a deep breath. Kirby stood behind her.

"Hello Mr. Ross."

Annie stepped aside so he could enter the room. She gave a little wave before she disappeared down the hall with her black skirt swirling around her legs.

Unsure if she was capable of carrying on a conversation, Lila almost called her back. But she reminded herself once again, he was only here about his sister.

"Miss Wentworth." Kirby nodded. "Please call me Kirby. We've been around each other enough to dispense with formalities, remember?"

"You're right, of course. I just wasn't sure it was appropriate here in the school." She took a breath and tried to stop rattling on like an empty rail car going full speed down the track. "I'm sorry, Kirby." She emphasized his name. "How is your sister? I should have asked you that right away."

"She's doing much better, thank you. And there's no need to apologize."

"I'm so relieved. I've been worried about her."

A soft knock at the doorway caught her attention, and she turned to see Rebecca holding a tea tray. How had she known to bring tea? And so quickly? Goodness, she must have started preparing it the instant Kirby entered the front door. But why? Before Lila could ask Rebecca about it, her friend slid the tray onto the table and disappeared from the room without a word. But not before Lila took note of the gleam in her eye. An inkling of suspicion teased her. Mrs. Whitley had been to visit Mrs. Collins this morning. Had Rebecca or Annie—there was no doubt the two were in this together—caught sight of Austen Abbey's most famous matchmaker and come up with a few ideas of their own?

If so, they'd clearly forgotten everything they knew about Lila's mother, or they wouldn't be trying to force a match. If Lila's mother ever caught wind of Kirby, he, like the others before him, would fall prey to her wiles. If Kirby Ross knew what was good for him, he would run as fast as he could from Austen Abbey, Lila, and one Lady Sarah Wentworth.

She turned to give him some excuse as to why she couldn't have tea with him, only to find him at the table pouring the tea. *Pouring!*

This would be where her mother would swoop in and make some witty remark, capturing Kirby's attention. But she wasn't her mother, nor did she wish to be. She was simply herself. Lila would rather remain the mouse in the corner than emulate anything resembling her mother.

So instead, she seated herself at the table then reached out and accepted the fine porcelain teacup that was filled right to the brim. She had to take great care not to slosh it on herself as she lifted it to her lips. "Thank you, Kirby."

"You're welcome, Miss Wentworth."

"Lila, please. How can I be expected to call you by your Christian name if you don't reciprocate?"

"But we weren't properly introduced."

Lila found herself laughing at his silly game. "Very well. Kirby Ross, I am Lila Wentworth. I'm pleased to make your acquaintance." She broke off, suddenly uncomfortable to realize he was staring at her.

"You have a beautiful laugh, Lila."

"Oh." She dropped her gaze and traced the delicate handle of her teacup. He couldn't have caught her more off-guard if he tried.

"I'm sorry. I didn't mean to embarrass you."

"No, please don't apologize. I'm just not used to—" She broke off, unsure if she wanted to admit she wasn't used to praise.

"Compliments? You deserve compliments." His green gaze was gentle and unwavering.

"That's very kind of you." She remembered her mother's letter and wondered if he was thinking about the cruel words he'd overheard.

"I'm not trying to be kind. I mean it." His lips curved into a soft smile.

Unsure what to say, she dipped her head. The silence grew awkward. Was he as embarrassed as she was? She glanced up again, only to find him still looking at her. She picked up her teacup, and hot liquid splashed over the side.

Kirby was out of his chair in an instant, one of the linen napkins in his hand. "Here, let me help."

Once the tea was blotted, she expected him to go back to his chair. Instead, he stood by her side and appeared to be debating something. Finally, he said, "I'd be honored if you'd accompany me on a stroll through the park tomorrow afternoon."

And there it was. She'd already decided she'd accept if he asked her again. But suddenly, looking at him, she froze. Was he asking because he felt sorry for her?

"I'm sorry, Kirby. I'll be attending church tomorrow." She wasn't sure why she said it. Unable to bear her mother's behavior in church, of all places, she hadn't been to church in a while. Now she'd have to go in order to keep from being a liar. "And then I must dine with my mother." No, that wasn't quite right. She'd almost forgotten her resolve *not* to eat with her mother.

It was hard to believe, but he actually looked disappointed. "I understand." He reached around her and picked up his cup of tea, then drank the last of it. She reached for the pot to pour him another cup. "No, thank you. I must get back to my sister." He turned toward the door.

"Kirby, wait." Her heart thundered so hard she was certain it could be heard throughout Austen Abbey. "I—" She broke off, unsure if she could go through with it. But when he looked at her expectantly, she rushed on. "I usually have to be somewhere after church. But I nearly forgot, I've cancelled for this week. I'd be happy to accompany you to the park after church." She sucked in a breath, waiting for his reaction.

"I'll call for you tomorrow after church, then." His smile nearly took her breath away and never dimmed as he put his hat on and slipped out the door.

Lila didn't go to church the next morning. She just couldn't. Every time she thought about walking through those doors and seeing her mother pursue any gentleman who looked her way, dread filled her.

Perhaps she should have gone. Perhaps it was time to turn it over to God. It wasn't like she could change the behavior on her own.

But instead, she lingered over her tea, said a prayer for her mother, and took great care to put on her best walking dress. It was her very favorite gown of white with dark blue trim at her waist, cuffs, and hem. A silver paisley design was spaced nicely across the white fabric, so as not to clutter the gown and draw attention away from the narrow waist and slim skirt. She tried not to indulge in vanity and seldom wore the expensive gowns her mother plied her with. In fact, the night she moved from Swan House to Austen Abbey, she'd left most of them behind. But this one—this was her favorite.

Looking in the mirror as she adjusted the smart looking blue hat that set it off so well, she was glad she'd kept it.

But wearing it for a stroll in the park? She'd agonized over it, of course, alternating between an ordinary walking suit of pale blue with a white blouse. She didn't want to appear overdressed.

Both Rebecca and Annie were attending church this morning so were unable to offer their advice. And she hadn't told them of Kirby's invitation the night before because the instant he'd walked out the door she'd been hit with a wave of anxiety about accepting. Even when she went to bed she wasn't sure if she'd actually go with him or send her regrets.

Kirby was escorted into the tea room promptly at one o'clock, where she'd been waiting nervously. One look at his smile, and she was glad she hadn't cancelled.

"How was church?" They were halfway down the drive when he asked.

Lila swallowed hard. She wasn't about to lie. "I didn't go."

He stopped walking and looked at her in concern. "Did something happen? Are you ill?"

Lila turned to face him. "I know you heard my conversation that day in the tea room."

The silence before Kirby nodded was long and uncomfortable. Finally he said, "I did."

"I haven't been to church in quite some time. For many reasons, all of them having to do with my mother and the attitudes she put forth in the letter you heard me discuss with my friends."

"You don't really think whoever reads those letters actually believes them, do you?" They'd started walking again, but it didn't stop Kirby from looking down at her.

"How could they not? I'm sure they make for good reading if one endorses salacious gossip. She talks about me as if I'm a toad. She told my uncle I'm too stupid to ever make a match."

"Surely you know that's not true?"

When she didn't answer, he took her hand and clasped it in his own. "I don't think you'd be teaching French for Mrs. Collins if you were stupid. And you're definitely not a toad."

"Thank you, Kirby." Lila sighed. "But she also talks in her letters about making a match for herself. Not that there's anything wrong with that, I suppose. Except the manner in which she approaches it is entirely wrong."

"What do you mean?"

"She always throws herself at men far younger than herself—men who haven't even been married. And sometimes at men who are married. It's disgraceful." *And* humiliating, but she didn't figure she needed to tell Kirby that. He would assume it.

"Why don't you change churches?"

Truthfully, Lila hadn't really given it any thought. She'd attended the same church most of her life. "Rebecca attends a different church. I suppose I could go with her. I'm sure she wouldn't mind at all."

"There, you see." Kirby sounded satisfied. "Or you could come with Mary Beth and me. We've found a nice little church. Everyone is very friendly, and I've even become friends with the reverend."

"That's very nice of you, thank you. I'll think about it." But she knew she wouldn't. There was a limit to how many uncomfortable situations she could tolerate at one time—mother first, church second. And somewhere in there was a very handsome man named Kirby.

They strolled along in silence for a while before Lila brought up a subject that made her curious. "Tell me about your work, Kirby. And those diagrams I saw on your desk. Do they have something to do with the moonlight towers the city is planning to install?"

He was about to answer when he was interrupted by a voice that made Lila cringe.

"Yoo-hoo, dear. Over here."

Before she could think of a reason to turn back the other way, her mother shouted out, "Lila. Can't you hear me?"

She waited for the familiar feeling of dread to overtake her. The feeling she got whenever her mother was getting ready to strike. But this time, the dread didn't come. It surprised her, but not half as much as the tears that pricked her eyes. Where had those come from? And why?

"Lila!"

Now her mother was standing up in the carriage. Did she even care what kind of spectacle she made?

Lila must have made a strange sound because Kirby gave her a curious look before he put a protective hand on her arm. "Let me guess. Your mother."

Before she could answer him, her mother called out, "Who's that with you, Lila?"

Lila sighed. "I guess there's no avoiding it," she muttered under her breath. Then louder, she said, "Come on then, Kirby. Time to meet my mother."

They approached the carriage and she nodded to Gilford, who was looking on without disguising his interest, before turning to her mother. "Mother, may I present Kirby Ross? Kirby, this is my mother, S—" She broke off at her mother's subtle glare, then corrected herself. "Lady Sarah Wentworth."

Her mother extended her hand, palm down. Kirby didn't have to bend far since she was still standing in the carriage, and he didn't hesitate to lean forward and kiss it.

They never do. Lila scolded herself the instant she thought it.

"Where have you been hiding this one, Lila?" Her mother fluttered her hand in front of her face as if she needed to cool off.

"I've not been hiding him anywhere, Mother."

"Is he the reason you haven't been to see me? I missed you at dinner on Friday evening. And last Sunday, too."

Lila bit her tongue to keep herself from spilling exactly why she had no intentions of dining with her mother again.

"Well never mind then." Her mother sat back down. "I've found you, and that's all that matters." She made it sound as if she'd been seeking her out. Lila knew that was preposterous.

"Gilford, please help my daughter and her handsome gentleman aboard the carriage."

"What? Mother, no."

"Yes, Lila, dear. I want you and Mr. Ross to join me for dinner. Now come along."

Lila wanted to refuse. Really, she did. But the scene could get quite ugly if she did, and she didn't want to subject Kirby to such a thing. Really, which was worse? To lose him due to a scene she caused? Or lose him to her disgraceful mother?

Either way, she lost.

Gilford stepped forward then, and she sighed and allowed him to help her into the carriage. She slid over as Kirby sat down next to her, feeling as if she were in a dream—nightmare, really.

How else was it possible that her mother tracked her down and influenced Kirby to dine with her at Swan House?

Eight

The dinner with Lady Sarah was awkward and uncomfortable for Kirby. Not because she behaved inappropriately. But because she didn't. Other than standing in the carriage calling to Lila in the park, she'd behaved like a lady and was an excellent hostess. It was far from what he expected, and it was difficult to picture her behaving in the manner Lila had described.

However, he did believe Lila. She seemed the very picture of honesty. Besides, the hurt in her eyes had been very real. Remembering it caused him to clench his jaw and force himself to be as polite as possible to Mrs. Wentworth—to treat her with Christian charity, even though he didn't feel the least bit inclined.

There was also the fact that she seemed familiar. It wasn't because she and Lila resembled each other. It was something he couldn't quite recall.

"Have you been to church lately, Mother?"

He knew what Lila was doing. She wanted to know if it was safe to go to church. But when he saw Mrs. Wentworth glance to the right without moving her head, something told him she was about to lie.

"I haven't been to church in weeks, Lila. You'd know that yourself if you were in attendance. Why, my dear child, have you not been going?"

"I really haven't felt up to it, Mother. Truthfully, I'm not sure when I'll be back—if at all."

Kirby listened to their exchange in dismay. He didn't like that Lady Sarah put enough fear and humiliation in Lila's heart that she'd quit going to church. He also didn't like that her mother had just lied.

He knew she'd lied because he finally realized why she seemed familiar. He didn't know her, but he'd seen her before.

Lady Sarah attended the same church Kirby and Mary Beth had been attending for the last few weeks. The same church Lila would attend if she took him up on his offer to join them at church.

Lila should know her mother was still attending church, but he couldn't very well tell her right now. To point out that one's hostess was a liar was far from polite. But he'd definitely have to tell Lila, especially if she decided to go to church with him.

For now, he'd keep silent and make sure he did nothing to disrupt this dinner. He didn't want to make things more uncomfortable for Lila than they already were.

Later, when they were alone, he'd make sure she knew the truth.

But as he sat through the dinner and small talk, he had another idea. Perhaps he could speak to Lady Sarah next Sunday afternoon and convince her to tell Lila herself.

Monday morning, most of the girls were seated in class and Lila was getting ready to give them an oral exam. She was just waiting for Mary Beth.

"Good morning, Mary Beth," Lila said when the girl finally walked through the door holding one arm behind her back. "How are you feeling?"

"Much better, *Mademoiselle* Wentworth. I'm so sorry about your teacup. I'd like to buy you a new one."

"That's incredibly sweet, Mary Beth, but so unnecessary. I'm just glad you weren't hurt any worse."

Mary Beth smiled. Then she pulled her arm from behind her back. "I found this outside the door." She handed Lila a pink rose and all of the girls practiced their French by repeating "*Oh, là, là,*" over and over again.

Since Mary Beth brought the rose, Lila knew there was no sense looking out in the hall. On impulse, however, she looked out the window and was surprised to see her mother being helped into the carriage by Gilford. Surely her mother wasn't visiting with Mrs. Collins again? Could the flowers be from her mother? It didn't seem likely. Still, she had to think back. When had the roses first appeared? Before, or after she'd moved out?

It didn't matter. There was no way her mother would be able to get in and out of the abbey with a rose in hand, without being seen—someone would have seen her and mentioned it. So why was she here?

"*Mademoiselle* Wentworth, are you all right?"

Lila turned back to her class, embarrassed. "*Oui*, Franny. I was just thinking about something. *Je suis désolée.*"

"About the man who sends you flowers?"

The girls laughed. Lila pretended to ignore them.

"Let's get started with the exam, shall we?"

Later that day, with the rose—and Kirby—still on her mind, she was surprised when an envelope containing a poem was delivered to her classroom. If they were both from Kirby, Lila found it a little strange that they weren't delivered at the same time. But it wasn't as strange as the poem.

Your lips shine like dew on the morning grass.

On Wednesday, following a quick knock at her classroom door, she received another rose. This time, like the first time, there was an envelope attached. She looked in both directions of the hallway, then out the window. She never caught sight of Kirby, and Mary Beth was in class. She opened the envelope carefully, fearful of another dreadful line of poetry, pleased instead to find another scripture.

"*Whatever is true, whatever is noble, whatever is right, whatever is pure, whatever is lovely, whatever is admirable—if anything is excellent or praiseworthy—think about such things.*" ~ *Philippians 4:8*

The verse touched her deeply. She had the sense Kirby was trying to show her what was important. The first verse he'd given her talked about inner beauty and gentleness. This verse talked about where to focus your thoughts. Clearly he was better at picking out scripture than he was at writing poetry.

Twice that week, Kirby had come to tea. And twice he'd taken her for a stroll. It was during the second stroll that she almost thanked him for the roses and the verses, but it was clear he wasn't ready to reveal himself as the giver.

It was harder still not to ask him about the poetry. She sighed as they walked slowly through the park.

"What's that sigh all about?"

"Oh, nothing. I was just thinking. You never did tell me about those diagrams on your desk. They are moonlight towers, aren't they?"

He looked genuinely surprised. "Moonlight towers, huh?"

So she was right. She couldn't suppress her smile.

"What do you know about moonlight towers?"

"I know enough. They're so tall people say they can touch the moon. Of course, I know that's an enormous exaggeration. But I do know they're going to be so bright, women will feel safe walking down the street unaccompanied. They're to be installed by the Fort Wayne Lighting Company. Oh, and I'm pretty sure you're the engineer who's going to figure out where each tower will be installed. That *was* a map of the city streets I saw on your desk."

Kirby blinked. "And you think you're stupid? Lila, you're undoubtedly one of the smartest women I've ever known."

Had he just said she was smart? Lila studied him for a moment, pleased to see sincerity beaming from his eyes and his smile.

This time she couldn't hold back her own smile. This wasn't like the other day when he'd said she was smart because she taught French. There was something else in his tone, something she'd waited a long time to hear.

The tears burned so hot and so fast at the back of her eyes, she had to look away. It was the perfect moment for the trolley to approach the stop just outside the park. The whistle drowned out the sound of her discreet sniffles. And even though they were still inside the park and not trying to catch the trolley, the exhaust blew their way, and it was the perfect excuse to wipe at her eyes.

"Here." Kirby tapped her on the shoulder.

A slight turn was all it took to see the crisp white handkerchief he held in his hand.

For some reason that made her sniffle even harder.

"Thank you." She took it and quickly turned away again so she could dab her eyes and then her nose.

"Are you crying?"

"No."

"Are you sure?"

Was that amusement she heard in his tone?

"I'm positive." She turned to him and smiled, blinking quickly in hopes the air would dry up any remaining moisture in her eyes.

"Good." He flashed her one of the grins she'd come to adore. "I can't have my sister telling her classmates that I made their favorite teacher cry while we were out for a stroll."

"Letting your sister tell them anything about our strolls in the park is the fastest way to spread rumors throughout the abbey. I can't have my students—" She broke off when she saw that he was trying to keep from laughing. She had to bite the inside of her cheek to keep from doing so herself.

As they headed back, she asked him about the moonlight towers again. "How long will it take to install the lights?" She was afraid of the answer. She'd just found him. She wasn't ready for him to go back to Indiana.

"Once we finish the planning, it will take a couple of years."

"Wow. I never would have imagined it would take so long."

"You'll have to come back to my office and see an actual photograph of one of the towers. They're a hundred and sixty-five feet tall. It will take a very long time to build and install, or to bring in by freight and assemble if we go that route. When we're finished, Austin will be lit brighter than a million candles."

"I was only a child when the Servant Girl Annihilator struck Austin, but people still talk about it today."

"How many women were killed?"

"Eight. All in the same hideous manner." *With an axe.* She shuddered.

"I imagine it's difficult to forget something like that."

"Yes. And it's still frightening to walk through the streets at night. I know the towers will bring a great deal of comfort to a lot of women."

They talked a little more about the towers and the murders, and Lila told him about the "cemetery ghost" scare they'd had at the abbey a few years ago and rumors that the axe murderer would return.

"I think we should talk about something more pleasant," Lila finally said. "Do you think the university will ever have a baseball team?"

Kirby looked at her, surprised. "You know about baseball?"

"A little bit, yes." What would he think of her now? "My father enjoyed it. There isn't much around here, but when he traveled to New York he liked to take in a game. Then when he came home, he'd tell me all about it."

"I've gone to a few games in Cincinnati, and one in Kentucky. There's nothing like it." Kirby's tone held a smile, and he seemed as happy to talk about baseball as he did the moonlight towers. Lila felt her heart tugging just a little more toward him with each passing minute.

They'd avoided talking about two things—her mother and church. Lila could tell Kirby wanted to encourage her, but he stopped short each time. She found that odd since it had only been a few days ago when he'd encouraged her. A few times it had almost seemed as if he wanted to tell her something but stopped himself at the last minute.

Lila tried to ignore the disquiet this caused to her newfound sense of self-worth that Kirby brought out in her. But because of everything that she'd been through with her mother, it wasn't easy and she feared the disquiet might just win.

Nine

The next Sunday, Lila walked to the little church about three blocks from Austen Abbey and not far from the park. Though she wished she wasn't alone, it was preferable to attending with her mother. As she neared, she couldn't help but think about Kirby. She should have taken him up on his initial offer to attend church with him and his sister.

She groaned as she drew near and saw her mother's coach sitting out front. Gilford sat in the shade of an oak tree, the image of patience though he likely didn't feel it.

Gradually she drew to a stop, dread filling her. Why was her mother here?

By her own admission she hadn't been to the church in weeks. It was the only reason Lila felt safe coming back here.

Now that she finally made up her mind to come back to church, she felt pulled between wanting to go inside so she could be refreshed in spirit, and wanting to turn and run. How could she truly focus on the Lord with her mother in attendance? She couldn't bear to have a confrontation or be embarrassed or belittled.

She had a sense of freedom, however tremulous, and knew it could slip away the instant her mother opened her mouth.

"Please, God. I'm so weary of all of this. I just want to live my life without being controlled and used by her."

Slowly Lila started forward. "And Lord, in spite of it all, I do love her and want her to be happy. Perhaps someday we can renew our relationship."

Lila found herself walking faster now, and her pace seemed to increase with the lightness in her heart.

As she neared the large oak tree, she nodded hello to Gilford and continued toward the door, praying she could slip in the back row without her mother seeing. But as Lila stepped through the door and into the narrow and crowded foyer, a young woman just inside turned around.

Mary Beth.

When she caught Lila's eye, she stared, wide-eyed.

So this was where they attended. What a lovely coincidence.

"Good morning, Mary Beth." Lila looked past her, trying to see Kirby.

"M-Miss Wentworth?"

Now that was an odd reaction. Granted, Mary Beth didn't know she attended this church, but it would have seemed she'd be happy to see Lila.

The organ music started playing the soft chords of "It Is Well with My Soul."

"I have to go. I'll see you tomorrow." Mary Beth hurried into the sanctuary, and Lila followed behind her. As much as she wanted to say hello to Kirby, Lila slid onto the back pew. She didn't want to take a chance of being seen by her mother.

She strained to see where Mary Beth sat, and if Kirby was with her. She couldn't, though, because there were too many tall people sitting in front of her. For that matter, she couldn't see her mother. She supposed she should be thankful for that. And for *that*, she should be praying for forgiveness.

Reverend Sullivan was an older man, still handsome, but not really the perfect age to be friends with Kirby. But Kirby didn't care about such things, and she liked that about him.

"Good morning, brethren." Reverend Sullivan took his place at the front of the congregation, diverting Lila's attention from something that was of little consequence. "This morning we're going to learn about Jesus's encounter with the woman at the well."

How interesting. Though Lila wasn't certain her mother had actually done more than throw herself at men, she hoped her mother would learn from the message that she should never go any farther than that until she had a husband—but she shouldn't be throwing herself at them at all.

"Before we say our closing prayer, I'd like to take a moment to do something a little different."

Lila looked up in surprise. Had she really been so absorbed in thoughts of her mother that she'd missed the entire sermon? She glanced around, feeling guilty. Everyone's eyes were on Reverend Sullivan. Relieved that no one appeared to notice she'd been caught up in her troubles rather than in worship, Lila turned her attention to the reverend.

"I want to talk to you for a moment about worth. Self-worth, to be exact. Over the last few weeks, I've been praying for someone who doesn't see their own value as a person. This was done at the request of someone in the congregation. And over a small period of time, a few others have joined us in prayer."

Lila recalled the scripture verses she'd received with two of the roses. Roses she'd been certain were from Kirby. She froze, scarcely able to breathe. Surely he couldn't be talking about her. Surely Kirby hadn't confided things about her to the reverend.

"This," she heard Reverend Sullivan continue, "is because someone who is supposed to love this person unconditionally has said and done things to tear down their sense of worth and continues to heap nothing but condemnation upon their head. Today I want to ask you, all of you, to please join me in praying for this person. For when two or more gather in His name, He is with us."

Lila's cheeks burned. She wanted to run out the door, certain everyone in the room was staring at her, certain everyone in the room knew they were talking about, and praying for, her. And while she should feel a sense of peace and gratitude, she only felt the sharp sting of betrayal.

Kirby and his friendship with Reverend Sullivan. Lila scoffed.

The second Reverend Sullivan and the congregation bowed their heads, she slipped out the door and into the tiny foyer. But before it could shut completely, she sensed someone else behind her. She couldn't bring herself to turn back to see who it was.

"Lila, wait."

Kirby.

His hushed voice was full of urgency, but it didn't matter. She had nothing to say to him. Absolutely nothing.

Exiting the foyer doors, she blinked in the bright sunshine and pulled her hat forward. It was good for decoration but not for shading one's eyes.

"Lila, please wait." This time Kirby's voice was loud but gentle. No more whispering. "Please? It's not what you think."

She walked swiftly away from him, not bothering to turn around as she answered him. "How could you possibly know what I'm thinking?"

"You feel betrayed. You think *I* betrayed you."

"You forgot mortified, humiliated, and embarrassed. Choose whichever word you'd like. And why do I feel that way, Kirby? Ask yourself that, why don't you? Oh wait. You don't need to ask. You already know. Because you took it upon yourself to ask your friend the reverend to pray for me. Worse, you told him personal things about me. How dare you?"

"Lila, if you would just listen to me, you'd see—"

She stopped then and whirled to face him, blinking fast in an attempt to dry up the growing moisture. "There's another word you can add, Kirby. Horrified. Do you know my mother is in there? Of all the times for her to decide to go back to church. She probably wonders if they're talking about us. Why, if she saw me she'd *know* for sure they really are talking about us."

"Lila, Mary Beth and I started coming here right after we moved here. She has been coming to church as long as we've been here."

Stunned, she sank down on a nearby bench. "She has? But she said she hasn't been to church in a long time. You heard her say that, and you didn't tell me she lied."

Sitting next to her, Kirby eyed her as if waiting for her to ask him to leave. Then when she didn't, he nodded. "I didn't recognize her at first. Certainly not when she stopped us in the park. In truth, I'd not met her before that day. I didn't really recognize her until she told you she hadn't been to church for a while. And then I didn't know what to say."

"How about the truth?"

"I'm sorry, Lila. I am. But I think your mother is, too. She's been spending quite a bit of time with Reverend Sullivan over the last few weeks. Or rather, I guess I should say he's called on her several times."

Lila gasped. "Has she— Are they—?" The thought was unbearable. She buried her face in her hands. Her mother had sunk to a new low.

"It's not like that, Lila."

"I wouldn't be too sure."

"I would. They've been talking and praying together."

This gave her pause, and she raised her head and looked at him. "Praying together? Really?"

Kirby nodded.

"Surely my mother's not the one who asked...?"

"No. It all started with an impish little mischief maker."

"Mary Beth?"

Kirby nodded.

"She did look kind of guilty when I saw her in the foyer this morning."

"Exactly. I didn't find any of this out until this week."

"I knew you were keeping something from me."

He looked away.

"That *is* what you were keeping from me, right?"

"Can we talk about that later?" Kirby didn't meet her eyes. "I was trying to figure out how to tell you your mother lied, when Mary Beth told me about her visits with your mother. She's been talking about this new friend of hers for several days. I had no idea it was your mother. Mary Beth even gave her a copy of *Lady Susan*."

Lila gasped. "You know about *Lady Susan*? And your sister gave her a copy of the book? But why?"

Kirby squirmed. "I may have told her about our initial meeting, and she may have compared the situ—er, ah, your situation to *Lady Susan*."

This was growing worse with every blink of her eyes. Lila groaned. Bad enough all of the adults knew. But one of her students, as well? Maybe more if Mary Beth wasn't one to keep a confidence.

Thankfully Kirby had the good graces to look chagrined. Still, it didn't give Lila any sense of satisfaction.

"Why did you tell her?"

"I was distressed. I didn't know how to comfort you. I didn't know what to do and I wanted to make things better for you."

"But why?"

"Why? Because you were hurting. You *are* hurting." Kirby opened his arms, beckoning her to find comfort.

Against her better judgement, she went.

He bent his head low, pressed it against hers, and when he spoke his breath brushed against her ear. "There was so much pain in your eyes, Lila. It hurt me to see it. You believed those things she wrote." He tightened his arms around her then. "I don't know how many years you've heard those horrible words, but I found myself wanting to undo them in your mind. They're not true. They're not. You're beautiful. But even if you weren't, you have a beautiful heart and a lot of love to give."

"I'm still mad at you, just so you know."

"I know," his voice rumbled against her ear.

Lila pulled out of his embrace and scooted away. She studied Kirby, trying to gauge his sincerity. The gentle pull of his eyes spoke truth. A lock of sandy colored hair brushed his forehead. His smile was tender, affectionate, and it was as if it was for her alone. She couldn't take her eyes off his mouth. She wanted to kiss him.

Did he want to kiss her? She scooted close again, almost close enough to be back in his embrace. But this time it wasn't for comfort.

His eyes widened. "Lila?"

Without hesitation, she gave him a slight nod. He put one hand under her chin, tilting it up, and then gently brushed the curve of her cheek with his other hand.

When he leaned forward and kissed her, his lips were soft and gentle and like nothing she could have imagined. Sweet, warm, needing, affirming—all for her.

"Kirby! *Mademoiselle* Wentworth! Come quick."

Mary Beth's voice hurried its way into her ear. Apparently Kirby's as well, because he groaned. They moved apart instantly, and Lila tried to slow her breathing.

Surely Kirby and Mary Beth could hear the beating of her heart.

"What is it, Mary Beth?" Did Kirby sound annoyed or alarmed?

"It's Lady Sarah. You have to hurry."

Now Lila was alarmed. "My mother? Is she hurt? Did she take ill?"

Lila was running toward the church steps. No matter how her mother treated her, she was still her mother.

As she ran, Lila prayed her mother would be all right.

Ten

Kirby was right on Lila's heels as she entered the building. She stepped through the foyer into the sanctuary and stopped, stunned. Her mother stood at the front of the church with Reverend Sullivan. There were a few people still in their seats, but most of the congregation was gone.

Lila turned and looked at Kirby in confusion. Had they really been out there that long? And who had seen them in what might be interpreted as a compromising situation? It was hard to believe they'd been so oblivious, but that's how it was whenever she was with him. Would she find herself yet again the subject of gossip?

"Your mother is asking for a special prayer," Mary Beth whispered.

Stunned, Lila started to slide onto the back pew, motioning Kirby and Mary Beth to join her.

"No." The female voice came from the front of the church. "I want you to sit up here."

It was her mother's voice. This was all very strange.

"Please, Lila, come up here."

Confused, but oddly not nervous, Lila did as her mother asked. But she pulled Kirby along with her, and Mary Beth followed. The girl's grin was absolutely wider than Lila had ever seen it.

In that instant, Lila remembered the day she'd heard her mother's voice coming from Mrs. Collins's office. Mrs. Collins gave her the first envelope of awful poetry. Mary Beth had given her the second one—the same day Lila had looked out her classroom window and saw her mother getting into the carriage. Mary Beth had been late to class that day.

It seemed suspicious then, but even more so now. No. It couldn't possibly be. Was Mary Beth writing poetry, if one could call it that, for her mother?

When Lila reached the front, her mother held out her hand. Uncertain, Lila glanced around. Reverend Sullivan, Kirby, and Mary Beth all wore smiles she interpreted as encouragement. But they also smacked of conspiracy. Erring on the side of encouragement because she couldn't stand the thought of being talked about, Lila slowly approached her mother and held out her own hand. Her mother clasped it, truly clasped it, with a firm and warm squeeze.

Lila's heart contracted. She looked up at her mother's face and saw— or thought she saw—a softening of her features and a smile on her face.

It couldn't possibly be.

But it was.

Then her mother glanced at Mary Beth and held out her other hand. "Come here, young lady." Her tone was gentle and pleasant, belying all Lila knew of her mother.

What was happening here?

"Lila, my daughter." Her mother's voice faltered for a moment and her smile faded. "My beautiful daughter." Lila saw moisture glinting in her mother's eyes. "There's so much I want to say to you, and I just don't know if I have all of the right words."

Lila's mouth went dry.

"First and most important, I love you. I've always loved you."

Next to her, Kirby squeezed her other hand. She drew strength from it.

"I got lost somewhere along the way. Lost in selfishness, prestige, money. And most of all, vanity. It took someone very special to make me see what I'd done to you. My darling daughter. I've been so destructive. I know I can't undo everything overnight. And I can't change overnight. But Reverend Sullivan has agreed to spend time with me, praying. And Mary Beth has been spending time with me. She's been telling me about her mother and what a special woman she was—what a good mother she was. I know I can't hold a candle to her, but I'd like to try. Please, Lila, will you let me?"

Swallowing hard, Lila ignored the twinge in her heart. The one that was trying to protect her from getting hurt again. Instead she chose to let go of Kirby's hand and pull her mother into an embrace. These were all things she'd longed to hear for years. She dashed at her eyes with the back of her hand, and she felt her mother do the same.

Next to them, Reverend Sullivan cleared his throat. "Lila, before we pray, your mother has something she'd like to read to you."

Lila watched her mother pull a slip of paper from her handbag. She listened without cringing to the complete poem.

Your eyes sparkle like the bluebonnets that dot the Texas hills.
Your lips shine like dew on the morning grass.
Your heart burns brighter than the moon.
You're kind, intelligent, and beautiful, and you're dearer to me than all the stars above.

There was no rhyme or reason to the words, except maybe that last line, and yet Lila knew they came straight from her mother's heart. But it was the last line that managed to wrench a sob from the very depths of her soul.

"*Ma belle fille. Je t'aime.*"

Her mother opened her arms, and Lila went to her gladly. "I love you, too, Mother."

She stayed close to her mother's side while Reverend Sullivan prayed the Lord's blessing and peace over the two of them.

When he finished and her mother let her go, she turned to Mary Beth and whispered, "Thank you."

Then she went into Kirby's waiting arms. He hugged her tight and whispered in her ear. "You thought those lines of poetry were from me, didn't you?"

"How did you know?"

"The look on your face."

"And fairly awful love poems they would have been." Her mother laughed and sniffled at the same time.

Lila sucked in a breath, horrified to realize her mother had overheard.

"Will you forgive me, Lila? Is it too late to start over?"

Lila turned to the woman who'd been her tormenter for so long. "I forgive you, Mother."

Reverend Sullivan cleared his throat again. "There's something else you should know."

Lila looked up at him, but it was her mother who spoke.

"Reverend Sullivan and I have been spending time together."

Lila tried to keep her expression passive, tried to suppress her groan, and squeezed Kirby's hand to keep herself from expressing her dismay. She was thankful for his calming presence.

"It's not what you think, Lila. Because of Mary Beth's suggestion, he's been teaching me the scriptures. Talking to me about God and His purpose for me. I have to find a new way, and I have to find satisfaction in doing good works for others rather than my desperate attempts at securing a future."

In all her life, Lila had never seen her mother appear shy. But just now, Lady Sarah Wentworth cast her gaze to the floor and her chin trembled.

"Did you mean the words you wrote?"

Her mother nodded.

"Oh, Mother, they mean the world to me."

"Lila, I can't undo the past. But I plan to go forward as a different person. I'll likely make mistakes, but I hope—no, I pray—any mistakes from this day forward won't be at the cost of my dignity."

"We'll go forward together, Mother."

"Thank you." Her mother's watery whisper brushed her ear, and Lila was certain her mother's eyes were as damp as her own.

Eleven

Late the next afternoon, Kirby met Lila and Mary Beth at Austen
Abbey. He arrived with Gilford in the carriage because they were
going to dine at Swan House with Lila's mother.

"Lila, could we have a few minutes alone before we leave?"

"Of course. Let's just step into the tea room."

"Perfect," Kirby said and followed her into the room with the curved
walls. "I can think of no more perfect place than where it all began. Do
you remember that first day we met?"

Did she? How could she forget? She nodded.

"There was a reason I'd come here. We never did get to talk about it."

"Are you finally going to tell me?"

He nodded. "As long as you promise not to be upset."

Now she wasn't sure she wanted to know. "Is it something bad?"

"You might think so, even though I don't. I mean, I didn't at the time.
I'm not sure about now."

"Kirby, what are you talking about?"

"France."

"What about it?"

"I came here that first day to ask you to stop filling Mary Beth's head
with stories about how wonderful it is."

"Oh, really?" Lila pretended to be insulted.

"It was only because she wanted to go there and study and I can't
afford to send her."

"Then you've changed your mind?"

He pressed his lips together. "Not entirely. I think I'd send her if it was affordable—and if I knew she was being properly chaperoned."

Someone tapped on the doorframe of the open doorway. Lila looked up to see her mother standing there. "Hi, Mother."

"Lila." Her mother nodded at her then turned to Kirby. "I believe I can help with that." She paused a moment, as if uncertain.

Kirby was already shaking his head. "I can't accept money from you."

"You haven't heard my plan yet."

Lila shot Kirby a glare. "We'd love to hear your plan, Mother."

Her mother gazed at her with an expression she could only call loving. Her heart warmed.

"I've been talking to Mrs. Collins. It seems as though there are several students who'd love to go to France, but find themselves in the same financial situation. I'd like to sponsor a trip. It's not school abroad by any means, but it would give them a taste of France and build their appreciation for other cultures."

"Mother, that's a wonderful idea. What do you think, Kirby?"

Kirby glanced from Lila to her mother, then back.

"I think it's a wonderful idea, as long as there are proper chaperones."

Clapping her hands together, Lila's mother laughed. "Would you consider yourself, Lila, and me proper chaperones?"

France. Lila breathed in a satisfied sigh. She couldn't wait to share it with the students. And with Kirby, too, of course.

Rubbing his knuckles across his chin, he appeared to be contemplating it. "I could be persuaded. Under the right circumstances."

Her mother glared at him. "And what do you consider to be the right circumstances, young man?"

Now he smiled, and Lila had the feeling she was about to find out the reason they were here in the tea room in the first place.

"Wait here."

Puzzled, she watched him disappear through the door. When he reappeared, he held an armful of blush-pink roses, each one more delicate than the next. Mary Beth, Annie, and Rebecca were with him. He tilted his head toward the ladies. "I found them eavesdropping."

The women both had the good graces to blush. Mary Beth, however, beamed. She was, no doubt, already imagining her trip to France.

"So the roses really were from you?"

This time it was his turn to look puzzled. "Is there someone else attempting to court you?" His tone was indignant.

Court her? "No," she said, instantly defensive. "I really did think they were from you in the beginning. But when the poetry turned out to be from my mother, and you said nothing about the flowers or scripture verses, I thought maybe I was wrong about the roses as well."

"Ahem." The loud cry for attention came from Mary Beth. "Did someone say something about a courtship?"

Rebecca and Annie both shushed Kirby's sister. Then the three of them stared at Kirby with eagerness flowing off them.

"None of you were invited, and if you want to stay you'll have to just be quiet."

"Does that include me?" Mrs. Collins appeared in the doorway.

Kirby groaned. "Lila, I'm beginning to think you're part of a package deal."

"You'd better believe she is," Mrs. Collins said.

"Thank you, Mrs. Collins." Lila pinned Kirby with a glare she didn't really mean. "Kirby, what's this all about?"

Waving his hand in the air, Kirby turned to face her mother. "Lila, I need to ask your mother something."

"Oh?" For some reason she felt like being petulant. "If it involves me, don't you think *I'm* the one you should talk to?"

He ignored her. "Mrs. Wentworth, I'd like to ask your permission to court your daughter."

All of the ladies in the room, except Lila, gasped. Lila's heart contracted.

Her mother turned and studied her for a moment that seemed to last forever. Then she looked back at Kirby. Was she about to decline?

Lila held her breath.

"I just have one question, Kirby. Are you sincere?"

"You'd better be sincere, Kirby Ross," Rebecca said. "Or you'll have to deal with all of us."

"I promise each of you, I'm not going to hurt Lila. She's the only one for me, and I can assure all of you that I've never been more sincere about anything."

"Then I grant my permission." When her mother turned to face her, Lila saw an expression in her eyes that she'd waited her entire life to see: love, devotion, and the kind of fierce protectiveness that only a mother could possess.

Kirby swept Lila into his arms and as he whirled her around the room she saw her friends and Mary Beth all looking on with smiles.

He leaned forward as if to kiss her, but before he did he stopped and glanced around the room.

He cleared his throat. *"C'est tout simplement toi, Lila, qui j'adore."* Then he focused his gaze on Lila. *"Simplement Lila. Je t'adore."*

Lila let the words settle on her heart. *It's simply you, Lila, who I adore. Simply Lila. I adore you.*

Maybe there really was something to Jane Austen...and happy endings were possible after all.

FULLY PERSUADED

NIKI TURNER

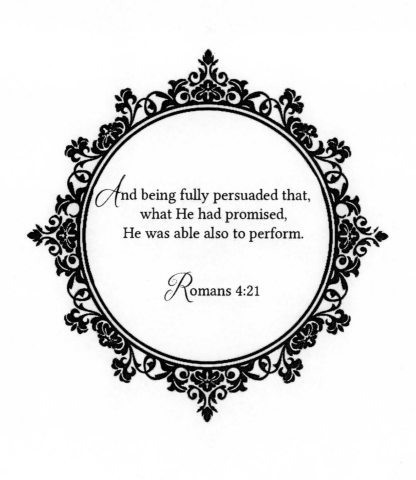

And being fully persuaded that,
what He had promised,
He was able also to perform.

Romans 4:21

A man does not recover
from such a devotion of the heart
to such a woman!
He ought not; he does not.

~Jane Austen,
Persuasion

One

May 1894
Austin, Texas

"I heard he's a gambler."

"Becky's cousin said he's an outlaw."

The Austin society matrons huddled in front of the Jeanette C. Austen Academy for Young Ladies—fondly known as "Austen Abbey"— resembled hens surrounding a grasshopper, ready to peck the poor insect to death. Annie swallowed and ducked behind a hedge that kept her out of sight, but not out of earshot. If they caught sight of her, she would become the hapless grasshopper.

"Bad blood, I'm telling you, there's no getting around bad blood. Annie Ellis ought to thank her pa and sister for their wise counsel all those years ago," announced one self-righteous voice.

Heat suffused Annie's fair cheeks as if she'd eaten one too many hot peppers. Careful to stay behind the concealing foliage, she hurried toward the back of the school.

She slipped through the gate in the wrought-iron fence, climbed the back porch steps, and entered her sanctuary. Classes were in session, so the hall was silent. She rubbed her knuckles against the hard, hot lump of emotions lodged in her chest. Part of her wanted to run away, but she had responsibilities to her students and to the Abbey. And, she sighed, nowhere to go. She couldn't even afford a train ticket out of Travis County.

79

Somewhere in the vast building the chime of a hand bell signaled the end of the current class session. Doors opened and girls fluttered into the hall like so many bright butterflies. Annie glanced at the watch pinned to her plain shirtwaist. She had enough time before her painting class to meet with Headmistress Collins and ask if the rumors were true. Was Ford Winters really returning to Austin after an eight-year absence? Ford was distantly related to Augusta by marriage, so her reports were less likely to be skewed by Austin's penchant for the sensational.

Annie threaded upstream through the flow of students on their way to their next classes. Reaching the headmistress's office, she caught her reflection in the window at the end of the hall and grimaced. She would never be a beauty, no matter how many times she sought out a mirror. She patted her drab brown hair to make sure it was suitably restrained and smoothed wrinkles from her serviceable gray serge skirt before she knocked on the polished door.

"Yes?"

"Headmistress Collins? It's Annie Ellis. Could I speak with you?"

"Certainly, my dear. Come right in."

Annie pushed the door open, struck anew by the room's welcoming atmosphere, bedecked in rich shades of emerald green. Seated behind an oversized desk, Augusta Collins wrote in her daily ledger in what Annie knew was perfect, precise penmanship—tracking student attendance and grades and who knew what else. Sunlight streamed through the half-moon window behind her, giving the vague impression Augusta was somehow not of this temporal realm. Annie was awkwardly aware of her feet sinking into the deep carpet.

"And what, pray tell, can I do for my favorite art teacher?"

A bit of the icy chill Annie had felt since hearing the rumors about Ford melted under the headmistress's kind reception. "I've heard Ford Winters is returning to Austin, and I wanted to ask if you knew anything about it." Her words tumbled out in a rush.

Augusta leaned back in her chair, her expression a blend of fondness and concern. "Annie, you should sit down."

Annie checked her watch. "I only have a few minutes until my class."

"It will be all right if you're late once."

Annie's heart fluttered against her ribs like a trapped bird. Augusta Collins would never suggest tardiness as an option under normal circumstances. She dropped into the tufted brown velvet chair opposite Augusta's desk and pressed shaky hands into her lap.

"Yes, ma'am?"

"Noah told me he spoke with you at length about options for funding the Kelly Ranch."

Annie flushed. Talking to the bank president had been embarrassing and unpleasant, in spite of his efforts to comfort her. The Kelly Ranch was all she had left of her mother's family, and Annie was determined to save it from bankruptcy. She'd finally acquiesced to the idea of offering investors an opportunity to purchase shares in the property. Thus far there'd been no takers.

"I'm sorry, ma'am, but what does this have to do with Mr. Winters?"

"I hope you will forgive me, but I took the liberty of telegraphing Ford to inform him of the opportunity."

Opportunity. She should have been affronted or angered by Headmistress Collins's announcement. Instead, anticipation quivered through her nerves and settled at the base of her spine in a warm hum.

"Annie, I know there has been talk around town about Ford's...er... activities since he left Austin."

And his former relationship with you.

Annie ignored the unspoken words. Eight years earlier she'd yielded to her father and sister's beleaguering about Ford's "questionable parentage" and "insufficient prospects for the future" instead of following her heart.

"I'll have you know," Augusta continued, "I wouldn't have contacted Ford about the Kelly Ranch if I had concerns about his moral code." She tapped her well-manicured fingers on the desk's surface in a steady rhythm.

Annie met Augusta's gaze. She was ashamed to admit that Ford's morality was the least of her concerns. She had loved him once. If she were honest with herself, she still loved him. Ford Winters invaded her heart and mind with debilitating frequency.

"Annie, dear, I give you my word, Ford has accumulated his wealth through legal methods, no matter what the local gossips say."

Annie considered Augusta's words and sucked in a breath. "So he's coming here to purchase shares in my...our...the Kelly Ranch?"

Augusta reached into her desk and withdrew a fat envelope. "Noah Whitley has scheduled the paperwork to be signed later this morning. I told him I would pass this along to you."

Annie reached for the envelope with a shaking hand. "That's so soon."

"Noah was under the impression your situation was urgent."

"Yes, it is. I just wasn't expecting..." Annie's hand dropped into her lap and her chin fell to her chest, stricken by what the contents of the envelope meant to her life.

Annie's grandparents had homesteaded the Kelly Ranch, and Annie loved the place as much as her mother and grandmother had. Her mother, Amelia, aware of her husband's and youngest daughter's weakness when it came to money, had given Annie legal control of what remained of the family's property before her death. Annie could legally refuse Ford's purchase of shares of the property, but for the sake of her mother's love for the ranch, Annie would endure anything.

"I don't have a choice." Her statement was laced with resignation.

Augusta rose from her chair and came around the desk, skirts rustling. Unbidden, she wrapped her arms around Annie in a gentle lemon verbena-scented embrace. "My dear, there is always a choice. Unfortunately, the right thing to do is rarely the thing that appeals to your flesh."

Two

Ford Winters glanced at the sleeping woman beside him. Escorting Noah Whitley's eighteen-year-old cousin from St. Louis to Austin as a favor to the well-respected banker was a gesture of goodwill, though she'd tried Ford's patience at every turn. The girl was a study in frippery, something he despised.

He reached into his coat pocket and withdrew a creased and tattered letter. He scanned its contents—written in Augusta Collins's notoriously perfect penmanship—for the umpteenth time, half expecting the words to be different. Her request, politely disguised as a suggestion, had come as a surprise. He had never imagined returning to Austin, much less returning as an investor in the Kelly Ranch, the family home of the woman who'd broken his heart.

The train's whistle sliced a shrill tone through the humid afternoon. Ford refolded the letter and tucked it back into his pocket. Beside him, Merilee yawned and stretched like a small, perturbed kitten. She turned big, blue eyes in his direction, her bow-shaped lips pursed.

"I must have drifted off. What were we talking about?"

Ford offered her a benign smile. "Nothing important, Merilee." Merilee's topics of conversation ranged from the trivial to the inane.

Brakes squealed as the train rolled into the station. They were scheduled to go directly to the bank upon their arrival in Austin. Ford planned to relinquish oversight of Merilee—with well-disguised relief—to her cousin, sign the official documents, and head directly for the ranch. His heart pounded at the thought of seeing Annie again.

When he'd left Austin he'd firmly slammed the door of his heart on Annie Ellis, her family, and all things to do with true love. Would seeing her again blow that door wide open, beyond his control?

Ford sucked in a breath of the stale smoke- and sweat-tainted air in the train car. He'd learned, over eight tumultuous years, to control his temper, his fear, and his desires in order to obtain the things he wanted the most. This, he told himself, would be no different.

Allowing Merilee to cling to his arm like a bur, he assisted her onto the platform.

"Ooh! Look at the trolley!" Merilee bounced up and down on her toes. "We simply must take the trolley to the bank, Ford, we must!"

He'd planned to walk from the station to the bank, hoping to regain his bearings before the meeting. Austin had changed a great deal since he'd last walked its streets as a troubled and angry young man.

Merilee continued to extol the virtues of the trolley, her voice rising in pitch and volume with each syllable until Ford winced and gave up his plan to walk to the bank. The trolley would enable him to deliver Merilee to her cousin much faster, and might preserve his hearing and sanity in the process.

When her last morning student left the Abbey's art studio, Annie pressed the heels of her hands against her eyes, seeking relief from the dull thud of a growing headache. She had struggled through her closing lesson on Baroque artist Caravaggio, seeing Ford's features where Caravaggio had painted the apostles.

Would he look the same? Perhaps he'd grown a paunchy belly and was prematurely bald. That might make it easier. She winced at the uncharitable thought as she untied her paint- and plaster-smeared canvas apron and draped it over an iron hook behind the door. It didn't matter how Ford looked now. There was nothing between them. She'd destroyed that.

She brushed at her gray skirt and white shirtwaist. They were still clean, thanks to the apron, although both garments were frayed at the edges and slightly over-large for her too-slender frame. She needed to set aside some of her pay for new clothes, she thought, her stomach knotting at the thought of money and budgets as she reached for her shawl and satchel.

She left the school the same way she'd come in: through the back. She had no desire for a face-to-face encounter with any of the gossip-hungry Austinites who might still be afoot. She wrapped a gray wool shawl around her shoulders for protection against the damp spring breeze, and headed for the bank.

Though her pace was slower than a condemned man's on the way to his own hanging, Annie was still early for the appointment. She shifted, trying to find a comfortable seat on the stiff horsehair sofa in the bank's lobby, as the carved mahogany clock in the corner ticked off the time. Noah had offered her a seat in his office, but that would have required polite conversation.

A woman entered the lobby, giggling behind one gloved hand. Annie watched her with a mixture of awe and envy. Some things—like golden blond hair and a fashionable figure—were not distributed evenly, in her opinion.

A man followed the woman, engaged in combat with her recalcitrant parasol. Only his boots and his pant legs were visible behind the flounce of pale pink silk. Annie, hidden from view behind a fancy potted plant, rolled her eyes. What was it about some women that turned men into imbeciles?

"Victory, at last!" he exclaimed.

The parasol snapped shut, and Annie's eyes widened. Black hair, eyes a startling shade of green, a strong jaw. No, unfortunately he wasn't bald, or paunchy. If anything, the years had embellished his good looks. A suffocating wave of nausea threatened to overtake her.

Ford Winters had returned to Austin as the captive escort of a silly blond.

"Thank you so much for rescuing my parasol, Ford. It's my favorite." The girl-woman simpered, her voice surely pitched too high for anyone but dogs to hear.

Annie's vision blurred, and she closed her eyes. As if having Ford play the role of rescuer for her beloved ranch wasn't bad enough, he'd returned with a woman who outshone Annie in every aspect of appearance, a cutting reminder that she'd rejected him and he'd moved on, while she remained alone.

"Annie?"

Oh mercy, his voice hadn't changed in the least. The deep bass tones resonated from her burning ears to the tips of her dusty shoes. She forced her eyes to open. Ford Winters, more gloriously handsome than ever, leaned over, putting their faces on a level plane.

"Annie?" Ford repeated, clearing his throat. "Are you all right? You're very pale."

Oh, how she wanted to fling her arms around his neck and hug him. It was so good to see his familiar features again. But years of Austin Abbey training came into play, and she rose swiftly to her feet. "I'm fine, Mr. Winters. Merely battling a headache. It's nice to see you again."

Ford arched one brow, glossy black as a raven's wing, in a too-familiar gesture. Could he still read her mind?

"Mm-hmm. Nice to see you also, dear Annie."

The only time she'd ever sidestepped Ford's uncanny ability to see into her soul was the night she broke his heart. He knew how awkward and uncomfortable this meeting was for her. Annie's mouth opened and shut like a fish gasping for air on the banks of the Colorado River.

"Close your mouth, darlin'. There are a lot of flies around this time of year."

Her mouth snapped shut as obediently as the parasol even as she folded her hands to keep herself from pushing that errant ebony lock of hair off his forehead. Old habits died hard. Ire over his teasing demanded a retort, but before she could answer, the blond appeared, gloved hand extended toward Annie.

"I'm Merilee. I'm sorry Ford has forgotten his manners. You'll have to forgive him. It was such a long train trip I feared I'd be an old maid before we arrived in Austin." Merilee drawled out the words "old maid" with a flutter of thick eyelashes.

The words stung, whether Merilee intended them to or not. Annie bit her tongue to silence a cutting response, if she'd been able to think of one. She'd come up with something later, probably that night, when she lay in her bed and remembered every word, every nuance, of the encounter. She shook Merilee's gloved hand. Ford had been traveling with this slip of a girl? Why?

"Annie, I believe this is the first time I've ever seen you without the power of speech," Ford said cheerily. "Merilee, meet Annie Ellis of the Kelly Ranch."

Annie's cheeks flushed, and she wished for the thousandth time she'd not been cursed with her mother's Irish complexion. Irritation sparked. How dare Ford tease her in the presence of this twit? Annie mustered her confidence, met his green-eyed gaze, and then turned what she hoped was a conciliatory smile on the blond.

"Welcome to Austin, Merilee. It's lovely to meet you. I hope you'll come to visit the Kelly Ranch. Now that Ford will be joining us as a shareholder, we expect to entertain Austin's finest citizens with greater frequency." She was lying through her teeth, and had to squelch the sharp twinge of guilt that accompanied her words. She had no intention of wasting their limited funds on foolish parties.

From the corner of her field of vision, Annie saw Ford's eyes narrow. She'd aggravated him. Well, one good turn deserved another, and all that.

Merilee smiled wide and clapped her little hands together. "I do love parties! I'm glad there will be some during my stay with my cousin."

Annie frowned in confusion. Cousin?

"Greetings, everyone!" Bank president Noah Whitley crossed the lobby, his handsome face wreathed in a wide smile. "Merilee, it's wonderful to see you again!"

Merilee skittered across the room and flung herself wholeheartedly into Noah Whitley's embrace. "Cousin Noah! You simply must buy Mr. Winters a meal, since he's been putting up with me for the entire trip from St. Louis. He was the perfect escort."

Annie blinked as awareness dawned. A muscle in Ford's jaw twitched, reminding her of a perturbed feline's tail swishing back and forth before it pounced. His emerald eyes were hard and glittering when he turned to her.

"I suppose I'll be managing the actual work at the ranch while you cavort with your father and sister?"

The edge in his tone made her shiver. So he, too, carried pain from their past.

"No. That's not what I meant—"

"Miss Ellis, Mr. Winters, shall we sign the official documents?" Noah tucked Merilee's hand in the crook of his arm with an affectionate pat and strode toward his office.

Ford extended his elbow. "Shall we? Or do you have a better offer?"

Annie flinched, stung. He knew she didn't have a better offer. The humiliation she'd dealt him eight years prior had come full circle.

Three

Ford clenched his teeth until they ached, striving to ignore his response to Annie's touch. She was, in light of her statement to Merilee about parties, as consumed with appearances and social standing as her vain father and sister. How, then, could he still react to her physically and—though he was loathe to admit it—emotionally?

She still had a temper. His teasing had ignited it, and unless he'd lost the ability to interpret her expressions, finding him in the company of the perky Merilee had made her a wee bit jealous.

Outside Noah's open office door, she pressed Ford's arm. He glanced down, willing himself to remain unmoved by soft caramel-colored eyes that brimmed with tears.

"I'm sorry, Ford. If you weren't here..." She sucked in a breath and Ford sensed the true depths of her discomfort. "Thank you for coming. The future of the Kelly Ranch depends on you now, and I am indebted to you." She released his arm and moved to sit in one of the burgundy brocade wing-backed chairs opposite Noah's polished banker's desk.

Ford frowned. He didn't want her indebted to him. He wanted... what did he want from her? He took a seat in the other chair, his mind spinning with unresolved questions.

Noah shuffled through a stack of papers and dealt the documents across the desk with the skill of a professional card shark. Ford waited patiently for Annie to read through each page before she passed them to him. Each successive page of legal jargon tightened the invisible bond between them, ratcheting up his tension until he felt like an overwound spring.

She gasped when she reached the paper that outlined the terms and conditions giving him a fifty-one percent share in the Kelly Ranch. He was sure that rankled by the way she gnawed at her bottom lip, a decidedly unladylike nervous habit Ford remembered well. He'd once successfully stolen a kiss when he caught her with her lip between her teeth. The memory rushed through Ford, accompanied by heat, and he clenched his fists.

"Mr. Winters?" Noah cleared his throat.

"Yes?"

"The papers, could you not...er..."

Ford frowned at the document crumpled in his fist. He released his grip, smoothing the paper as best he could against his leg.

"I apologize, Mr. Whitley." He sensed Annie's curious gaze on him and knew his color was high. Swallowing, he placed the wrinkled page on the desk and took a deep breath before speaking. "Purchasing these shares is an honor and a responsibility. I take this very seriously." Ford spoke to Noah, but his words were for Annie's ears. "I'm well aware of the respected history of the Kelly Ranch, and I hope to restore it to the prosperity which it once knew." He turned to face Annie. "I'm going to need your help, Miss Ellis."

She blinked, obviously surprised. "I appreciate that, Mr. Winters. Whatever assistance you need will, of course, be made available."

Her formal response belied the tears sparkling in her eyes and her trembling hands. It took every ounce of Ford's strength not to reach out and gather her into his arms. She seemed fragile and vulnerable, a shadow of the vibrant girl he remembered.

But he couldn't fall into that trap again. He'd loved her once, she'd broken his heart, and he'd promised himself he would leave Austin again as soon as he'd turned the Kelly back into a thriving cattle ranch. He wouldn't give her, or her family, the chance to reject him again.

"Well," Noah interjected. "Let's get the rest of these papers signed, so you can get on with it." He reached for a pen and pushed it toward Ford. "If you could sign at the bottom, please."

Ford complied and passed the pen and paper to Annie. She added her name to the document in her fine, meticulous penmanship.

Almost like a marriage license.

Ford rejected the thought outright. He had offered her everything he'd had eight years earlier and she'd turned him down. If she hadn't found something better yet, that was none of his business.

Noah clipped the papers into a neat stack.

"Excellent. I'm quite certain this will be beneficial for all concerned." Noah rose to his feet. Ford and Annie stood as well.

"Cousin Noah, can Ford take me to the house? I'm sure you've got more work to do here." Merilee flounced behind the desk and attached herself to her cousin like a needy house cat.

Ford tensed. In such close quarters with Annie he'd forgotten all about Merilee.

"If you will all excuse me," Annie interrupted. "I have other business to attend to." She turned to leave and collided with a regal vision in emerald silk who entered the room without bothering to knock. Annie would have lost her balance, but Emmeline Whitley had the quick reflexes that can only be attributed to a mother of five busy children. Emmeline grasped Annie's arm and steadied the younger woman.

"Mrs. Whitley, I'm so sorry," Annie started to apologize, but Emmeline cut her off with a pat on the shoulder and a shake of her auburn head.

"No harm done, Annie. And will you please start calling me by my given name? Besides the fact we're both Austin Abbey alums, being called Mrs. Whitley makes me feel elderly." As if that settled the matter, Emmeline waved a binder full of fabric and wallpaper samples at her husband. "I've had the loveliest idea for your office, darling," she said.

Noah rolled his eyes, and Ford smothered a grin.

"My office is fine as it is, Emmeline. And I'm in the middle of a meeting."

"Oh, I know, your secretary told me," Emmeline replied, dropping the heavy binder on the desk with a thwap. "Merilee, my dear, it's so good to see you."

Ford felt a mite sorry for Noah, who looked like he'd been caught unprepared in a Texas dust devil.

He swiveled to see Annie's reaction to Emmeline's interruption, but Annie, to his dismay, was gone. Turning back, he saw Emmeline's calculating gaze on him, her head tilted to the right and one gloved finger pressed against her lips. Sensing danger, Ford looked at Noah, who shrugged helplessly, then reached for his wife and pulled her close.

"Mr. Winters, would you care to join us for lunch?" Noah asked.

Ford suppressed a groan. He wanted to get to the ranch, assess the state of things, and get to work. Eight years ago he would have given his eyeteeth for such a warm welcome into Austin's elite society. Now he couldn't have cared less.

"Ford, you'll join us, won't you? Please?" Merilee stretched out the long "e" sound in "please" like a small child begging for candy, and fluttered her lashes in his direction.

Ford's heart warred with logic. Part of restoring the Kelly Ranch to its former glory would necessitate reclaiming its standing among the members of Austin society. This was a prime opportunity.

"I would be honored to join you. Thank you."

Four

Ford surveyed the Whitleys' beautifully appointed dining room. There'd been a time in his life when he would have paid any price to be an honored and welcomed guest at such a table. Now that he'd arrived at his long-held dream, reality didn't hold the same intoxicating appeal. It made him more determined than ever to accomplish his goal and get out of town.

The Whitleys—Noah and Emmeline and their five children—were charming and polite and generous. No, it wasn't the Whitleys that soured the experience, or their guests, Will and Eliza Delacourt and their three children, visiting from Memphis. It wasn't even Merilee, who fawned and fluttered at his side. The food was delicious, the setting aesthetically pleasing, the conversation engaging. The children's laughter carried from the parlor, where they'd been served their meal spread out on blankets on the floor like a picnic.

Ford shook his head, shoving back his nagging discontent, and forced himself to focus on what Noah Whitley was saying to him.

"...I would expect you're quite anxious to get started out at the Kelly."

"Yes, although I really have no idea what to expect. I haven't seen the ranch or visited in eight years."

A silent pall fell over the table. Emmeline turned the full force of her golden brown gaze on him.

"I'm sure you know about the death of Mrs. Ellis?"

Ford nodded. Augusta's letters had informed him about the goings-on in Austin. When he'd heard of Annie's mother's passing a few years after his departure, he'd been sorely tempted to pack his bags and head back to Austin. But the next day the mine he'd invested in near Telluride had struck a silver vein. He'd been swept up in the rush.

"Since Mrs. Ellis passed away, things at the ranch have gone astray. I fear Mr. Ellis, in his grief..." Emmeline shared another telling glance with Eliza. "He has made some questionable choices in the management of the property. Annie started working at the Abbey immediately after her graduation to help cover the expenses at the ranch."

"Annie is working?" Ford's throat constricted. Augusta hadn't shared that bit of information with him in her otherwise effusive letters.

"She teaches art classes. She's an excellent instructor," Eliza said.

"She actually lives at the Abbey now," Emmeline added. "In case you need to ask her something about the ranch."

Ford's face grew hot.

Noah cleared his throat. "I think that's enough talk of business, Emmeline. Rest assured, I'll fill Mr. Winters in on the details of the property if he has any questions."

Emmeline speared her husband with a gimlet eye that would have turned a lesser man to solid Colorado granite. After a moment, she smiled. "Of course, darling. What shall we discuss instead?"

Will Delacourt folded his napkin and laid it beside his plate. "I'm looking forward to this year's regatta. Are you planning to attend, Noah?"

Merilee perked up. "Is it like a party?"

"It's a rowing competition," Will explained. "Teams come from around the world to compete. It's a challenge for sportsmen. I've thought about putting together a team."

Eliza elbowed her husband in the ribs. "I don't think so, Will."

Ford straightened, grateful for a change in conversation. "That actually sounds like fun."

Eliza and Emmeline turned matching expressions of disapproval on him. Ford's gaze dropped to his plate.

"It could be a fundraiser for the academy. A local team could garner donations to compete in the name of the Abbey." Noah sounded thoughtful.

"You aren't actually considering this?" Emmeline demanded.

Noah smiled at his wife. "Think what we could accomplish for your beloved Austen Abbey."

Emmeline leaned back in her chair. "You have no training, no preparation, and no skills."

"We can recruit the other alumni husbands and sons," Will said. "I'm sure they would be more than happy to dedicate some time and energy to the school."

Emmeline stared at Noah, then at Will. Finally, her generous mouth curved into a smile. "I'll talk to Augusta about promotion and getting a letter out to all the alums and their husbands."

Ford raised his linen napkin to dab at his mouth to hide his own smile. He'd unwittingly discovered his first new friends in Austin. Perhaps his return wouldn't be as awkward and uncomfortable as he'd imagined. But he still had to make things right at the Kelly.

"If you all would be so kind as to excuse me, I really need to get out to the ranch tonight. If I leave now, I should make it by dinnertime."

He left the Whitley residence amid a chorus of friendly farewells and instructions to the nearest livery.

He rented a wagon and collected his trunk from the train station, returned to the bank and opened an account, something he'd forgotten to do in the unexpected invitation to lunch. He stopped at a general store and bought two flannel work shirts, dungarees, and three new kerchiefs, then settled the outstanding debt on the Kelly Ranch tab. Several hours later, wallet lighter, Ford snapped the reins and set the rented team into a steady trot.

As he neared the property, he noted how little the area had changed. While Austin had flourished, it seemed the Kelly had been frozen in time. He smelled something tantalizing, and his mouth watered. As he'd suspected, he'd arrived just in time for supper, unannounced and uninvited. But that didn't matter. He'd bought his right to join the Ellis family table fair and square with money—the only thing Walt Ellis ever recognized as valuable.

Five

By the time she left town, the sun was low in the sky. Dark clouds rolling in from the southwest mirrored Annie's black mood as she urged her beloved mare forward. After leaving the bank, she'd gone back to the Abbey, intending to pick up her overnight bag and leave. Franny Sue Price—one of her favorite students—had waylaid her, distressed over a grade. Annie comforted Franny Sue and then trekked to Weed's Livery to collect Baby Gray.

She kneaded her belly with a clenched fist as she rode. The hard knot of bitter regret in her soul was a constant ache. She'd once been so quick to believe that her father and sister had her best interests at heart where Ford was concerned.

A mile outside of Austin, the clouds opened and drenched her in rain. She nudged the mare's sides with her heels, urging her to speed up. The road became slick, slimy mud under Baby Gray's hooves, and the mare stumbled more than once. Mist hindered Annie's vision. She wiped moisture from her face and let the reins lie slack, grateful the horse knew the way home with or without visual cues. Thanks to Ford's training, she thought with a pang.

The landscape was shrouded in a sodden gray blanket when light finally pierced the gloom. Monroe, the Kelly's aging foreman, had the lantern out. She'd called from the livery to let him know she was coming home for the night.

Annie patted the mare's neck. "Monroe will give you some oats, sweetheart. You've earned them."

As they approached the barn, the mare pricked her ears. Her hooves, clotted with mud, moved more easily. Monroe scurried toward them on bowed legs, the lantern in his hand swaying from side to side in a wild arc.

"Miss Annie, you've no biz'ness out in this weather," he groused. "And this late in the day, no less." He caught the mare's bridle in his free hand. His teeth and the whites of his eyes glimmered in the lantern light.

"I told the storm to hold off, Monroe, but it wouldn't mind me."

Monroe rewarded her teasing with a genuine smile as she dismounted.

"I'm glad you're here safe. I dunno if the master held supper for you, but I 'spect my darlin' wife will have set something aside for you." He paused and cleared his throat, shuffling his feet in a way that told her he was anxious about something. "You should know, Mr. Winters arrived a little while ago."

Light flashed over Annie's vision. "He's here already?"

"Yes, miss. Explained the situation to me, and I 'spect stormed the castle and told your pa and sister all about it." Monroe's voice held no censure, only concern.

"Thank you for warning me. I came home to give my father and Edie the news, but I guess Ford beat me to it." She slogged toward the house in the continuing drizzle. "Good night, Monroe," she called over her shoulder.

She paused outside the front door to peel off her wet gloves. Squaring her shoulders, she twisted the doorknob and stepped across the threshold into her own personal purgatory.

He'd fallen into some alternate version of hell, but at least he wouldn't starve.

His unannounced arrival at the ranch had been less dramatic than he'd feared. He'd simply shown Walt and Edie the documentation that outlined his lease. Walt, already well into his cups, had blinked and sputtered. Edie had regarded him with calculating eyes and invited him in for supper.

Ford grimaced behind his napkin as Edie recounted—for at least the third time—her extensive social connections in Austin. He smoothed his features and returned the threadbare linen square to his lap.

Edie stared at him across the polished walnut table. He hadn't been paying close attention to her monologue and was unsure what she hoped to hear. He opened his mouth to compliment the meal when a gust of wind—damp and cool from the rain—whooshed into the stuffy dining room.

Edie's head, tilted at a coquettish angle, snapped up straight. She prodded her father's arm with none-too-gentle fingers.

"Father, someone is here. Perhaps you should see who it is."

Walt huffed and rose on unsteady legs.

A bedraggled Annie entered the room. "Oh, for heaven's sake, Father, sit down before you fall down."

Ford cursed his pulse-pounding response to Annie's voice and rose.

Walt collapsed into his chair and retrieved his half-drained glass of whiskey.

Annie dropped her soggy gloves on the table with a wet slap and eyed the room's occupants, her fire-lit gaze settling on Ford.

"Well now, isn't this cozy?" she muttered, pulling out a chair before Ford could do it for her.

Monroe's wife, Berea, waddled into the room with a steaming mug and a full plate which she placed on the table. She draped a woven shawl around Annie's shoulders and disappeared into the bowels of the house without a word.

Annie wrapped both hands around the mug and lifted it to her mouth. Despite the shawl and the hot drink, she shivered, and Ford was tempted to demand she take a warm bath and go to bed. Instead, he sat back down, picked up his fork, and began to work his way through a decadent piece of chess pie.

"Annie," Edie's nasal whine pierced his internal prayer.

Annie sighed and set the drink down.

"We simply must have a dinner party for Mr. Winters, to celebrate his return to Austin." Edie fluttered imploring eyes at Ford. "We will be inviting Miss Merilee and her family to the dinner party, won't we? I understand the two of you are an item."

Ford choked. A circuit-riding preacher he'd met in Colorado had once told him, "If the Gospel message spread as fast as gossip, the whole world would have heard the Good News in less than a month." Never had Ford realized how true that statement was until now.

"Miss Whitley and I are not an 'item.' I escorted her to Austin as a favor to her family, that's all."

"Still, she's expected to be quite a catch this season, Mr. Winters. The man who wins her hand will have a great deal of influence in Austin society."

"That's all well and good, but I'm not in the market," Ford growled. "Nor am I here to gain influence in the Austin society pages."

Ford wondered if Edie remembered he'd been little more than a servant himself when he left Austin, on the same social level as Monroe and Berea.

"Of course we'll host a dinner party for Mr. Winters. We'll invite the whole town." Walt's words slurred as he banged his now-empty glass on the table and slumped toward Edie. "My dear, you make whatever arrangements need to be made. I'll see to it that the bills are paid."

Annie snorted. "Ford will be handling the accounts from here on out, Father. Do as you will." Without another word, she left the room.

Ford endured a barrage of questions from Edie and Walt about his availability, whom he would invite, and whether to order French champagne or take a risk on the latest trend—wine from California. When father and daughter began to argue the merits of red versus white, Ford escaped the dining room and went hunting for Annie. He'd squelch the party plans later.

He took the stairs to the upper floor two at a time. Light glimmered under Annie's door. He tapped with two knuckles and counted to fifteen before the door jerked open.

"Ford." Her tone was cool.

"Annie." Ford peered over her head into the room. Clothing was strewn across the bed and draped over a chair. Her carpetbag stood open on the bed.

"Packing?"

She shrugged. "I don't live here anymore."

Ford ran a hand over his face and through his hair. "I have no desire to fight with you."

"Nor I you." The set of her jaw belied her words.

"Can we be friends, at least?"

"We're business associates now, Ford. That will have to suffice. You can reach me at the Abbey if you have any questions."

He felt the rift in her soul as she said the words. Her heart was at the Kelly, and they both knew it. He ransacked his brain for an argument, noting at the same time the soft flush on her mouth. Uninvited and decidedly unwelcome memories of kissing her trampled rational thought and he stepped back, putting her out of reach.

"What's happened here?" he asked.

Her eyes flashed. "Here?" She gestured to herself. "Or here?" She waved her hand around in a circle to include the ranch. The raw pain in her eyes unnerved him.

"First, here..." He mirrored her movement, encompassing the ranch as a whole. "Because I think that's directly related to what's happened here..." His hand stilled, one finger pointed at her heart.

She paled, but when she spoke, her voice was strong. "What's happened here is that my mother died, and I'm not strong enough or good enough or virtuous enough to keep my father and sister from going off the rails. They persuade me to do their will, but I have no power to persuade them to do anything."

She choked on a sob and Ford started to reach for her, but she held up a hand, palm out, to ward him away.

"I'm not the person who needs to be running this ranch, Ford. I've failed. Please, do better than I've done." She closed the door and shut him out.

Six

In the cold hours before dawn, the front door creaked open and banged shut. Ford clenched tangled sheets in his fists. He would not chase after her, would not beg her to stay. He rolled to face the window. The storm had passed, and moonlight silhouetted the buggy as it disappeared down the lane.

After he'd spoken to Annie the night before, he'd searched out Monroe and asked him to take Annie to town in the buggy instead of letting her ride back to the livery alone.

The old man's whiskers had twitched like a rabbit's. "She'll fight me, Mr. Winters. The girl does what she pleases."

Ford had replied, "She's got no business traipsing to and from Austin alone. Austin might think itself civilized, but no place is that civilized."

"I'm agreeing with you, son. Tell you what: My wife's been hankering to visit her sister in town. I'll tell Miss Annie she can ride in with Berea."

Ford had thanked the old man. It was good to have an ally. He'd been prepared to march into the stable in his union suit and throw the stubborn woman into the buggy by force, if necessary.

As the sun crept higher in the eastern sky, the weight of his new responsibility settled upon him. For the first time in his adult life, he was accountable to someone besides God and his own conscience. A man should be up by now, and busy with work.

Five minutes later, Ford scraped his razor over his cheeks and chin, praying with each sharp, careful stroke for wisdom regarding the ranch's future. He'd returned to Austin half out of ambition, half out of a desire to satisfy his wounded pride. He grimaced in distaste at his reflection in the mirror above the dresser. Those were questionable motives on a good day.

"Too late now," he muttered.

When he made his way downstairs, he found Walt Ellis snoring on the velvet chaise in the parlor, still clad in last night's rumpled attire. Ford's mouth tightened. Making his way through the house, Ford noted the tattered upholstery, accumulated dust, and faded wallpaper. The front door whined like a cranky cat. The paint on the porch was peeling, and his boot caught on a loose board as he jogged down the steps and headed for the barn. The place was falling apart, and yet Walt and Edie were planning a party. On credit.

The wholesome scent of sweet, dry hay welcomed him into the barn. His eyes flickered to the loft. He'd stolen his first kiss from Miss Annie Ellis there when they were in their early teens. She'd slapped him, and he'd tumbled from the loft and broken his arm. Ford chuckled and rubbed his forearm. It still ached sometimes when it rained.

A grizzled gray head poked out of a stall. "That you, Mr. Winters?"

"Yessir, it is."

A warm smile cracked Monroe's weathered face. "Good t'see you in the daylight, boy." Monroe closed the stall door behind him and ambled toward Ford on bowed legs. Ford allowed the older man to wrap him in an embrace. Monroe and Berea had never shown Ford anything but kindness. "My Berea and Miss Annie set off in the buggy more than an hour ago."

"Thank you for tending to Miss Annie."

Monroe stepped back and cocked his head to the right, his one good eye focusing on Ford with unerring accuracy. "Love the gal as if she was my own daughter, you know."

"I know, sir," Ford replied, and then changed the subject. "How are things here, then?"

Monroe cleared his throat noisily and spat on the dirt floor. "Terrible. But I expect you know that, since Miss Annie's sold out her inheritance."

Ford's eyebrows lifted in surprise at the bitterness in Monroe's voice.

"I'm thankful it's you, don't get me wrong, boy," Monroe said, shaking his head. "But it sore grieves my heart that it's come to this. Her pa..." Monroe caught himself. "I expect you'll be wanting to see the stock, then?" Before Ford could reply, Monroe swiveled away. "I'll saddle yer horse, and we'll get going."

The sun scorched the western horizon deep orange by the time Ford and Monroe dismounted again. Ford gathered the horse's reins in one hand and led the animal inside. Fatigue—and discouragement—settled over him like a heavy blanket. The conditions at the Kelly were dismal. Fences were down. The cattle that hadn't been auctioned off were malnourished. Even the chickens in their coop seemed weary.

He'd jumped at the chance to buy shares in the Kelly with the idea of swooping in as its savior, showing off his acquired wealth and worldliness, and riding away when he was done, letting all of Austin—and especially Annie—know what they'd lost when they rejected him. Now, he didn't know what he wanted, exactly. Riding the land had reminded him how much he loved the work, loved the place. And, though he didn't want to admit it, seeing Annie again had resurrected his feelings for her.

The sounds of horses chomping grain and the whistle of brushes over slick horsehide were the only noises to be heard in the barn for a long while.

"Monroe?" Ford's currycomb stilled mid-stroke, and he pressed his forehead against the animal's warm flank. He inhaled comforting scent of horseflesh, warm and alive.

"Mr. Winters?"

"Just call me Ford, Monroe, you've known me too long to call me mister anything." He recognized the snorting sound as Monroe's acknowledgment. "What's to be done to save this place?"

Silence stretched between them. Prodding Monroe for quick answers was fruitless. He liked to formulate his responses.

The sound of Monroe's currycomb thudding into a tack box preceded his reply.

"Money's the solution, of course. Not merely pouring money into the place, but keeping Mr. Ellis—" Monroe paused to expectorate over the stall door. "—and Miss Edie away from the money."

Ford closed his eyes. Monroe's answer wasn't a surprise, but neither was it a welcome solution. It would create more strife in an already tense situation.

Ford patted the gelding's neck, tossed his own currycomb into the box with Monroe's, and left the stall. Monroe was waiting for him outside. Dusky evening light turned everything a muted shade of gray. Monroe pulled out a pipe and packed it with tobacco from a stained leather pouch. Ford leaned against the side of the barn and watched lights begin to flicker on in the house, not quite ready to go inside.

"What might your intentions be toward Miss Annie, if you don't mind my askin'?"

He did mind, because he didn't know the answer. He'd returned with some sort of distorted idea of justice—or retribution. And then when he saw her again, everything shifted. He turned toward the older man.

"I'll be honest with you, Monroe—I've no idea."

Monroe guffawed. "Well, boy, I'd say you're in trouble at least as big as the state of Texas. And you ain't likely to solve the problem on your own. Are you a prayin' man?"

"I am. For several years now."

Monroe clapped a hand on Ford's shoulder. Tears glittered in the man's cloudy eyes. "Glad to hear it, son, because I'm thinking you'll need to be spending plenty of time on your knees."

Seven

Annie awoke with the sound of her mother's laughter echoing through her mind. She pulled the coverlet over her face and pressed her hands to her ears. She hadn't dreamed of her mother in months. Why now?

Oh, she knew why. Because Ford was back. Her mother had loved Ford. When Annie yielded to Walt and Edie's persuasion, Annie's mother had been heartbroken. How Annie wished for a way to redeem the time, to make her mother proud of her again.

She knew her mother would approve of her work at the Abbey, where she poured her energy into lesson plans and spent her evenings hunched over lumps of clay or paint-spattered canvasses, sharing her love of art with the students. But she also knew her mother had hoped Annie would one day run the Kelly Ranch.

Tears trickled out the corners of her eyes, down her temples and into her hair.

It had been three days since she'd fled from the ranch. Three days of throwing herself into her classes, into extra hours in the studio, into volunteering to design and paint huge canvas banners for the upcoming regatta. And three days in which she hadn't been able to stop thinking about Ford. His proximity had flung her backward in time to the hours and days when they'd been friends, when they'd first begun to see each other through the filter of young love. How she had loved him!

And then to the weeks of being harangued by her father during meals; the late night visits from Edie—well-versed in the art of manipulation—to warn her away from Ford. They'd worn her down in every way, until their arguments seemed reasonable. Until she couldn't hear the voice of her own heart.

A sharp rap at the door startled her. She dragged herself off the bed and pulled a plain wrapper over her thin lawn nightdress. The visitor knocked again, and Annie opened the door.

Ford, eyes spitting green dragon fire, was not the visitor she expected.

"What are you doing here?" She jerked the wrapper snug around her midsection. Male visitors were only permitted in the Abbey's public rooms downstairs. "You know better than to come up here. Mrs. Collins would have an apoplexy. Get out, you'll get us both in trouble."

"You think you can abandon me in the midst of the mess the Kelly has become and run off to play school and sleep late?"

Annie's eyes widened, first with shock and then with indignation. "Excuse me? Did you say I was 'playing school'? I'll have you know, Ford Winters, that I take my responsibility to the school and to my students seriously. I'm not 'playing' at anything." Her anger escalated with every word, and she caught herself wagging her index finger at him in teacherly disapproval. Old, spinster-like disapproval, she thought in horror.

Before she could jerk her hand back, Ford wrapped one warm, callused hand around her finger, sending a jolt of heat through her.

"I apologize. I shouldn't have belittled your work. I've heard nothing but good things about what you've accomplished at the Abbey."

Annie's eyes met his, testing for sincerity. She saw no deception in his green gaze.

"However, the school year is nearly over." His grip tightened. "Therefore, there is no reason for you to stay at the Abbey when you should be at the ranch."

His voice was calm and even, but Annie noted the telltale muscle twitch in his cheek and knew he was primed for a battle of wills. She frowned. She couldn't tell him the truth. Staying at the ranch wasn't an option when his presence reminded her of all the things she'd felt for him once, and her own folly. Frantic, she scanned the room for a suitable excuse to stay at the Abbey as long as possible. The regatta flier peeked out from beneath a stack of books on her desk. She plucked her hand free, snatched up the paper, and thrust it toward him.

"I have responsibilities here."

She had been considering ways to beg off her role as chaperone, to avoid attending the ball, but Ford's demand for her to return to the ranch upped the ante.

Ford glanced at the flier without taking it. "I'm well aware of the regatta. I'm on one of the rowing teams."

Annie blinked at him. "What?"

He smiled. A Cheshire cat's grin if she'd ever seen one. "We've formed an amateur team. All proceeds will go to the Abbey."

"We?"

"Noah, Will Delacourt, Harmon Gray, and a few others."

"That...that's very generous of you."

"I'll be at the regatta, and available to personally escort you home to the Kelly afterward, unless I can convince you to come back with me now."

Bossy. Ford had always tended toward bossiness. It was one of his least appealing traits and never failed to spark her anger. She stiffened her spine, ready to revolt.

"Annie, I need you."

His words sucked all the starch out of her. Her arms dropped to her sides. Ford picked up her right hand and pressed it to his chest. His heart pulsed beneath her palm, and something warm and soft and altogether lovely began to unfurl in her soul.

"I love the Kelly Ranch, I always have, but I don't know it, or love it, the way you do. I need you to help me bring it back to life."

The warmth blossoming within her shriveled and died like a shooting star. Annie snatched her hand back. "It's obvious my help at the ranch has only served to drive it toward destruction," she said.

Ford shook his head. Inky-black hair scattered haphazardly across his forehead, begging her to sweep it back into place. She clutched at her wrapper to keep her fingers from yielding to that urge.

"That's absurd, Annie. I've been through the books. The only people driving the Kelly toward destruction are your father and sister and their predilection for buying on credit and making foolish decisions."

Her eyes flickered to his. Father and Edie had long blamed her for their financial difficulties. Having someone—anyone—take her side was balm to her wounded soul, yet doubt and fear hovered in the back of her mind.

"That doesn't mean I can help you. I was willing to sell shares in the ranch because I finally realized I don't have what it takes," Annie whispered.

Ford grasped her shoulders. "That's ridiculous, and you know it. No one knows the land and stock like you do. But from what Monroe tells me, ever since your mother passed, you've basically washed your hands of the place."

Her eyes widened. "That's not true!" Even as the words left her mouth she knew he was right. In her grief, she'd refused the role her mother had groomed her for with such diligence.

"Stay through the regatta, if you like, but once it's over, I'm taking you home." With that edict, he strode away, boots clattering down the wooden steps. When the door slammed shut behind him, Annie let herself breathe again.

Ford barreled out of the gatehouse and nearly trampled a visitor, a woman. He lunged backward, apologizing. She waved a gloved hand at him.

"No harm done." Kind, curious eyes scrutinized him. "I'm Lila Wen... Ross." A blush suffused her cheeks. "I'm recently married."

"Ford Winters. I'm glad I ran into you. I have a call in to your husband about joining an amateur rowing team to benefit the Abbey. Would you ask him to get in touch with me? I'm at the Kelly Ranch."

Lila blanched. "Oh. You're Ford. That Ford. Annie's Ford."

Annie's Ford. The phrase disconcerted him. "Not exactly."

Lila shook her head. "I heard... But that's not what I meant..." She raised her hand to her mouth, as if to stop herself from saying more. "It's nice to meet you, Mr. Winters. I'll let Kirby know you'd like to speak with him." And with that, she scurried past and disappeared into the gatehouse.

Ford gazed into the cloudless Texas sky. It was a perfect day to be out on the ranch, but he'd spent the last three days not in the pasture mending fences, or tending to sick livestock, or even fixing up the house. No, he'd spent three long days trapped in the study, mired in past-due notices, with Walt and Edie hovering behind him making demands he couldn't, or wouldn't, satisfy.

The call to meet with Noah and the other gentlemen who'd agreed to form a rowing team had been a welcome means of escape. After the meeting, wherein he met a young and brash Eddie Mansford and reconnected with his distant step-cousin, Harmon Gray, he'd gone to the Abbey, determined to convince Annie her place was at the ranch.

Finding Annie in her wrapper, hair loose around her shoulders and face flushed with sleep had been a jolt to his system. The girl he'd fallen in love with was as stubborn as she'd ever been. As always, her stubbornness made Ford bossy, and the bossier he got, the more mule-headed she became. He needed help and he knew it. And who better than Augusta Collins for advice on the female psyche? Besides, he should explain his visit, lest she hear he'd invaded the holy sanctum of the teacher's apartments from someone else.

He bounded up the steps two at a time. The front verandah welcomed guests with its white wicker chairs and plump chintz cushions. The boards under his feet were sturdy and recently repainted. Fragrant flowers bloomed in baskets along the railing, lending their sweet scent to the humid air. The polished brass plate around the door handle gleamed in the early summer sunshine.

He frowned. No wonder Annie would rather be here at the Abbey than at home. The school grounds—well-organized, ordered, peaceful, settled—must feel like a sanctuary in comparison to the ranch. All the tasks to be accomplished at the Kelly overwhelmed him. It was a heavy burden to bear, too heavy for any one person, male or female.

He reached for the knocker.

"Ford? What a lovely surprise!" Augusta Collins intercepted him, her arms laden with fresh-cut flowers.

Ford kissed both her cheeks in the European fashion. "I should have come by here before I headed to the Kelly Ranch. I've missed you."

"Come inside," she said, ushering him into the foyer. "We have much to discuss."

"Do we ever," he muttered, entering the cool interior of the Abbey. Augusta delegated the flowers to a student and waved Ford toward her office.

Eight

The second soft knock on Annie's door that morning startled her more than the first. She hesitated, wondering if Ford had returned. Finding Lila Wentworth Ross on the other side of the threshold was such a relief that Annie gathered her friend into an uncharacteristic hug.

"Annie, are you unwell?" Lila maintained a steady grip on Annie's upper arms and searched her face.

"No, I'm fine. I slept late. It is Saturday, you know."

"But...that man..."

Annie gasped. "Ford! Did he bother you?"

Lila frowned. "No, of course not. He was a perfect gentleman when I met him outside. I do believe the man is interested in you, Annie, and I have no idea why you would refuse him if he has come calling after all this time."

Annie dragged her friend, none too gently, into the room, closing the door behind them. "Don't be ridiculous, Lila. Mr. Winters hasn't come calling. We've naught but a business relationship." Annie offered Lila a wide, toothy smile. Lila crossed her arms.

"I don't think I believe you."

"I'm serious, Lila. He bought a share of my family's property, not a share of me."

Lila's brows rose at that statement. "And you're all right with that?"

"I have no choice about the shares. I don't even want to see him. In fact, I rebuffed him even this morning."

"Perhaps he cares for you, Annie," Lila's eyes softened with the romantic illusions harbored by a happy newlywed.

"Maybe once, but no longer."

"I don't believe that." The starch in Lila's usually mild tone surprised Annie.

"Lila? Are you upset with me?"

Lila shook her head. "No. I think—" She pressed her lips together and seemed to weigh her words. "Everyone deserves a chance, that's all."

Lila knew her history with Ford as well as anyone. Did she mean Ford deserved a second chance? Annie had been the one to reject Ford, not the other way around. Besides, she would never expect Ford to give her a second chance after the way she had treated him.

"Maybe it's not Ford who needs a chance, Annie. Maybe you need to give yourself one," Lila murmured, reading Annie's face.

"I don't want to talk about it."

Lila patted Annie's shoulder sympathetically. "Oh dear, I'm sorry. I didn't mean to upset you. And you're right, that isn't why I came by. I finished reading the May edition of Ladies' Home Journal and I wanted to bring it to you." Lila reached into the bag she carried and withdrew the magazine. "I know you love Emma Haywood's column on art every month. And this month there was a wonderful story about Queen Victoria, as well."

Guilt flooded through Annie. "Thank you for thinking of me. I'm sorry I'm such dreadful company. I've not been myself since this whole business with Ford coming back to town." She took the magazine. "Can you stay for a bit? Tell me all about Kirby and married life, and take my mind off my troubles?"

Lila smiled, then giggled. "Talk about my handsome husband? Of course! And while I talk, let me do your hair. Don't you have a meeting with Mrs. Collins and the other teachers today?"

Annie groaned. "I'd forgotten all about that. Thank you for reminding me." She settled herself on a stool in front of the dresser and reached for her mother's silver-handled brush, which Lila snatched from her fingers.

"Let me."

The sheer pleasure of having someone else brush her hair, then braid and twist and pin it into place, swept Annie out of her own head and into Lila's glorious new life as a married woman. She loved her friend and Kirby too much to feel anything but joy for the two of them.

The two friends chatted for more than an hour, and then Lila prepared to leave. "I should get going, I'm supposed to meet Kirby for lunch downtown. I'll talk to you soon, all right?"

Annie nodded.

"I mean it, Annie Ellis. You call on me if you need anything at all, even if it's only a shoulder to cry on. Lord knows I've cried on yours often enough."

Annie grinned. There was some truth to that statement. After she closed the door, she pressed her back against it. She did feel better, although Lila's words about second chances echoed through Annie's soul. Was there such a thing, truly?

The bell on the clock tower chimed, and she realized how late it was. Stripping off wrapper and nightdress, she dressed herself: chemise, petticoat, the despised corset, a high-necked, severe black serge dress, fraying at hem and cuffs and collar. She added stockings and shoes, grabbed a hat and a pair of gloves, and darted out the door, immensely glad her hair was already coiffed.

The other teachers and a few of the older students had gathered in Augusta's study. Some were seated around the small table with its fantastic spread of hors d'oeuvres, some perched on tufted ottomans and sofas. They all cradled delicate china cups between thumb and forefinger, sipping at appropriate intervals. Annie resisted the urge to groan. She loathed tea, far preferring the strong, black "cowboy coffee" she'd grown up with at the ranch.

"Annie, dear, I've had coffee prepared for you," Augusta said when she spotted Annie in the doorway. Annie flushed, humbled by the woman's innately gracious behavior. Franny Sue handed her a thick white mug. Annie took a sip of the rich, dark brew that never failed to remind her of her mother, thanked Augusta and Franny, and found a seat.

Augusta called for attention. "As you all know, the regatta is the highlight of Austin's social season. It's a grand opportunity for the students of the academy to present themselves to a wide variety of influential individuals—"

"Eligible individuals," Franny Sue whispered. Those nearest tittered behind their gloved hands.

"Hush," Augusta said. "Matchmaking is not the directive of this academy, as you all know. Educating and refining young women so that they may succeed in whatever course God's calling dictates for them is our purpose."

The whispers and giggles evaporated.

"With that said, there may well be opportunities for some of our graduates to meet suitable gentlemen. Or to renew old courtships."

A dozen eyes turned on Annie, sending a rush of heat to her face that threatened to set her hair on fire. Mrs. Collins, much to Annie's surprise, merely smiled and tilted her elegant head in a gesture of assent before continuing to speak.

The headmistress outlined the events and activities the girls and their chaperones would be attending, but Annie could scarcely pay attention. The implications of her earlier words whirled through Annie's mind like a Texas tornado.

She'd convinced herself her feelings for Ford were a girl's infatuation, but having him suddenly thrust into her life again had her questioning her own arguments. Annie took another sip of the bitter black coffee and forced herself to pay attention.

"...I've sent invitations to many of our graduates and their families," Mrs. Collins was saying. "Many of them plan to attend the regatta anyway, and several of our alumni husbands and family members have created their own team, which provides an ideal occasion to celebrate this year's commencement with a ball."

And a perfect chance to promote the academy by presenting a united front of successful, happy women who attributed their success to the Jeanette C. Austen Academy for Young Ladies, Annie thought.

Augusta's lips curved into a smile. "Having the commencement ball during the regatta is an ideal way to promote the benefits of the academy, but we wouldn't be so gauche as to call it advertising, now would we?"

Someone who didn't know Augusta Collins might not have recognized the sparkle of humor in her eyes, or the shrewd wisdom of her plan. Annie grinned at the headmistress and earned a conspiratorial nod in return.

The ball was scheduled for Friday evening, following the regatta festivities. Annie suppressed a sigh. Where would she come up with a suitable dress? As a chaperone during the regatta, her plain, well-worn, everyday attire would be excused, but as an academy alum and example to her students, appropriate attire for the ball was expected, if not required. Her mind ran through her meager bank account. There was no way to justify the purchase of a new gown.

Asking Ford for the money since he was now in charge—as she'd so belligerently announced—irritated like a cactus thorn in her shoe. There was no way she would ask Ford Winters to subsidize her wardrobe, even if it was for the sake of the Abbey. Asking for his financial help would be worse than the alternative of raiding her sister's wardrobe, and that was not an option. She'd have to make do.

Would that be the story of her life? The girl who "made do"?

"I've spoken with the regatta officials. We have to be registered by week's end," Ford told Noah over lunch. "Do you think you can come up with three more names?

Noah dabbed his mouth with a napkin. "If all else fails we'll pull in some of the local ranch hands and younger fellows."

"Thank you. I'm afraid my connections are rather limited."

"I understand. I commend you for your willingness to step up and participate in the regatta so soon after coming back to town."

"It's for a good cause."

Noah tilted his head in assent. "And a good way to gain the favor of a certain art teacher?"

Ford choked on the mouthful of water he was attempting to swallow. Noah pounded his back until Ford held up a hand, indicating he could indeed breathe on his own.

"I'm sorry," Noah said. "You have to understand something about my wife. Emmeline fancies herself something of a matchmaker. Has for years. After the meeting in my office she insisted there was something between you and Annie Ellis. I confess, usually she's right, but if she's not I'll be sure to tell her to stay out of it."

Ford took a small, safe sip from his glass and placed it back on the table. "No apologies are necessary. There was something between Annie and me, a long time ago. Before I left Austin."

"I've heard something of the story, the Abbey grapevine being what it is," Noah replied. "And now that you've come back?"

Ford fidgeted with his water glass. "I don't know. A lot has changed." He paused, remembering the jail cell in Santa Fe. "I do know I would like to see Annie restored to her rightful place at the Kelly Ranch, and if I can help make that happen, I will."

He felt the older man's gaze on him. "That's a good place to start."

"We made it, finally." Will Delacourt joined them, breaking the thread of conversation between Ford and Noah. "One of the children has a fever."

"Nothing serious, I hope?" Noah asked.

"Eliza doesn't think so, and I trust her judgment." Will pulled out a chair and sat down. "How are our plans for the regatta coming along?"

Ford sat back. What he would give for a marriage like Will's, or Noah's. The thought startled him. He'd long preferred adventure and the open road, and yet he found himself envious of these two gentlemen. He wanted what they had.

Nine

Ford's unexpected appearance outside the Abbey's front gate on Sunday morning irritated Annie. Shouldn't he be at the ranch, fixing the mess she'd been unable to repair on her own? She tried to focus on her annoyance as he approached, but Ford Winters in his Sunday-best attire was something of a distraction. It was difficult to reconcile the boy she'd known with the man he'd become.

As was her Sunday habit since her mother's death, Annie relaxed on the verandah with a mug of coffee in her hand and her unopened Bible in her lap. She'd convinced anyone who asked that the big Austin congregations were such a contrast to the small clapboard church of her childhood she found it impossible to concentrate on the Lord. Mrs. Collins was not convinced by her excuse. Annie was certain she was on Augusta's prayer list, but the lady—in her graciousness—had never confronted her about her avoidance of Sunday worship.

Ford stalked up the steps. He wouldn't be so easy to dissuade. She knew from the snatches of conversation she'd overheard around the Abbey that Ford had encountered God somewhere during his travels. She wished her own convictions were as solid as his were reputed to be, but Ford was the last person on earth with whom she wanted to discuss matters of faith and forgiveness and love. Especially love.

Without so much as a greeting, Ford settled into the wicker settee beside her, forcing Annie to shift her legs and feet so they wouldn't brush against his.

"I missed you at church. I left a few minutes early to see if you were all right."

"I generally don't attend when I'm in town," she replied. "I prefer a smaller congregation."

"From what Reverend Albright tells me, you've avoided all church congregations for a very long time."

Annie wrinkled her nose. How dare the portly little pastor talk about her behind her back? "Are you checking up on me?"

"I ran into him yesterday. He, for whatever reason, remembers me, and he asked after you. Come to find out, you haven't darkened the door of a church since your momma died."

"Leave me alone, Ford."

"I can't." He reached over and covered her hand with his own. "We're partners, you and I, and we need to be in agreement about the future of the Kelly."

"Fine. I agree." She snatched her hand away, perturbed by the heat that remained.

"Not good enough, Annie. The troubles at the ranch are going to need more than good intentions to solve. Church is a good place to start when your troubles are bigger than you are."

The hair on the back of her neck bristled.

"No." She fought valiantly against the tears that prickled the backs of her eyelids. He didn't understand. She couldn't go back to church. She was guilty. Condemned. Judged and found wanting.

To her horror, he wrapped an arm firmly around her shoulders and tugged her against his side.

"You're much too thin," he commented, running his hand from her shoulder to her elbow. The touch was inflammatory, both to her senses and to her temper.

"Leave me alone!" Hot tears trickled down her cheeks. Ford stilled, and silence thickened the air between them. Then he groaned and pulled her into his embrace, pressing her against his broad chest.

Annie's too-slight frame stiffened, but Ford couldn't let her go. He buried his face in her hair, empathy flooding him with such force it was like a physical blow to the gut. He'd suffered after her rejection, but what she'd endured far surpassed his mostly self-inflicted misery. How he wished he'd been man enough to stay and fight for her, with her.

"I'm so sorry, Annie," he whispered. "Can you ever forgive me?"

Her body, wound tight as a drawn bowstring, went limp. Her hot tears seeped through his shirt, and he prayed his heartfelt words were powerful enough to lance her toxic wounds. Perhaps this was the ultimate purpose for his return to Austin. Not to redeem his reputation, or even to resurrect the Kelly Ranch, but to restore Annie's faith, so traumatized by the people and circumstances around her.

"Oh, Ford, whatever has happened to Miss Ellis?"

At the sound of Merilee's singsong voice, Annie jerked away from Ford as if he were a hot branding iron. He tugged a handkerchief from his pocket and slipped it into her hand. She turned her back on him and the approaching crowd. And it was, indeed, a crowd.

Merilee, resplendent in a pale pink silk gown, was accompanied by Augusta and a veritable catalogue of the Abbey's most prominent alumnae and their respective spouses: Emmeline and Noah Whitley, Harmon and Kathryn Gray, Eliza and Will Delacourt, Brandon and Marion Tabor, and newlyweds Lila and Kirby Ross, the latest addition to the rowing team. A ruckus in the yard alerted Ford to the presence of more than a half-dozen children of various ages and sizes tumbling over one another like puppies in the grass.

Augusta climbed the porch steps with haste and approached Annie with outstretched arms. Ford stood guard between Annie and the averted eyes of the guests who filed quietly into the Abbey for the impromptu Sunday meeting about the upcoming regatta. That was why he'd left church before the service ended. He'd wanted a few moments with Annie before the meeting.

Emmeline Whitley pinned Ford with the same scrutinizing look she'd given him at dinner as she passed. Noah stepped behind her, gripped her shoulders, and whispered, "No, Emmeline," just loud enough for Ford to hear, before steering her inside.

Ford turned. Augusta had taken Annie to the opposite side of the verandah and sat with her on a cushioned bench, holding her hands and speaking low. He hadn't come here to make Annie cry. He'd only wanted...what had he wanted? He'd wanted her at church this morning. He wanted her back at the ranch. With him.

He watched Augusta lead Annie away, toward the apartments, and wrapped his fingers around the railing like a man on a ship's deck in a hurricane. He'd come to discuss her spiritual condition, and instead exposed his own heart: he was still in love with her. Despite the wound she'd delivered him eight years ago, despite the desperate situation in which they now found themselves, he was still in love with Annie Ellis.

He remained on the verandah until someone called him inside.

Over a dinner of cold chicken, fresh asparagus, and warm baking powder biscuits straight from the Abbey oven, the assembled group discussed plans for the regatta. When the children grew restless, everyone headed outside.

Ford resumed his position on the verandah, dazed by his epiphany about Annie and wondering what he was supposed to do about it. Merilee brushed up against his side as the children scattered across the lawn.

"We're all going to play hide and seek. Won't you join us?" She laid a dainty hand on his arm. He glanced down and pulled his arm away.

"No, thank you, Miss Merilee."

She pouted prettily before she flounced away.

"You sure, Ford?" Noah joined him at the railing. "We could use a sharp pair of eyes to find all the little ones. Some of those boys have a knack for getting into strange places."

Ford hesitated. "I guess I could join in for a round or two."

"You're worried about Annie?"

"It's that obvious?"

Noah chuckled. "Knowing something of the history between you two, if you weren't concerned about her welfare I'd be surprised to find you still here, now that you've seen the state of the Kelly Ranch."

Ford's chin dropped to his chest. "There is a lot to be done."

"Come on, we're getting started!" Will jogged past, waving at them to follow.

"I guess we should get moving," Ford said, relieved to change the topic. The two men ambled down the steps and onto the lawn, following Will's path.

The children, Merilee, a few of the Abbey students, and some of the more adventurous parents were clustered around the large live oak behind the Abbey. Rules were discussed, teams were chosen. A small girl in a white dress announced she'd counted to ten that day and should be "it" first. The adults chuckled, the young people groaned. The little girl turned her face toward the live oak, crossed her arms, and began to count in a hesitant, cautious voice. Ford, who was on her team, closed his eyes as children and adults scattered around him.

When the count reached ten, he opened his eye. A smile curved his lips at the shrieks and squeals of two little ones he spotted hiding in the lilacs, mere feet from where he stood. They leapt to their feet and darted toward the live oak. Ford shoved his hands in his pockets and ambled after them, thinking of Annie.

Even if he was still in love with her, he couldn't expect to roll back into town, take over her family's ranch, and have her fall at his feet. No, his original plan was the best one. He would restore the Kelly, give it back to her, and leave. She could marry someone else...

Pain gripped his heart at the thought.

"Psst. Up here!"

He stopped still and looked up. Balanced on the branch of a tree, he spotted a profusion of pink ruffles and stifled a groan.

"Merilee, you aren't supposed to tell me where you are."

She giggled. "I know, but I'd rather you find me than someone else, and I can't stay up here all day."

"It's not safe. You should come down."

"All right. Catch me."

And she launched herself off the branch.

Ford lunged forward, arms outstretched in a vain hope that he'd reach her in time, but the foolish girl had underestimated her distance from him. The frilly hem of her gown brushed his fingertips as she crashed to the ground like a wilted peony, broken and silent.

Ten

Annie woke from her nap relieved, refreshed, and embarrassed. Remembering how she'd sobbed and sniveled all over Augusta, Annie inched farther under her quilt. The venerable headmistress had walked Annie to her room with instructions to have a nap and come down for supper later. Annie had been more than willing to acquiesce.

Now she realized whatever Ford had jangled in her soul had needed to be disturbed. It was like having a dislocated joint reduced. It still hurt, but the joint was working again. When Augusta came on the scene with her gentle words and shrewd advice, all the emotional baggage Annie had been hauling around roiled to the surface. Regret, grief, fear, even her spiritual confusion, had tumbled out. Now that emptied-out-space in her soul was occupied by the most delicious sense of peace.

"Thank you, Jesus," she whispered into the empty room.

Someone knocked on her door.

"Annie? It's Lila."

Annie hauled herself out of bed and opened the door. Lila, her face wreathed in worry, gripped the doorjamb.

"I'm all right, Lila dear," Annie said, feeling guilty for worrying her newlywed friend. "I think I needed to let it all out. I'm feeling quite refreshed." When her friend's expression didn't change, Annie's brows drew together. "What's the matter?" She dragged Lila inside.

"While you were resting, some of the men organized a game with the children. Merilee Whitley fell and hit her head. They're taking her to the hospital now."

Blood drained from Annie's head and limbs. "What happened?"

Lila crossed the room, pointed out the window. "They were all playing hide and seek. Merilee climbed into a tree, and she called to Ford to catch her..." Her voice trailed off.

"Oh no." Annie raised a hand to her mouth, picturing the scene.

"She was just beyond his reach. He was right there when she...landed. He hasn't left her side since."

"He must feel terrible," Annie murmured.

Lila nodded solemnly. "He looked stricken. Augusta has organized a prayer meeting here at the Abbey, but a few of us are heading to the hospital. I thought you would want to come with us."

"Of course. I'll come right down." Annie cringed. Images of Ford and Merilee together at the bank, on the street, Merilee's dainty hand tucked into Ford's massive arm, assailed her. Was there more to Ford's relationship with Merilee than he'd let on? Her gut clenched.

"We'll wait for you," Lila said, tapping Annie's shoulder.

Ford bit his tongue to keep from shouting at the driver to speed up the team of horses, knowing it would do no good. Merilee, ghastly pale, lay still, pink ruffles smeared with blood from the gash to her scalp. Emmeline sat opposite Ford in the ambulance wagon, chafing one of the girl's limp hands between her palms.

"She's going to be fine, Ford, I'm sure of it," Emmeline said, her voice calm.

Ford shook his head. "I should have been paying more attention." Guilt racked his soul. Merilee had been flirting with him, teasing him, and he'd done nothing to stop her.

"It wasn't your fault," Emmeline said. "It was a foolish thing for her to do."

Guilt maintained its grip on his belly like a vicious claw. He willed himself to shut out the horrific image of Merilee's body fluttering toward the earth like a doomed butterfly.

At the hospital, attendants whisked Merilee away, leaving Ford, Noah, and Emmeline in a waiting area. Ford paced. Noah and Emmeline held hands and prayed.

Half an hour passed, then an hour. Ford wanted to ram a fist through a wall. When he thought he might implode, a white-coated physician appeared.

"You're here for the young lady?"

"I'm her cousin," Noah stepped forward. "How is she?"

"She's coming around. The blow to her head has caused some confusion and memory loss, but I believe she'll have a full recovery."

Noah sagged. Emmeline propped him up. Ford rubbed his face with both hands.

"Right now she has a terrible headache. She'll need plenty of rest and quiet. I'd like to keep her here for a few days for observation."

"Certainly," Noah responded.

Ford's peripheral vision registered motion and he turned toward the corridor. Annie, accompanied by Lila and Kirby Ross, had arrived with Augusta. Ford felt as though he'd swallowed ground glass.

Augusta went to Noah, Lila to Emmeline. Annie remained frozen in the orifice of the hallway. Her eyes met his, and held.

"Which one of you is Ford?" the doctor asked.

Ford's heart dropped into his stomach. "That would be me."

"The young lady is asking for you."

Ford broke the connection with Annie and focused on the doctor. "Now?"

"It might help jog her memory." The doctor motioned Ford to follow him, then turned. "You seem to be important to her."

Eleven

Bleary-eyed, Ford returned to the ranch at dawn. He'd spent most of the night sitting on a hard wooden bench at the hospital, swamped with guilt. Augusta, Noah, and Emmeline had all tried to tell him there was no reason to feel responsible for the girl's actions. He didn't believe them. Merilee had even apologized, but he hadn't been able to see beyond her bandaged head and blackened eye to receive her words.

He reined in his horse and dismounted. Monroe hobbled out of the barn to meet him. "I wondered what you'd gotten up to when you didn't come home last night." Monroe took in Ford's rumpled attire in a measuring glance. "Everything all right?"

"There was an accident at Austen Abbey yesterday afternoon."

Monroe clapped a hand against his chest. "Miss Annie! Is she all right?"

Ford shook his head. "Miss Annie is fine." Physically, at least. "Noah Whitley's cousin fell from a tree and had to be taken to the hospital."

"The little gal you brought into town on the train?"

"Yes. Merilee." Ford pulled off his derby and slapped it against his leg to shake off the dust. "I need to take care of things here and then head back to the hospital." A dull flush climbed up his neck and face. The guilt he'd been carrying since Merilee tumbled from the tree multiplied and grew like dandelions in springtime. He kept making mistakes. First Annie, then Merilee. Why had he thought he could make things better for anyone by coming back here?

"You should know I tried to talk to Annie about God, about faith, and I think I ended up hurting her." Ford scooped up an armful of fresh hay and chucked it into one of the stalls.

"Maybe you're going about it the wrong way." Monroe scooped level measures of grain and dumped them into buckets in each stall.

"What do you mean?"

"I mean, you're trying to get back in Miss Annie's good graces, trying to convince her that she's what needs fixin', when really what needs fixin' is this ranch."

Ford dumped an armload of hay into a stall and paused. Hadn't he thought that same thing? "So you're saying the ranch is the way to Annie's heart?"

Monroe shrugged. "Mebbe so, my boy, I don't rightly know. But if what you're doing ain't working, it's time to try somethin' new."

A flicker of hope bloomed in Ford's heart, along with an idea. It was a crazy idea, but an idea nonetheless. "Monroe, I think I know what to do."

"Then get to it, boy. I can manage the rest of the chores jes' fine."

Ford charged from the barn into the house and locked the office door behind him.

An hour later he opened the door and called for Walt and Edie. When they shuffled into the hall, he ushered them into the office, steeled for a fight.

"Take a seat, please, we need to talk."

Walt huffed, and Edie frowned at the dusty chair. Ford closed the door and waited. When they were seated, silent, and focused on him, he opened his mouth.

"As of today, you are under a spending freeze. There will be no purchases made, no money spent, unless I approve it first."

Edie shrieked. "You can't do that!"

Ford raised a brow. "I most certainly can. I checked the contract this morning." He pushed papers across the desk. Neither Walt nor Edie reached for them.

"In addition, you will either begin putting in a full day's work, or you will move out." Walt seemed to shrink before Ford's eyes. Edie, on the other hand, went red.

"I do not have to work! We aren't servants!" she hissed. A vein throbbed in her temple.

Ford gave her his best steely glare. "This is not the English aristocracy, Edie, and it never was. This is a working ranch. That means everyone works. Everyone pulls his, or her, own weight."

Edie lunged to her feet. "I. Will. Not. Work."

Ford smiled. "Then you will not eat."

Walt shuddered. Edie sat back down and held out her hands. "I don't know how to do anything," she whined. "And Daddy is too old."

"I am not!" Walt harrumphed. Ford suppressed a grin. Walt's vanity would get the best of him yet.

"Edie, I'm not expecting you to milk the cow or plow a field," Ford cajoled. "You can start with dusting and polishing the furniture, and straightening the bookshelves. Cleaning this room alone could take a week."

Her face reddened another shade. "I'm not stupid, Ford Winters, no matter what you think. I can clean a room as well as Berea, or Annie, or anyone else."

Full house, for the win.

"Walt, you'll begin with some simple projects around here..."

Walt lurched to his feet. "I'll get right on that, as soon as I have a drink." He stumbled toward the cabinet that held his whiskey decanter. Ford beat him to it.

"Nope. No more drinking. It's costing a small fortune." Ford raised the decanter over his head, out of Walt's reach. The older man lunged for it, but then seemed to wilt.

"I don't know if I can do without." He moved a trembling hand over his forehead and then snatched it back, gripping it in the other hand to steady it.

Compassion stirred in his belly for the man who'd helped cause him so much pain. "Walt, I'd be happy to pray with you."

Edie snorted, and Ford glared at her. Walt, however, grasped Ford's arm. "I'd appreciate that."

Everyone turned toward the window at the sound of the buggy. Ford pulled back the curtain and peered out. Relief flooded through him.

Annie had come home.

The door banged open. Annie swiveled and sucked in a breath. Ford, in all his masculine glory, stepped onto the porch, fists on hips. He marched down the steps and gripped Annie's elbow. "Could I speak with you?"

Annie shook her arm free. "I didn't expect you to be here."

"Where else would I be? This is my job now, remember?"

"I thought you'd be with Merilee."

"I was, all night. I'll go back when I'm done here for the day."

Annie flinched. He'd stayed at the hospital all night? He must care for Merilee even more than she thought. "I...I'm sorry. Is there anything I can do?"

"You could be here."

Annie's temper sparked. "I have duties at the Abbey, duties which have kept food on the table here for the last few years."

He gripped her arms, causing heat to run up her arms and into her head, setting her senses aflame. She thought of Merilee, and cooled at once.

"Annie! Come in here!" Edie's voice rang through the air. Ford released Annie, but their eyes met and held.

"I'm coming," Annie replied, her voice high and thin.

Ford stalked away without another word.

She found her father and sister in the parlor. When Edie saw her sister, she lurched to her feet, hands on fists.

"Ford is putting us to work!"

"What?"

"Ford, your wretched old beau, told Daddy and me that we have to start working at the ranch. Every. Single. Day. And he's freezing our spending accounts. We can't buy anything unless he approves it. He's a tyrant."

The warmth Annie had felt when Ford touched her returned, and magnified, and she smiled.

"What are you smiling about?" Edie hissed. "Daddy is too old to work, and I...I'm not made for that. You have to change his mind."

Annie's smile broadened. "I have no intention of changing his mind. It's about time someone put you two to work. I should have thought of that." She left her sister standing in the hall and returned to the parlor. Of course she hadn't thought of it, she berated herself. She'd been so consumed with her own misery she hadn't done anything at all.

She carried her things to her room. At least for one night, she would stay. She'd come out of concern for Ford's state of mind—she would stay for the ranch.

Twelve

"That is the most wonderful idea I've heard in months, Ford." Augusta Collins tapped her pencil against her desk.

"When do you think we could arrange something? Next month, maybe?" Ford asked.

"Oh goodness, that's too far away. This needs to be taken care of posthaste."

"But with the regatta coming, and graduation, I know how busy you are."

"Never too busy for a good deed. Besides, everyone is in town, which means we'll have more hands to help." She flipped open a book on her desk and ran a finger down one page. "This Saturday. That gives us a few days to prepare." She frowned suddenly. "Do you want it to be a surprise?"

Ford considered that. He didn't know how Annie would react to dozens of her fellow alumnae and their families showing up for a ranch resurrection. "No. I think I'd better tell her."

Augusta smiled. "You know her better than you think you do." She reached for a piece of paper. "I'll need a list of supplies."

"I'll get that to you. Thank you for helping me with this."

Augusta cocked her head. "This isn't only about the ranch, is it? This is about Annie. And you."

Ford opened his mouth to explain, but Augusta raised her hand. "You don't have to tell me. I can see there are still feelings between you two."

"I want to do right by the Kelly Ranch. For Annie, for her mother, and maybe help Edie and Walt find a way out of the pit they're in."

Tears sparkled in Augusta's eyes. "You were a dear boy, and you have become a wonderful young man." She waved her hand at him. "Get the rest of your business done in town, and then go get some sleep."

Ford rose. "I have to visit Merilee."

"Why?"

"What happened is my fault."

"What happened to Merilee is her own fault. She climbed that tree. Don't take blame where blame is not due, Ford."

It was the same thing she'd told him at the hospital. He tried to let the words sink in, but they bounced off. All he could see was Merilee falling from the branch and hitting the ground in front of him.

"If you continue to pay attention to her out of guilt, you will break her heart."

That got through. He had no interest in Merilee. She was a child. "You are a wise woman."

She dipped her graying head regally. "To God the glory."

Annie wasn't sure what was wrong with her father, but it was beginning to concern her. Walt had been sober all day.

Edie was morose and sullen. That wasn't terribly odd, but she seemed unusually despondent.

Annie was worried about Monroe, too. She'd found the foreman earlier seated at his mostly unused desk scribbling away on a piece of paper. Something was going on, and not knowing what was making her irritable.

Berea entered the dining room and placed steaming platters of roasted chicken, vegetables, and mashed potatoes with gravy on the table. No one moved. Ford ambled in. Annie's concerns snagged in her throat when he pulled out the chair beside her and sat down. His scent—sage and cedar—blurred her worries.

"Where have you been? And what's going on? Everyone is acting strange."

"Business," he replied. "I'll fill you in later." Ford turned his attention to Walt, who stared into his empty plate. "Walt, Monroe was working on a list. Could you go check with him and make sure there's nothing to add?"

Walt's eyes widened. "Certainly. I'll go find him."

He looked genuinely pleased, Annie thought. "He's in the tack room," she offered.

When Walt left the room, she turned on Ford. "What did you do to my father?"

"Do? Nothing. I did offer to pray for him."

Annie blinked. "He hasn't had a drink all day."

Ford shrugged. "Prayer works?"

Annie pushed away from the table and stood.

"I need to talk to you. I have a plan, and I don't want you to be surprised."

Annie's lips tightened. "What plan?"

"Sit down, Annie dear." Ford patted her chair.

"I think not. What have you done?"

"Some of the Academy alums and their families will be coming out Saturday to help restore the Kelly Ranch to her original grandeur." Ford forked up a mouthful of chicken and potatoes.

Annie cringed, even as her temper burned. "You set this up without my permission?"

"I don't need your permission, according to our contract."

"This is different. This involves my friends, my community. I never asked them for help, not even once."

"Why not?"

Annie dropped into the chair again, defeated. "Because it's not their problem."

"As far as I can tell, everyone is excited to help, whether it's 'their' problem or not."

She pressed her hands to the sides of her head.

"Annie, if one of your friends was in the same situation, how would you respond?" His tone was kind.

"I don't know."

"Yes, you do. You'd be at the front of the line, seeking to help, no matter what it took."

"I wish that were true, but it's not. You of all people should know that when push comes to shove, I give in." Her voice cracked and she bit her tongue.

He covered her hand with his own. How she wished he would quit finding ways to touch her. The warmth coming off his skin radiated through her and made her crave more. "Annie, you were too young to know your own mind."

"You weren't that much older. You knew your own mind."

"Did I? I thought I knew what I wanted. But if I'd known my own heart, I would never have walked away."

Oh, what was he saying? Annie's heart twisted cruelly in her chest. He'd realized he hadn't really loved her back then? That it had all been a silly crush? She tried to withdraw her hand from beneath his, but he curled his fingers around hers and pulled them to his mouth, forcing her to look into his mesmerizing green eyes.

"I've learned a lot, Annie, and maybe the most important lesson is that I no longer give up so easily when I want something." He kissed her fingertips gently, and her heart went into triple time.

"Oh. So that's how it is." From the doorway, disdain rolled off Edie's tongue like bitter water. "I take it she won't be forced into manual labor like Daddy and me?"

Annie snatched her hand back as her sister stormed away. Annie stood with such haste she nearly upended her chair. "How is Merilee, by the way?"

Ford inhaled. "She's fine. But I need—"

"It's all right, Ford, I understand." Annie gathered dirty dishes from the table. She didn't understand at all. How could he dote on Merilee and then kiss her fingers? "I need to head back to the Abbey. I have a class early tomorrow."

"Annie..."

"I'll leave the buggy here and ride Baby Gray."

"Annie, would you stop?"

She paused. Exasperation was so clearly carved on his features he could have been one of Notre Dame's sneering gargoyles.

"Merilee is not—"

"Annie?" Berea hustled into the room, puffing like she'd run halfway across the ranch. "Come quickly. It's Mr. Walt."

The dishes Annie held slipped to the table with a clatter, and she ran after Berea, Ford on their heels.

They found Walt collapsed against the barn; his usually florid face a sickly gray. Monroe knelt beside him, fanning the man with his hat and praying aloud. Berea, Annie, and Ford reached the scene at almost the same time. Annie dropped to her knees opposite Monroe.

"Daddy?" Annie hadn't called him "Daddy" in forever, and the word felt strange on her lips. His breathing was harsh and raspy.

Ford felt Walt's neck for a pulse.

"Is it his heart?"

Ford surveyed Walt with an objective gaze. "I don't think so. We can send for the doctor to make sure, but I think he's suffering the results of not drinking. His body is reacting to the lack of liquor in his system."

Annie frowned at him. "How would you know that?"

He quirked one raven-colored brow and smiled wryly. "Because I've been there. Fortunately, a very kind sheriff found me, hauled me to a jail cell, and left me there until I dried out enough to listen to what he had to say. And he had a lot to say."

Walt mumbled something unintelligible and waved his hands ineffectually in front of his face, as if warding off a swarm of unseen insects.

"Monroe, let's get him upstairs," Ford said.

Monroe and Ford lifted her father to his feet, draping his arms across their shoulders. She watched them head to the house and saw her sister come running from the other side, hovering around Walt until Ford commanded her to get out of the way. Annie sat down hard in the dirt, mindless of her skirt.

How had it come to this? Why hadn't she seen how broken her father and her sister were? Instead, she'd judged them, while blaming them for her own broken heart—and to a lesser degree, for her mother's death.

"He'll be all right, Miss Annie." Berea's gentle face appeared in Annie's field of vision. "Getting that man off the drink is the best thing we can do for him."

Annie nodded. She knew that was true. But she wasn't grieving for her father. She was grieving for herself. Ford was wrong when he said she would be first in line to help someone in need. She had, in fact, been the first one to run away.

Thirteen

Ford enjoyed the strain in his shoulders and back, the sun's warmth, and being part of a team. That last thought came as a surprise. He'd always been a loner, always gone his own way without asking for help.

This rowing team had changed his perception of what it meant to be part of a unified body. Together, Noah, Brandon, Harmon, Will, Kirby, Eddie, young Hank Crawford, and Ford were recording excellent times.

With early summer sunshine glittering off the water's surface, Lake McDonald was filled with rowers. As the number of days till the regatta decreased, the number of teams practicing increased exponentially.

When they'd stowed the narrow boat at the rowing club, Noah gathered them together.

"Emmeline has come up with uniforms for us."

Someone groaned, and everyone else laughed. Noah held up a hand. "Never fear. I've approved the design. Simple shirts with Austen Abbey embroidered on the backs, and matching shorts. I'll bring them with me for our next practice."

Right now their team was a rag-tag group clad in everything from old football uniforms to riding breeches to flannel trousers.

"What color are the uniforms?" Eddie asked.

Noah didn't answer, and a buzz of mild panic rippled through the group.

"I talked her out of pink. That's all I can say."

Ford breathed a sigh of relief. Pink made him think of Merilee tumbling to the ground. He checked his pocket watch. He needed to get to the hospital. Do his duty.

Ford was full of gratitude when he left the lake. He'd never expected to find genuine friendship in Austin again. Annie had been his first friend, his best friend. He caught glimpses of that connection still, but she was so closed off in her self-made prison he wondered if she'd ever be free. Perhaps the outpouring of love he'd been warned to expect on Saturday would help.

"I can't wait for the regatta," Lila said. "I'm looking forward to seeing Kirby in his uniform."

Annie folded the last rowing team shirt she'd ironed and added it to the stack with a laugh. "Lila!" Annie admonished, tossing one of the pressing cloths at her friend. Lila caught it and grinned.

"I'm a married woman now, I can enjoy seeing my husband in his rowing team costume."

"Well, I'm not, so spare me!" Annie made herself sound stern, but she couldn't hide her smile. It blessed her to see her friend happy.

"How is your father?"

"He's better every day. We had the doctor come out and examine him, and he concurred with Ford's diagnosis. Daddy needs to quit drinking."

"Daddy? I don't think I've heard you call him that."

Annie blushed. "Since Ford arrived, things have been changing. I've been changing." She sat down on the bed and smoothed her skirt. "I was so upset over what happened with Ford, and then my mother's death, that I shut everyone out. I stopped seeing anyone's pain but my own. Oh, Lila, I probably did that to you, too, and I'm sorry."

Lila sat beside her. "You have been nothing but a good friend to me, Annie. Without you I wouldn't have been able to stand up to my mother and find my way to Kirby. There's no reason for you to apologize to me! If anything, I should apologize to you."

"For what?"

"For not being more supportive of your struggles with your family."

"I've been blind about my own family, Lila." Annie laid her head on her friend's shoulder for a second. "Now that we've both apologized for no reason..." They both laughed.

Lila patted her arm. "Are you ready for Saturday?"

Annie cringed. "No. I'm embarrassed and humiliated."

"Shame on you, Annie. You should be honored. We're all excited to be able to do something to help."

"I'm sorry. I don't mean to sound ungrateful..."

"I understand. For someone as proud and independent as you are, accepting help is hard. But whether you like it or not, we're coming to help. It's going to be fun."

Annie heard the sincere goodwill in her friend's voice, and knew Lila spoke from her heart. Annie resisted the idea of being a charity project, but she had to admit, it was the best plan anyone had come up with for getting the Kelly Ranch back in shape in a hurry.

Her father, though still a little shaky, had started helping out, and doing the work seemed to encourage him. His collapse had frightened Edie into a blessed silence. She spent almost all her time in her room, or tending to her father.

"I should get going. Kirby will be finished by now," Lila said, failing to hide the smile that lit her face every time she mentioned her husband.

"Are you meeting him somewhere?"

"No, he's picking me up here."

On cue, bells chimed, letting them know someone was outside the Abbey.

"I'll walk out with you," Annie said. "Someone is going to take care of the uniforms, right?"

Lila nodded. "Yes. Noah has been charged with handing them out to the team members at their next practice."

"Why don't you give Kirby his now?"

Lila glanced at the pile of purple and green uniforms and shook her head. "I'll wait."

Annie laughed. "I don't blame you. Whose idea was that color combination?"

"I'm not sure, but Headmistress Collins had the final say. And because of that, none of the men on the team will dare to complain." Lila closed the door to the study behind them. "Have you decided what you're wearing to the regatta ball?"

Annie groaned. "I have nothing. I'm thinking I'll slip away before the festivities start. No one will notice if I'm not there," she said, facing Lila as she opened the front door.

"I think you're mistaken."

She jumped at the sound of Ford's voice. There he stood, hair slicked back in such a controlled way she knew it was still damp.

"Wh...what are you doing here?"

"Kirby said he was picking up his wife here after our team practice. I thought I would see if you were ready to head back to the ranch. We could ride out together, like the old days."

Was that hope she heard in his voice? "What about Merilee? How is she doing today?" The words were out of her mouth before Annie knew she was speaking.

"Annie?" Lila caught her arm. "Kirby and I have an appointment for dinner. I have to go. Will you be all right?" Her eyes flicked from Annie to Ford and back again. Lila could be quite protective.

"Yes, Lila, I'll be fine." She leaned in to hug her friend's neck. "Hurry up, or you'll be late for your meeting. I'll see you Saturday."

She and Ford watched the couple leave.

"I hoped you'd agree. I picked up Baby Gray for you." Ford pointed toward the side of the house, where her mare was tethered beside a huge black gelding she didn't recognize.

"That makes it hard to refuse. Where did you get the gelding?"

"I bought him yesterday. Pretty, isn't he?"

Pretty was an understatement. Annie moved toward the horses as if compelled by an invisible hand. The gelding, at least sixteen hands, was ebony black.

Annie reached into her pocket and pulled out two peppermint candies. With a candy on each open palm, she offered both horses the treat.

"He'll be useless now," Ford teased. "Following you around, looking for sugar."

"Oh stop. You taught me that trick."

"I didn't think you would remember that," Ford replied.

Annie ducked her head. "You trained her. Of course I paid attention to your methods."

He helped her into the sidesaddle and then swung easily onto the gelding's back.

"What's his name?" she asked.

"I haven't decided. I'm thinking about Rez."

Annie frowned. "Rez? Why?"

"Short for Resurrection. Or Restoration. I haven't decided."

"Oh." Annie swallowed. She wanted to ask him how he had found his way to God. She wanted to ask about his life over the last eight years. Instead, she bit her lip and stayed silent.

When they reached the outskirts of town, Ford leaned over and poked her arm. "Can you really ride in that sidesaddle? I never remember you using one."

"I hate it, but as a teacher, I have to maintain appearances. I only ride astride at home."

Home. It was the first time in a long time she'd referred to the ranch as home.

"So..." Ford said slowly. "If I challenge you to a race, like we used to do, I'm guaranteed to win, right?"

Annie shot him a glare through narrowed eyes. "Sidesaddle or not, you trained this horse. You'd be betting against yourself."

"Fair deal." He prodded the gelding forward, pulling ahead of Annie.

"Wait! What's the prize?"

He shouted over his shoulder. "Same as when we were kids. Winner's choice."

Annie choked on her next breath as he urged the gelding into a gallop. Ford's choice had always been a kiss.

There was no way she would win, but her pride and their shared history wouldn't permit her to concede. Fixing herself in the despised sidesaddle, she snapped the reins, sending the mare into a full run.

Ford was waiting for her at the gate to the Kelly.

"That wasn't fair. You got a head start. And your horse is bigger," Annie protested. "And you should try riding sidesaddle sometime."

"Same old Annie, always trying to hedge her bets," Ford said.

"That's not fair..." Annie nudged the mare alongside the gelding. Her knee bumped against Ford's.

"It's perfectly fair. I won, I get a kiss."

"Fine." Annie turned her face upward, lips pursed. A hot flush rolled over her entire body and her pulse quickened in anticipation.

"Nope. Not good enough." Ford whisked her off the sidesaddle, onto the gelding's back, and into his arms.

"This isn't what I remember," she breathed, as one of his hands curved around her neck and the other splayed across her spine.

His mouth was on hers before she could stop him.

Truth be told, she didn't want to resist. She didn't want to react the way common sense and propriety demanded. She wanted to enjoy the feel of his lips on hers, the tight-leashed strength in his masculine form.

Eight years earlier Ford's chaste kisses had made her tingle and tremble with excitement. Those kisses had belonged to a boy. These were different. These were the kisses of a man who knew what he wanted and intended to have it. If their shared kisses in their youth had sparked a flame in her, these threatened to engulf her in a head to toe inferno. With the slightest pressure from his fingers, he tilted her head farther to the side to gain better access to her mouth. The subtle—and experienced—movement shattered the spell. Annie shoved her hands against the broad expanse of his chest and jerked her mouth from his.

"Release me," she demanded. Her voice came out in a squeak. He slipped two fingers under her chin, tipped her head back and forced her to meet his gaze, still holding her close with his arm around her waist.

"I'll release you, dear Annie, on one condition."

She pushed against his chest again. Her actions were as ineffectual as a child's. "You can't demand conditions. I've paid my bet."

When he didn't relent, she sighed. "All right, what? What condition?"

"Give me a chance."

His eyes were the luminescent green of the tender moss that grew along the banks of the creek. The words were those of the boy she'd loved, spoken through the mouth of a man. She trembled in his arms. She'd loved the boy. She still loved the man.

"What happens after Saturday? What happens then?" she whispered, and immediately regretted her words.

"All I'm asking is a chance. Don't give up on us, Annie." His grip on her tightened, and then she was back in the hated sidesaddle. Baby Gray shifted beneath her.

"Monroe," Ford murmured.

"Ford."

Annie forced herself to relax.

"Wasn't expecting the both of you," Monroe drawled.

"It wasn't planned," Ford replied, swinging out of the saddle.

Annie tried to ignore the niggling voice that said his kissing her was nothing more than a whim, tried to discount his words. She dismounted, gathered the reins, and handed them to Monroe. "How is my father today?"

"He's doing much better, Miss Annie. Better every day. He came out and helped with morning chores. I 'spect by Saturday he'll be right as rain."

"That's good news." And after Saturday, then what? The question she'd asked Ford nagged at her. Would he leave? Was he preparing the ranch for a wife, a family?

"We're all ready and lookin' forward to the help," Monroe said. He added the gelding's reins to his massive grip. "You young'uns go on inside. I'll take care of the horses."

"Thank you, Monroe."

Annie watched the old foreman lead the two horses away.

"I'd appreciate it if you would review the tasks we've laid out for Saturday to see if we've prioritized everything correctly," Ford said.

"I...I can't."

Ford's brow creased. "Of course you can. You know this property better than anyone."

Annie squeezed her eyes shut. "I knew this property."

"Don't sell yourself short. You knew the ranch in its heyday, when it was succeeding. That's what we need now—someone with a vision for what it can be again."

Annie shook her head, eyes still closed. "I don't trust myself. I've made too many bad decisions." A shudder rippled through her. The first of those horrible decisions had been to reject Ford all those years ago. "I have to go."

Inside, she dragged herself up the stairs. It was like being trapped in an irreversible eddy. No matter what she did, she kept coming back to Ford. And she suspected he was planning to slip the stream and leave again.

Fourteen

Saturday dawned gray and misty. Upstairs, in the comforting familiarity of her old bedroom, Annie leaned into the window. The cool glass against her forehead provided a distraction as a steady stream of wagons and buggies rolled through the Kelly's gates.

The front door squealed on its hinges and slammed shut with a resounding bang. The sound of boot heels on weathered boards echoed upward, and Ford appeared in her line of vision, broad of shoulder, narrow of hip. He strode across the open space between the house and the barn to greet their guests.

His guests, she amended. Her lips formed an "O" as she realized how many people had come out. In a few short weeks, he had managed to ingratiate himself into a group that included Austin's elite. She shook her head, remembering the tousle-haired boy who charmed extra baking powder biscuits out of Berea and teased sweet kisses from Annie with little more than a wink and a smile. None of those talents had faded. Ford's charm had only become more potent with age.

"Annie? You need to get downstairs. People are here, and Ford is asking for you," Edie's voice pierced the air.

"I'm coming," Annie called. She turned away from the window, caught a glimpse of herself in the cheval mirror, and groaned. "Give me a few minutes."

"Hurry up! I'm tired of telling people I don't know where you are."

Annie flung open the wardrobe and scanned its contents. Plain gray skirts and well-worn white shirtwaists dominated the contents. The black dress she'd worn to her mother's funeral hung on the far side, untouched. With a sigh, she reached for her standard skirt and shirtwaist combination.

It wasn't that she didn't like beautiful clothes and fine things. But she hadn't allowed herself the luxury of enjoying anything for a long time. When she was dressed, she twisted her hair up at the back of her head and shoved one of her mother's shell combs into it to secure the knot.

"Annie?" Ford banged on her door. "I need you."

She stared at her reflection. Suddenly, her cheeks had color, her eyes sparkled, and her drab brown hair shone. Her hands flew to her face, palms cool against her heated skin.

"I'll be right there," she said, her voice too high. She wiped her damp palms on her skirt and opened the door.

"I need you to be in charge of organizing the ladies." At her confused look, his fingers curled lightly around her elbow and he steered her toward the stairs. "The ladies want to help, but most of them aren't suited for fence repair, calf branding, or replacing the rotted boards on the front porch," he explained. "They've brought enough food for an army, and they want some assignments. Can you give them something to do?"

When they reached the bottom of the stairs, Annie saw Lila in the foyer.

"Consider us your spring cleaning crew. Where should we start?" Lila asked.

Tears sprang to Annie's eyes. Ford squeezed her arm. His warm breath tickled her neck when he leaned in to whisper, "You're in good hands here. I'm off to the barn." He disappeared faster than she could concoct a reason to keep him in the house.

"Oh my goodness, Annie." Lila breathed, eyes wide. "He is the second most delectable man I've ever met."

"Second to Kirby, I presume?"

Lila wrapped an arm around Annie's shoulders. "Of course! Kirby is perfect. Now, there are half a dozen ladies out there who need something to do. Are you ready to be mistress of the manor?"

Annie swallowed the lump in her throat. That had been her mother's role.

"It's time, Annie. She would want this," Lila whispered.

Annie inhaled deeply and straightened her shoulders. "You're right."

Annie opened the front door and stepped onto the porch. "Good morning, everyone," she said. "First, I want to thank you all for coming. Your kindness and generosity means more than I can express." The lump reappeared, and she swallowed hard as tears bit at her eyes. "I apologize for my lack of organization today. I don't even know where to begin..."

To Annie's relief, Berea climbed the steps and stood beside her, papers fluttering in her hand. "Here are lists of the things that need to be done inside."

Annie stepped back and let Berea organize the women. Within a quarter hour, three groups were on task and the air was filled with the sounds of productive labor.

Annie dropped onto the creaky old porch swing, head swimming, and closed her eyes. She felt alternately blessed and humiliated.

"You're going to have to move, miss."

Her eyes snapped open. Ford towered over her. He'd rolled his shirtsleeves to his elbows, exposing well-muscled forearms.

"Move?" she muttered.

He grinned, and her breath caught in her throat.

"I'm on swing duty." He pointed to the frayed ropes that attached the swing to the porch roof, and then leaned over to flick off a chip of peeling paint on the seat.

"Oh. All right. You've thought of everything," Annie said, rising to her feet.

"Actually, repairing the swing was your father's idea."

Bittersweet memories of her parents, snuggled close on the swing on a cool evening, sipping coffee and laughing, assailed her.

"I wanted to thank you," she said.

He cocked his head and raised an eyebrow in query.

"For...what you've done for my father." She shrugged her shoulders. "I think you may have saved his life."

She was surprised to see a warm flush spread across his cheeks.

"Your father needed a push in the right direction, that's all. He still has a ways to go."

"Annie! Annie? Where are you?" Edie banged through the screen door with a squeal and a slam. Ford and Annie both flinched.

"That's next on my list, after the swing. That stupid door," Ford murmured.

"I'm right here, Edie. What's wrong?" Her sister's complexion was pallid, skin drawn tight over her cheekbones, and her hands clenched into fists.

"One of the ladies went in mother's room."

Blood drained from Annie's face. No one had gone into their mother's room since the day of the funeral. They'd closed the door and pretended the room didn't exist.

"I know we have to clean it, Annie, I know we do, but I can't do it alone. Will you come help?"

Ford's warm hand curved over Annie's shoulder. "We can leave it as is."

Annie glanced at the swing and thought of her father. If he could take a step toward healing, so could she.

"No. We've been putting this off far too long. Come on, Edie." Taking a leap of faith, she reached for her sister's hand and led the way inside, surprised when Edie's cold fingers curled into her own.

In the room upstairs, dust motes drifted lazily through the beams of light like tiny stars set adrift. Annie waited for the familiar pang of grief, but it didn't come. In fact, with the light and fresh air coming in, the room felt...new. No, that wasn't the right word.

"It feels like hope," Edie whispered. "Mother was always so hopeful, even when things were going terribly wrong."

Annie squeezed her sister's hand. "It does, doesn't it? Oh, we should have done this so long ago."

"We weren't ready."

"You're right. But we are now. Where do we start?"

"I would suggest starting with the jewelry case." Annie swiveled to find Augusta in the doorway.

They went through the jewelry, sorting rings and earbobs and brooches. Annie and Edie alternately laughed and wept. An hour later they moved on to the wardrobe.

"Oh. My." Edie breathed. "I'd forgotten she had these things."

The door opened and Augusta breezed inside. "Your mother was quite a fashionable woman," she said, fingering a particularly lovely lilac silk gown trimmed in ivory lace and satin piping. "I believe these could be made over quite easily for the two of you. Why don't each of you pick one out now and we'll get them to my seamstress. With luck, they'll be ready in time for the gala."

"That would be wonderful!" Edie exclaimed, then stilled. "But I've got plenty of dresses. I don't need a new one right now."

Annie's eyes widened. Perhaps her sister was changing, too. "Edie, I want you to have one. Pick your favorite."

Edie's fingers fluttered over the rainbow of colors, coming to rest on a sage green silk. "This one, I think."

"That's perfect, my dear," Augusta said. "Now, which one for Annie?" She pressed a finger to her mouth. "I don't believe I've ever seen our art teacher in anything except gray and black."

"This one. This one is perfect," Edie said, withdrawing a rose and gold shot silk evening gown. "The color will set off your hair and eyes." She held the dress up to Annie.

"You have an excellent eye for fashion, Edie," Augusta said. "I agree, that's the ideal dress for our Annie." She reached for it and draped it over her arm with the sage green. "I'll take these back into town with me."

Ford used his kerchief to mop sweat from his forehead and tucked the cloth back in his pocket. Experimentally, he opened the screen door. No squeal. Then he jerked it open. Still no squeal. Releasing the handle, the door slammed shut with its customary bang. He frowned. At least the squeak was gone.

The use of wire mesh in windows was a new development, and a welcome one. The mesh kept out mosquitoes, gnats, chiggers, and other unwelcome insects, while still allowing airflow. The addition of a screen door—a wood frame lined with the fine mesh—installed in front of the main door, was even more recent. Unfortunately, no one had come up with a way to keep the lightweight doors from snapping shut.

He turned to the swing. He'd swapped the fraying ropes for sturdy metal chains, sanded the swing, and painted it Caladium Yellow. It glowed. He'd painted the front door, too, in Newport Green.

He heard laughter coming from the open windows in the kitchen. Monroe. Berea. And...he cocked his head. Walt. His mouth curved into a smile. Walt was a changed man.

The sound of feminine chatter drifted out of an upstairs window and filtered through the sultry air to his ears. Was that Edie? He listened for a moment. Edie had been different since Walt's collapse. Yes, and

Annie, he realized with pleasant surprise. He'd know Annie's voice, her laugh, anywhere.

He considered the question she'd asked after he'd kissed her: What would happen after today? He didn't know, not for certain. There were too many variables: Merilee, Walt, Edie, Annie, and his own heart.

Fifteen

Annie woke early the next morning. She scrambled to dress and hurried downstairs, but Ford was already gone.

"Where did he go, Monroe?" she asked the foreman when she found him in the barn.

"He didn't say, Miss Annie," Monroe answered, scratching his grizzled head. "Shall I saddle Baby Gray, or would you rather take the buggy?"

"The buggy, please!" Edie interrupted.

Annie turned to find her sister, still in her dressing gown, hair loose about her shoulders.

"Mrs. Collins said I could come in and meet her seamstress. She wants me to see her work and show her some of my designs for the dresses she took to town. I asked her about it before she left."

"Designs? What designs?"

Edie flushed pink and pulled a handful of papers from behind her back. Annie took them, looked at the sketches and gasped. "This is me!"

Edie snorted. "Not in those shirtwaists and dowdy skirts you wear. This is what you could look like. This is what I was thinking the seamstress could do with the shot-silk."

Annie flipped through the sketches, marveling at the skill level displayed. "These are amazing."

"Oh, I can't do real art. Not like you. This is it. I draw dresses."

Annie squeezed her sister's shoulders. "This is real art, Edie. Get ready, because if I must have a new gown for the gala ball, I want one my sister designed."

Ford bought a small bouquet from a vendor on his way to the hospital. Merilee's physicians were keeping her in the hospital as a precaution, they'd told him.

Today her parents were waiting for him.

"We need to talk to you, Mr. Winters," Merilee's mother said. She was a sweet, plump woman with hair so blond it seemed white.

"Of course, what can I do for you? Is everything all right with Merilee?" His heart stuttered. Had she taken a turn for the worse? He still couldn't shake the guilt.

"No, no. Don't fret. Merilee is doing fine. In fact, we expect her to be released tomorrow."

Ford exhaled. "Thank God."

Merilee's mother smiled at him. "You've been a most...diligent... friend."

"It's the least I can do, considering my role in her injuries."

"Merilee talked to us about that," her father said. "Mr. Winters, you bear no guilt in her accident."

Ford closed his eyes to block out the memory of Merilee falling. "No, sir, I do. If I'd been paying better attention..."

"What we're trying to say, Mr. Winters, is that you don't have to keep visiting," Merilee's mother said, a blush coloring her cheeks.

Ford was slightly offended. The sound of Merilee giggling made him look up. Her parents exchanged a glance.

"You see...she has a beau from St. Louis. They had a falling out a few months ago, but when he heard of her accident, he came to be with her as quickly as he could," Merilee's mother said.

A dull roar started in Ford's ears. "So you're saying I'm...excused?"

Merilee's father sighed. "Yes, exactly." He paused, cleared his throat. "You seem to be a very nice young man, Mr. Winters, but we aren't looking for a relationship of obligation for our daughter. She deserves a relationship based on love. And so do you."

Ford caught himself before he flung the flowers to the ceiling with relief. Instead, he laid them on a nearby table and extended his hand to

Merilee's father. "Thank you, sir. You're right. Your daughter deserves more than guilty obligation. Please, give her my best."

With that, Ford rose, feeling lighter than he had in days.

Sixteen

A nnie twisted in front of the mirror, uncertain.
"I don't know."

"What do you mean you don't know? It's beautiful!"

Annie squirmed under her sister's scrutiny. "I'm not accustomed to wearing—"

"Anything fashionable that fits," Edie snipped. Annie frowned.

"You have to admit, it's a beautiful gown," Edie offered, her tone conciliatory. She'd been a meeker, kinder Edie for several days.

Annie faced the mirror. It was a gorgeous dress. That was true. Augusta's seamstress had snipped and trimmed the old gown into a modern marvel based on Edie's design. The rose-colored shot silk, with fine gold threads in the weave that made it seem to glow, complemented Annie's hair and eyes in a most becoming fashion. She turned to the left, then to the right again. She tugged at the bodice.

"Do you think it's cut too low?"

Edie snorted. "Hardly. It's quite modest." She pointed to the pile of dresses on the bed. "You'll need at least two day gowns. Which ones?"

"I was going to wear my school clothes. I'll be chaperoning, after all."

"You will do no such thing." Augusta's voice came from the door. Annie jumped. Augusta held a hand to her breast. "Oh Annie, my dear, you look so very much like your mother."

Annie flushed, and hot tears prickled the backs of her eyes. It was the kindest compliment anyone could have paid her.

"I took the liberty of ordering coordinating gloves, hats, and underthings as well. They're in the box."

"Mrs. Collins, that's too much. I can't afford those things..."

"I'll remind you an Abbey girl receives gifts with grace."

Annie blushed all the way to the roots of her hair. "Yes, ma'am. Thank you."

Augusta chuckled. "Aren't you meeting Kirby and Lila? You should get going."

Annie checked the clock. She and Edie had been dawdling with the lovely gowns. "Edie, can you help me out of this?" She turned her back to her sister for assistance.

When Annie left the Abbey to meet Lila and Kirby, her heart was full. First the changes in her father, and now Edie. God was at work. It had started with Ford's return to Austin. She wanted to speak with Ford, but with exams, and preparation for commencement, and the coming regatta, she'd been too busy to get out to the ranch. He hadn't stopped by the school either, though she knew he'd been in town. She missed him.

That realization had her hurrying down the sidewalk, beads of sweat popping out on her forehead before she'd made it all the way down the block. Summer had arrived in full force, complete with heat and humidity. But she'd been trapped indoors all week with her classes, and she wanted to be outside, even if it was only for a walk to the Driskill Hotel.

By the time the hotel came into view, Annie was a sweaty mess. Damp strands of hair clung to her forehead, cheeks, and the back of her neck with sticky persistence. Her fingers were slimy inside the cotton gloves, and rivulets of moisture trickled down her spine at random intervals.

A familiar flash of movement across the street halted her mid-stride. Ford. Perhaps he could join them for dinner. Annie raised her hand to wave, and then froze.

Ford was exiting one of Austin's high-end jewelry stores. Joe Koen & Son Jewelers was exclusive to Austin's wealthiest citizens, and even they reserved their visits for the most important of purchases. Yet there was Ford, waving to whatever shop clerk was within.

Her hand dropped to her side. He could have any number of reasons for stopping at Koen's. Yes, it was the primary source for engagement rings among Austin's elite, but Koen's also sold watches and earbobs and...

But he hadn't come to see her since the work day at the ranch. And he hadn't answered her question about what would happen after the ranch was restored to a healthy state. Perhaps she'd misunderstood his kindness, his kiss. Or perhaps not.

He ran one hand through his perpetually tousled hair before he popped his derby on his head and disappeared in the growing throngs of people heading home after work.

At the hotel a black-coated doorman opened the door for her. She thanked him on her way inside. She spotted Lila and Kirby right away, heads bent together over a menu, and knew a sharp, painful flash of jealousy. Annie slipped into the seat across from them, acutely aware of her singleness.

"Annie!" Lila reached across the table for Annie's hands. "It's so hot outside, did you walk?"

Annie was aware of her sticky gloves, her damp locks, and her sweat-darkened clothing. "It seems summer is upon us in earnest."

"Today it was so hot at regatta practice we all went for a swim in Lake McDonald when we were finished," Kirby said, reminding Annie once again of Ford, and that he'd been in town every day but hadn't come by the Abbey.

"Frizzled ham, mashed turnips, and Boston brown bread," she mumbled when the waiter came to take her order. She hated turnips. And brown bread.

"Are you all right?" Lila questioned.

"I saw Ford leaving Joe Koen & Son."

Lila gasped. "We ran into him earlier today. Outside the hospital."

Annie's brow furrowed. An icy glaze, hard as stone, coated her heart and quelled her hopeful imaginations.

"Merilee. He was visiting Merilee."

Lila nodded. Kirby stared into his soup.

Annie's hair rose on the back of her neck, like the hackles on a rooster. How dare he kiss her so sweetly and then...consort with Merilee?

"Annie, dear, I'm so sorry. I had no idea things between Ford and Merilee were so serious," Lila offered.

"Nor did I." Annie muttered. Rage threatened to overwhelm her, but then she thought of her father's sudden sobriety, her sister's sudden camaraderie, and Ford's part in those minor miracles. She would choose to be thankful, she decided.

Seventeen

The morning of the regatta dawned with rain. Not a sprinkle, not a shower, but a tedious, steady downpour that kept the ladies of the Abbey indoors. They'd congregated in the parlor to sew, read, and socialize. Mostly socialize.

Annie was glad for the reprieve.

She didn't want to see Ford now, much less talk to him. The idea of congratulating him on his impending engagement made her itch. Absently she scratched her arm.

"Annie? Are you all right?" Franny Sue Price, one of her favorite art students, bumped against her side.

Annie smiled at the girl. "I'm all right. Just feeling a bit... claustrophobic."

Franny Sue turned her face to the raindrop-pelted window. "Me, too."

"I'm sure the weather will clear soon."

"I hope so. I don't want to miss the ball."

Annie thought of the gown hanging in the wardrobe. She'd wanted to attend the ball right up until she realized Ford was probably proposing to Merilee.

"I'm sure the ball will go on, regardless of the weather," Annie mumbled.

"Mr. Winters will be there."

"I know."

"Will you dance with him?"

"I doubt it," she said. "I believe he has a fiancée now."

Franny's hopeful expression collapsed. "That's terrible news."

Annie smiled sadly. "I agree, but it's what Mr. Winters wants."

"Then he's a fool," Franny Sue snapped. "I think he should marry you."

"I don't think I'm the marrying type, Franny, dear."

Franny Sue snorted. "That's silly. Everyone is the marrying type when they find the person they want to marry. You should eat. You look pale." The girl sidled toward the buffet.

Annie turned back to the window. To her dismay, there was a break in the clouds to the west. The storm was moving out.

Ford pulled the rowing uniform over his head with a grimace. He was mature enough to wear a purple uniform for a good cause, even if it delayed his plan. Again.

The previous day's rain had kept the Abbey ladies, including Annie, away from the regatta, along with most of the spectators. Despite the downpour, the races had gone on as planned. To everyone's surprise, the Abbey team performed well and progressed to the next round.

"Ready, man?" Harmon clapped Ford on the back. They both winced. Everyone on the team was sore.

"I'm ready. At least today the water will be under the boat, not in it," Ford said.

Harmon laughed. "True. And we'll have the entire contingent of women from the Abbey cheering us on."

Ford thought of the tiny velvet box in his jacket pocket. He was free from his sense of obligation to Merilee. The ranch was progressing back toward health and prosperity. There was only one thing missing, but he found himself afraid to take the next step. Did she want him? Or would she push him away again? Could he risk having her break his heart for a second time?

He followed the rest of the team outside to join their crew. He wanted half an hour alone with Annie, but between her Abbey duties and his role on the rowing team, it seemed he would have no opportunity until after the regatta. Ford scanned the lines of spectators.

"The ladies said they'd be at the finish line, so there's no use looking for them now," Noah said cheerfully. "Let's make them proud, boys!"

Ford picked up his oars and climbed into the boat with his teammates. They maneuvered to the starting line.

"We should pray," Will said as they waited for the starting gun.

"We should have thought of that before now," Noah quipped.

"I'm serious. C'mon, boys, bow your heads."

They complied, and Will's strong voice rang over the water. "Lord God, we ask your blessing on this race. Protect every team, every competitor from harm or injury. We pray that You would be glorified by our performance as a team, no matter where we place in the end. In the name of our Lord, amen."

The men murmured their assent as the race announcer called them to their oars. Peace rolled over Ford, and not just about the outcome of the race. He'd done his best for the Kelly Ranch so far and would continue to do so. But just as he couldn't postpone the start of the race, he couldn't postpone his feelings for Annie any longer, no matter the outcome. He'd fixed up the ranch, and delayed. He'd bought the ring, and delayed, finding one excuse after another.

He wrapped his fingers around the oars, taking comfort in their smooth grip. This was it. After the race he would find Annie and propose again. It was time.

The Austen Abbey team picked up their oars and positioned themselves. The shot that signaled the start of the race set them in motion. Like a wind-up toy they churned across the water in perfect union. Muscles strained, sweat glistened, and they pulled together. Stroke, pull, stroke, pull.

Ford thought of Annie as the oars circled into the water, out, and back in. If only his relationship with her was as straightforward as a race to the finish line.

It was the cheering that snapped him out of his reverie. Arms rhythmically rotating the oars in unison with his teammates, he glanced from side to side. They'd taken the lead, he realized, with a sizeable lead. Their competitors trailed them by several yards. Ford's muscles burned, his chest ached, and he wanted to quit, but quitting wasn't an option when you were part of a team. He picked up his pace.

They crossed the finish line to a roar of applause, and at that moment, Ford knew he was willing to risk everything to win the hand of the only woman he'd ever truly loved.

Eighteen

The Abbey crew astonished everyone by handily winning the amateur division of the regatta.

Ford joined his team on the winners' podium and raised the trophy high overhead to the cheers of the spectators. Somehow he had been elected crew captain. Or mascot. He wasn't sure which. He kept searching the crowd, seeking one particular face. He spotted her at last, handed the trophy to Kirby, and plunged off the platform.

By the time he waded through the mass of humanity, she was gone.

"Nice uniform."

He jerked around, and found himself confronted by a girl in her late teens.

"Who are you?"

"Franny Sue Price. You're Ford, and you're looking for Annie."

"Where did she go?"

Franny Sue shrugged. "Haven't a clue. She left when she arrived." The girl-woman jutted her chin and Ford followed the direction she indicated. Merilee sat to one side in a wheeled chair, with her parents—and a stranger who must be her suitor, judging by the way he hovered at her side.

"Ford! You have to join us!" Will called. Ford winced. Chasing Annie down clad in his green and purple rowing costume—they really couldn't be called uniforms, as that implied some degree of dignity—was probably not the best way to woo her.

"They want us to give a victory speech at the ball tonight. Would

155

you be our speaker?" Kirby asked.

Ford sucked in hot, humid air. "Wouldn't Noah be a better representative? I've barely returned to Austin."

"Putting this crew together was your idea. It makes sense for you to give the speech."

Ford squeezed his eyes shut. Was there ever an instance when giving a speech was pleasant? He imagined the ball-goers assembled before him, and an idea blossomed in his mind.

Annie tugged on elbow-length white gloves and faced Lila and Edie.

"Will I do?" She didn't want to go, but she had an obligation to the Abbey to attend.

Lila's eyes sparkled. "You look wonderful. We should hurry, though."

Annie allowed her friend and sister to herd her through the door.

She'd caught a glimpse of Ford in the ridiculous green and purple uniform, muscles straining as he dragged the oars through the water. A flash of him with the members of the rowing crew, rejoicing over their win. And then she'd watched Merilee be wheeled in, a broad smile on her youthful face, accompanied by her parents and a handsome young man Annie assumed was her brother. She'd fled.

Now her feet propelled her into the buggy even as her heart contracted with pain. She settled into her seat and shifted her skirts to make room for Lila and Edie. The wheels clattered as they set off.

"It will be all right, Annie," Lila murmured.

"What will be all right?" Edie looked from Annie to Lila.

Annie squeezed Lila's arm to silence her, but Lila was already talking. "It appears Ford is going to propose to Merilee. If he hasn't already."

"What?" Edie was aghast. "That's impossible."

Annie groaned aloud. "Can we please not talk about it?"

"How dare he? I can't even..." Edie sputtered.

"Really, it's not a surprise," Annie replied. But even as she said the words, she was remembering kissing him, the times he'd sought her out. She should have told him how she felt, instead of running away from their shared past and from her own mistakes. And he shouldn't have kissed her and paid attention to her. Now it was too late.

"I'm going to have words with him," Edie said.

"No! Stay out of it, Edie."

An uncomfortable silence settled upon the buggy's occupants.

When the wheels crunched to a halt in the gravel outside the gala site, Annie spoke up.

"I gave Ford up eight years ago. I'm glad he has come back to Austin, and I'm grateful for the things he's accomplished at the ranch. But I have no claim on him."

"Of course," Lila assured her. Edie nodded, but her lips were pressed in a thin, tight line.

The women climbed out of the buggy, shook out skirts, adjusted gloves, and checked hairpins before turning to the huge canvas tent, illuminated by torches outside and strings of electric lights inside.

"It looks magical," Lila breathed.

"Let's get this over with," Annie muttered. Picking up her skirts and lowering her head, she trudged forward.

Nineteen

Ford watched Annie come into the tent, flanked by Lila Ross and Edie. Annie could have been walking to the gallows, judging by her expression. Lila sought out her husband. Edie remained at her sister's side, a murderous gleam in her eyes. A tremor rippled down his spine. Had Edie gotten to her sister and persuaded her to reject him yet again?

The musicians on the platform picked up the pace of the music, and couples whirled onto the temporary dance floor. He moved toward Annie, but Augusta halted his progress.

"Your speech is next. Are you ready?"

"I was going to ask Annie to dance." They'd shared their first dance together at an Abbey ball. It seemed appropriate.

Augusta shook her head. "Trust me, it would be better if you gave your speech first."

Ford frowned. "Why?"

"News travels fast in Austin. You were seen leaving two places the other day, and that has the rumor mill grinding out theories. Whatever you say this evening, I recommend it clear up any question about your relationship with Merilee."

"All right," he said slowly. "Do you recommend anything else?"

"Tell Annie you love her and ask her to marry you."

"Do you think she'll have me?"

"If she doesn't, then she's a fool twice over. But I know our dear Annie Ellis, and she's no fool." Augusta leaned in and kissed his cheek. "My prayers are with you." As if she knew—and she probably did—she

158

patted his jacket pocket, where the engagement ring rested. His heart started to pound.

Noah took the stage, and the crowd fell silent.

"We're all gathered here in support of the work that is done every day, every month, every year, at the Jeanette C. Austen Academy. We all support the school, but sometimes it takes new ideas to grow a project. This year, Ford Winters, newly returned to his hometown, had an idea..."

His hometown. Ford hadn't thought of Austin that way. It justified his return somehow. Noah explained the fundraising plan and held up the trophy.

"Ford? Would you please say a few words?" Noah asked.

Ford took Noah's place on the platform and cleared his throat.

"You're all here tonight for the sake of the Academy—Austen Abbey—and it's a cause worthy of your support. It's not only the young ladies of Austin who benefit, it's their future husbands and children and employers and coworkers. My life has been changed by the Abbey, and I've never taken a single class."

The crowd laughed at that, and Ford relaxed a bit.

"Some of you remember me from my childhood, most of you—thankfully—don't." Whispers erupted behind gloved fingers. Ford held up a hand.

"I've heard all the gossip about myself. Most of it's true."

Some of the men guffawed, only to be elbowed and shushed by their wives.

"When I was a boy, I fell in love with a girl." Annie's head jerked up and their eyes met. He held her gaze.

"I wanted to marry that girl, but the timing wasn't right. I wasn't ready." He saw her eyes go round. He knew she blamed herself, but he knew better. "It's my opinion that the prodigal son of Bible fame learned some important lessons when he was out there in the world." Heads nodded. "It would have been nice if I could have taken classes at the Abbey and learned those lessons, but some of us are too hard-headed for that."

"Amen, son."

Ford blinked, recognizing Walt's voice. Walt stood behind Annie. His back straight, his eyes clear. Annie jerked around in her chair. Her father placed his hands on her shoulders and turned her gently back to face Ford.

"Since I've returned, I've been welcomed with open arms. I've made new friends, and rediscovered the importance of family. There's only one thing missing. The girl I fell in love with all those years ago is now a strong, beautiful woman. And I'm still in love with her. Maybe more so now, because I know what it's like to live without her."

There was a little gasp from several of the ladies in the room, but Annie remained still. Ford jumped off the dais and strode across the dance floor. At Annie's chair, he dropped to one knee and withdrew the ring from his pocket.

"Annie Ellis, I offer myself to you again with a heart even more your own than when you almost broke it, eight years ago. Will you please marry me?"

Annie stared at the ring, eyes wide. She looked at Ford. Sensed her father's silent acceptance and heard Edie's soft sigh of approval. She nodded. She couldn't speak.

"You have to say something, darling. This is a terrible time to run out of words," Ford whispered.

In response, she flung herself into his arms, where she'd always belonged, and whispered a "yes" in his ear. The tent erupted in applause, whistles, and laughter around them.

"Thank God," Ford muttered, his voice hoarse.

She leaned back far enough to look into the green eyes she'd loved for so long. "You didn't think I'd refuse again, did you?"

He cocked his head. "I hoped not, but one never knows."

She held out her left hand and let him slide the ring over her gloved fourth finger. "You bought this at Koen's."

"How did you know that?"

"I saw you coming out of the store on my way to dinner with Lila. I thought..."

Ford shook his head. "You thought I was going to propose to Merilee."

She swallowed, nodded. "I was so angry with you."

"That young man with Merilee and her parents? That's her beau. He came all the way down to be with her as soon as he heard she was injured."

"Oh."

"I'd tell you to close your mouth again, but I have a better idea." He kissed her, to the immense glee of the crowd. "I wanted to do that the moment I saw you at the bank," he murmured, pulling her against his chest.

She breathed in the scent of him, warm and familiar, and silently thanked God. Despite all her doubts, her lack of faith, her outright avoidance, God had kept His promises. And she was fully persuaded He would continue to do so.

MANSFORD RANCH

DINA SLEIMAN

He will bring to light
what is hidden in darkness
and will expose the motives
of the heart.

I Corinthians 4:5

If one scheme of happiness fails,
human nature turns to another;
if the first calculation is wrong,
we make a second better:
we find comfort somewhere.

~Jane Austen,
Mansfield Park

One

Austin, Texas 1897

"So, did ya kill anyone today?"

A muddy boot thumped down beside Franny Sue Price where she sat outdoors upon a pristine patchwork quilt, but she kept her eyes glued to the paper in front of her. "Not yet, but I'm working on it."

"Who's the lucky fella?"

Franny lowered her parasol and frowned at Eddie Mansford as her eyes adjusted to the bright afternoon sun. No point in admonishing him on his unrefined speech. Ten years of harping hadn't corrected it. Despite his wealth and connections, he seemed determined to remain a cowpoke of the lowest rank.

"I haven't quite pinned that down." She tapped her pencil against her journal. "Perhaps it shall be a woman who dies this time."

"Which story are you working on? The puritanical pirates or the pirating puritans?" His warm hazel eyes gleamed with laughter, but he held his lips steady.

"Funny." She never said the man was stupid. "I outgrew pirates long ago. I want to delve deeper into human nature and the depravity of mankind with my new tales."

"A Gothic it is. I sure do love that there Edgar Allen Poe."

"Gothic romance, I would say. But I find myself in need of the perfect villain."

"Villain, huh. How about some big city fella?"

Franny pressed her pencil to her lip as she pondered that. "Perhaps you have a point. *We do not look to our great cities for our best morality,*" she said, quoting a favorite author.[1]

Fortunately, the nearby city of Austin, which was yet new and small, did not qualify for such a description.

"Well, I'll be hogtied if you don't have a quote for dern near every occasion." Eddie took off his hat and slapped it against his chaps, sending forth a swirl of dust.

"Goodness, Eddie." Franny coughed and waved the dirt away from her white day dress with its yellow silken sash. She should have known better than to wear such a frock about the ranch, but it was her favorite. "Lord knows *you* shall never play the hero in a romance novel."

"Sorry about that. I still need to wash up for supper."

"You had best, or Uncle Manny is sure to tan your hide. Company's coming. Did you hear? Hank Crawfield has returned at long last." A smile twitched at her lips. Between her attendance at finishing school and Hank's going back East, they'd barely seen one another in years, but the few glimpses she had caught were quite satisfactory.

"Now there's a villain for your story. Something about that one just ain't right. Fancy east coast university or not."

Franny paused to contemplate. "Interesting. On the surface his manners are charming, his wit flawless, but you might be onto something. He has a bit of the blackguard about him. Remember the way he'd pull the wings off fireflies just for the fun of it when we were children?" Franny shivered. Something had indeed not been right about the gleam in his eye as he committed the act.

"Mmm. And shoot the barn cats with his slingshot."

"Don't remind me." She had feared the awful boy would hunt down her beloved Nibbles.

"He always was in some heap of trouble when we was young."

Franny resisted the temptation to correct Eddie's grammar. "Well, we barely know him anymore. And we managed to find plenty of trouble ourselves during childhood. He's changed, no doubt. Who could fail to with such a fine education?"

"Book learnin' will only get you so far." Eddie rubbed his jaw. And quite a nice chiseled sort of jaw it would be, if only he bothered to

---

[1]   *Mansfield Park,* Jane Austen 1814

shave once in a while.

Old Rusty hobbled by on his peg leg, a bucket of water sloshing at his side. He shot Eddie the oddest look. "Evenin', folks."

"Good evening to you, Mr. Forbes. Can I offer some assistance?" Franny asked.

"Thank ye kindly, ma'am, but I'll be just fine." He shook his head at Eddie before heading to the bunkhouse.

"Now there's a mysterious character. I wonder what that was about." She redirected her attention to the dusty young man beside her. "And how would you know about 'book learning' anyway?" Eddie had barely finished the eighth grade before he traded in his slate for a lasso, whereas she herself had attended the Jeannette C. Austen Academy for Young Ladies, the finest finishing school west of the Mississippi. She now volunteered there as a creative writing teacher one afternoon a week and remained after school to help lead a new drama troupe.

Once upon a time, Eddie had been her Ivanhoe and Sir Walter Scott all tied up in one. Too bad he was so determined to waste his life on the trail.

"You of all people should realize that ain't fair, Franny Sue. Didn't I just yesterday give you an earful about that Darcy fella?"

Okay, so he was well read. Mostly at her insistence. She repressed a chuckle. Never had she expected him to complete the entire Jane Austen novel, but she had hoped he might learn a thing or two about proper manners before returning it. "Now, Mr. Darcy. There's a hero for you. Perhaps you should take a lesson, Edward Reginald Mansford."

He winced at the use of his proper name. "I maintain he was right stuck on hisself. Reminded me too much of Hank by half, that one did."

"So which is it then? Is Hank a hero or a villain?"

Eddie offered a sly grin and pushed rumpled hair in a sandy shade of blond from his forehead. "I suppose we'll find out soon enough." He turned and walked off toward the bunkhouse, slapping his hat against his leg once more.

Franny Sue bit on her pencil, an alarming habit she could not bring herself to break for the sake of her creative process. Then she proceeded to begin a new and unexpected entry in her journal.

And so we shall see, dear reader, soon enough indeed, the true character of one Henry Crawfield of Austin, Texas. For it is such in the nature of mankind, that though he attempt to hide his true proclivities, in due time they shall trickle forth in telling detail, if one but patiently attunes oneself to observe such minute inconsistencies.

Eddie entered the bunkhouse and chuckled to himself. He never tired of teasing that young lady. The smell of ham and beans tickled his nose. He wished he could just have dinner with the cowhands tonight instead of donning that suffocating evening coat in an attempt to please his father and the ridiculous Crawfields.

Rusty eyed him warily from the stove where he stirred a boiling pot of beans. "What was that there dern fool accent you was usin' with Miss Price?"

The irony of the comment clearly escaped Rusty.

"What's it matter to you?" Eddie snatched the spoon from Rusty's hand and sampled the soup. "Needs salt." He gave the crusty old man a friendly shove before returning the spoon. Rusty had been cooking up beans ever since he lost his leg as a young man in the War Between the States. But he didn't like to be coddled.

"You might just stand a chance with that young lady iffin you didn't act like such a dunderhead around her."

"Stand a chance? Who said I wanted a chance? That squirt is like a sister to me." Eddie's stepmother and father had taken in Franny Sue, a distant step-cousin, over a decade ago when her family landed on hard times. The eight-year-old girl had looked so lost and alone. Eddie never could resist melting at the sight of those big, doe eyes. From that first night when he had heard her crying herself to sleep and snuck into her room to tell her stories, she had become the younger sibling he always dreamed of.

Rusty raised a bushy gray eyebrow his direction. "You expectin' me to believe that nonsense?"

Eddie pictured her as he had seen her moments ago—all gleaming golden-brown curls with those perfect bow-shaped lips smiling up at him from beneath the lace of her parasol. His heart did a funny flip in his chest. "Fine, she's turned into the fairest maiden in all of Texas. Is that what you want me to say? But we're not suited. She's made that abundantly clear. So why not enjoy a bit of fun?" He chuckled again, sitting at the table. "It annoys her to no end when I talk like a cowboy."

"Hmm. And you're not at all interested in winning her for yourself?"

"She's right. We don't belong together. She wants a fancy city life with a man wearing a three-piece suit and a pocket watch. Of course she's caught my eye. She's caught every man's eye within a hundred miles. I care about her, yes. I care about her enough that I want her to be happy, and she would never be happy married to a cowboy like me." He needed a solid, practical wife. Not one given to fripperies and whimsy.

"You're right about one thing. Any man within a hundred miles would be thrilled to rope that pretty little heifer."

Though Rusty clearly meant his statement as a compliment, Eddie grinned as he imagined the horror on Franny Sue's face if she'd overheard it. But he turned the subject to more pertinent matters. "The girl won't pick a husband without my father's approval. I know she's grateful to him and all. She should be, but I can hardly stand the way she worships the man."

"So who is suitable for Miss Fancy-pants Price? That Hank Crawfield?" Rusty slammed his spoon down on the table.

Eddie rubbed a hand over his brow. "Don't even joke about it." Hank had always turned his blood cold in his veins. The devilish spark in his eye still haunted Eddie. No one changed that much during a few years at a university.

"Well, if not you, it may as well be him." Rusty flashed a gap-toothed smile.

"That Hank's no good. I swear I'd move to town and take a job at the bank myself before letting Franny run off with the likes of him." Eddie crossed his legs and tugged at his boot.

Rusty hobbled toward him, pulling a dishrag from his pocket and smacking Eddie's shoulder with it. "To the house with you, boy. Your father will have my skin as well as yours if he catches you gettin' ready for his fancy dinner party out here with a bucket of lye soap."

"Fine." Eddie stuffed his moist, aching foot back into the boot.

Rusty shook the rag at him. "And don't think I didn't notice when you started making yourself at home in the bunkhouse. Precisely three months ago, that's when. When that there young lady you're supposedly not interested in came home from her hoity toity finishing school. What are you running from, boy?"

"Rusty, you're too observant for your own good." It was true. When she returned, the house became too stifling. Every time she walked into the room with her milky skin and tinkling giggle, his heart would race.

His throat dried up. And since his father considered her a daughter, they were all too often left unchaperoned.

No, better to make teasing banter outdoors and remove himself far from the temptation of one Miss Franny Sue Price. Despite her supposed acuity concerning human nature, she had no idea the feelings he struggled with and seemed innocent to them herself. He intended to maintain the illusion of brotherly annoyance. He was more than happy to hang around the bunkhouse and could hardly wait to take the cattle to the farther pastures that would keep him away for days at a time. Give him the musk and leather scent of his faithful mustang over Franny's honeysuckle enticement any day. Besides, as Rusty so pointedly observed, she'd be married off and out of the house soon enough.

Best to change the subject.

He thumped his foot to the ground, driving it deeper into the boot. "Maybe you should be the one writing Gothic novels, Rusty. I'll send Miss Price your way the next time she gets stuck with her character motivations."

Rusty plopped into the chair across from him, beady eyes staring from a wrinkled and grizzled face straight at Eddie. "I betcha she don't even know you went to that newfangled university in Austin while she was right nearby in town."

"A few useless classes in literature and philosophy do not a university education make. And that was supposed to be our little secret." Eddie shoved his Stetson on his head, and as easily slipped back into his cowboy accent. "Just keep it to yer own doggone self."

He shot Rusty a warning glare before heading toward the house to dress for dinner.

Franny Sue smoothed down a loose curl, admiring herself in the long mirror of her armoire. In the distance, hooves clicked against the drive. She dashed to her dressing table, snatching up her journal and pencil, and dove for her window seat overlooking the expansive front lawn. A lady should never run, but there would be plenty of time for such civility later. She didn't want to miss recording this moment for posterity.

Tucking her feet beneath the bustle of her buttercup silk gown, she settled herself upon the cushions. The childish position proved yet another appalling habit she dare not forsake for the appeasement of the creative muse. Tonight she would be all manners and refinement, she promised herself. Nothing would prevent her from pleasing dear Uncle Manny with the portrait of the perfect lady, for which he had invested a small fortune.

As the man exited the house and appeared on the drive before her, love swelled in her chest. How could she ever repay Uncle Manny for gift after gift he had bestowed upon her? Her own father had abandoned his family for the lure of the trail. When his life ended senselessly, hers might have all but ended as well, if not for the generosity of the precious white-haired gentleman awaiting the carriage.

Despite Thomas Mansford's stoic nature, Franny perceived in the set of his square, manly features the importance of this evening. He had hinted on more than one occasion that it would please him if she settled down with Hank Crawfield, the son of his best friend and business associate.

She tapped on the window and waved down at Uncle Manny. His face softened as he gazed toward her, waving in return. She wasn't about to let some vague memory of a wayward child prevent her from granting her uncle his heart's desire. She determined to give Hank Crawfield every opportunity to prove himself worthy of her affection.

Although she had immersed herself in romance for much of her childhood, she had since put such juvenile nonsense far behind. At Austen Abbey, as the girls called their school, she learned the importance of duty and honor, respect for one's elders, finding one's proper role in society. Just as she now fit the role of training future young ladies, even as she waited for her uncle to choose a suitable husband for her.

Franny had learned to value a man of manners and education. A man who might provide security and stability. Never an irresponsible cowpoke to be lost in the next pointless gunfight. And Eddie had the audacity to recommend Hank as her next villain. Preposterous!

As the carriage rolled closer, she noted the exquisite detailing. The crafted leather. The carved woodwork. The Crawfield emblem emblazoned on the side like an English coat of arms. When it pulled to a stop, Franny sat poised and ready to write.

The moment had arrived. Hank was finally back to stay.

The door swung open, dear reader, and at first all one could distinguish was the form of a Stetson outlined against the backdrop of a golden Texas sun. Then the man himself alit from the carriage. A shadowed silhouette of male perfection bedecked in a tailored evening suit sauntered toward one Thomas Mansford with the utmost confidence and grace, causing my heart, I must confess, to flutter in my corseted chest. He reached and clasped Mr. Mansford's hand with the precise balance of affection and decorum befitting the reunion. Soon enough, we shall discern, my friends, if such etiquette resides only upon the surface of his demeanor or if it springs from some deeper wellspring of true refinement.

Two

Franny Sue dashed down the stairs with her heeled shoes clicking. No one witnessed her brief breach in etiquette, and she wanted to be ready and waiting when the men entered. At least she had foregone sliding down the bannister, which was in fact the quickest route to the first floor. While she was quite adept at that mode of transportation, she wouldn't wish to wrinkle her gown.

Once in the foyer she re-puffed her thick sleeves and straightened her small bustle. Thank goodness the huge, figure-distorting bustles of last decade had fallen out of fashion. Certain styles were meant to die. Perhaps these exaggerated mutton top sleeves would be the next to go. She seemed to have a special knack for deflating them only on one side or the other, though she must admit she preferred them in the shorter length this evening dress required. Combined with her tight corset, which, truth be told, caused her no end of discomfort, she knew the sleeves created the perfect hour-glass figured currently en vogue. Sometimes one must suffer for beauty.

She calmed her breathing after her mad dash down the stairs and lifted her chin. Flipping open the lace fan attached to her wrist, she fluttered it gently just beneath her lips to add an air of mystery. That skill she had learned from the other girls at Austen Abbey, for Mrs. Collins never did encourage such overt flirtation. But as Uncle Manny had already made clear his intent that she snag Hank Crawfield as a husband, she could see no harm. The flow of air combined with her heated skin sent her honeysuckle perfume drifting about her.

Perfect!

At that moment, Eddie came careening down the bannister and nearly crashed into her, no doubt using the unseemly mode of transportation more to annoy her than for any other reason. She stepped aside just in time. Though she would not permit herself to appear flustered, she was unable to resist slapping him with her fan. "Do you really wish for the Crawfields to see you behaving like a child?"

"Don't even pretend you didn't want to slide down the rail yourself. That's the difference between you and me. I don't put on airs."

She grimaced at the incorrigible man who knew her all too well, who had in fact been the one to teach her that risky maneuver. "You say airs, I say manners, but clearly you fail to distinguish between the two." He might look stunningly handsome with his fresh shave and evening coat, but she was not fooled by outward trappings for one moment.

A thump on the porch brought them both to attention. By the time the knob turned, Franny Sue had resumed her feminine pose with fan in place.

Uncle Manny entered first and then waved their guests inside. A portly Mr. Crawfield came next, and finally the man of the hour: Hank Crawfield himself.

He straightened his pristine white bow tie as he surveyed the elegant entryway, then proceeded to sweep off his top hat with perfect decorum, all the while holding one arm behind his back in a debonair manner. His thick dark hair was slicked back just right and his mustache curved to the perfect degree. The maid approached, and he offered her his hat with an elegant nod. Eddie suddenly appeared the rough cowboy he was in comparison to Hank with his east coast polish. When at last Hank's gaze fell upon her, he smiled with delight.

"There is the lovely lady." He walked her way and scooped up her hand to place a kiss upon it.

She almost wished she had gone to the extra length of wearing opera gloves, but surely that would have seemed too formal for a dinner at home with friends, and she would have missed the brush of his lips upon her skin.

"It has been far too long, my dear Franny Sue," Hank said as he continued to bow over her hand.

Delightful little bubbles filled her at his pretty speech. "I feel the same way. I hope your time back East has treated you well."

"Sublimely," he said in a deep, raspy voice, finally relinquishing her hand. "And it seems your time at our own Austen Academy has agreed with you. Turned the young spitfire into the elegant lady."

She giggled as she fluttered her fan. "Not such a spitfire, truly."

The older gentlemen both watched their exchange with obvious enjoyment.

Eddie emitted a muffled noise behind her that sounded like a repressed laugh.

"She simply admired her step-cousin and wished to be like him in all ways," said Uncle Manny.

"Ah, yes, I remember." A cold edge crept into Hank's voice, and he shot Eddie a chilling glance to match.

Eddie just snorted in yet another unmannerly display.

Hank pulled a beautiful bouquet of Texas bluebonnets from behind his back and handed them to Franny. "For you, my dear."

"My favorites! I can't believe you remembered that as well." Franny sighed, recalling that she and Hank had picked them together once as children, on a rare day when he deigned to behave. She pressed the flowers to her nose and drank in the sweet scent of Texas in spring, which she hadn't smelled nearly enough during her years in the city at finishing school. "Thank you so much. I'll have the maid put them on the dinner table."

She turned and handed the lovely blossoms to the middle-aged Maria, who yet stood in attendance nearby.

"And good evening to you, Mr. Crawfield," Franny said, offering her hand to Hank's father, which prompted greetings all around.

Even Eddie seemed to make an attempt at civility.

"Come," Franny said, "let us all go to the drawing room for a drink before dinner." She indicated in that direction.

Hank, of course, gallantly offered her his arm.

Yet as she linked her hand through the crook of his elbow, she could not forget that cold look in his eye. Surely he was entitled not to like his childhood rival. Yet she should not be too quick to trust him nor become enamored. She would reserve her judgement for now. Stiffening her spine along with her heart, she proceeded toward the drawing room with her defenses firmly in place.

Eddie carved into the last portion of his prime rib with all the violence he would like to administer to that Hank Crawfield. Everything about the man irked him. From his dandified clothes and speech, to his fawning manners, to the smoldering way he looked at Franny from beneath his hooded eyelids.

Across the table from him, Hank draped his arm around the back of Franny's chair and leaned close to whisper something in her ear.

Eddie felt as if some small, prickly creature crawled beneath his skin.

Franny Sue's responding melodic giggle tinkled like wind chimes, making him more miserable than ever. Oh how he hated that magical giggle. Except that he loved it and couldn't imagine his life without it.

He shoved the no doubt delectable piece of meat into his mouth and chewed without tasting, then forced himself to swallow it down.

"What are you two conspiring about over there?" asked Mr. Crawfield with a wiggle of his graying brows.

Father nudged his friend with an elbow. "Let them have their fun, Richard. It seems they're getting along splendidly just as we hoped."

"Perhaps by the time you return from your trip to Dallas, we might have a joint announcement to make. Now that Hank's home for good, it's high time he took a bride and settled down. I can't tell you how ready I am for grandchildren." Mr. Crawfield raised a glass toward Hank and Franny Sue.

Glancing at the pair, Eddie noted that Hank's arm was still draped over Franny's chair, and he now fingered the lace edging her short sleeve in an all too familiar way.

"Gentleman, let's not rush matters." Hank gazed down at her, although he spoke to the men. "Franny and I might have played together as youngsters, but we've barely seen each other in years. While I would like nothing more than to join our respective families, the young lady and I need time to become reacquainted."

Franny batted her lashes up at Hank. The girl always had been a sucker for pretty words. He'd like to blame the writer in her, but the truth was, she was a sucker for pretty things in general, as her frothy concoction of yellow silk and white lace attested.

"Well, young Mr. Crawfield, I officially give you permission to court my daughter. Three weeks is a long time. Who knows what might happen before I return?" Father winked at the two, and Eddie's stomach heaved. "Speaking of becoming reacquainted, you've told us all your tales from back East, but what are your plans now that you're home, son?"

Eddie jolted at the term son, and checked to make sure that his father was indeed speaking to Hank. Sure enough the man stared directly at the blackguard, whom he wished to welcome into the family fold. Eddie was suddenly glad his mouth was empty, because otherwise he might have choked. He dropped his fork to the table in disgust.

"I plan to begin by working for my father here in Austin at the bank, but I hope to expand my interests and holdings as well, and begin to build my own empire." Hank shot Franny a look that seemed to suggest it might be hers too someday.

She gave him a playful swat. "I have always admired a man who seeks to improve himself."

"What do you have in mind?" asked Father. "Ever consider ranching?"

"In fact, I purchased some land about twenty miles east of here on my last trip two years ago. But it's more of a cotton plantation than a ranch. Man shall not live by beef alone, you know."

"Blasphemy!" Father chuckled good naturedly nonetheless. "That's excellent forward thinking. Textiles are always in high demand, especially with so many cities springing up in our beloved Texas."

"Precisely." Even Hank's subtle nod was pretentious. "Why import it from another state when we have the climate to grow it in our own?"

Although Eddie and his father didn't always see eye to eye, he usually trusted the man's judgement. How did Father fail to see the darkness hiding just under the surface of Hank's slick exterior? In the past few days, they'd had several arguments over the subject. Eddie understood the advantage of a ranching family marrying into a local banking family, and of course Father had always liked Mr. Crawfield, but still.

"He's a self-starter, this one here." Mr. Crawfield gave his son's shoulder a shake.

"And what do you do for fun?" Father asked. "Still collecting weapons?"

Eddie well recalled Hank's chilling fascination with weaponry.

"Ah, yes. I've recently acquired an ancient Samurai sword." Hank smiled with only one side of his mouth, but Franny seemed enamored by the effect.

"Interesting," Father said. "You know Eddie just got the new Springfield rifle."

"Really, the Krag-Jørgensen?" Hank turned Eddie's way with interest for the first time tonight. "I've been thinking about purchasing one. Might you show it to me? I'd like to see it in action."

"Of course, but you know, I actually use my gun rather than just mount it like some fancy wall-hanging."

"Touché," Hank said smugly. "Bankers don't have much call for toting about rifles. That's more the role of the bank robber, but I assure you I know how to use a weapon properly. I've gone hunting a number of times while back East. Hunting there is much more formal in nature."

Franny Sue quirked a delicate golden-brown eyebrow his way. "Eddie wouldn't know about anything formal. Don't let the evening attire fool you—he is still a cowboy through and through. Try as I might, I can't keep him off the trail."

"Now, Franny dear." Hank patted her hand. "Each man must follow his own path. We can't all carve out the financial future of this great nation."

Hank's suave laugh grated on Eddie's last nerve. How had the man managed to defend him and insult him in the span of two short sentences? Hank had been stirring up trouble for as long as Eddie could remember, probably because his parents traveled so much and spoiled him on the rare occasions they were home. After his mother had passed away, the last vestige of soft playfulness had been stripped from the man. Although Hank had now added a sheen of refinement over top, the villain was still as plain as day in his pale blue eyes.

If Father couldn't see it, Eddie must convince Franny.

"Why don't you youngsters take a short constitutional before dessert," Father suggested, patting his mouth with his linen napkin and setting it on the table. "Eddie, you can show Hank that new rifle, and Mr. Crawfield and I can discuss business matters for a few minutes."

Eddie tossed his own napkin on the table and shoved his chair away from it. Anything to get out of this stifling dining room and catch a few breaths of fresh air. Maybe outside of the watchful gazes of their fathers, Eddie might be able to provoke Hank and unmask him. "I'll go get it and meet you on the porch."

Three

"My dear, you look all golden perfection in this setting sunshine. Your hair gleams with the touch of Midas." Hank reached out to tuck a curl behind Franny's ear and then scooped her two hands into his own.

Both instinct and years of training bade her to yank them away, but Uncle Manny had just given them permission to court, and to her amazement, marriage had already been mentioned forthrightly in reference to them. Besides which, Hank had taken her hands with the utmost gentleness and spoke like a true romantic, and so she resisted instinct and gave his hands a warm squeeze. Could it be that the wayward child had indeed grown to be an upstanding man?

As he continued to gaze down at her with his icy blue eyes, her eyelashes fluttered of their own accord. She felt the heat creeping into her cheeks and hoped they had tinged a becoming shade of pink. Throughout dinner his charm and sophistication had pleased her to no end, melting away her reservations, although she was still determined to guard her heart.

The door flew open and banged against the side of the house. Hank dropped her hands as Eddie tromped onto the porch—plus one rifle but minus his evening coat. The lean muscles in Eddie's arm bulged against his crisp white shirt from gripping the gun so tightly. At least he'd kept his vest and tie and had not completely abandoned decorum.

"Let's get this over with," he grumbled and strode toward the barn, behind which he kept targets for practice. He shot a glare at Hank. "If a city fella like you can keep up."

"Naturally." Hank's tone remained calm, but his eyes registered challenge as he followed Eddie down the steps.

Franny stood alone for a second before realizing she would be left in the dust by their competitive posturing if she didn't move quickly. She managed a somewhat ladylike trot in their direction, but they seemed too wrapped up in each other to even notice her.

She inserted herself between the two men and surveyed each of them with her author's eye. One might never know that Hank was annoyed, except by the slight rigidity of his shoulders and the briskness of his step.

Meanwhile, Eddie was clearly upset. Although he loved to spar with her and often assumed the role of surly cowpoke, this emotion was on a different level entirely. His jaw was clenched, his face flushed, a vein stood out prominently against his neck, and when the wind ruffled his sandy hair, she detected sweat beading along his forehead.

She glanced over the rest of him and noted that his state of undress, along with the vest nipping in close at his trim waist, lent him a rather rakish appearance. Not unlike the pirate hero she had created two novels ago.

Had she subconsciously written Eddie into the role of Jean Luc?

No, that was ludicrous.

As was her continued trot to keep up with them. Not that with her long slim legs she couldn't easily run circles around the ranch if needed, but ladies did not do such things.

"Gentlemen," she said, using the word loosely in the case of Eddie. She slid an arm through each of theirs. "Please slow down. You wouldn't wish for a young lady to injure an extremity."

Hank immediately pulled to a stop. Eddie kept going and yanked her like the rope in a tug of war before dropping her arm and turning to her with disgust plastered across his face.

"My dear, I do apologize." Hank patted her hand where it looped about his arm. "How thoughtless of me. I fear my love of weaponry has outdone my better judgement. There is no rush."

"Your *legs*," Eddie said, emphasizing the less delicate term, "look right fine to me."

"Uh!" the sound escaped from her without forethought.

Eddie had no right looking at her legs like so. Although she knew her skirt and several layers of petticoats passed her ankles, and although she and Eddie used to swim together in their undergarments, she felt as if she should cover said legs.

"And there is a rush if you want to see this gun in action before the sun sets." Eddie held up the gleaming weapon, the only thing about him polished a tenth as much as Hank himself.

"A lady's well-being always comes first." Hank now wrapped his arm around her, as if shielding her from the crass man before them. "And must I remind you that there are certain things a gentleman should not mention?"

Franny tucked herself tighter into Hank's side. "Eddie never claimed to be a gentleman."

Eddie's surly face crumpled at that.

Which made no sense at all, but suddenly she felt an urge to soothe whatever was troubling him. "But you must forgive him. He thinks of me as a sister after all these years and forgets about such niceties."

"Yeah..." Eddie seemed to stumble over his words. "Like...a sister. Right, squirt?"

Franny frowned at him but was relieved to see him relax a bit.

They continued in awkward silence past the barn and around the back.

Eddie stopped before a fence rail. About a hundred feet away stood a target.

"How are your eyes these days, Hank?" asked Eddie.

"Exceptional, of course."

"Then watch close." Eddie fished a bullet from his pocket, slid it into the loading door, and slid the bolt home. Lifting the Krag to his shoulder, he took aim.

Franny would never mention that her own fingers itched to get ahold of the rifle. Though she had put such interests far behind her, Eddie had managed to instill a love of firearms in her as well, which she had never quite shaken.

She jolted as the gun exploded and the bullet made a fresh hole in the center of the target.

"That Norwegian certainly does have a way with a gun," Hank said, displaying his knowledge of the weapon's designer. "May I try it?"

Eddie eyed Hank skeptically. But evidently even he did not think Hank capable of true harm, for he handed over the weapon without a word. He tossed Hank a fresh bullet with a hint of challenge.

But of course a gun expert like Hank knew just how to load it. He turned it over and around to better study it. "How many grains of black powder in these bullets? Two-thirty, isn't it?"

Franny pressed her lips together to disguise her sudden intake of breath, for the question immediately belied Hank's supposed expertise. Even she knew that the Krag was the first rifle to use the new smokeless powder in its cartridges—although she winced at her own awareness of such indelicate issues.

Eddie snickered, and smiled for the first time that night. "It's a thirty caliber round, with forty grains of nitrocelluose powder."

"I see," Hank said with an extra dose of superiority.

For the first time Franny paused to wonder if perhaps he used his polish to distract from his weaknesses. She had used that tactic in a character once. She began to view Hank through different, more cautious eyes.

"The general opinion is that Mauser outclasses the Krag," Hank said.

"'Where an opinion is general, it usually is correct,'" Franny added a favorite quote by way of support.[2] Though to be fair, the Mauser only out-performed the Krag in tropical climates, from what Eddie had said.

Eddie's jaw went tight, but he said nothing.

Hank finally lifted the gun and fired it. He hit the target, although from what she could tell at this distance, the bullet struck about eight inches left of center.

She said, "Excellent shot," although she knew she could do better than he had, given the opportunity.

"It's nice," Hank said, examining the gun again. "I like the weight and the recoil. Although it seems to skew a bit to the left. I suppose you know to compensate for that."

"If you say so." Eddie smirked.

Hank tossed the gun back to Eddie, and Eddie snatched it neatly from the air.

"How about you, Franny Sue? Want a turn? It's a dandy. You can check out the aim for us."

Eddie held the gun to her, and she stumbled backward pressing a hand to her chest as if the weapon were a snake that might bite her. "Why, I could never. I might muss my dress."

Hank wrapped an arm about her waist this time. "Don't be afraid,

---

2   *Mansfield Park*, Jane Austen 1814

darling. If you like, someday I can teach you to shoot. Or perhaps you might wish to accompany me on a fox hunt. There are no guns involved in that style. Can you ride sidesaddle?"

Eddie rolled his eyes at that.

Of course she could ride: sidesaddle, English saddle, Western saddle, or no saddle at all. And although she was out of practice, once upon a time she could perform tricks worthy of a rodeo cowboy. Surely Hank remembered, although perhaps he had never seen her ride in the more lady-like fashion. "That sounds lovely," was all she said in reply.

"Hank, quick!" Eddie shouted. He tossed the gun back to Hank. "Barn cat at two o'clock."

Hank chuckled. "Ah, I was quite the scamp." Playing along, he took aim and pretended to pull the trigger. "Boom!" He jerked the gun backward as if it had fired.

Again, something harsh and cold flashed through his eyes that caused Franny Sue pause.

"Come my dear, I've seen enough, and I'm sure I caught the scent of apple dumplings drifting this way." Hank wrapped an arm about her again, as had quickly become his habit, and began leading her toward the house. As they passed Eddie, Hank roughly shoved the gun in his direction and slammed him in the gut.

Eddie did not so much as groan. Franny Sue knew his stomach to be solid muscle impervious to both punches and tickles, although again she winced at her own knowledge.

"I tell you, there is no gourmet French pastry in the world that can rival a down home apple dumpling." Hank chuckled, but Franny did not know what was humorous about that.

She studied him again. He seemed by any casual observation to be a true gentleman, yet she had noted a few subtle inconsistencies. She glanced back at Eddie, who was now hunched over and gripping the fence rail with two hands.

Eddie's behavior had exhibited some marked inconsistencies as well this evening. She would have to ponder that. Stumbling over a root, she forced herself to look forward. Hank took advantage of the opportunity to pull her closer and attach his other hand to her elbow. She could not decide if she felt protected or trapped.

Eddie slipped out his old bedroom window and onto the balcony. He leaned against the timbered wall and slid, or rather collapsed, down the side until he was sitting. Once upon a time their home had been a simple but spacious white-washed rancher's house, but when his widowed father had remarried to Franny Sue's aunt when Eddie was a mere five years old, the house had morphed into something far grander.

First they'd added wings to each side, then a second floor above the original structure along with columns, archways, and balustrades, and finally this balcony overtop the old porch, unfortunately linking his room to Franny Sue's.

He yanked off his bow tie and twisted it in his hands while staring out into the inky sky twinkling with stars. Reason told him he should have hurried back to the bunkhouse the second the Crawfields' gilded carriage had pulled away. But right now he needed to be near her. Just a little bit longer.

Pain cut through his gut as he considered Franny in the clutches of Hank Crawfield forever. He must convince her that the man was no good, and while he was at it, compile a list of suitable bachelors to replace him.

Let's see, James Ferris was a man of good character. There was Elliot Turner, and of course his old friend Clay Whitfield who was now a lawyer. She'd fancy a lawyer. A man in a three-piece suit with a pocket watch who sat behind a desk was precisely who she was looking for.

But at that thought, pain nearly doubled him over again. Who was he trying to fool? No one would be good enough for Franny Sue.

The girl might be given to a certain amount of shallowness and pliability, not to mention her obvious issues from her father. However, she had ample wit and intelligence, a deep well of love and strength, and a hidden spunky nature he loved to prod to the surface.

Darn it all! Now he sounded like Franny. He'd been spending too much time with the girl for his own good lately.

He twisted the bow tie around and around in his hands, frustrated beyond measure with this situation and taking it out on the silken accessory.

And to add the finishing touch to his torture, Franny herself climbed out her bedroom window, just like she had in the old days. So many times she had slipped out here in her nightgown to meet him, and he would tell her stories and show her the stars. Fortunately, she'd had the good sense to put on a dressing gown. She stared down at him and smiled.

His gut twisted yet again. The ruffles of her white gown shining in the moonlight should bring to mind that little girl who had been like a sister to him. Instead, they sent his mind spinning in a different direction entirely. A decidedly unbrotherly direction.

She leaned over the railing and left him in silence for a moment. The truth was, she was not his sister, as his reaction to her slim yet rounded bottom attested. She was merely a step-cousin, if such a ridiculous relationship even existed.

He took a deep breath and braced himself against her easy charm and femininity, for another, more relevant truth remained. They were not at all suitable. The mangled bow tie in his hand should be proof enough. Franny wanted a society husband and a fancy life. She would never accept a cowboy. And he had no intention of changing his ways.

Finally, she sat down cross-legged beside him. She stared out over the vast expanse of prairie as she spoke. "I'm sorry for whatever upset you tonight. As much as I love to irk you, I hate to see you hurting."

Hurting? So that's what that pain in his gut was, but he would never admit it.

"I can't stand to see you with that man. There are plenty of bachelors in town. Let me make a match for you."

"But Hank is Uncle Manny's choice. I must respect that if at all possible. And I rather like the new Hank."

Eddie tamped down all the anger and—yes—hurt, roiling inside of him. "So you plan to see him again?"

"He's going to come and pick me up for brunch and a carriage ride on Saturday."

"Brunch?"

"You know, late breakfast or early lunch. He claims it's all the rage in England."

"Of course he'd come up with something pretentious like *brunch*. It pert near kills me to see that man put his slimy hands on you." Eddie reinstated his best cowboy accent by way of defense. "He's a dirty old pole cat, I swear. Why can't anyone see it?"

Four

"E ddie," Franny laid a gentle hand upon his arm, hoping it might bring him some small comfort. "You can drop the *dern fool* accent. I know you just use it to bother me."

He leaned his elbows onto his knees and turned his head to smile wryly at her.

Something about that smile in the moonlight made her heart do an odd little flip. Then again, as her uncle had pointed out this evening, she had worshipped Eddie for years. She had esteemed him above any literary hero, even her favorites like Oliver Twist, Robinson Crusoe, and Mr. Darcy himself.

"Fine," Eddie said. "Hank is a villain and a scoundrel worthy of a Dickensian novel."

Could it really be the mere thought of Hank Crawfield that vexed Eddie so much? "If you feel so strongly about this, I suppose I must take your opinion into account. I did note the slightest inconsistencies in his demeanor tonight."

"Slight?"

"Slight. But that could have meant anything. Perhaps the memories of his childhood mishaps embarrass him. Or they bring to mind his lonely upbringing. Either of those would provide motivation for the anomalies I spotted."

"Well, his father seems to dote on him now. My father too for that matter. But please, Franny Sue, I beg of you. Don't be fooled by him."

"It's clear that we must get to the bottom of this mystery, for both of our peace of mind. But I will not deny Hank on such flimsy evidence as your grudge against him. It would not be fair to him or to Uncle Manny."

"There must be some way to bring his true nature to light."

"Hmm..." She tapped her lip as she did when pondering the next words to put to paper, but surely Eddie would not even notice the subtle lapse in manners. "When faced with trying circumstances, one's true nature does tend to reveal itself."

"Then we need to create some trying circumstances."

"I've got it!" She bounced and turned to him, rising to her knees in her excitement. "You know about my drama troupe, of course."

"The one that's met every week for six months and still hasn't managed to put on a single show?"

They met after school on the days she taught creative writing at the abbey, but true enough, they had not yet put on a single performance. She twisted her lips. "I haven't deemed them ready yet. They need to develop more expertise, but this could provide the perfect opportunity."

"Uh oh, not a scheme."

"Not just any scheme. A perfect scheme." Her mind brimmed with ideas. Oh, this would be too much fun.

He arched a brow at her but seemed to be catching her amusement. "Are you sure about this?"

"Positive."

"Well, if it stands any chance of keeping you away from that slimy Crawfield character, count me in."

He offered her his hand, and she gave it a firm shake.

The oddest little bit of electricity seemed to sizzle between them. How strange. A peculiar tenderness washed over his features. Suddenly she wondered if there might be a deeper, more complicated source to Eddie's angst. Perhaps he...

But no, it was too ridiculous to even consider. Eddie had always been a brother to her, and the good Lord knew they were by no means suited for each other.

She simply would not give the issue another thought.

"Well, good night then," she said, still somewhat flustered from the strange sizzle. She scrambled to her feet and back through the window.

Whatever had she been thinking to crawl onto their shared balcony like they were still children? In the future she would strive to keep the same decorum and boundaries with Eddie Mansford as she should with any single man. She had been far too lax in her treatment of him. Thank goodness he slept in the bunkhouse most nights. She had never appreciated it until this moment.

Uncle Manny was a wise man to send her to the Austen Academy for Young Ladies when she turned sixteen, and he was wise to now seek a husband for her. Not just any husband, but an ideal man such as Hank Crawfield. Matters with the undeniably handsome though gruff Eddie could easily grow awkward if they were left alone too often.

She sat down at her desk where a lamp yet flickered on this dark night. Picking up her fountain pen, she began to scribble in her journal in an attempt to still her racing heart.

Dear reader, I must confess that Mr. Hank Crawfield exceeded the loftiest expectations that a gently reared young lady might hold dear within her heart. In him I find a man of education, dignity, grace, re-finement, and style to be surpassed by no other. The packaging on this gift, which seems to have been handed to me upon a silver platter, is flawless and exquisite. Worthy of naught but the highest compliments. However, a shiny red coat has too often been known to disguise a rotten apple. What lies at the core of Mr. Crawfield? Only time and my carefully devised plans shall tell.

"I can't believe I let you talk me into this," Eddie said, picking up a tiny, crustless cucumber sandwich and eyeing it warily. He took a bite and then raised an approving eyebrow. "Not bad. Just don't tell Rusty you saw me eatin' this here sissified food."

"My plan is brilliant, just you wait and see," she said, ignoring his comment about her perfectly prepared sandwiches. "Writers know how to set up a scenario to their liking."

Franny must admit, Eddie looked oddly juxtaposed in these current surroundings. Although she'd insisted he remove his spurs on the front porch, he hadn't even bothered to take off his dusty chaps before entering the elegant drawing room of Austen Abbey. A room as "sissified" as the sandwiches with its rust colored velvet couch, sage walls with flowered accents, and fringed curtains along the alcove of windows filling the rounded turret. "For the love of all that is holy, would you please remove your hat and attempt to appear pleasant?"

Eddie removed his hat as bid but slapped it against his chaps and denim pants, no doubt intending to elicit the cloud of dust that billowed about him. He grinned mischievously her way, but at least he was no longer frowning.

She ignored his bad manners and scanned the room. At just that moment, Frank Mallory walked through the door rubbing his bad shoulder and completing their small troupe of players. He was always the last to arrive, which, Franny supposed, was the price one paid for coercing the older man here based upon the close friendship they had formed over late night cups of cocoa while she attended school here at the abbey. But their drama exercises had proven that he had quite a knack for character acting, being the deep-thinking and empathetic fellow he was, despite his tough demeanor.

"Captain, how good of you to join us!" Although Frank had served as a general handyman at the Abbey for many years, she always felt a person who had served in the army deserved his formal title, no matter how much time had passed. And she certainly knew him to be a man worthy of respect.

She clapped her hands together and emerged from behind the table. "If you will be so good as to gather your refreshments quickly, I would like to get started. I have a special project for us today."

"And a new leading man, I see!" Nellie Sprague, a mercantile owner's daughter, appeared ready to eat Eddie whole. Whether due to his good looks or their admittedly dire need for male actors, Franny did not wish to venture a guess.

"Now, now," Eddie grumbled, taking a seat in the circle of finely carved wooden chairs that had formerly been around the table. "Don't you go getting any bright ideas."

"Eddie Mansford! Well, I'll be." Frank looked over from where he was filling his plate with sandwiches and pastries. "Someone push me over with a feather. I never thought I'd see the likes of you here."

"That makes two of us." Eddie shook his head.

Franny stood in front of the chair to the left of Eddie and pressed her hands together, hoping that somehow the restrained gesture might bring them all to order. "Which is precisely what I wish to speak to you about. But before I proceed, I must ask you all to agree to secrecy concerning this project."

"I can keep a secret!" shouted Benjamin, Nellie's younger and very enthusiastic brother. Nellie tugged him back down into his chair by the bottom of his trousers.

"Oh, I'm not sure about that." Annie Winters tugged at the high collar of her shirtwaist. "I do so hate to keep secrets from Ford."

Annie, their resident artist, was not quite as adventurous as the thespians in the group. However, family pressure and misunderstandings had kept her apart from her beloved Ford for far too long. Now that they were safely married and expecting their first child, Franny had compassion for her dear friend's concern. "Well, perhaps secret is not the right term. Perhaps discretion. Allow me to explain and I think you shall better grasp my meaning."

As she told the story of her impending match with Hank Crawfield, she looked out over the gathered assemblage. With herself and Eddie, there were fifteen people, mostly young women, and mostly, she hoped, trustworthy. There were a number of Austen Abbey students, of course, as well as several graduates in the room, like Annie Winters and also Emmeline Whitley, who would make an excellent director once Franny actually wrote a script.

But as they needed both males and females of varying ages for the troupe, they had opened it up to the community at large, which explained the presence of Nellie's younger brother Benjamin. Kathryn Gray was also a regular attender. The Easterner now married to Mrs. Collins's nephew had always loved a good story, and had outgrown her shyness since becoming a married woman.

Cora Browning, a farmer's daughter from outside of town, was the only person new to Franny. The Browning family had moved to the area last year, but the girl had a true love of theater and had been looking for a troupe to join. Despite her mousy brown hair, Cora had a flair for the dramatic and the voice of an angel. Her inconspicuous looks would allow her to play a variety of roles like a chameleon.

Once Franny had concluded her carefully planned speech, Benjamin's hand went into the air. "So you want us to put on performances to test this Hank Crawfield?"

"Precisely. I shall write the lines like short skits, although naturally you shall have to do some improvisation based upon his reactions."

"That will put our exercises to excellent use!" Nellie said, catching Franny's excitement.

"Oh, it all sounds so romantic," said Kathryn Gray, a notorious fan of dime novels.

"I agree." Megan Conroy, with hair like a copper penny, clutched her hands to her chest and fluttered her lashes. "I'll help in any way you need me."

"But I want to perform in a real play, and I want to be the bad guy," the twelve-year-old boy stood again and pretended to spin a six-shooter in his hand. Then he shot in the direction of Frank, who was now seated in the circle, eating happily. Benjamin blew an imaginary puff of smoke away from his gun with just the right mix of disdain and bravado. The boy was a born actor, and in that moment, reminded her so much of Hank as a child.

"Benjamin, please!" His seventeen-year-old sister pulled him back into his seat. "We all want to perform a play, but we have many details to yet pin down. For example, a venue and more male actors." She shot a pointed look at Eddie.

"And trust me," Franny said with a wink to Benjamin, "I have a wonderful role in mind for you."

"I'm game," said Emmeline Whitley. "To be honest, I'm uncertain about Hank myself. He's Noah's nephew, as some of you know, and I had such hope for him at one point. But since he's returned, I admit, I've had some concerns."

Franny's face heated. She pressed her hands to her cheeks. "Oh, Emmeline, I had forgotten. It's been so long since he was in town. What you must think of me."

Eddie snorted beside her, and she managed to turn and step upon the tip of his booted toe without appearing obvious.

That seemed to remind him of his manners, for he said, "No offense intended, Mrs. Whitley. My reservations started all of this, but maybe I've gotten matters wrong."

Emmeline, an auburn haired beauty in her middle thirties with five school-aged children, giggled like a girl and waved away their concerns. "No worries. I find a man who protects the women in his life to be quite admirable. And I admire a young lady who takes initiative, Miss Price. Although, I must say, I was known as quite the matchmaker once upon a time, and I don't feel at all certain that you and Hank suit one another."

Emmeline cast a curious glance Eddie's way, and then seemed to shake off whatever thought she'd had. "Either way, I say we proceed with this plan. You shall be the writer, dear Miss Price, and I shall be the director. Why don't you let me take over from here? Now I say our

Mr. Frank Mallory is perfect for our first skit."

"But Hank might remember me," Frank said. "Even if he doesn't, other townspeople will, and they'll give me away."

"Not when I'm done with you." Annie's eyes now shimmered with anticipation. Evidently she had gotten past her earlier concerns. "I'm as good with makeup as I am with paint. And I've been collecting old wigs ever since we started the group."

"And what will your role be?" Nellie batted her long, curling blond lashes Eddie's way.

Franny pressed her lips together to prevent herself from chiding the girl. She was too young to be trying to catch the eye of Eddie—she ought to be focusing now upon her education. But Franny would not embarrass the girl publicly, and soon enough Nellie would mature and realize that a cowboy like Eddie was not as romantic as he seemed. As Franny herself had. Or at least should have by now.

Franny took note of all the gazes upon her and of the awkward silence in the room but could not recall where the conversation had left off.

Eddie cleared his throat. "I'll be watching from a distance, Miss Sprague. This whole charade is worthless if no one is there to see how Hank reacts."

Franny sighed her relief, thankful that Eddie had come to her rescue. "Precisely, and if I am not with Hank, I shall be watching with Eddie."

"I understand your concerns, dear," Emmeline smiled. "Truly I do, but I hope the new Hank Crawfield shall pass your tests with flying colors."

"And I hope he's a villain and gets what he deserves." Benjamin bounced in his seat. "Maybe he'll have a showdown with Eddie."

"Now, now." Franny wagged a finger his way.

"I'm with the boy." Frank let out a low chuckle.

Eddie just turned his head up to her and winked. "This is gonna be a hoot."

Good heavens, what had Franny gotten herself into now?

Five

By late Saturday morning, all the plans were in place, although Eddie still could not fathom how he'd let himself be drawn into these shenanigans. He peeked over his newspaper as Franny entered the fancy sitting room where his stepmother had always insisted breakfast be served promptly at 9 a.m. In the bunkhouse they chowed down on bacon, eggs, and oatmeal shortly after the sun rose, but there was no accounting for the rationale of a fancy lady like his stepmother, Franny's aunt. And her protégé clearly aspired to live up to the woman's memory. Although today Franny was arriving late since she would be dining elsewhere.

Franny pulled out a chair across from him, puffing the ruffly skirt of her light blue linen day dress, which oddly brought out the roses in her cheeks, before settling herself at the table. Having suddenly lost his interest in the latest agricultural updates, he continued to watch her from behind the paper. She twisted her lips and eyed him skeptically as she poured coffee into a china cup and added two lumps of sugar and the perfect amount of cream.

"You know," she finally spoke, "I don't need you to chaperone me. Besides, Hank shall only be stopping by a few times over the next weeks to pick me up for outings. It's not as if he's staying here."

"Can't a man have breakfast in his own home for once?" He folded his newspaper and sat it on the table, reaching for a pastry in the center. He took a bite of the flaky, berry-filled concoction. "We don't have these in the bunkhouse, you know," he said, chewing as he spoke just to vex her.

"You don't fool me for one minute, Edward Reginald Mansford."

He grimaced. She knew he hated his middle name.

"And you don't need to sleep in here just because Uncle Manny is out of town. Juan and Maria can take care of me just fine."

As much as Eddie respected their faithful servants, he would not trust them with keeping Hank from any funny business. He would see to that job himself. Not that he had reason to question Hank's character in the area of women, but he wasn't taking any chances.

"Just look at you." Franny Sue gestured to his outfit.

He took a minute to glance down over himself, although he still wasn't sure what had possessed him to don a suit complete with the trendy new sack jacket she had insisted he buy—which was surprisingly comfortable—and his best boots with their intricate stitching. "I didn't think you'd let me eat in the fancy sitting room in my blue jeans."

"As if you've never tried it before."

"And I need to blend in once we're in Austin."

"Because there are never any cowboys in the city." The skepticism in her eyes settled into flat out suspicion. "Don't you work the horses every morning at this time?"

"Not today."

"Then why not head into the city now?"

"I don't plan to leave you here alone with that Hank Crawfield. Someone needs to put the fear of God in the man."

"Ah ha! So you do fancy yourself my chaperone. Uncle Manny has already given his permission that Hank court me. Come now, Eddie. You have a different role to play in today's theatrical."

"I can handle two roles. I'm adaptable like that. Just don't tell Nellie Sprague." He grinned at her, and she surrendered a smile his way for the first time that morning. A smile full of light and grace to rival the sunshine beaming through the window.

"Well, I like your suit. You look downright handsome," she conceded.

His gut twisted as he tried to convince himself that he had in fact not donned the tan suit—which he knew to bring out the green in his eyes—to elicit such a response.

An odd rumble outside brought them both scrambling to their feet and jogging for the front porch. Eddie loved it when Franny Sue's excitement made her forget her fancy new manners. How he missed the old Franny. He might have married a girl like that.

In their race for the door, they both wedged into the frame together. Finally he relented and pulled back. She shot through the opening first, beaming back over her shoulder in triumph.

"What in God's green..." he said, scratching his forehead as he stepped onto the porch.

In front of him was the strangest darn contraption he'd ever seen.

"Oh!" Franny clapped in delight, bouncing on her toes and causing her curls, as well as other feminine attributes, to bounce prettily with her.

Eddie practically groaned in his agony.

Franny grabbed his arm. "It's one of those new automobiles."

Eddie knew what an automobile was, had seen pictures and read articles, but the shiny horseless buggy in front of him somehow surpassed his imagination. And he certainly hadn't expected Hank Crawfield to be the one to introduce the new invention to their city.

Hank smugly hopped out of his car, even as he left the noisy motor to continue rumbling through the peaceful countryside. Patting the newfangled machine, he shouted, "Quite a beauty, isn't she? How's that old Kragg rifle looking to you now, Eddie?"

Was this some sort of competition to him? Eddie had no intention of playing along. "I have to admit, this is quite a surprise."

"It's a Haynes-Apperson!" Hank said with a heaping dose of pride.

Franny moved closer and ran a hand over the bright green paint as she peeked under the leather roof. "I've never seen an automobile in person before."

Unable to resist this rare opportunity, Eddie moved closer as well. "I heard they only make a few of these a year."

Hank's chest puffed out as he twisted the edge of his mustache. "It pays to go to the best schools and meet the most important people."

Eddie just eyed him quizzically. He could not for the life of him imagine why Franny needed some elaborate series of tests to realize that Hank was a pompous fool. But perhaps that was not enough basis for her to deny his father's request. They had yet to prove Hank an actual scoundrel.

"Give me a moment while I grab my hat and gloves," Franny said to Hank. Then she whispered to Eddie as she brushed past, "I told you, you should have been in town already."

But the fancy automobile had pulled up to the house at a slow crawl. Eddie had no doubt he could beat them to town on his mare, Sally. In fact, he could cut directly across the range and beat them by a long shot while they wound about on the main road to town.

Eddie and Hank stood in uncomfortable silence for a moment.

"So you're taking her to brunch," Eddie grunted.

"Yes, at the Imperial."

"I reckon that will be acceptable. But have her home by mid-afternoon. And be careful with that thing." Eddie resisted an urge to kick the tire of the beastly machine. Automobiles were still in the experimental stages and quite dangerous. Perhaps he shouldn't allow Franny to ride in it at all, except that he had seen the gleam in her eye and knew she would never listen to him if he tried to stop her.

And then there was her scheme awaiting them in Austin.

Franny proved him right by skipping past him. "Oh, I can't wait. I haven't done anything this exciting in ever so long. Let's go!"

Hank helped her up into the automobile with a flourish. She waved to Eddie, an expression of pure bliss covering her pretty face.

Surely the girl had no idea the torture she was causing him.

Hank folded his linen napkin and placed it neatly on the table after brunch.

Franny likewise folded her own napkin. "That was delicious. Thank you."

"Again I apologize for the debacle along the way. I promise that we shall take Papa's carriage home."

Franny giggled. "And again, do not apologize. It was quite an adventure, and I loved every moment of it. Including our unplanned delay." She had to admit that though Hank had been undoubtedly frustrated when the car sputtered to a stop, he had maintained perfect decorum and had it up and running again in a matter of minutes.

"I like your spirit, Miss Franny Sue Price. You are the perfect mix of lady and companion. I hope you don't mind if I say that I could envision myself making a life with a girl like you. We could travel to places like Paris and Rome. Have a grand world-wide adventure together. I would enjoy revisiting those sights and seeing them through your eyes."

"Oh, Mr. Crawfield. That sounds divine." Franny had never expected to take a grand tour. Uncle Manny was finishing school rich, but not *that* rich.

"Do call me Hank. Despite my long absence, we have known each other for quite some time. And I hope you shall allow me to call you Franny."

"It only seems natural, I suppose." She lowered her chin and batted her lashes at him.

He sat back and crossed one leg over the other, displaying the perfect crease in his trousers. Then he took a mannerly sip from his coffee cup.

The entire morning had gone perfectly, even if the slow speed of the car had gotten them to town closer to lunchtime than brunch time. She had barely needed the velvet ties on her fashionable bonnet style hat to hold it in place at that pace. And its ostrich feathers had barely stirred. But something about Hank Crawfield certainly set her heart to fluttering. Still, she would make no decisions until he had passed her tests. Perhaps afterward she could tell him all about it, and they could share a laugh over how he had proven Eddie wrong as they shopped at Koen's for a huge diamond engagement ring.

"Shall we take a stroll about town before I return you home?"

Perfect. Her cue. She waved to young Benjamin who had been lounging outside the large picture window of the restaurant since shortly after they arrived. Benjamin caught her message, nodded subtly, and dashed off down the street.

"Someone you know?" Hank asked.

"Yes, the young brother of a friend of mine."

"I have lost touch with so many people here in Austin."

"Well then, a walk would be lovely. In fact, I was meaning to ask if we could stop by Daisy's millinery shop. I have a new hat on order that I'd like to pick up." She did not mention that the hat had arrived Thursday, and that she had purposely left it for this ruse.

"I would be happy to oblige you Mis...rather, Franny." Hank stood and offered her his hand.

She took it and stood as well. As he donned his hat with a swoop, she took her gloves from her reticule and put them on. Together they headed out into the fall sunshine.

And Hank suspected nothing.

Franny smiled at the Austin street she so loved. The limestone capital loomed at a distance, and one never knew whether a streetcar or a stray cow were more likely to lumber past.

They strolled in the direction of Daisy's—a well-established landmark that even Hank would remember. As they reached the corner of Pecan and Congress, a greasy, grizzled old man sprawled upon the ground with his legs blocking much of the sidewalk.

Even she had a hard time believing it was Frank, and she had concocted this scheme.

Beside her, Hank took in a sharp breath. She tipped down her hat to shade her face, and turned her gaze to study him closely. He froze in his spot for a moment and seemed to collect himself. "I say, good chap, would you mind clearing a path for the lady?"

Ah ha! Very nicely done. But there was more yet to come.

The vagrant, rather Frank, reached with his arms to pull his legs out of the way one at a time, dragging them heavily across the limestone sidewalk.

"Oh, sorry," Hank said. "I didn't realize it would put you to so much trouble, but you shall be safer this way nonetheless. We wouldn't wish you to be trampled, now would we?"

"No, I'm sorry," said the vagrant. "But might you be able to spare some change for a wounded old soldier?" He held out his hand and leaned toward them, tugging at the hem of Franny's pristine blue day dress.

Hank stepped to form a human shield between her and the man. He turned to her and gripped her by the shoulders, moving her a few feet away from the groping hands. Fire snapped in his eyes, and she wondered if he might be about to explode. He ground out his next words through gritted teeth. "Allow me to handle this, my darling."

He turned back to the man. "You should not accost the lady so," Hank said sharply, but still under control.

Frank managed a few tears. He truly did have a future in the theater. "I'm real sorry, mister. But I'm so hungry, and the lady...she has kind eyes."

Hank took in another sharp breath. He paused for a moment as if considering the matter.

A part of Franny wished to beg him to help the man, but she remained neutral as her prescribed role demanded. Eddie would never believe the results if she mucked up the test.

Finally Hank reached into his pocket. He tossed the man a quarter. Not much, but enough to purchase a decent lunch. "There you go, good chap. But do stay out of the path. If you're new to town, perhaps one of the churches might help you. My family has long been members of the First Church of Austin."

Hank returned to Franny and offered her his arm. This time he carefully steered her around the man.

She smirked under the shadows of her hat. Hank had passed test number one with flying colors.

Drat! Eddie pounded his fist backward into the side of the building, but otherwise continued to lean against it in an appearance of non-chalance.

Not only had Hank maintained his composure, he had shown Christian kindness and charity, the very traits they had hoped to test. And Eddie could find no fault with either Franny's performance nor Frank's. But of course the man would behave well in front of the woman he wanted to impress.

They had gone too easy on Hank, but the next test would be even better, and he would see to it that Franny was not at Hank's side.

Now that would be a true test.

Six

Unbeknownst to him, Hank had accommodated their plans quite nicely by inviting Franny to the box social and dance the following Saturday before dropping her off at home. Not that she hadn't been prepared to prod him in that direction if necessary. And he had behaved the perfect gentleman throughout the week, keeping his distance but telephoning her twice to check on her well-being in her uncle's absence.

Now they sat on a pristine quilt in the lawn of the capitol building finishing up the boxed dinner—which, truth be told, Maria had cooked for her. Hank had bid the exorbitant sum of ten dollars for it, thereby thwarting any competition before it was even presented.

She waved to her neighbors Brandon and Marion Tabor as they strolled by with their youngest in a baby carriage. They both looked so happy, and Brandon barely limped as he pushed the pram.

"I hope you enjoyed your dinner," Franny said to Hank, patting her mouth with her napkin. For her part, she had needed to utilize quite a bit of self-control to keep from completely devouring the succulent beef brisket and mashed potatoes, and even more so to restrain herself to a single piece of Maria's cherry pie. Hank had certainly eaten the larger portion, but had done so in a mannerly way as always.

He smacked his lips. "Well worth every penny, as was my lovely company. Thank you for the excellent hints on which box was yours. Elsewise I might not have been so bold with my offer."

"You might have at least played along with the bidding. I know your father and my uncle have high hopes for us, but it wouldn't hurt for you to assess the competition."

"My dearest, I'm Hank Crawfield. Who can compete with that?" He lifted her hand from the blanket and placed a kiss upon the back.

But both the endearment and the kiss left her cold in light of his pompous statement. She supposed she must forgive it, though, as it was true. No other bachelor in Austin shared Hank's education, his vast experiences, nor his wealth. "The mission society will appreciate your generous donation, but truly you should not be quite so certain of your charms."

He just tipped back his head and chuckled. Much as she loved his manners and his pretty speeches, apprehension gripped her as she imagined life with such a spoiled and entitled man. Would he expect to have his way with her as well?

Not that she was stubborn nor controlling by nature. She had readily let her aunt and uncle form her into the young society woman she had become, but they had never opposed her on issues that truly mattered to her. Then again, little mattered to her in light of their love and generosity. Perhaps she would grow to feel the same way about Hank.

He scanned the area around them, looking up and down Mesquite Street. "Can you imagine it? They say in a decade the streets shall be swarming with automobiles. No more horse nastiness to scrape from the streets each night. No more smell. Isn't progress amazing?"

Franny did pause to imagine that, and she wasn't entirely certain. The automobile, while exciting, had been noisy and emitted far more fumes than even the oldest, smelliest horse. And she had heard that injuries from auto crashes were far more serious than those from carriages and wagons.

Hank peered at her. "You hesitate. And what is your opinion, Franny Sue?"

Not being one to stir up trouble, except with Eddie of course, she said, "I am sorry to disappoint you, Hank." She nearly stumbled over his first name, which still felt too intimate, but managed to continue. "I'm afraid I do not have a ready opinion on this issue."

He chuckled again. "I suspect you are almost entirely composed of ready opinions not yet shared."[3]

Franny spotted the challenge in his eyes. Despite her agreeable

3   *Mansfield Park*, Jane Austen, 1814

manner, she did so hate to back down from a challenge. "Well, if you insist. Change is not always progress. With each new invention we experience new opportunities and new freedoms, it's true. Yet we also create new problems and face new challenges."

He eyed her keenly now. "Might you offer some examples?"

"Factories are a clear example. We are all blessed by the goods they produce, yet the workers suffer and small farms diminish."

"I see that they taught you more than just how to set a table at that fancy finishing school of yours."

Franny could feel the blush creeping up her cheeks. She could hardly believe he had managed to draw her down this path. She lowered her head and fluttered her lashes. "Or perhaps a better example would be the telephone, for without it you might have come to call on me in person this week rather than merely calling on the phone."

He smiled and tipped up her head. "Well played, my dear. While I admire a woman of education and would never wish to be saddled for life to a dimwit, I also admire that you know when to hide such an education behind a demure smile and act the lady."

Though that had been exactly her aim, somehow Franny felt insulted to hear him speak the words aloud.

But she was rescued from further comment by Megan Conroy with her penny red hair glistening in the evening sunshine. "Franny, there you are. I was looking for a friend to accompany me to Austin Abbey for a brief while, so that we might...um...freshen ourselves after dinner."

Having already been reintroduced to Megan earlier that day, Hank shook his head with a chuckle. "Women. You are all the same. Not a one of you can, um...'freshen' yourselves alone. Go right ahead, darling. I shall clean this up. You should touch up your curls before the dance."

Again she felt ever-so-slightly insulted. There was only a faint breeze this day; surely her curls couldn't be too mussed.

He leaned over and kissed her cheek in a proprietary manner before she realized his intentions.

Megan's eyes grew huge like saucers.

Hank stood and helped Franny to her feet, with perfect manners of course, and yet she still stung from his comments.

Megan linked her arms through Franny's and hurried her away. Once they were out of earshot, she whispered, "I cannot believe he kissed you like that. In public! Unless... Franny, did you accept his proposal? It's all just so romantic!"

Franny swatted her friend's arm. "Don't be silly. He hasn't even asked yet. I doubt he will before Uncle Manny returns."

"Then that kiss was a bit scandalous, don't you think? Oh, I love it!" she squealed. The daring Megan was typically in favor of shirking society's strictures in the name of romance.

Franny paused to consider that. It was the first true breech of etiquette Hank had displayed. Yet he had done it out of his growing affection for her. She supposed she shouldn't hold that against him. "Do you think people will talk?"

"If Hank Crawfield takes to kissing young ladies on the cheek, everyone will likely assume it is the latest fashion, and think us all provincial for not adopting the trend sooner."

Franny shook her head and tucked in closer to her friend. "Sadly true. He is Hank Crawfield, after all." Polished man of society or entitled over-grown child? She had begun to fear the latter was true. Still, that did not mean he was a villain. Soon they would see how he stood up to a test of his patience and self-control.

Megan turned and looked behind her. "He's not watching us. Let's duck behind that tree over there."

They both lifted their skirts and dashed the few feet to the huge maple tree, whose trunk was broad enough to hide them both.

Franny peeked out from her tree at the far west end of the lawn and waved to Eddie, who lounged against a different tree directly in front of the capital and across the street. Even at that distance, the devilish lopsided grin he shot her way caused her stomach to do a little flip. He looked all too handsome again today, wearing another stylish day suit, which he must have purchased for himself. His hair was slicked neatly to the side, and since he had shaved properly, his dimples danced beneath his sculpted cheekbones.

She took a deep breath and ducked back behind the tree. What odd thoughts to be having about her cous...or more precisely her step-cousin, Eddie.

"Is everything okay?" Megan asked.

"Yes, the plan is underway. Matters should proceed shortly."

Eddie would pass along her signal to Frank, who would nod to Benjamin.

She peeked out from the tree again and watched Hank lounge back upon the quilt and turn his face up to the evening sun. Megan watched from around the other side. At least Franny could see that he was patient enough to await a lady, and that he had the good grace to find joy even in the waiting. But that joy might not last long.

Franny studied him further. The crisp white pants, the light blue and white striped jacket. The dapper straw hat upon his head. Her lips twitched with a grin as she awaited Hank's fate. Truly, this was just a little too much fun to be ladylike.

Right on cue young Benjamin Sprague came streaking across the lawn with a giant, furry, and outrageously muddy dog. Goodness, the boy must have bathed him in the stuff. Bravo, Benjamin! He feigned as if the huge dog was out of his control and dragging him by the leash, but Franny knew well that Goliath loved his owner Benjamin and obeyed his every command.

Unwittingly, Hank played along. His eyes were now closed, and he appeared far too relaxed to note a bit of ruckus around him.

Eddie held his breath as he awaited the inevitable with far too much anticipation.

Goliath careened directly into Hank, running over his legs and pressing against his chest, toppling him to the ground.

"Ho! I say!" Hank pushed the dog away and scrambled to his feet.

"Goliath, no!" Benjamin shouted, but he subtly prodded the dog forward again. "Tell the man you're sorry, Goliath. Give him a kiss."

Goliath jumped up on Hank, plunking his muddy paws on Hank's pale jacket and licking his face.

Hank pushed against the dog again. "Child, please, get your beast under control!"

"Sorry, mister. We were playing down by the river. He slid into the mud and got spooked something awful. Pulled me all the way up Congress Street. I thought I'd never get him to stop."

Hank's face was as red as a tomato. He clenched his teeth and fists tight. A vein in his throat looked as if it might burst.

But then he took a deep breath. "I had a rowdy dog once," he said. "But you really must do better."

"I'll try, mister. Really I will." But he nudged Goliath with his toe, and the dog began to bounce about, flinging mud once again.

"Boy, I must insist you take him from this place immediately. There are ladies present."

"I'm trying." Benjamin fumbled with the leash as Hank took out a tiny white handkerchief and began to dab at the mud on his suit.

Except that the mud had completely overtaken the suit in huge splotches and the pathetic handkerchief stood no chance.

"Give me that leash," Hank snapped. He grabbed the leash from the boy's hand, though not quite roughly. "You, dog, sit," he commanded.

Goliath immediately obliged.

"Better," said Hank. "Now where do you live, boy?"

"Over Sprague's mercantile."

"Ah, well I'm afraid your father shall have to hear of this. There shall be no disguising the evidence. Come along, let's get you both home."

"But what about your picnic?" Benjamin gestured to the now muddy quilt and toppled box with dinner remains spilling out.

"I can't finish it like this, now, can I?" Hank sighed. "I'll need to clean up before tonight's dance."

Hank looked down Mesquite Street, where he believed Franny had gone.

"Were you here with a lady?" Benjamin asked.

Hank continued to survey the area, and his gaze landed square on Eddie. He headed his way.

Eddie pulled himself up straight and strode across the street to meet Hank at the edge of the lawn.

"I suppose you rather enjoyed that little performance," Hank said, causing Benjamin to freeze in place and Eddie's gut to clench.

But then he realized it had only been an expression, for Hank did not look at all suspicious.

"Can't say that wasn't fun to watch." Eddie folded his hands over his chest.

"Well, obviously I must get this menace back home so the boy can clean him up. Then I'll need to clean myself up. Would you please let Franny know where I've gone?"

"Of course. I'll do you one better and clean up the mess over there. That's right nice of you to help the boy home."

"I can hardly leave the beast here to ruin the whole picnic."

Eddie frowned as Hank led boy and dog away. Franny peeked out further from her tree. Not only had Hank managed to restrain himself and not strike out at the boy or the dog, he had been honorable enough to think of the well-being of others and take charge of the situation.

This was not at all the result Eddie had hoped for.

Though it nearly killed him, he had to admit that Hank had improved, at least somewhat. What if they never did prove him a scoundrel? What if he had changed? And worse of all, what if Franny did marry him?

He nearly crumpled over with the pain that thought brought him, but he managed to catch himself. Franny was heading his way now, and he had to pretend everything was normal. That she was just his squirt of a cousin, and he the cowboy who loved to torment her. The only role he would ever have in her life. Still, he could never let her marry Hank Crawfield.

Hank had two more tests to face tonight. Eddie couldn't give up hope yet.

Seven

Franny Sue tapped her toe to the quick tempo of the tune. Although she could perform the stateliest ballroom dances with flair, a part of her preferred a good old-fashioned country romp. It was, after all, the sort of music she'd been raised with, and besides, tonight's dance was for charity. The gathering had drawn rich and poor alike. She noted past Academy students Eliza Delacourt and Lila Ross both dancing with their handsome husbands.

She glanced about the huge barn located on the fairgrounds where the state fair had been held for a time. Lanterns on the walls gave the place a warm, cheerful glow. Colorful bunting brightened the stark wooden room, and the many swirling and stomping bodies filling it kept the chill night air at bay. Everything seemed to be in place.

Nellie Sprague, waiting nearby, wiggled her brows at Franny. Cora Browning, playing the role of one Scarlet Johnson for the evening, had just arrived and leaned against a wooden beam, wearing a dress and a curling wig to match the name she had created for herself. Between the dazzling red hair and the abundant makeup, no one would recognize the normally mousy girl, even if they had met the newcomer previously.

And Eddie smirked at Franny from across the dance floor waiting for the show to begin.

Hank, fully recovered in a clean suit, sauntered toward Franny with two cups of punch. Though appropriately casual for the relaxed occasion, he appeared as dapper and polished as always. Franny smiled to him, thankful that he had excelled at today's test. Just two more tonight, and she would insist that Eddie drop this nonsense.

It was in everyone's best interest that Hank pass. Hers, Uncle Manny's, and Hank's as well, for she wished the best for the man, even if he was a bit stuck on himself. His upbringing had not been the most pleasant, and with that she could relate. Hers had not been so ideal until Uncle Manny and Aunt Lottie had rescued her.

Her gaze shot to Eddie again. Well, perhaps not everyone's best interest. But Eddie would get past this. Whatever *this* was.

"Here you go, darling. You mustn't over exert yourself," Hank said.

She smiled politely and accepted the punch. They had only taken a few romping turns about the barn. She had barely warmed up. Hank had been the one who appeared winded and fatigued. "It's kind of you to look out for my welfare," she said nonetheless.

"If matters proceed in this direction, that might be my job for life. And yours shall be to make my home, rear my children, and charm my business associates. You shall be perfect, I have no doubt. Thank goodness you have no career aspirations like some of those silly girls I met back East."

Franny took a sip of her fruity punch as she considered that. Though Hank was partly correct—and she and her uncle had both assured him repeatedly that her volunteer teaching was only temporary—perhaps he did not remember her literary aspirations. They were not such a large issue, but if she and Hank were to consider marriage, they should know such things about each other. "You do recall that I wish to write novels."

"Oh, that." His brows shot upward. "You hadn't brought it up these past weeks. I assumed you had put such childish ambitions behind you."

Engaging all the self-control she had acquired at finishing school, Franny managed not to glare at him. "There is nothing childish about a literary pursuit. Was Charles Dickens childish? Mark Twain? Henry James?"

"But dear, those are all men."

"Fine. Jane Austen, Charlotte Bronte...Kate Chopin!"

He sputtered and covered his mouth to keep his punch from spewing at her mention of the controversial feminist author. "Chopin! My, you do have quite a bit going on in that pretty little head of yours. I suppose there's no real harm in a bit of scribbling, assuming you keep your priorities straight. Before long I'm certain the busyness of family life will banish such aspirations. You'll see."

Franny narrowed her eyes, not at all sure she did see. She saw little more than the pompous man Eddie kept warning her of. The same Eddie who had, in fact, always encouraged her writing. Still, many men felt like Hank. It was hardly a crime. And she had a way of being quietly stubborn when she wanted to. He would not thwart her so easily. Eventually he would come to understand how important her writing was to her. Wouldn't he?

Either way, they might as well get on with this night. Perhaps he would fail their tests, and she'd have nothing to worry about.

She linked her free hand through his elbow. "Come, Hank, I see a friend of mine I'd like to introduce you to."

Nellie Sprague, with blond curls spilling over her brow, waved excitedly to them. "Good evening, Franny Sue. And who is this handsome fellow you've found?"

"Nellie Sprague, this is Hank Crawfield, just returned from an extended stay on the East Coast. And Nellie was like a little sister to me during my last year at the Abbey."

"How nice." Hank lifted her hand for a polite kiss. "Sprague, you say. I believe I had the...pleasure of meeting your brother and your... dog this afternoon."

"Goodness, that was you! On behalf of my family, I apologize again." She shot a sly look Franny Sue's way. It seemed her acting still needed a bit of work. "But the East Coast. How interesting. Did you attend a university?"

"In fact I did. Then I spent a few more years attending to my father's business concerns in New York City."

On cue, Eddie approached and tugged at Franny's sleeve. "Excuse me, everyone, but could I steal Franny from you for a few minutes? Family concerns. You understand."

"Of course," Nellie smiled. "I'll take good care of Mr. Crawfield for you. In fact, I have the juiciest gossip for him." She laughed wickedly.

"You don't say." Hank quirked a brow. "I have been rather out of the loop for some time."

"Nellie, behave!" Franny admonished.

"Always." Nellie batted her lashes a bit too enthusiastically. Yes, that one needed a few more acting lessons before she took to the stage. Although her younger brother's performance this afternoon had been flawless.

Eddie led Franny a short distance away and spoke in low tones. "I hope this works."

"Just pretend to be telling me something important."

As Eddie continued whispering nonsense about cattle and diseases and hooves, Franny Sue attuned her ears to the conversation a few feet away. Nellie obligingly spoke loudly over the music.

"...really," she said. "Can you believe the audacity?"

"That one over there?" Hank nodded his head toward Cora Browning, known to him only as Scarlet Johnson.

"Indeed. Can you believe the nerve of her, showing up at a respectable function like this?"

Hank paused to consider.

Now they would see if he would exhibit goodness, or dive head first into a round of salacious gossiping.

"Perhaps you're mistaken, Miss Sprague. Not all girls who work in a drinking establishment are, as you so delicately put it, fallen women. It is unfair to make such an assumption. And while her dress and demeanor are a bit bold, they're still within societal norms. This is the sort of community event where everyone, society and working class alike, should feel welcome."

"Bravo, Hank," Franny whispered.

"Not so fast," Eddie said.

"Hmph." Nellie swept a hand Scarlet's way. "Just look at the way she's eyeing the men. And it appears she's got Frederick Clooney in her sights. Have you heard about his latest scandal? Shady business dealings."

Frederick was a fellow banker and Hank's biggest competition in town, not that Frederick's local bank could quite compete with Hank's father's growing national one. Still, this would prove the ideal temptation.

Hank followed the man with his icy blue eyes. He took a deep breath, and that hard look fell over him.

"What's he doing?" asked Eddie, whose back was to them.

"Shh!" But Franny shifted, took his arms, and adjusted their stances so that they both could see them.

Finally Hank shook his head. "I'm sure the story is quite fascinating, but Frederick Clooney is beneath the mention of a fair lady like yourself. Perhaps we might dance instead."

Nellie offered her hand, and Hank led her to the floor.

"Darn it all!" Eddie said.

"I told you. Hank is a gentleman through and through."

"I don't buy it. Maybe he just felt awkward hearing the story from a young girl. I bet he'll have a private investigator on the matter by tomorrow."

"Perhaps, but you can't deny that he's passed yet another test." Although Franny did not mention how miserably Hank had failed her test when she'd shared her heart's fondest desires with him.

"I'll deny whatever I please." Eddie scuffed his boot against the floor.

She giggled. "Don't be surly."

"These tests of yours are too easy. Let me take him out back. I'll give him a real test."

"That might prove your physical superiority, but nothing else."

"I forgot, you're the so-called expert on human nature."

"That I am. Hank just had the perfect opportunity both for gossip and for underhanded business tactics. He has passed our tests of generosity, kindness, patience, self-control, and now goodness. And clearly he has given up pulling the wings off fireflies and shooting barn cats. What more do you want?"

"A lot more. You deserve everything, Franny Sue. The very best. A man of honor and valor and strength."

Something about his statement made her gut clench. Eddie was all those things, but he had chosen a life that would never suit her. "Goodness, sounds like you've been reading too many of my novels. Besides, I trust Uncle Manny's judgement."

Eddie clenched his jaw.

Franny followed the dancing couple with her gaze. Though the seventeen-year-old Nellie was a bit young for the twenty-five-year-old Hank, they made a fine looking couple with her golden curls and his dark, brooding charm. They were both excellent dancers and moved gracefully across the floor. And...and she felt not even the slightest stir of jealousy. That was odd, but she shook off the thought as Nellie nodded to her over Hank's shoulder.

"They're ready for the last test. Let's get into position."

Eddie followed Franny as she tugged him around the periphery of the wooden barn and out the back door. "I swear, Franny Sue," said Eddie. "I've just about had it with skulking around like a doggone criminal."

Nearby Cora, otherwise known as Scarlet Johnson, leaned against a fence rail in the moonlight.

Ignoring Eddie's comment, Franny waved to the girl. "It's almost time," she whispered.

Scarlet waved back. She'd exited the barn shortly after Nellie had pointed her out to Hank to prevent suspicions by the townsfolk. Thankfully no one else was outside, although Franny had come armed with plans to chase any onlookers away.

"What now?" Eddie asked.

She peeked over his shoulder. "Shh...They're coming. Put on your hat and pull it over your eyes." She dragged him down the side of the barn farther from the door and deeper into the shadows.

He slapped his ever-present cowboy hat onto his head, and then leaned against the barn with a hand to each side of her. "We could pretend we're a courting couple sparking in the dark. That'd throw him off for sure." But the moment the words were out of Eddie's mouth, heat flooded him. His gaze honed in on her pert lips, and he immediately regretted his statement.

Franny swatted his arm with a strength that belied her delicate Southern flower act. "What if someone saw us? Just keep your head down."

But she did, in fact, tuck close to him and press her hands against his chest to better see over his shoulder. Suddenly he couldn't care less about Hank...what was his last name? The stupid fellow could do whatever he pleased, as long as Eddie could stand so close to Franny and bask in her honeysuckle perfume. It took every ounce of his self-control not to move his chin the fraction of an inch that would be required to nuzzle her soft, gleaming hair.

She lifted her head, and for a brief moment, her lips were but a whisper away from his. With the slightest shift, he could easily...

But just then, he heard a scuffle and peeked over his shoulder as well.

"Thank you so much, Mr. Crawfield." Nellie dramatically fanned herself with her hand as she exited the barn. "I never swoon like that, truly. But I appreciate you taking me outside for some fresh air."

"I'm happy to help, Miss Sprague."

Nellie feigned as if spotting Scarlet for the first time, although she knew the actress would be waiting for her outside. She huffed as she stomped in Scarlet's direction. "Scarlet Johnson!" she said. "What are you doing here? Don't you look at him that way! This is Franny Sue Price's suitor. You just keep your filthy paws off of him."

"But I didn't...I was just..." Scarlet stuttered, looking impressively embarrassed.

"Seems like you've found yourself a good actress in that Cora," Eddie whispered.

"Much better than Nellie." Franny's warm, moist breath tickled his neck. How he wished to draw her even closer.

But the performance nearby was just warming up.

"I'm sick of you showing up at polite functions and plying your trade. Have you no decency?" Nellie spat the words.

"How...don't...I'm not what you think. I was just waiting for a friend who promised me a dance."

"Why don't you let him dance you on home?" Nellie brushed her away with a condescending flick of her wrist.

"Please, ladies," Hank sputtered.

"I've had it with you...you...you Jezebel!" Nellie punctuated the insult with a resounding slap across Scarlet's cheek.

As Nellie turned on her heel, lifted her skirt, and flounced back into the barn, Scarlet collapsed against the fence. She covered her face with both hands and commenced to weeping.

Hank stumbled to and fro for a moment, not sure what he should do next. At last he seemed to gather himself together. He pulled a handkerchief from his pocket and took it to Scarlet. "Don't cry, Miss Johnson." He offered her the scrap of white satin.

Scarlet accepted it and dabbed her eyes. Unless Eddie's eyes deceived him in the moonlight, the cloth came away wet. How had she managed that? Eddie himself had no knack for acting. Other than trying to act like he wasn't falling further and further every day for Franny Sue, an act he feared was not at all convincing.

"I apologize on behalf of my companion," Hank said, moving closer. "She's young, and I do not for one moment believe those vicious rumors."

"Why are people so cruel?" Scarlet asked, her full bottom lip trembling and her big eyes gazing up at Hank as tears trickled down her cheeks.

Hank stepped closer. "My dear, you are breaking my heart." He reached out and cupped Scarlet's cheek with one hand, running his other hand gently down her arm.

Eddie's pulse picked up speed and his senses shot to high alert. What was this?

"You are a beautiful woman, Miss Johnson, and beautiful women always inspire jealousy. I imagine it's nothing more."

Scarlet wiped her cheeks again with the handkerchief, and then pressed it into Hank's hand. "You are very kind, sir. Might I ask your name?"

"Crawfield. Hank Crawfield."

"As in the *Whitley-Crawfield Savings & Trust?*"

"One and the same. I've been back East for some years, but I'm home now, and I won't suffer to see you mistreated again."

"Thank you so much."

"Where, might I ask, could I expect our paths to cross again?"

"I wait tables at the Golden Griffin Saloon. I realize it's not the ideal job, but..."

"Then I shall have to pay you a visit sometime and make sure the patrons are treating you with proper respect."

"I would like that." Scarlet smiled.

Hank stepped back. "It was a pleasure to meet you. Now I'm afraid I must look for Miss Price."

"Of course, you're her escort?"

"Yes, and perhaps more before long."

"Then enjoy your evening."

"You too." Hank bowed his head before sauntering into the barn.

"Did you see that?" Franny batted Eddie's arm again. "I told you, the perfect gentleman."

"What?" Eddie raised his brows. "Did *you* see that? Were we watching the same man? He got fresh with Scarlet."

"He did not. He was kind and gentle and comforting."

"That's not how a gentleman comforts a woman of poor virtue."

"She told him the rumor wasn't true."

"He had no reason to believe her. At best *Scarlet's* virtue was questionable."

"You're being ridiculous now." Franny dug her fists into her hips.

Once Hank was well out of sight, Cora, dropping her Scarlet persona, dared to approach them. "Did you see that?" she asked.

"Yes!" Eddie and Franny answered at once, scowling at each other.

"Cora, you didn't think he got fresh with you, did you?" Franny crossed her arms over her chest now.

Cora pursed her lips. "Not in an overt sort of way, but..." She seemed reluctant to go on.

"But?" Eddie prompted.

Cora just shook her head. "I did my part. Yours was to evaluate him."

"You see!" Franny slapped his arm. How many times did she plan to do that tonight?

"I saw a man who was caressing a beautiful woman and setting up a second meeting with her." Eddie raked his hand through his hair, wanting to yank it from his head in frustration. How blind and stubborn could one woman be?

"He told her forthrightly that he was attached to me," said Franny. "Besides, that wasn't even the test. I would never stoop to such a crass assessment."

"Maybe it should have been the test. Maybe we need another test."

"No! This is finished." Fire sparked from Franny's golden brown eyes.

Cora, still standing uncomfortably beside them, cleared her throat. "Well, I should be going then. I plan to change back to my normal self and join Nellie for the rest of the dance." As she walked away, she shot Eddie a look that said that she knew he was right, but that she wanted to stay out of the matter.

"Franny, be reasonable." Eddie reached out to stroke her arm.

She jerked away. For the first time he noticed that she looked rattled, and he spied a sheen to her eyes. "I'm done discussing this. Hank's looking for me," she said in a suspiciously raspy voice. Then she turned and stormed away.

Back at home and snuggled safely in her window seat, Franny clutched her journal to her chest for comfort.

She opened the book and nibbled on her pencil for a moment, that appalling habit that always seemed to appease the muse.

Tonight Hank Crawfield revealed, I must admit, a new side of himself to me. A rather callous side that would quickly dismiss my passions. A side that might perhaps seek to control my life and relegate me to the role of the "little woman" in every way that term might imply. In addition, dear reader, it seems he may be a bit of the lady's man, although upon that issue I remain unconvinced, yet firm in my resolve that I shan't stoop so low as to test his morality.

Though he has passed all of my tests, my conclusion is thus: Hank Crawfield is far from perfect. He is pompous, entitled, and domineering, to say the very least. And though I shall never confess as much to my dear cousin, a small part of me fears he might be worse. Yet here is the rub: no man is perfect. We must each of us only select the sorts of imperfections with which we might accustom ourselves. A woman must choose to marry with her eyes wide open, knowing the man has flaws aplenty, but choosing to accept and love him nonetheless.

On that final comforting thought, she closed her book. But as she gazed out into the starry night, the thought occurred to her that each day Eddie's imperfections had been shrinking and shrinking in light of Hank's more glaring ones.

Eight

"I'm so glad you could join us for tea today," Mrs. Collins, the head-mistress of the abbey, said as she bent over to refresh Franny Sue's cup.

"Thank you for allowing me to drop in unannounced. I suppose I could have telephoned, but I didn't want to call during the school day." Franny Sue smiled as she inhaled a whiff of the delightful, relaxing lavender blend.

"Nonsense, you know you're always welcome." Mrs. Collins smiled in her own genteel way.

"And of course you knew just when to expect tea time. I'm so glad Mrs. Collins brought this tradition with her from England. There aren't many places in Texas to find a proper tea." Evangeline Danwood, a friend of Franny's who had stayed on at the Abbey as a full-time teacher, took another prim sip. Evangeline had always been reserved and even a bit cool, although Franny knew her to have a gigantic heart beneath it all.

"This has been just lovely," Franny said. "Other than Maria, I don't have any female interaction at Mansford Ranch."

"And here we are surrounded by females night and day. We can hardly get away from them." Evangeline waved to the girls rushing through the hallway filled with squeals and laughter as they hurried to their next class.

Franny Sue had needed this company today. After five days of frigid silence between her and Eddie, the girls' comforting chatter brought her true peace. She had even suffered through the uncomfortable ride beside him in the buggy just to escape him for this short time. But perhaps he knew that she needed a friend, for he rarely offered to take her to town, Juan being the one who drove her when she taught.

At least Uncle Manny would be home in two more days.

"I must be going." Evangeline stood. "My break is finished."

"Don't let Nellie Sprague give you any guff. Remember, these girls might have been your friends not long ago, but you are the authority now." Mrs. Collins shot Evangeline a firm look which demonstrated how such an authority figure might maintain control.

"I will, I promise." Evangeline whisked away to make it to her next class on time.

Franny just smiled her encouragement. The girls never gave her any guff, but of course she was the special once a week "fun" teacher who came in a whirl of stories, imagination, and creativity. The girls in her class had chosen to take it as an elective. Whereas Evangeline worked day in and day out teaching required classes.

"Now." Mrs. Collins turned that same firm look to Franny. "What is this that I've heard about you putting poor Mr. Crawfield through some series of tests?"

Heat crept up Franny's neck. She felt like a young schoolgirl all over again, although she had never been one to garner Mrs. Collins's censure. "Actually, I wanted to speak to you about that, but not in front of Evangeline."

"Evangeline never was one for game playing and such silliness, but I hadn't realized that you were." Mrs. Collins continued to watch Franny with an intensity that made her wish to squirm in her velvet armchair.

"I suppose I owe you an apology. I should have paused to consider that you expect more from your instructors, and from the drama troupe even loosely linked to the school's name. I'm not quite sure what possessed me to undertake such shenanigans."

"I appreciate that, dear, although it's no great matter. What I truly wish to know is why? There must be a reason."

Franny paused to consider. "Well, I realize it is no excuse, but my cousin Eddie has quite a knack for bringing out my childish side."

At the mention of Eddie, Mrs. Collins relaxed, and a smile danced over her lips. "Ah, Eddie. Now it makes more sense. I take it the over-protective step-cousin does not wish to see you with another man."

"It's not another man—it's Hank. They never liked each other."

"I seem to recall that. Well, I suppose it is healthy to have someone in your life that brings out your spunky nature. I confess, I hadn't realized you possessed one."

Franny cocked her head to the side. "But I thought you wished to curb our tempers."

"Curb, yes, teach you the proper time and place, but not eradicate. Some circumstances require a woman to find her spunk in order to overcome."

"I'm not certain this was one of them. Eddie was so sure that Hank was a villain, and I was so determined to prove him wrong that I'm afraid I went to rather questionable lengths."

Mrs. Collins sat her cup and saucer on a side table. "And did he pass these tests? I do recall he was quite a scamp as a child."

Franny sat her tea aside as well. "That's the problem. Though he passed the actual tests, I noticed other causes for concern, but I do not wish to admit that to Eddie now."

"My dear girl! Do not let stubbornness determine your fate."

Franny Sue looked down to her hands which twisted upon her lap. "You're right, of course. But now I don't know what to do. I've realized that these tests were ineffective, but how can I tell for certain if Hank is the man of good character he purports himself to be?"

"A woman must trust her instincts, especially concerning matters as serious as marriage."

"But Uncle Manny wishes for me to marry Hank, and I would so hate to disappoint him with no good reason."

Mrs. Collins leaned forward. "Dearest Franny Sue, while respect for one's elders is always admirable, your uncle shall not be the one married to Hank. He shall not live with him day after day for the rest of his life. And he shall not be nearby in the middle of the night when you're crying yourself to sleep. You must take ownership of this decision."

A cold chill washed over Franny. Those words struck her with a prophetic sort of significance, but she attempted to push it all away. "Maybe I'm overreacting. Maybe Eddie has gotten into my head. How can I know for certain?"

"You might never know for certain, but I suggest you pray about this. God is the only one who knows Hank's truest nature."

And that quickly the cold chill melted into warm comforting tingles. "Pray. Of course, we should have done that from the start."

She would pray, and she would apologize to Eddie just as soon as she had a chance, for her stubbornness was certainly getting her nowhere.

"So, Eddie, I've been wishing to talk to you," Franny said shortly after they passed through the busy part of town and into the quieter countryside.

Eddie chuckled. "I'd say you've been wishing *not* to talk to me." Although, he had been taken aback by her almost warm greeting when he picked her up from Austen Abbey. She had spoken a good ten words to him, more than she had all morning.

"Don't be difficult. I wish to talk now."

"Fine, what is it?"

"You were right, of course. Something about Hank has niggled at me all week, and not just his arrogance, nor his treatment of Miss Johnson, which I still find inconclusive."

He took in a deep breath of relief. He had been afraid she might marry Hank just to spite him, and that would be a tragedy indeed, both for Franny and for Eddie. "Then what?"

"He seems rather controlling."

"I thought you liked having a man in your life to tell you what to do." He could hear the bitterness toward his father in his voice, but he couldn't hold it back. This had all been that man's crazy idea to begin with.

"Uncle Manny guides me. He makes requests, but he never dictates. He's quite wise, and he always considers my wishes, which is why I'm yet hesitant to disappoint him. But Hank seems different. And..." She bit her pretty lip as if she didn't want to continue.

"And what?"

"And he doesn't want me to write."

"That's plum stupid. Writing isn't just what you do, it's who you are. It's like breathing to you." His heart twisted for her. Now more than ever, he could never let her marry that scoundrel.

"Hank seems quite willing to smother me then. But perhaps it's my fault. I didn't speak of writing for quite some time. Perhaps he'll come to understand how important it is to me."

"So what do we do now? More tests." His words came out surly again. He just wanted Franny Sue away from that man. But maybe part of his frustration came from the fact that he was coming to realize that he wanted her for himself.

He could marry her, and his instincts told him that he could win her with a bit of effort. That would solve everything.

But she would try to domesticate him, and he wasn't at all certain he was ready for that.

"Actually," she said, "Mrs. Collins suggests that we pray. I don't know why we didn't think of it sooner."

Somehow that broke his tension. He laughed, a true laugh this time rather than a surly chuckle. "Why do a simple thing like pray when you can scheme and connive and get half the town involved?"

Franny just looked up at him with her big doe eyes and grimaced.

"Just kidding." He nudged her playfully with his shoulder like the old days. Then he pulled the horses to a stop.

"What are you doing now?" she asked.

"I'm fixin' to pray."

"Here?"

"Why not?"

"Okay." She appeared hesitant at first, then she swiveled on the leather seat and offered him her hands.

His mouth grew dry as he stared down at them. Of course she would want to hold hands. Their family always held hands during prayer. He should have seen this coming.

Taking her gloved hands into his larger, rugged ones, he took a deep breath. They felt so right there. Then he bowed his head. "Father God, Franny Sue and I come humbly before you asking for wisdom and guidance. We ask forgiveness for being set on our own stubborn paths and trying to solve this problem in our own wisdom. We surrender our wisdom and ask you to be in control."

Franny gave his hands a squeeze and whispered, "Yes, Lord."

"God, please give us direction. We don't trust Hank, we don't feel everything is right there, but we need to know for sure. Give Franny a clear sign, and give both of us peace about whatever your will is for her life and her future."

She sighed, and then said, "Amen."

He opened his eyes and saw her staring up at him from just inches away. Trust and hope radiated from her eyes, and something more. She seemed to be asking, imploring him for something, though she did not seem to know what. Her lips turned up just slightly toward his, so inviting, so kissable. Just a few inches and he could claim them as his own.

But he jerked away. Franny was young and innocent. Surely she had no idea the signals she was sending. And once he kissed her, they could never just go back to being Eddie and Franny, practically siblings. Their relationship would change forever in an instant, and he was not yet certain he wanted that.

Sure, he'd thought about spending extra time in town to take more classes at the university. Sure, he wasn't needed on the trail so much now that they sent most of the cattle north on trains. And he even had to admit that he hadn't hated dressing up these last few weeks in his new, comfortable sack coats.

Just as he thought he might give in and began to lower his lips a fraction of an inch, Franny bounced and clapped. "I know what we need to do!"

"Do?" he asked confused. "Do about what?" About getting married? About kissing?

"About Hank. I sensed God speaking to my heart. We've been looking in the wrong place all along!"

He shook off his crazy thoughts. Of course, Hank. Franny hadn't been thinking about Eddie at all. "So where do we look?"

"Somewhere that he isn't surrounded by society." She wiggled her brows mischievously.

He faltered for a minute, then he understood. "His plantation."

"Exactly! But we don't have much time before Uncle Manny comes home."

"Hank said it's about twenty miles from here. That's at least a half day travel, if we push the horses hard."

"We'll need a plan." Her eyes lit.

"But I have a feeling this will work." Although he could not say why. She just laughed merrily, and his heart took flight at the sound.

Nine

Franny pulled up beside Eddie on her mare as he tugged down his hat against the sun to better scan the horizon. "If our intelligence is correct, we should be there soon."

"You needn't make us sound like a couple of spies."

"But we are." He wiggled his brows at her.

She just giggled and pulled her own cowboy hat low to survey the area along with him. The sun was bright and glaring with not a cloud in sight, but since they were well into fall, the air still held a nip, which was one of the reasons they had decided to take what should be a two-day journey in one day. But the more important reasons were appearances and the need to make excuses for her absence to Juan and Maria, and even to Uncle Manny if they didn't return before him. One day was much more easily explained away than an overnight trip.

"Let's stop and water the horses," she said. "I know we need to hurry, but once we get there we might need to stay out of sight for a while."

"Good idea." He led the way to the nearby stream, which was full and rushing this time of year.

She slid off the saddle with ease, being dressed in denim pants and a man's plaid shirt. They had agreed that they could travel less noticeably if she didn't flaunt her femininity. Once they had devised their initial plan yesterday, they had turned back to town to gather information and supplies, including these boy's clothes for her. They had left this morning before dawn, as much to avoid questions as to get here quickly, and they had alternately cantered and walked their horses the whole way.

Franny stretched against the strain of the long ride before walking her mare to the edge of the stream.

"So how is it to be back in the saddle?"

Franny smiled. "I almost hate to admit it, but I've really enjoyed this day. I adore the outdoors, and I've missed horseback riding." She smoothed down her denim pants. "And I loooove these clothes! They're so comfortable. I might take to wearing them more often."

"I certainly wouldn't object. You look surprisingly charming. Can you understand why I love this so much?" Eddie swept his hand across the open plain.

"A part of me can. But after seeing the way my father wasted his life on the trail, I think it should be a rare treat, not a regular lifestyle."

"I understand those memories must be hard on you, but you do realize I'm the rancher, right? I take good care of my men."

Franny took a hard look at him. For some reason she always thought of him as just a cowpoke, but in truth, he was much more. "I suppose so. Speaking of which, shouldn't you be on the trail right about now? You've been home all summer and fall."

He gazed at her quizzically. "I thought you knew we'd started sending the cows north by train a few years ago. I avoided it as long as I could, but the new homesteading laws have made it nearly impossible to drive cattle over distances, and besides, it's just good business sense."

Now she gazed quizzically back into his handsome face. Stared directly into his warm hazel eyes and lost herself for a moment in the swirl of brown, green, and gold. "So then..."

"I don't go on the trail anymore. We graze the cattle all over Mansford land, but I'm rarely gone more than a day or two."

She felt her mouth form an O as she considered the ramifications. Then she shook herself out of her stunned state. "I didn't realize, but I'm glad to hear it. What do you do with all that free time?"

He brushed his foot back and forth across the stream bank. "Well... you have to promise not to tell my father."

She grasped his arm. "We've kept plenty of secrets for each other over the years."

He grinned sheepishly. "I've been attending a few classes at the university. Just general ones for now, but I've been considering earning a degree in business."

Now Franny's mind reeled. He no longer went on the trail. He was getting an education. He spent time in town. It changed so much. "Why not tell him? He'd be thrilled to hear it."

"He's been nagging me to go to school for years. I can't give in that easily."

She swatted his arm. "Stubborn as always. But as Mrs. Collins so wisely said to me just yesterday, 'Do not let your stubbornness determine your fate.'"

"Maybe I've been doing too much of that lately." Something about the shift in his voice caught her by surprise. She thought she knew him inside and out, but she had never heard him use that wistful tone before.

So she turned up her face to him and searched his eyes as if for answers. Still confused, she leaned in for a closer examination, until they were mere inches apart.

With no warning, Eddie crushed her to his chest. With his free hand he caressed her cheek, causing a shower of tingles to travel through her.

"I'm tired of being stubborn," he said.

Then his mouth swooped down and caught hers. For a moment shock froze her, but his lips felt so right, so familiar, so exhilarating. Though she had never been kissed before, her body seemed to understand how to respond of its own volition. Before she realized what was happening her arms had looped around his neck and her lips were melding with his, seeking, inviting.

After an eternity and no time at all, Eddie pulled away and leaned his forehead against hers, while he yet held her in his arms. He sucked in a ragged breath.

"I..." she stumbled over her words. What did this mean? Where did they go from here? "I'm not certain what I'm supposed to say."

"How about we say nothing for now? We need to get to Hank's plantation soon if we want to make it home tonight. Just keep this in mind, okay? No matter what happens today, factor that kiss into any decisions you make."

A part of her wanted to tease him. To ask him if he was throwing his hat into the ring. This was Eddie after all, and that had been their relationship for years. But that kiss, along with the new information he had volunteered this afternoon, had changed everything. She wasn't ready to deal with what it might mean for her future.

Right now they were on a mission to convince Uncle Manny that she shouldn't marry Hank. But she was forced to wonder how her uncle might feel about a marriage even closer to home. Had he ever considered it? Was it too odd and awkward? Although she and Eddie had been like siblings, in truth, they were no real relation at all.

With such confusing thoughts spinning through her head, she said nothing and silently mounted her horse. Eddie did likewise, and they continued east toward Hank's plantation.

When they finally caught sight of their first cotton field, they stayed hidden and made their way around the edge of the property toward the houses at a distance. Once closer, they dismounted and tied up their horses, crouching down and scurrying in for a better look.

They both hid behind a large bush and peeked over top. Eddie sighed with relief. Although the last mile of their ride had been silent, everything seemed normal enough now. They were working as a team, reading one another's thoughts like they always had. Franny did not shy away from him, but instead pressed close to keep out of sight.

"Here goes nothing," Eddie said, as he took off his hat and crept upward for a better view.

He could hardly believe his eyes.

Franny gasped beside him.

Before them spread a collection of ramshackle huts. He could see through huge cracks in the walls straight inside to the tiny, stark interiors. A few black workers roaming the area wore ragged, threadbare clothing and no shoes.

"It's awful," Franny said. "Like slave quarters. Maybe worse."

"I thought the Northerners fought to free them from conditions like this," Eddie whispered with a shudder.

"We learned at school that often sharecroppers are treated worse than slaves, for the owners have no loyalty to them," Franny said. "Maybe Hank doesn't know. Maybe he's just been gone too long."

Eddie's stomach churned now. Even he hadn't realized Hank was such a scoundrel. Thank the good Lord they had found this in time. Franny could never be happy with a man like that. "But look at the main house."

The large central structure was ornate, expensive, perfect, and pristine. Hank had been taking care of this place, or at least the only part of it that mattered to him.

"But will it be enough to convince Uncle Manny?" Franny asked. "As confusing as this all has been, I still don't wish to disappoint him. From what I hear, this sort of treatment is not unusual. Uncle might just ask Hank to make improvements."

"We'll have to...wait!" Just then an odd sight met Eddie's eyes. A beautiful young black woman, dressed better than the others and looking like an African princess with a bright patterned scarf wrapped about her head, stepped out of the main house. Her rich mahogany skin glowed with health over exotic, yet perfect, features. On her hip she held a small child, about a year and a half old, with a paler complexion like coffee and cream.

Eddie turned to Franny.

Her eyes were glued to the pair as well.

"When did Hank say he bought this place?" Eddie asked, not wishing to state the obvious.

"About two years ago, in the summer, so a little more."

Eddie reached for her hand and gave it a supportive squeeze. "The timeline would be right."

"But surely he has a white overseer."

"Maybe, but she came from the owner's house. The overseer's would be the smaller one over there." He pointed to a more modest, though sturdy, home.

Franny still seemed unwilling to relent to the truth. "Perhaps she works in the main house. A cook or a housekeeper."

As the woman and child came closer, the child turned directly toward them.

The tiny boy gazed their direction with wide eyes in an icy shade of blue that could only have originated from one person.

Poor Franny. Eddie gave her hand another squeeze. Even he hadn't expected this.

Franny bit her lip. Tears puddled in her eyes. "We have to talk to her. We have to find out for sure."

Clutching Eddie's hand, Franny made her way down the slight incline to the woman. "Excuse me, ma'am," she called in as friendly of a voice as she could muster.

The woman spun toward them, gasping and pressing a hand to her chest. "I didn't see you there."

Franny chose not to explain that they'd been hiding.

"Sorry to startle you, ma'am," Eddie said. "We're friends of Hank Crawfield, and we were passing by this way."

At that she tensed and turned the child away from them as if to shield him with her body, although clearly it was too late to hide the boy. Fear clouded her soulful brown eyes. "Mr. Crawfield ain't here right now. He left yesterday afternoon."

So Hank had been here, recently, and still the place looked like this. She hadn't wanted to believe it possible.

The small child tugged at the woman's shirtwaist. "Mama, down."

Still gazing at them with frightened eyes, the woman lowered the child to the ground.

Franny let go of Eddie's hand and stepped forward. "I don't wish to bother you, but is there any chance we might trouble you for a glass of water?"

The woman appeared to relax a bit.

"I have some lemonade in the kitchen. Follow me." She regally led them back to the house with the little boy toddling behind them.

"Have a seat on the porch. I'll be right back." She tried to pick up the boy and take him with her, but he fussed and pulled toward where a few toys lay scattered about the porch. Not the sorts of toys poor sharecroppers owned. The woman relented and let him play.

Franny eyed Eddie as they sat side by side upon the porch swing.

His returning look seemed to question when she would admit what was staring her right in the eye, quite literally, for the small boy pierced her with his stunning blue gaze. He toddled over and placed a carved wooden toy in her hand. "Hosey!" he declared with excitement.

Franny turned over the small animal he claimed to be a horse and smiled at him. "I think this is a cow."

"Cow?" he asked, twisting his head to an exaggerated angle.

"Yes, it's definitely a cow."

"Cow!" he shouted with just as much enthusiasm.

By that time the woman had reemerged, carrying a tray with two glasses of lemonade.

"Your son is so beautiful," Franny opened cautiously. She accepted her glass and took a few bracing swigs.

"Maybe you should just finish your drink and be going," the woman snapped.

"I'm sorry. I didn't mean to offend you. He truly is stunning, and so very sweet."

The woman softened as she gave Eddie his glass and sat down the tray. "It's just that you shouldn'a seen him." Fear surged through her eyes again. "Please promise me you won't say nothin' to no one. He'd be crazy mad at me."

"Do you mean Mr. Crawfield? Does he get crazy mad often?" Franny asked.

The woman rubbed at her arm in a telling sort of way. Clearly Hank intimidated her. Possibly hurt her. And surely he would not be *crazy mad* if the child belonged to someone else. "I can't talk about any of this. Please just promise you won't say nothin'."

Franny couldn't promise such a thing, for she needed this information to convince Uncle Manny that marrying Hank would be a huge mistake. At the same time, she did not wish to endanger this precious woman and her child.

"We promise." Eddie made the decision for her.

"B-but..." Franny stuttered.

"We'll think of something." Eddie wrapped a reassuring arm around her shoulder. "We always do."

Ten

Franny tapped her toe impatiently. She paced to one side of the Austin hotel room, turned at the cheap, peeling wallpaper, and headed back in the other direction. Eddie seemed to have nothing better to do than hold up the wall near the door. Meanwhile Uncle Manny and Mr. Crawfield stared at her with curiosity and no small bit of annoyance from their matching chairs at a table in the corner.

"How much longer must we sit here, darling?" Uncle Manny asked.

"I don't know." She looked to the door, and then to the window, and back again. "What time is it now?" she asked.

Eddie pulled a pocket watch from his sack coat. "Four thirty."

She frowned at him, for it was not the answer she had wanted.

Wait...a pocket watch? He had changed so much recently. Then gazing at him, she recalled their kiss. Then as she had a hundred times in the past day, she pushed the memory aside.

Ever since they discovered Hank's secrets, they'd been planning and preparing for this moment, and they had yet to speak about the incident at the stream.

"He's a half hour late. Maybe he isn't coming." She sagged onto the quilt-covered bed in defeat.

"I can't take the suspense anymore." Mr. Crawfield pounded the table. "And I don't understand why we're in this shabby hotel."

"And I want to know how things are progressing with you and

Hank," Uncle said. "You promised me an answer if we met you here."

Franny sighed. The time had come to admit defeat. "I'm sorry, Mr. Crawfield, Uncle Manny. I was so sure this would work."

"What would work?" Uncle Manny sounded as frustrated as his friend.

She looked to Eddie, but he shrugged. The time had come for her to speak her mind.

She took a deep breath. "During Uncle's absence I spent time with Hank. He's a very impressive young man on the surface, but I had some reservations. Then yesterday Eddie and I went to see Hank's plantation. His workers live in squalor and he treats them terribly. Did you know that?"

Uncle Manny looked to Mr. Crawfield.

"I didn't." Mr. Crawfield folded his hands on the table. "But I can't say I'm surprised to hear it."

"And there's more," Franny continued. "But we made a promise to someone, and we can't tell you what it is."

"Which is why we're here," Eddie finally spoke up. "It's a long story, but we sent Hank a rather suggestive letter from a woman he met recently inviting him to her—or rather this—room. We thought we could reveal what we suspect to be his true character that way."

Franny hadn't wished to stoop so low, but in the end she saw no other option, and what they had seen at the plantation warranted extreme measures. "I'm sorry, Mr. Crawfield. I hope we haven't offended you."

He frowned. "I can't say I love the idea, but Hank hasn't exactly been known for his upstanding character. I suppose I understand, but I'm glad he's passed your test."

"I don't understand." Uncle Manny stood. "If you didn't wish to marry Hank, you could have just told me."

"You know how I do so hate to disappoint you."

Uncle Manny thought for a moment before he spoke. "Well, it is a disappointment. If not Hank, then who do you plan to marry? I wanted someone exceptional for you. Someone from our close circle of friends. And no one questions that he's the finest catch in town. I have to think about your future, you know. This plantation situation isn't ideal, but we believed perhaps you might soften and guide Hank. That was part of why we suggested the match. I still think marrying him is the best course of action."

Eddie moved to her side now and wrapped his arm around her

shoulder. "I have an alternate suggestion. She could marry me."

They all three gasped. Franny had not for one moment expected this. And yet, again, it felt so right.

But what would Uncle Manny think of the idea? Her stomach tied in knots.

Uncle Manny stared at the two of them for a moment.

But the reaction that came next was the last thing Franny might have ever imagined. Uncle Manny and Mr. Crawfield both broke into uproarious laughter.

Uncle Manny sank into his chair and doubled over. Coming back up, he reached across the table and gave his friend a shove. "I told you!"

"That you did! I believe I owe you five dollars," Mr. Crawfield said between his loud guffaws.

Gripping her shoulder tighter, Eddie said, "Would someone please explain what's so doggone funny?"

"I..." Uncle began and then fell into laughter again. "I..." He tried again and laughed all the harder. Finally he patted his reddened face and tears with his handkerchief and managed to pull himself together with a deep breath. "I wanted the two of you to marry all along. But I knew if I suggested it, Eddie would go all stubborn and refuse just to spite me. What better way to get you two together than to toss Eddie's biggest rival into the mix?" He shook Mr. Crawfield's hand. "We're geniuses, my friend."

"Evil geniuses!" Mr. Crawfield said.

Indignity rose up in Franny Sue. "Evil indeed!" She crossed her arms and stomped her foot. "You played with all of our hearts. Hank's most especially. He didn't deserve that."

"Oh, dear," Mr. Crawfield said, sobering now. "I'm not at all certain Hank has a heart. The boy is all arrogance, and he needed taken down a notch. He's used to getting everything he wants, and while he did want you as a trophy to display on his mantle, I promise he never loved you. I was careful to watch for that."

Poor Hank. How could he ever succeed in life if his own father thought so little of him? Yet perhaps the man was right.

And it wasn't until that moment that Franny paused to realize she had never once spoken to her uncle harshly before just now.

Yet she felt no inclination to apologize.

"I can't believe you." Eddie shook his head in disgust.

"But it worked!" Uncle Manny said and began to cackle again. "Just look at the two of you. You're perfect for each other. Everyone knows it. I've given you years to figure it out on your own, but you behaved like a pair of stubborn dimwits."

"Hey!" Franny protested, but then realized there was some truth to it. "I just didn't want to marry a cowboy like my father, but now that Eddie plans to—" She clapped her hands over her mouth, remembering too late that it was supposed to be a secret.

"Eddie plans to what? Spit it out!" her uncle demanded.

Eddie spared her. "I plan to go to the university and get a degree in business. In fact, I've already started taking some classes. But I will continue to be a rancher. I have always loved it and always will."

Uncle eyed him warily. "And would you care to explain why you haven't told me until now?"

Eddie shuffled his foot.

Franny patted his chest to encourage him.

"Fine," Eddie said. "I was too stubborn to admit you were right."

"You see!" Uncle Manny clapped his hands together. "That proves my point exactly and demonstrates why I went to such extreme measures to get you two together."

"Speaking of extreme measures." Mr. Crawfield glanced about the hotel room. "They seem to run in the family."

"I'm afraid we do have a tendency toward drama." Uncle Manny shrugged.

Just then, someone knocked at the door.

They all startled and looked to one another, but no one moved to answer it.

The knock came again. "Miss Johnson, are you in there? It's Hank. Hank Crawfield. Please don't be mad at me. I've been looking forward to our...our time together with great anticipation. I'm so sorry that I'm late. My meeting at the bank ran long." He pounded now. "Please, oh please, Miss Johnson. Don't deny me. I do so crave your gentle touch."

"I've heard quite enough," Mr. Crawfield grumbled. He stormed toward the door and whipped it open, revealing a stunned Hank on the other side. "You are supposed to be courting Miss Price. But that's over now!"

Hank's stunned expression seeped to mortified as he glanced about the room and registered all of their faces.

"If you will all excuse us," said Mr. Crawfield, "I need to have a long hard talk with my son. At home!" He shouted the last two words.

Hank just gaped at them all, then turned and followed his father down the hallway without so much as a word.

"So." Uncle Manny nodded to Franny and Eddie, still glued to each other's sides. "What now?"

An excellent question, which Franny had not allowed herself to pause and consider previously. She turned her gaze up to Eddie.

He looked tenderly down at her.

"I suppose there's no need to rush anything now," Eddie said. "And I never did stop to ask you how you feel about all of this." He let go of her shoulder and backed away a step.

How did she feel about this? She always admired Eddie despite his gruff cowboy ways. Always thought him one of the handsomest men in Texas, when he bothered to clean himself up. He understood her like no other and had always sought to nurture and encourage the true Franny. And she had come to realize these past weeks that outward refinement counted for little; it was inward character that mattered. Eddie was a man of godly character and integrity to his very core.

What more could she want?

"I feel...I feel..." But she couldn't put words to it. She did not wish to say she loved him. It was at once too much yet not enough, for she had loved him most of her life. She took a moment to examine him. He appeared tense and uncomfortable. He had suggested not rushing. What if he didn't love her that way at all? What if he had only wished to rescue her? Worse yet, what if he had only wished to best Hank?

Finally she knew what to say. "I fear that you were forced into suggesting marriage. I don't want you to be bound by those rash words. I admit this whole situation has caused me to see you in a new light, but I do not wish you to marry me just to rescue me. This afternoon has proven that's no longer necessary. Do you even love me...in that way?"

He expelled a breath he must have been holding throughout her entire speech. "Oh, Franny Sue! How can you not know? I love you in *every* way. As man and woman, as hero and heroine. As I could never love anyone but you."

He took a step toward her, but then froze in place.

She had never seen the bold cowboy appear so terrified. "Oh, you stubborn fool, I love you too!" She rushed toward him and threw herself into his arms.

He spun her in several circles before placing her back on the ground and kissing her soundly.

In the background she heard Uncle Manny clapping and shouting, "Bravo! Encore! My daughter and my son, truly and for always!" But she just waved him away and continued kissing her new fiancé. The man of her dreams. Her perfect match.

How could she ever have missed it?

She could hardly wait to return to Mansford Ranch and begin their new life. Together.

$\mathscr{S}$ENSE AND NONSENSE

LISA KARON RICHARDSON

It isn't what we say or think
that defines us,
but what we do.

~Jane Austen,
Sense and Sensibility

One

May 16, 1899

E vangeline Danwood paged through the Sears & Roebuck catalogue until she found the guns. A revolver ought to work—a small one that could fit in her handbag, or maybe even a pocket. Not too expensive though, she couldn't afford to squander her savings.

Caught up in the intricacies of the offerings, Eva only distantly registered the sound of feet pounding along the corridor. She made a mental note to speak to the girls about decorum in the hallways then happily lost herself in the minutiae of the decision again. Heavy-handed rapping on her door made her start and lose her place.

Popping to her feet she scrambled to answer the door.

"Eva!"

Hand at the knob, Eva paused. Megan. There went her pleasant evening of planning for Ceylon, the teardrop shaped island that looked like it was falling off the tip of India where she would soon be teaching in a missionary school. She opened the door to her closest friend.

A whirlwind of chiffon, red curls, and eau du cologne engulfed her as Megan rushed in and grabbed her arms in a pincer-like grip. "Eva, it's gone. It's all gone."

Eva pulled back. "What's gone?"

"All of the missions money. It's all gone. I don't know what happened. I had it at the mission office, then I was thinking about some things Mama asked me to pick up for her. Then I remembered about James's birthday coming—"

Hands cold despite the early evening warmth, Eva took hold of Megan's shoulders. "Tell me what happened."

"I don't know," wailed Megan. "I just know the money is gone."

Eva snatched Meg's impractically small handbag from her and inspected it. The minute bag held a single quarter, a folded bit of paper, a handkerchief, and a pencil stub. It most certainly did not contain one thousand dollars.

"Not there," Meg said.

Eva ignored her as she upended the bag over her pale blue quilt. The money did not magically appear among the meager contents.

Eva picked up the folded paper, but before she could look at it closely, Megan whisked it from her hand. "That doesn't have anything to do with this. And the money wasn't in the bag when it was lost."

Half wishing she'd thought to buy a gun earlier, Eva planted her fists on her hips. "Megan Victoria Conroy, you are going to find that money if we have to ransack all of Austin to do it."

Tears filled Megan's wide eyes. "Don't be angry with me. I didn't do it on purpose."

Eva kneaded the bridge of her nose. "I know that. But without that money, I'll never make it to Ceylon. I'm supposed to book my passage this coming week." Her mattress springs screeched in protest as she plopped down on the bed.

Megan sat more tentatively. "I'm so sorry." She put an arm around Eva's shoulders. "But if anyone can find that money, it's you. You're the smartest person I know."

Eva plucked her handkerchief from her sleeve and handed it to Megan. "I'm not one of your beaus to flatter, Meg." A smile softened the reproach. "But who am I to sniff at a tactic that works on all of them?"

Megan offered a beatific smile in return and laid her head on Eva's shoulder. "I knew I could count on you."

Eva pulled away. "You're not off the hook. We're going to have to find this money together. Now start at the beginning and tell me what happened. Wait, when did you last have the money?"

"Well..." Megan said, "I definitely had it after the fair."

Eva tried not to scream. "Of course you did. I was there when Mr.

Ferris gave it to you." Although how anyone ever thought Meg would make a good chairwoman of the missionary board's fundraising committee, she'd never know. "What did you do after the fair?"

Meg's fingers began to pleat the delicate fabric of her skirt.

Eva narrowed her eyes. "Meg—"

Meg sprang to her feet. "I stopped by the missionary society offices. I left it there. I'll tell you all about it." She reached for Eva's hand. "But please come on. We have to go look or I'll never get a wink of sleep tonight."

"But I'm responsible for the girls."

"Pish, they should all be going to bed soon."

Eva raised an eyebrow. "You act as if you never attended this school."

"Oh, all right. But surely one of the other teachers could help you out for a change. You're always doing everything for them."

"I shall have to tell the kettles that the pot had something to say about their conduct."

Meg swatted at her arm. "You know what I mean. I'm sure someone would be willing to repay your many kindnesses by giving you an evening's respite."

"I suppose Miss Allan—"

"Miss Allan is perfect. Let's call upon her now."

Eva allowed herself to be all but dragged down the hall to the deportment teacher's room. In typical tornado fashion, Meg made short work of Miss Allan's defenses, and almost before she knew it, Eva was on the sidewalk in front of the Jeanette C. Austen Academy for Young Ladies.

Twilight softened the city's sharp edges, and a little thrill slicked along Eva's spine. The unsanctioned outing felt daring in the extreme. She was not the stick in the mud her students believed.

The walk to the offices of the missionary society took only a few moments. It was slightly eerie being the only pedestrians on the street. She couldn't even hear any of the usual clatter and bells from the trolleys. Eva picked up her already quick pace, until Meg was almost running to keep up. When they arrived Eva looked expectantly to Megan.

"What?" Meg responded as if confused.

"Do you have a key?"

"No."

Eva's lips compressed together.

"Don't give me that look, Eva. I know I can be flighty, but I'm not addlepated." She raised a delicate fist and knocked in a decidedly indelicate fashion.

Eva had no time to ponder what this new development might mean. The door swung in to reveal a figure, backlit by the gaslights glowing inside.

James Ferris.

His height always seemed to take her by surprise on first sight because he had such a self-deprecating manner. Although she could not see his deep brown eyes due to the light behind him, she knew he would be regarding her with the same serious attention he always showed. For the second time that evening, Eva had the sickening sensation of falling into an abyss.

He shifted to make room for them to enter, and the light illuminated a slightly too-big nose and the brown hair that never quite lay flat. His gaze found Eva's, and she could not look away or even blink. She had not seen him except from a distance for at least two months. Not since the announcement of his engagement to Miss Megan Conroy.

"Oh, James." Meg slipped past him into the office. "We're sorry to disturb you, but I had some committee business to complete and dear Eva agreed to assist me."

From somewhere deep in her well-mannered soul, Eva dredged up a smattering of polite conversation straight from her adopted mama's lips. "Good evening, Mr. Ferris. I understand congratulations are in order. I wish you every blessing." Her knees wobbled ever so slightly as she stepped past him.

He made a sound like a fishbone had caught in his throat then inclined his head. "You're very kind, Miss Danwood. It seems I haven't seen you in awhile."

"I had not noticed." The untruth seared her throat, but she could think of no way to recall the words and so let them hang like a fog in the air between them. Not that it mattered. The air was already choked with a million words that had not been said.

"Eva," Meg called from the inner office.

"Please excuse me." Eva swept around him and hurried through the spare, slightly shabby front room to join her friend.

"I missed you." James's words were tentative, and had her senses not been straining toward him, she'd have missed them.

God help me. She squared her shoulders. There was no use thinking of what might have been. She had to contend with one final Megan crisis then she would go to Ceylon. The thought soothed her. Very soon she would be in a whole new world, and all of the entanglements of her life in Austin would fade away as if they had never been. She would be able to immerse herself in helping her students. If it meant giving up the delights of marriage and a home of her own... Well, so be it. Surely God would ease the ache over time. And it wasn't as if she had the promise of those things if she stayed in Austin anyway.

"I had it right here in an envelope." Megan sat at a roll top desk. "There were a bunch of receipts from the fairs. I had to reconcile what bills were still owed with the money that came in. I was all excited because we earned so much, and I knew it was for your trip."

Eva bent over the desk and they began to open and rifle through the myriad drawers. For a long moment the only sound was the slide of wood and shuffle of paper.

She straightened. "Wait! Don't these desks usually have a secret compartment?"

"Yes! Maybe someone just moved it!" Megan fiddled with an apparently solid panel and opened it. She revealed a dark little cubbyhole. Megan reached inside, but came away with nothing.

Eva grimaced. "Let me guess, you decided against using it because you thought it would be too obvious, didn't you?"

"Am I that transparent?" Meg's tone was sharp with disappointment.

"Only to me. And only because never in your life have you taken the easy route when a complicated one was available."

"You needn't rub it in." Megan crossed her arms and slumped back against the chair.

"Just tell me what you did."

"I thought that a thief would be looking for something like a safe or a secret drawer, so I purposely avoided those things. I wrapped the money up in the bills and put the envelope in the outgoing mail."

Eva lunged for the mail tray. "Taking a page from Mr. Poe's book?" She flipped through the accumulated pile of letters. None was thick enough to hold a stack of bills and cash. She reached the end and then started over again. No, no, no. It must be here. "Are you certain that's what you did with it?" She started through them a third time. "Did you write anything on the cover?" She took each envelope out of the basket as she examined it.

"I addressed it to Mrs. Collins." Megan took the wire basket from her and sat on the edge of the cracked, inlaid-leather surface of the aged desk.

Eva stopped pulling envelopes from the basket. "Why ever did you do that?"

"I don't know. It seemed fitting at the time. She let us read mysteries because she said they would make us think, and if that was the only way to encourage us then so be it. So when I think of Poe I always think of her—"

Eva held up a hand to forestall the rest of Megan's explanation. "Were any of these other letters here when you put the envelope in the pile?"

Megan looked at the envelopes. "Yes. I think so. I put my envelope in amongst the rest. I didn't just set it on top."

Eva plucked out the last letter. "Well we can say with certainty that it isn't here."

"It must be. I know without a doubt that I put it there."

"I believe you." Eva patted Megan's arm.

"But what are we going to do? I'm so embarrassed. Everyone will think I've lost the money, or even worse that I took it." Megan covered her face with her hands.

Eva bit back a sharp retort about the fact that her entire future had rested on those funds. Instead she said mildly, "You have to tell James."

Megan looked at her with horror-stricken eyes. "Eva, I can't."

"Yes, you can."

"But what if he calls off the wedding?"

An unkind frisson of anticipation shot through Eva's heart like a little bolt of lightning. Even as she prayed for forgiveness, she tried to reassure Megan. "James is an honorable man. You do him a disservice to think he won't stand by you at a trying time."

"You're very kind, Miss Danwood." James's voice, rich as coffee, came from the open doorway.

Eva straightened so fast she sent the tray flying.

James stooped to help her gather the scattered correspondence. "I'm sorry to have startled you."

"Please don't apologize. It is nothing."

"What's this about trying times? Is something wrong?"

Eva looked at Megan. She wasn't going to rescue her this time. Megan could explain to her fiancé how a thousand dollars had disappeared.

Two

James took the news so well Eva wanted to kick him. How could he be so...so bland about it all? To preserve their privacy, she turned her back as he patted Meg's shoulder. Meg began crying again, and Eva busied herself with picking up the despoiled letters and rearranging them in the basket.

Her feet itched with the need to walk away. But she couldn't leave them unchaperoned. The wedding was months away yet.

James's voice sounded tentative, as if he didn't quite know what he was dealing with. "There now, Meg. It will all be well. The money is bound to turn up. No one will think you took it. People know your kind heart too well for that. And besides, you have no need of the money." This attempt at reassurance elicited only a dismayed hiccup. He soldiered on. "I bet someone saw it and thought to deliver it to Mrs. Collins in person rather than pay postage. We can ask her about it in the morning."

"Oh, James, do you think so?"

In spite of herself, Eva's heart lightened too. She hadn't thought of that possibility, but it would be just like one of the ladies who helped around the mission society to try to save a penny any way they could. She turned. "That is very sound logic, Mr. Ferris. Meg, we ought to be going."

James was quick to play the gentleman. "Let me get my hat and I

249

will walk you home."

Eva opened her mouth to protest, but Meg was already thanking him for his thoughtfulness.

As Meg turned toward her, Eva reaffixed a congenial smile. Of course Meg would want James along. It was sensible. Not that Meg ever took action based on what might or might not be sensible. Still, Eva could hardly begrudge her very natural desire for protection on the streets at night. There had been all those tales of the Austin Axe Murderer when they were little girls.

James fetched his hat, and within moments they were on the sidewalk. Eva lagged behind, allowing the others to precede her. As she noticed the way Meg's head tilted toward James, almost but not quite touching, she half wished the Axe Murderer would come and put her out of her misery.

She focused instead on her feet, pretending close attention to potential defects in the walk. So intent was she, that when he stopped unexpectedly she walked right into James.

"I'm so sorry." She jumped back as if scalded.

"I was about to offer you my arm. The gaslights are helpful, but it's awfully dark in between them." He crooked an elbow.

Eva wouldn't have minded if the street was darker still. Her cheeks burned furiously, and she was certain they could both tell she was blushing. "I..." She could think of no graceful way of declining. "Thank you." She accepted his other arm and, linked together like schoolhouse chums, they made their way to Megan's grand colonial house with its sweeping verandahs and tall, white Corinthian columns.

Megan slipped inside without waiting for a servant. In the sudden vacuum created by the loss of her chatter, the world seemed bereft of sound. Then James cleared his throat and offered his arm again.

"That's really not necessary. I'm quite capable of walking home without escort."

"I've never doubted it, Miss Danwood. But it would speak poorly of my character if I were to expect it of you. Please allow me to assuage my conscience."

Eva bit her lip to keep from telling him how much his conscience ought to require assuaging. Reluctant to create a scene, even though there was no one about to see it, she accepted his arm once again. Nearly dragging him along behind her she strode purposefully toward the school. There was certainly no point in prolonging their mutual misery.

Within a couple of steps James had matched his stride to hers and enquired politely after her students.

The dulcet breezes of a lovely spring evening did nothing to cool Eva's heated cheeks. She murmured something insipid and proper. Then she couldn't restrain herself any further. "Do you really think the money will show up at the Abbey?"

He started to shrug and then stopped himself. "I don't know. I'd certainly ask Mrs. Collins to be on the lookout."

Eva nodded once, and an uncomfortable silence nudged up between them.

"What if—"

"You know—"

Their words collided with the abruptness of a train wreck. Eva ducked her head. "Please go on."

"No, please Ev—Miss Danwood. Please say what you were going to say."

She made the mistake of glancing up at his face. A curious mixture of earnestness and tension scored his features and made her throat feel as dry as a tumbleweed. Would this walk never end? "I was only going to ask what you thought we should do if Mrs. Collins does not receive the money?"

"I suppose I would need to inquire with the office staff. See if anyone perhaps mailed the envelope or did something else with it." His voice seemed to lighten and grow brisker. "Perhaps you could assist me with that? I fear that some of the ladies may think me too gruff and believe I am accusing them of some wrongdoing, but you are the soul of tact and gentleness. I'm certain they would respond more willingly to your questions."

Eva blinked. "Do you really think so?"

"I do. And it would allow Megan to stay in the background. She feels so dreadful about all this, and I know it would be a strain on her to have to face all these people, knowing they worked so hard on the missions fair."

Deflated, Eva nodded. "Of course, we wouldn't want Meg to be uncomfortable."

He winced. "I'm sorry, Eva, it's not that I value her feelings more—"

"You ought to. She's your fiancée. She deserves your every consideration."

"I owe you an explanation, I know that." James took his hat off, slapping it against his leg. "I've never been able to get you alone so that I could explain what happened."

Eva was aware of that. In fact, she'd made quite sure of it. She walked even faster. The school was just around the corner. "I'll go around and talk to the ladies tomorrow after church."

His voice grew quieter, rougher. "Please let me explain."

"It's not necessary. And I fear it would do neither of us any credit. I'm quite sure I read too much into our friendship." She kept her own tone brisk. There was no need to rehash it all. James had made his choice—she wasn't it. And when she compared herself to Megan, she couldn't fault his judgment. So she had to be sensible.

If only it didn't hurt like her insides were being parboiled.

She let go of his arm. "Here we are. I'm going to go in the back entrance through the garden. No reason you should have to walk me around to the front. I'll see you tomorrow." The words came at a gallop. But even before they were out she'd managed to wrench open the generally disused iron gate and step into the lush sanctuary of the school garden. "Good evening." Her gaze skimmed the tops of his shoes, unable to rise to his face. What would she have found there? Relief? Pain? Either one would have hurt too much. She closed the gate firmly behind her before he could say anything.

In the green and leafy heart of the garden, she plopped down onto the end of a bench. She must have sounded like an idiot. Her poise had completely deserted her and left her rambling. All she needed to do was stop caring—to turn that part of her heart off. She inhaled and held the breath for a long moment. Everything would be better when she got to Ceylon.

If she got to Ceylon.

She wanted to wring Megan's neck. How could anyone lose that much money? What if they didn't find it? Eva could not tolerate staying. Being invited and having to attend the wedding. She shuddered and let herself fall back onto the bench, lying flat in a posture that would have earned one of her students a scolding. Everything had become so complicated.

The stars above her winked and twinkled as they had been doing for thousands of years. The breeze shuffled through the leaves all around her, bringing with it the scent of creation. She stilled herself, breathing in deep lungfuls of air and then letting it out again.

Events might have grown unexpectedly complex, but all she had to do was latch on to the bright thread of her mission, like Theseus in the Minotaur's maze. It would guide her through. She had a mission to accomplish in Ceylon, so she could and would overcome whatever obstacles arose. Feeling more herself, she sat up.

It was rather late. The school would have been long since locked up for the night. She could ring the doorbell and wake someone, or...

Eva hurried to the side of the grand old building. Sure enough the great old oak stood sentry as it always had. More importantly, the wrought iron bench encircling it remained a prominent fixture.

She hadn't done this since she was a student and then only once, but it was a night for bold action. She looked around first to make sure no one was about to observe her then fixed her handbag firmly over one arm. She lifted her skirts and climbed up on the bench. With a little hop she could reach the lowest branch. Now to walk her feet up the trunk, then swing a leg over.

It was a bit like riding a bicycle. Her body remembered what was needed.

A little laugh caught in her throat. If her girls could see her now they wouldn't think she was a fuddy-duddy. Higher and higher she climbed until she came level with the third floor window. A light from somewhere on the second floor seeped up the walls, providing just enough illumination that she could tell the corridor was empty.

Now came the test. She edged out onto the longest limb. It really did seem as if it had been custom designed to provide schoolgirls with a means of covert entry. She paused, holding her breath. There were no ominous creaks or cracks. She slid farther along, holding a higher limb for balance. Now it was almost as if she was suspended over empty space.

Farther still and the limb was growing thinner. It bent ever so slightly beneath her weight. Another step. More sagging. She swallowed. She might need to refrain from gobbling up Graciana's delicious pecan pie for a time. Two more shuffling steps and she was within arm's length of the window. Now came the real test. She had to let go of the branch above in order to reach for the sash. She tried it with one hand, but couldn't get the leverage she needed under the window. Balancing on the swaying branch, Eva released her death grip on the limb above and ever so slowly reached for the window. This was far more dangerous than she had appreciated as a girl.

Heaven help her if it was locked.

Her fears were in vain. The sash rose easily and silently, as if someone had been liberally applying grease to make sure there was no telltale squeak should this window be raised. Eva took note.

Silently as she could, she clambered inside. Panting, she turned to close the window behind her.

"Good evening, Miss Danwood." A pleasant contralto voice from the stairs sent her into palpitations. She whirled.

"Mrs. Collins!" Her hands fluttered about her person caught between brushing stray bits of bark off her dress, and straightening her twig snagged chignon.

Her employer's smile was placid. She stood regally with back straight, hands clasped gracefully in front of her. "An unorthodox means of entry. If you had but rung, the door should have been opened for you."

"Yes, I know. I, um, I didn't want to trouble the household so late. And it seemed a bit of research was called for."

Mrs. Collins waited politely.

"If I can enter this way, the girls could do so as well."

"I seem to recall that girls have done so in the past."

Eva's already burning cheeks managed to heat a little more. "I'll ask Frank to trim the limbs back away from the building."

"Thank you, dear. I'm sure he'll attend to it promptly."

"I wasn't out doing anything inappropriate, I promise."

"I know that, dear." Mrs. Collins turned to descend the way she had come.

Pausing only briefly to wonder how Mrs. Collins could know any such thing, Eva headed toward her own room. Then she hurried back to the stairs. "Mrs. Collins," she said in a stage whisper.

"Yes, dear?"

"Did you perhaps receive an envelope from the mission society this evening?"

"No. Ought I to have?"

Eva's heart sank. "No. It was just a possibility. Thank you. Good night."

"Good night."

If no one had delivered the envelope to Mrs. Collins, then what had they done with it? Eva hated to think of it, but if it hadn't been taken with innocent intention, then it must have been taken for less savory reasons and any hope of finding and reclaiming the money would come to nothing.

Three

James walked home at the same reluctant pace he had used as a boy when he knew he would have to own up to some youthful indiscretion. Eva hadn't looked back before she had been swallowed by the darkness. He wasn't sure if he'd wanted her to or not. But he did know that he hadn't wanted her to go. He hadn't spoken to her in months. Being near her again had filled him with that particular rush of warmth he experienced only around her. Seeing her appear in the office had made him feel like he'd been tossed into a pool of lava.

She had a way of returning him to the moment of his first foray as a gentleman. His headmaster had arranged with Mrs. Collins for a ball to be held. He and his comrades had arrived with clean nails, sweaty palms, and their hair pasted to their heads from the over application of Macassar oil.

They had been ushered in to where the girls waited giggling in the ballroom. Then they had been expected to ask one of the girls to dance. He'd wanted nothing more than to melt away, until he had spotted Eva. His chum. A girl, true. But she didn't rub it in his face by giggling at him then hiding behind an oversized fan. Looking back, he couldn't say when exactly things had started to change between them. All he knew was that upon his return from seminary she had given him a hug as she had a hundred times before, and yet it was completely different. He had, for a time, thought that perhaps there could be a future for them. At least until his father had made him see that he had a duty to his family and his parish.

A single light remained illuminated in his family home. Father was still awake. As the president of the mission board, he needed to know of the missing funds right away. James would have given a great deal not to be the one to have to tell him.

He let himself into the house quietly and stood for a moment outside the partially open door of his father's study. The matter could wait until morning. It wasn't as if there was anything to be done at this late hour. But he also knew his father. If he wasn't informed of the loss of the money tonight, he would be apoplectic when he did find out.

James poked his head around the door and then knocked.

Looking as if he had been buried in a pile of books that came up to his chest, his father took a moment to float to the surface and respond. "Yes?" He squinted over the rims of his half-spectacles. The downward pointing arrow of his nose looked sharper and longer than ever in the shadows cast by the gas lamps.

Long experience had taught James that it was best to break bad news quickly and cleanly. He stepped fully into the room. Spine ramrod straight, hands at his side, and definitely not fidgeting, he delivered his report.

When he was done his father removed his spectacles and wiped them slowly with his handkerchief. "Who all knows of this development?"

"At the moment, myself, Megan, and Miss Danwood."

His father's eyes narrowed. "It would be her. Is she going to be a problem?"

"Eva? What do you mean by 'problem'?"

A heavy sigh made it clear that James was incredibly naïve. "Will she be vindictive?"

"Eva's never been that kin—"

"She's never before been handed the opportunity to embarrass someone she may feel has wronged her."

"What do you mean?"

"Is she going to blare the news about like some sort of female foghorn?"

"If she did, it would be with good cause. She has been the most injured by this affair. Her journey to Ceylon is in jeopardy now."

"You are wrong, it's your own fiancée with the most potential for injury. This matter could become a major scandal if word of it gets out."

Now James knew what this was all about. "And since Megan is now linked to our family, that would be unacceptable."

"At last." Sarcasm dripped heavily from his father's voice. "You've realized the obvious."

He prodded his father a bit. "We should distance ourselves entirely then. We wouldn't want to encourage the appearance of nepotism. I'll take the matter to the police in the morning."

"Don't be absurd." His father flung his glasses on the table. "You will do your utmost to protect Megan for her family's sake and for the sake of your marriage. This alliance is too valuable to lose or allow to be tarnished. We don't even know that there was a theft. Calling in the police would be ridiculous. Not only would there be a scandal, you would look foolish on top of it." He rubbed the bridge of his nose, obviously ruing the fate that had cursed him with a son so simple that such elementary matters had to be explained. "Even your position as administrator of the mission society could be in danger."

James couldn't tell whether the disgust he felt was primarily for his father's venality or for his own cravenness since a part of him still longed to find a way to gain this man's approval. "Good night, Father. I'm tired." He turned on his heel.

His father's words chased him down the hall. "You must find the money and set this right."

James agreed wholeheartedly. He would find the wretched money and finally earn some measure of standing on the mission board in his own right. With that done, he could move out of his father's home and start a life of his own. He would certainly never force his bride to live in this mausoleum.

His bride. Megan.

Not Evangeline.

In fact, recovering the money would mean enabling Evangeline to leave for good. He sighed as he trudged up the stairs to his cell. He didn't deserve for her to stay. All he could do was try to give her the gift of her freedom and enjoy his last moments with her.

Eva had difficulty focusing on the sermon the next morning. Her mind refused to be reined in. It flitted from one worry to another and back without coming up with any answers. Two pews ahead, Megan looked drawn and pale, with dusky smudges under her eyes, and Eva suspected that she didn't look much better herself.

She fiddled with a loose thread coming from the ring finger of her left glove. One of the other teachers caught her eye. She straightened her shoulders and folded her hands neatly in her lap, resolutely ignoring the loose thread that continued to taunt her. She could—would—focus.

And she did. Sort of. Luckily the sermon ended a few moments later without testing her resolve too severely. As soon as the final benediction was given she jumped to her feet and nodded to Miss Sharp, the mathematics teacher who had agreed to shepherd Eva's students back to the school. Miss Sharp nodded back, and Eva made her way out of the pew to find Megan.

Her stomach growled. It was likely that she was going to miss Sunday afternoon dinner, but she consoled herself with the recollection of the apple and hunk of cheese wrapped neatly and lying in her handbag. It was no succulent roast with potatoes and carrots, but she wouldn't starve.

Megan excused herself from her family, but before she reached Eva's side a golden haired man—tall and lean, wearing a brocade vest under a finely tailored jacket—stopped her. He gave a bow of his head, and Megan smiled up at him, her many ruffles all seeming to flutter at once. Eva tapped her foot and glanced anxiously about the rapidly emptying church. At last Megan sashayed over to Eva, her red curls bobbing, a beatific smile on her face and the unknown gentleman at her heels.

"Have you met Mr. Deveraux Williston? He's new to town and recently bought a ranch." She turned back to the fellow. "Mr. Williston, this is my dearest friend in the world, Evangeline Danwood."

He placed his hat on his head and took her hand in his. Raised it to his lips. "Miss Danwood, it's a pleasure to meet any friend of Miss Conroy. She and her family have been remarkably kind to me since my arrival in town."

With an infinitely complacent smile, Megan looped her arm through Eva's. "Let's talk to Miss Haddix first, she always tears away from here like her kitchen's on fire. We'll have to be quick to catch her."

Indeed, as they stepped from the dim coolness of the church into the sun, they spied their quarry almost at the sidewalk.

Megan called to her. "Miss Haddix."

There was no response.

Mr. Williston stepped up beside her. "Miss Haddix!"

Every head in sight turned toward them. Luckily this included Miss Haddix, though her cheeks burned red as she turned her head. It was difficult to tell whether she was embarrassed or angry as the sun glinted off her spectacles, masking the expression in her eyes. Her precisely parted and knotted chignon and perpetually pursed mouth gave no other hint as to how she might have reacted to the summons. Having spotted them she paused, hands clutching her purse at her waist as if it were a life buoy.

Eva decided it would be best to try to smooth matters over before they proceeded. "Good afternoon, Miss Haddix. We're sorry to have startled you. May we walk with you?"

A suspicious tightening of pursed lips and furrowed brow was followed by a hesitant affirmative. "I suppose so."

"Is that a new hat, Miss Haddix?" Megan asked sweetly.

"It's the same hat I've had for four years."

"It looks especially pretty today. Perfect for spring."

Miss Haddix sniffed. "Can I do something for you folks?"

Megan's smile turned a touch stiff. "It's nothing much. We were wondering if you can tell us if you saw an envelope in the outgoing mail tray yesterday evening."

"You want to know if I remarked a particular envelope in a pile of envelopes?"

Eva stepped in. "I know it sounds silly, but it's important or we wouldn't bother you."

"Was there anything special about it?"

Eva looked to Megan who shook her head. "It was addressed to Mrs. Collins and it was quite thick."

Miss Haddix gave a slight shrug. "'Fraid I don't remember anything like that. What did you do, post something you didn't want to send after all? No, that doesn't make sense. The mail won't have been collected yet."

It was time for a change of topic. "Did you happen to see anyone else in the office late yesterday?" Eva asked. "You know, anyone else who might have seen the envelope?"

This made Miss Haddix purse her lips until they all but disappeared. "Except for yourselves, I saw Harry Kettle, the greengrocer. And of course there were quite a few of the volunteers milling about still.

Some people seem to have nothing better to do than hang about after an event." She cast a brief glance over her shoulder at the churchgoers who still clustered in chatting, laughing groups outside the church. "I believe I saw Franny Sue Mansford too. You know she just had her baby. That husband of hers is over the moon."

"Oh, yes. I remember seeing Franny Sue too, now that you mention it." Megan sounded thoughtful and looked up at Mr. Williston, who stood slightly too close to her side.

Eva emphatically did not roll her eyes. Megan might have mentioned Franny Sue sooner. They could have started with her. "Was there anyone else?"

"I hardly have time to keep track of everyone's comings and goings." Miss Haddix gave a little shrug.

"So no one who shouldn't have been there?"

"No." Once again suspicion flared in her features. "What's gone missing?"

"There's no need for concern. Just a silly mix-up. We'll get it all sorted in a jiffy."

Miss Haddix looked unconvinced.

James approached with frizzle-haired, pink-cheeked Miss Palmer on his arm. She was another regular volunteer at the mission society office. Miss Haddix greeted her with a jerk of her chin. "Lavinia, these folks are wanting to know if we saw an envelope in the outgoing mail tray yesterday."

"Oh dear." Miss Palmer's hands fluttered to her mouth. "I don't know. I mean it's difficult to recall. There are usually envelopes in the tray, and I don't always pay attention. Of course, I should. My late father was forever warning me to pay attention. I just have such difficulty. I mean there are ever so many things to pay attention to, if you see what I mean. Some people have the knack of knowing what to pay attention to, but I find that I don't, so I try to—"

Eva patted her free arm. "It's quite all right, Miss Palmer. There's no need to distress yourself. We were just wondering."

"Did you happen to notice anyone who was in the office that afternoon?" James's tone was gentleness itself.

The frilly edge of Miss Palmer's sleeve seemed to tremble in agitation as her hands once more flew into explanatory motion. "Well let me see. I do try to take note of the folks I meet. I always try to get to know folks and put them at ease. Makes things so much more pleasant and easy. And of course, people are so interesting if you know what I mean. They're always coming up with clever things to say. And they do—"

Megan and Mr. Williston exchanged a supercilious smirk. Megan gave an impatient huff of air. "Miss Palmer, who did you see yesterday?"

"What? Now let me think. There was Miss Haddix of course." Eva glanced toward where that lady had been standing to find that she had made good her escape. "And of course there was the elder Mr. Ferris." Miss Palmer gave James a little simper. "Your father is such a nice man, dear."

"Yes, ma'am."

"Was there anyone else?"

"Well I think Mr. Norton and his wife, Isabelle—she is a lovely lady, isn't she?—I think they were there. He's a state senator you know. And then of course there was yourselves, but I don't suppose you want to hear about that." She laughed merrily. "I don't know if I can recall anyone else."

"Well, thank you, Miss Palmer." Megan turned to go, her hand on Eva's arm pulling her to go as well.

"Of course, you could check my list."

"Your list?"

"Yes. Didn't I say? I keep a list of everyone who comes into the office. My memory isn't what it used to be, and if I have to follow up with someone I find it's helpful if I just have that little list."

"Why couldn't she have said that first?" Megan demanded in an undertone. Mr. Williston chuckled indulgently. Eva nudged Megan into silence with the sharp end of her elbow and James gave her a censorious look, but it seemed that Miss Palmer did not hear her.

"Would you mind if we look at your list?" James asked.

"Oh certainly, dear boy, if you want to. It's not very interesting, I'm afraid."

"Thank you, Miss Palmer, that's very kind."

"Not at all. Not at all. It's in the top drawer of my little desk. I do hope you find what you're looking for. I can come with you if you like, to show you where it is."

"That won't be necessary. We are quite capable of finding it on our own." Megan hastened to dissuade her.

"I see." Miss Palmer's glance fell to the sidewalk. "I quite understand. I can be such a pest to young people, I know. Well—" A sweet smile bloomed in her plump, pink cheeks—"I do wish you luck. Please let me know if there is anything else I can do for you." She hurried away, leaving them to watch her go.

Eva turned to Megan. "How could you have been so disrespectful?"

Megan sighed. "She rambles on so. And she didn't even notice."

"She did notice, and she didn't deserve your unkindness."

Megan looked stricken. "I didn't mean to be unkind. Do you really think she noticed?"

Eva and James both nodded.

"Oh, I must go make things right with her. She makes me impatient, but I know it's just her way. Do you mind if I catch up with you all a little later?" Picking up her skirts she hurried after Miss Palmer without waiting for a reply.

With Megan's abrupt departure, Mr. Williston also drifted away. Eva realized too late that she and James had once more been left alone. How did she keep getting into these scrapes? She took his proffered arm reluctantly.

James knew he should just walk Eva home and then go about his own business. It would be far better for everyone concerned. It was the wisest course of action. "Were you planning to go to the mission society today?"

Her eyebrows jumped and she squinted up at him against the sun. "I thought it might be worthwhile to have a look around in the daylight."

"I will accompany you, if I may. I thought it might be prudent to capture fingerprints before the beginning of the work week."

She cocked her head. "Fingerprints? Like in Life on the Mississippi?"

His cheeks warmed. "Yes. I thought perhaps they could be used to identify someone who had no business in the mission society office."

"How does one collect a fingerprint?"

James waxed eloquent at this, describing the required steps with great technical detail and equal fervor. Eva looked up at him with that tilt to her head that always signaled that she was truly listening, not just waiting for her chance to speak as most people did. His heart gave a painful sort of kick to his ribs.

He had never made any declaration, he reminded himself. She had never had a claim on him. It had only seemed for a while that they might be headed in that direction. The statements he had been reciting to himself for months were growing ever thinner and shabbier in his head.

Resolutely he faced forward, letting silence fall between them, trying to admire the profusion of spring flowers in bloom. Showy pink Crape Myrtle vied for attention with a profusion of buttery-yellow roses and brilliant blue columbine, and the long purple spikes of Texas sage were not to be outdone either, piling high in a hedge along the walk.

Eva let her fingers trail along a stately wrought iron fence. "I'm going to miss Austin when I leave. This is the only place that ever actually felt like home. It was like the whole city adopted me, not just my parents."

James cleared his throat. "Austin will miss you too." He picked up his pace, casting about for a way to fill the silence between them. They no longer had the sort of relationship where silence was a comfortable companion.

The plain brick face and paneled black door of the mission office looked much as normal except for the blank stare of darkened windows.

"It doesn't appear that anyone is here," she said.

"That's all right. I have a key."

"I'm sure Megan will be along soon, too."

James paused to unlock the broad black front door. "I've got to say, you've been kind to her. If I were in your place I don't know that I could be so forbearing."

A deep blush climbed up her throat and into her cheeks. She shrugged. "She didn't do it on purpose."

He held the door open for her and she brushed past, heading straight for the inner office. "I'll double check for any hiding places in here." She didn't wait for an acknowledgment.

James opened the satchel that contained his carefully collected items. He lined up on the desk a jar of finely ground charcoal dust, a very soft brush, and a stack of small, smooth white paper cards. The idea that God had put so much care into the details of His creation that He had even given each person a unique fingerprint seemed amazing. Maybe there was a sermon in there somewhere, though Father didn't like him to use many modern examples. He felt traditional citations were best.

Sighing with the thought, James unscrewed the lid of the jar. He'd never work out his problems with his father by mooning about. He needed to figure out where the money went. From the research he had done, fingerprints were most easily obtained from flat, smooth surfaces.

He dipped the brush into the jar and with gentle sweeps began swirling black dust along the top of the desk.

Back in the inner office, Eva opened the windows and turned on the electric lights in the office then put her handbag in the chair and her hands on her hips. If the money had not gone in the mail and no one had taken it, it must still be here. She simply needed to figure out where. Perhaps someone had stumbled upon the money and put it someplace safe. Her gaze scoured the room looking for any potential hiding places.

The desk itself would have to be searched thoroughly. And so would the tall wooden file cabinet. In addition, there was a bookcase stacked high with a miscellany that ranged from learned treatises on doctrine to travelogues.

Perhaps the money had been slipped into a book. Wherever it was, Eva had an idea that she was in for a dusty job. She unpinned her hat, took off her gloves, and rolled up the cuffs of her spotless white shirtfront.

She tackled the bookcase first. Methodically removing one book at a time, she paged through each. Unless each bill had been hidden in a separate book—and surely no one would go to such lengths—then the money, if hidden among these volumes, should be obvious. Her hope dwindled when she was halfway through the shelf. By the time she got to the bottom shelf it had petered out altogether. But doggedly she flipped through every single volume. She moved on to the file cabinet, then the desk. She could hear James moving about in the outer room, but he did not disturb her.

At least not on purpose. His mere presence had a way of generally disturbing her equanimity.

She was at last reduced to lifting up the rugs and checking behind the framed picture of a sailing ship that hung on the wall behind the desk. Nothing, nothing, and nothing.

Sighing, she stepped into the outer room to find James hunched over one of the three desks. Black powder was smeared everywhere, and he held a small brush in his hand. A stack of smudged white cards sat on the desk next to him. At her arrival he turned to her, revealing a face as smudged as the cards.

He looked half-abashed, half-relieved at the interruption. "Any luck?"

"Afraid not. You?"

He shook his head. "This is harder than the manual made it sound."

"And messier?"

"What?"

She rubbed the side of her own nose and he gave a start, his hand flying to his nose. "Drat." He pulled out a green and purple plaid handkerchief and began scrubbing.

"I've never seen a plaid handkerchief before."

He colored even more furiously. "Megan. A gift."

Eva nodded and turned away, not wishing to make him any more uncomfortable. She sat before the nearest desk and pulled out Miss Palmer's list of people who had visited mission society.

With the fair there had been a surprising number of people through the office. Eva recognized most of the names.

"Can I ask you a question?"

Eva looked up from the list. "I suppose."

"Why Ceylon?"

Very carefully she set the list down on the desktop, smoothing it out as if it were an exceedingly precious document. "I heard about it from a missionary who came through. They have a school. A place where I can be of real use. Where I can make a material difference for my students."

He nodded, his face grave and painfully sincere. "I'm glad to hear that. I would hate to have thought that you felt the need to leave because of my engagement to Megan."

The blood whooshed in Eva's ears, and her face felt scorched. She bit back the first sharp retort that came to mind. "Believe it or not Mr. Ferris, your engagement—" She sucked in a breath and sought to calm herself. "I will not deny that I once considered you important to me. However, God is more so. I'm going to Ceylon because I desire to please Him. Your engagement is irrelevant except that it cleared my path of any temptation to stay. You could say that you did me a favor."

Beneath its sun-bronzed cast, his face seemed to pale slightly. "I am happy to have been of service," he murmured. He bent once more over his task, his back to her.

Silently, Eva stood and tucked the list into her pocket.

A few moments later there was a clatter at the front door and it burst open on a wave of riotous laughter. The abrupt disruption to the heavy silence made Eva spin to face the door.

Megan and Mr. Williston barreled into the mission society offices. He had his hand on the small of her back, allowing it to linger longer than necessary to usher her before him. In fact, the gesture bordered on possessive.

Eva frowned and stepped back.

"Why are you looking so dour?" Megan's question sounded more like a challenge.

"I'm not..." Eva trailed off, knowing she sounded defensive, and that her protests would mean nothing anyway. Megan wasn't even listening. She had already turned to James.

"I went and apologized to Miss Palmer. She's sweet, but not very bright."

Mr. Williston snorted. "That's an understatement. She wouldn't know a deep thought if it lassoed and hogtied her."

Eva was gratified to find that James was looking as stony as she felt.

"She tried to tell me about her whole day. As if I was interested in the minutiae of her life."

Williston started laughing and nudged Megan with his elbow. "The tea."

Megan began giggling again and pushed back at his arm. "Oh yes, she started out by telling me she made a pot of tea when she arrived here yesterday. Right down to the type and number of scoops and how long she let it steep. I had to cut her off or we'd still be there listening to her drone on."

James's voice was slightly deeper than usual and as stiff as if he'd swallowed a cupful of starch. "We didn't tell her why we were asking her questions, so she likely thought she'd tell you everything and you could judge what was important."

"It would be easier to listen to her if she didn't dither so much."

Eva shut the desk drawer she had been examining a little too forcefully. "By continuing to speak unkindly about her you are making your apology a nullity."

"Oh ho. It sounds like we've gotten under Miss Danwood's skin. We better try to be good." Williston's mocking tone made Eva wish he was a student she could discipline.

Megan sniffed. "Don't mind Eva, she's been cross with me since this started. I'm sure nothing I do will be good enough."

Eva swallowed back a retort, almost choking on the bitterness. She exhaled slowly until she finally felt able to speak. "I already searched the inner office. Assuming you have come to help, why don't you take the storage room?"

"Oh, I'm sure it couldn't be there." Megan looked as if Eva had suggested that they hire camels to search the Sahara Desert. "I didn't go up there at all yesterday."

Eva didn't bother to explain her theory that someone else may have moved the money for safekeeping. "Then you search down here and I'll go up there."

Mr. Williston looked from one of them to the other. "What is it we're looking for?"

Eva crossed her arms and waited for Megan to explain. Meg's gaze slid from her to James but he too waited for her to give her account.

"I made a little mistake." As briefly as possible Megan confessed about the lost money.

"I had no idea this place pulled in that kind of money." Williston sounded duly impressed.

"People were especially generous because they knew the money was earmarked to help E—Miss Danwood's mission." James's voice sounded much more natural now, but when she met his gaze he glanced quickly away. "She's helped a lot of people over the years and they made their appreciation known."

Eva's annoyance dissipated, and a warm glow seemed to start at her navel and spread outward.

Megan patted Williston's arm again. "Saint Eva always does the right thing."

The annoyance was back.

"Now be nice, or they'll want you to apologize to Miss Danwood too." Williston's flash of a grin in Eva's direction did nothing to defuse the sting of his words.

The fact that Megan laughed and said nothing in her defense stung far more than any words that might have come from him anyway. As if she were, even with her friends, a prim schoolmarm who lived for the unreasonable pleasure of sucking the most innocent fun from her charges.

James cleared his throat. "I will give you a hand upstairs, if I may, Miss Danwood."

"Certainly." Her lips felt a little numb, but she was able to maintain her dignity as she moved around the desk and up the tiny stairwell set into the corner.

She could hear whispering behind her, but mercifully could not make out the words.

As she reached the top she could hear James's careful tread behind her and then there was a clatter.

Megan's voice rattled up to her. "I really didn't go up there Eva; you don't have to search that dirty old place."

"I would feel better knowing we didn't leave any stone unturned."

It might not matter very much to Megan that the money had been lost, but Eva's future was at stake.

Four

Eva could summon no enthusiasm for her classes the next morning. The money had still not turned up. And she kept rehearsing the conversations she'd had with James and Megan. Half a hundred times she came up with things she ought to have said to both of them. It would have been immensely satisfying to put them in their place.

Even as she thought it, she knew it would never happen. She just wasn't the sort of person who excelled at repartee. She could draft a scathing letter with the best of them—letters she never mailed—but put her on the spot and she was worse than useless.

"Miss Danwood?" One of her students tapped her shoulder, and from her tone it was clear that this wasn't the first time the girl had addressed her.

"I'm sorry Adelaide, what is it?"

"Is anything wrong, miss? You seem...out of sorts."

Eva managed a brief smile. "Not at all." She turned to the rest of the girls. "Five more minutes on your class assignment. If you're already done, you may bring them up to me."

Before anyone could move, Lizzie Woodhouse raised her hand. "I'm glad to hear everything is all right, Miss Danwood." She exchanged a smug smile with her bosom chum Camille Ford. "I had heard that you were caught climbing a tree and trying to sneak into the school the other night and that you're being sacked."

269

Eva's throat felt like someone had lassoed her right 'round the jugular and was trying to drag her to the ground. Her cheeks burned, but she managed to stand slowly. "That just goes to show how foolish we sound when we listen to malicious gossip. It appears you all have far too much time for idle chitchat, so in addition to the class work you've already done, we are now going to have a quiz."

There was a low groan, which she quelled with the gimlet stare she had perfected in the last two years of teaching.

"On a clean piece of paper, in your finest hand, I want you to name all the states and their capitals, all the countries of Europe and their capitals, and all the countries of South America and their capitals. And do be certain to thank Lizzie for bringing your lack of beneficial occupation to my attention."

A great sigh was heaved on all sides, but the girls dutifully opened their desks and pulled out fresh paper and pencils. Eva was pretty sure she saw a spitball sail and hit Lizzie in the back of the neck. Thankfully she hadn't seen where it had come from so she felt no need to intervene.

Why in heaven's name had she ever given in to the impulse to climb that blasted tree? It was hardly the action of a responsible and serious young woman. Lesson learned. She would be more careful in the future. She fought the inclination to bury her face in her hands. She wanted to get away from here, from the school, from Austin, from all of the expectations and all the people.

Maybe instead of being a missionary she should become a hermit.

It seemed six months had elapsed before the lunch bell finally rang. Once more, Eva decided to skip the midday meal. Instead she munched an apple on her way to visit Franny Sue Mansford. She'd elected to start with her for several reasons. She was living just a few blocks away in a neat, brick-faced townhouse with gauzy white curtains in the window and impeccably tended flower boxes, and she was an Austen Abbey alumna. Franny Sue had been one of the kind girls who tended to take the younger ones under her wing. She knew and liked Megan, and Eva trusted her not to gossip about the situation.

Eva mounted the clean-swept granite front steps and rang the bell.

A maid answered promptly and admitted her, ushering her straight into the parlor where Franny Sue sat poring over a manuscript and looking tired.

"Well isn't this a nice surprise. But isn't this a school day?"

Eva bent to kiss her cheek. "It is, but I have neglected you too long and yesterday I heard that you gave the world a new little Mansford. So I couldn't resist coming to see you any longer."

"I'm glad you did. I've been going stir crazy. Eddie is determined not to let me lift a finger for weeks."

Eva smiled. "Well you do need to keep your strength up."

Franny Sue sighed. "No danger of me doing otherwise."

The baby was produced from a bassinette positioned beside Franny Sue, and Eva nuzzled him close. He was tiny, and beautiful and perfect, infinitely fragile in his nest of blankets. Oohing and aahing over him came naturally, but all too soon his little eyes began to drift shut and he fell asleep. The maid came in to take him to his crib.

Franny Sue moved to the settee and patted the seat beside her. "Sit and tell me about what you've been up to. I heard they raised more than enough to send you out on your mission. You must be delighted."

There was no more putting it off, so Eva squared her shoulders and explained as briefly as she could. She tried not to be too critical of Megan in the recounting, but Franny Sue shook her head, all too acquainted with Megan's flightiness. "She was thinking of the wedding or some such, wasn't she?"

Eva gave a small shrug.

"I have to say this does take the cake even for Megan."

"She didn't mean to cause any trouble."

"She never does. And she will of course do everything in her power to make things right, but she could avoid scrapes like this if she simply gave a little thought to what she is doing in any given moment." Franny Sue sighed. "Does the board know?"

"Jame—Mr. Ferris's father knows."

Franny Sue nodded sagely. "He will delay telling the others as long as possible in hopes of recovering the money and allowing Megan to save face."

"I was hoping that you might have happened to see the envelope or notice something?"

Franny Sue reached over and gave her hand a squeeze. "I only wish I had. It would give me the greatest pleasure to help you, but unfortunately Eddie was harassing me to come home so I could rest, and I wasn't paying much attention to anything."

Eva couldn't help the little pang of disappointment that sliced her heart, but she managed a smile. "Oh. Well if you do happen to think of something, could you let Megan or I.... Perhaps it might be best if you would let me know."

"Oh." Franny Sue sat bolt upright, tea sloshing over the lip of her cup and into her saucer. She looked dismayed at the unaccustomed clumsiness, but simply set aside the tea and wiped her fingers delicately on a napkin. "I did see Megan. She was with that rancher. You know the fellow. He only moved to town about three months ago. Handsome fellow. Nice manners if he thinks you're worth his time."

"Mr. Williston?" Eva ventured.

"Yes, him." Franny Sue jabbed the teacup toward her with an exultant air. "Mr. Williston." She rolled the name about in her mouth as if testing it. Her nose curled slightly as if it tasted moldy. "I...I hesitate to say anything. You know I'm not a gossip—under normal circumstances."

"If it's not relevant, I promise it will go no further."

Franny Sue's cheeks colored. "He was with Megan. I recall thinking at the time that he was being too familiar with an engaged young woman. With any young woman indeed, unless she were his own fiancée. But Megan did not seem at all offended. I don't think she even acknowledged my greeting. She was too wrapped up in her conversation with him."

Eva swallowed the hard lump that had somehow lodged itself in her throat. "I see."

"It may be worth speaking to him."

"I have. He did not mention being there."

"Oh. Well." Franny Sue looked down at her teacup as if surprised to see she held such an object and set it aside. "I'm sure that he didn't say anything because he felt he didn't have anything worth contributing."

Eva didn't argue. Largely because she was feeling a bit queasy. She had noticed Megan's unwonted intimacy with Mr. Williston but had hoped that it was merely her own stuffy notions that made the behavior seem at all untoward. This confirmation of her judgment from a source she trusted implicitly made her want to cry. James did not deserve such treatment and Megan knew better.

"I'm so sorry I never saw the money or what Megan did with it."

Once again, Eva summoned a smile, though it felt stale on her lips. She made up for it by squeezing her friend's hand. "I forbid you to worry about it. You have more than enough fresh concerns of your own. I'm certain it will turn up somewhere."

"I'm certain of it."

"Well, I better head back to class. I can hardly discipline a student for being tardy if I'm committing such sins myself." She stood, then stooped to kiss Franny Sue's cheek. "Don't pester the maid. I can show myself out. I know the way well enough."

Pulling on her gloves, Eva hurried from the room and down the hall. Head down, she heaved on the heavy oak door and let out a strangled squawk as she plowed into someone.

There was a grunt as her face made contact with a wall of solid broadcloth. Strong hands steadied her. "Are you all right, Eva?"

James.

Of course it would be.

"I'm so sorry." She raised a hand to her chest as if she could restrain her racing heart by pressing on it. "I would reprimand one of my girls for running about so pell-mell."

He smiled down at her, looking almost indulgent. "No harm done."

She had a brief vision of him as a playful and gentle papa. That needed to be dispelled at once. She grasped for straws. "Have you come to see Franny Sue and her new baby? They're both doing beautifully."

He nodded. "That and"—he lowered his voice—"I hoped to ask her about whether she saw anything at the mission society office."

Eva matched her tone to his. "I just spoke to her."

"You look troubled."

Eva cast about for what to say, and James seemed to sense her reluctance.

"May I walk you back to the school? I'll return to call on Franny Sue afterward."

Eva acquiesced, allowing him to lead her from the shade of the porch. She could not—would not—repeat all that Franny Sue had told her. It would hurt him, and she had no desire to do that. But she could tell the pertinent parts. "Mr. Williston was there, and she saw him speaking to Megan."

James frowned.

Eva nodded. Through years of familiarity she was able to trace the course of his thoughts. "I know. Why didn't he mention it to us?"

"Do you think it's possible?" James couldn't seem to bring himself to complete the thought.

Eva shrugged. "I don't know him well at all and he has no people here in Austin. I don't know if he's capable of such a theft or not."

"He presents himself as well-to-do."

"Yes, why would he steal money he had no need of?"

"How do we know he has no need of it? Appearances can be deceiving."

Eva paused and turned to face him. "That's a good point."

James looked grave as he resumed their stroll. "I hate to think ill of anyone, but I'm afraid Mr. Williston bears further investigation. I can think of no reason he would fail to have mentioned his presence at the mission offices."

Eva bit the inside of her cheek. She could think of no reason Megan should not have mentioned it. Even she was not so scattered as to forget the kind of encounter Franny Sue had described. Had she been trying to hide the fact of the meeting? "Perhaps we could talk to Mr. Olson at the bank? He'll know."

James nodded. "I'll go this afternoon."

Eva sighed.

James looked down at her, his gaze shifting to the hand that rested lightly on his arm. "Would it be all right for me to come by this evening and report what I find?"

"It's not an evening for guests, but I can request leave from Mrs. Collins."

"I'll see you this evening then." He tipped his hat and left her standing at the school's decorative front gate.

Evangeline pushed through and then turned to watch his figure as he strode briskly away. Things used to be so easy between them. And even now, heaven help her, while things weren't easy or comfortable between them, working with him held a certain bittersweet charm. It would be the leaving him behind that would be painful. She turned to continue on inside. Still it would be better than staying to watch him marry Megan.

Five

There had been a time when nothing mattered more to Eva than her drive to be the best teacher she could be. Today, for the second day in a row, all she wanted was to escape her classroom as quickly as possible. The afternoon lessons dragged by like they had lead weights pulling them down. If there was anything worse than being a student trapped in a dull class, it was being the teacher. Things she might normally have found mildly amusing or turned a blind eye to, found her growing shrill and irascible.

When at last the final bell rang she beat most of the students out the door. She headed straight for Mrs. Collins's office. That good lady looked up at her knock and waved her in warmly. Being in Mrs. Collins's presence always made her feel like a student again. She stood as straight as a poker and clasped her hands gently in front of her.

"Good afternoon, Evangeline, is there something I can do for you?"

The emerald green of the office was at once restful and regal. The half-moon window added a touch of whimsy to the otherwise businesslike atmosphere while the brown tufted chairs were just worn enough to be comfortable.

"I was wondering if perhaps that letter we spoke of might have arrived with today's post?"

Mrs. Collins drew her lips down in a frown. "I'm so sorry, dear, but nothing has come."

Eva had known that was probably the case, but she still felt a sinking sensation in her middle. "Thank you." She turned to leave.

"Won't you tell me what this is all about, Eva?"

Evangeline turned back to her old mentor.

"Do have a seat, my dear." Eva turned to the cozy sitting area to find that Mrs. Collins had already had tea things laid out. How did she always know when someone wanted to talk to her? Eva took a seat in one of the tufted chairs, and Mrs. Collins sat across from her. While Mrs. Collins poured, Eva told the short, dismal story.

"Oh dear." Mrs. Collins's look of pity deepened as she handed over a cup that was just as Eva liked it.

"You did hire someone to take my place, didn't you?" Eva asked.

"I'm afraid so. She's moving here from back East in a few weeks so that she can become acclimated to Austin before the school year starts." Miss Collins cocked her head. "But of course, we'd be happy to keep you on. I can find something for you, I'm sure."

Eva's smile felt as fragile as a pie shell. "I couldn't put you out. I know full well you won't need me." She couldn't stay and she couldn't go. Why had God let this happen? She had been praying about it since Megan's unwelcome announcement. "I have my savings. I could..." She paused as an idea began taking shape even as she spoke. "I could make it as far as San Francisco. It will at least be a step toward Ceylon. And if you would be willing to write me a letter of reference, I can try to find a position at a school out there. I could simply work to pay my own way to Ceylon."

"I will write you a letter of course, but Evangeline, do you think that's wise? You'd be leaving all your people to try to make your way in a strange place alone."

Evangeline raised her hands in a gesture of futility. "I don't know. I don't know what to do. I haven't sensed any clear direction from God. But I'll be leaving everyone I know when I go to Ceylon anyway, so I can't see that there's much difference." She did not try to list the reasons why staying would be intolerable. She had a feeling Mrs. Collins required no explanation.

Mrs. Collins made no further attempt to dissuade her. "My dear girl, we will miss you a great deal."

Eva left Mrs. Collins's office several minutes later with an unsettled feeling in the pit of her stomach.

"Eva!"

She turned around to find Megan standing behind her. The wretch didn't even have the grace to look miserable; she was practically glowing with health and beauty.

"You do know there are rules about when visitors are allowed," Eva snapped.

"Oh." Megan stopped in mid-stride, her outstretched hand drawing back as if it had almost been bitten. She glanced at the students bustling about and watching them with interested eyes. "I wanted to check on the progress."

Eva regretted her sharpness but couldn't seem to help herself. "I see no reason why I should be required to give you a report."

Hurt flashed in Megan's eyes.

Eva sighed. "Let's go to my room."

They did not speak as they wended their way through the students and other teachers. Unusual for Megan to stay silent for so long. Maybe the seriousness of the situation was finally sinking in.

Eva did not offer any refreshments as they settled into their accustomed places. Megan perched on the edge of the bed and Eva in the desk chair. They had sat this way countless times over the years. But never before had they been at such odds.

Before Megan could ask any questions, Eva pounced. "Why didn't you mention that Mr. Williston was at the mission offices with you?"

"Wha—I don't know what you mean."

"You know very well what I mean and don't try to pretend otherwise." Eva was having none of it this time. "Williston certainly never said anything, and you must know how suspicious that looks in light of what happened."

"Who said he was there?"

"This isn't like you, Megan. You've got your faults, but you've never been sneaky or manipulative."

Megan blushed. "Oh, Eva, I'm sorry. It's all such a muddle. But I can't go on deceiving you. I've been so miserable, you can't even guess."

Eva crossed her arms and waited for Megan to explain.

"It's just that... It's this engagement to James. I—it was never my idea. It is what my parents want. I have been trying to hold up my end, and I was doing a pretty good job of it, but then..." She paused and looked at Eva with imploring eyes grown suddenly large with unshed tears.

Eva merely waited.

"But then I met Mr. Williston, and he snatched the very breath from my lungs. It was so very dramatic. I was out riding at our ranch and I was exploring this little gully when a squall came up and there was a flash flood. He saved my life. Oh, Eva, he makes my heart sing like no one else could. When I am with him, the world is a brighter place and I want to dance and sing. He understands me like no one else ever has. And he doesn't think me shallow. He understands the way my soul longs for deep connections."

All of a sudden Eva was cold; so cold that it seemed she was frozen in place.

Caught up in her raptures, Megan didn't seem to notice. "I'm afraid that was why I was so thoughtless about the money. He happened to come by and we were speaking. But there is nothing suspicious in it. I was with him the whole time. I can vouch that it wasn't he who took it. I'm surprised that you would even consider it. Anyone can see his heart is true just by looking at him."

"What I see when I look at him, is someone who isn't above mocking a kind elderly lady or flirting with a young lady who is engaged to someone else. If he was truly a man of character he'd never do such things."

The color that rushed into Megan's cheeks this time was an angrier red. "You just don't understand. You're entirely cool and unfeeling. You have no idea what those of us with more passionate natures experience. Our sensibilities are so much more alive to others."

In the same measure that the blood had rushed to Megan's face, Eva could feel it fleeing her own. "You must stop this or you are bound to hurt someone who has done you no wrong. How can you go about talking to other men behind James's back?"

"There is no harm in talking. We did nothing wrong, Eva. Give me a little credit."

"That's where you're wrong. Please be sensible."

"I can't be like you. I'm not heartless. I don't even believe you cried over James, though I know you had set your cap for him before he began courting me. Yet you never murmured a word but to congratulate me on a fine match. Knowing you didn't really care was the only reason I even agreed."

Eva snapped her jaws together against the words that wanted to rush out. She breathed in once. Twice. Three times. "Megan, I think it would be best if you would go before we both say a lot of things that we might regret. We haven't found the money, and I'm coming to believe that it's not likely we will."

Megan stood. "For that I am very sorry. I will speak to my father and confess all. Perhaps he will be able to help replace at least a portion."

"Good night." Eva held the door for her.

"Good night." Megan looked as if she wanted to say more, but Eva feared that if they remained in conversation she would begin screaming, so she made no sign that would encourage her friend to speak.

When she had gone, Eva shut the door quietly behind her then plopped on the bed. She had no desire for any supper. She tried to pray, but the words seemed to jam up in her throat. There were certainly no blinding flashes of insight giving her a clue as to how to proceed with her life.

She pulled her knees up to her chest and rested her forehead against them. She had hoped to do such good in Ceylon. It was utterly unfair that Megan had managed to steal two dreams from her—and without even trying. Even in her disgruntled state, Eva couldn't say that Megan had acted with any malice or intent. She had never meant to hurt Eva.

But she had.

Eva wanted nothing more than to crawl under the covers and go to bed, but James had promised to come by and report on what he'd learned from the bank manager. She would have to stay dressed if she wanted to hear what he had to say, and she really did.

As angry as she was with Megan, she was concerned for her friend as well. Her heart ruled her head, and if Mr. Williston proved to be something other than the paragon she believed, it would crush Megan.

Eva's thoughts revolved over one another again and again until she jolted awake. Her tongue felt fuzzy, and she had a crick in her neck and drool on her blouse.

Grumbling, she groped her way out of bed. The girls' essays would have to wait until tomorrow to be marked. She was going to put on her nightdress and then she would lie down. Stretching out would feel amazing. She'd have a fresh perspective when she awoke in the morning.

Also, she'd give James a piece of her mind. Why hadn't he ever come to report what he had learned?

A pattering sound came from the window. With a burst of realization, Eva knew that it was the noise which had awakened her. Shifting course, she went to the window, pulled up the sash, and looked out.

From below a stage whisper carried up to her. "Oh good, you weren't in bed yet."

"James?"

"Yes." He stepped a bit closer so that the light from her window illuminated his face.

"What time is it?"

"Eleven thirty."

"What do you want?"

"To tell you about the bank manager." He looked about him as if afraid that someone was eavesdropping.

It was improper enough that she was talking to him at all so late at night. There was no way she was inviting him inside. "Well?"

"He would only speak in the most general terms. Williston doesn't have much in the way of assets in the bank. But some folks are funny like that. They want to keep their money nearby. Or he may not have moved his holdings to the bank here in Austin yet. He's only been here about three months."

"So we learned nothing."

"We learned that he has an account."

"Does he have any debts?"

"His property is mortgaged."

"More and more people are doing that though—I don't know that it means anything. Unless—is he paid up?"

"Yes. He was late with his last payment, but nothing serious. All ranchers do that at times. Sometimes they can't make it into town."

"So it's possible but not probable that he needs extra money?"

James shrugged. "You know I've never talked to a girl at her window before. It's not really like I imagined it would be."

"No?"

"No. I'm getting a pain in my neck from looking up. And my voice is getting scratchy from this whispering."

"Romeo you're not." With that Eva shut her window and pulled the curtains.

Despite its obvious drawbacks, the conversation had not been a total loss. She'd had an idea. She would go to the bank and get a loan. She could send the money back in small installments out of her teaching stipend at the mission. Maybe she could still make it to the mission. She sat down at her desk to compose just what she wanted to say.

Once more the next afternoon, Eva tore out of class at the end of the day and up to her room where she changed into her most dignified shirtwaist and jacket. She tucked up all the stray hairs that had come loose during the day and then retrieved her handbag.

As she walked to the bank she perused her carefully penned words from the night before. It had taken a number of drafts, but at last she had captured what she wanted to say. She rehearsed the words over to herself.

The polished marble of the floor echoed as she crossed the lobby. The enormous, intricately worked mahogany counter gleamed and gave off the smell of bee's wax polish. From behind the high brass grill one of the clerks, Mr. Pennyroyal, looked mildly surprised to see her. "Miss Eva, how are you? We usually only see you come time to deposit your savings." He smiled to show he was still willing to wait upon her.

She approached him gratefully. "I was hoping to speak to Mr. Edmonds about a loan."

Mr. Pennyroyal's eyebrows rose a notch. "I see. If you'd care to wait a moment, I'll go see if he's available."

"Thank you."

Eva took a seat in a stiff, cane-backed chair set in a corner and placed her handbag primly in her lap. She wanted to pull out her speech again but felt that it wouldn't strike the properly confident note, so she settled for reciting it in her head.

She waited some fifteen minutes before Mr. Pennyroyal fetched her. Sucking in a breath, Eva followed him to the manager's office and allowed him to usher her inside a room that reeked of cigar smoke.

Mr. Edmonds stood at her arrival. "Good evening, Miss Danwood, I trust you're well."

"Yes sir. And you?" She stuck her tongue against the roof of her mouth to suppress a cough.

"Well enough. Well enough. But what is this I hear about you wanting a loan?" He stubbed out the nub of cigar he held, the red embers almost close enough to singe his fingers. "I thought you were heading out to foreign parts with the missionaries."

"Yes, that's precisely why I need the money." She launched into her speech. "Unfortunately, the expectation of funds I had been relying upon has been disappointed—"

Shaking his head, Mr. Edmonds broke in. "You want me to loan you the money to go off to foreign parts?"

She nodded but couldn't help but notice that he looked skeptical. She drew in a breath to continue with her discourse.

"How much are you wanting?"

"What? Oh, one thousand dollars."

He let out a low whistle, and his eyebrows got even more athletic than Pennyroyal's had.

"I shall pay you back every penny. I have it all planned out. I will send money from my teaching stipend."

"Have you got anything that could be used as collateral?"

"I—no. Not really."

"Didn't your parents own a store?"

"It was sold to pay the medical bills after they passed away." In truth her adoptive parents' medical bills had exceeded the price of the store, and she had had to work diligently to pay off the remaining amount.

He started to shake his head.

Eva popped open her purse and pulled out a small jeweled brooch that had been her mother's. "Wait. I have this."

He accepted it from her hand. He rummaged about in his desk drawer for a moment and then pulled out a jeweler's loupe. He held the brooch up to the light and examined it.

"Glass," he said finally. He passed it back. "Worth a few dollars at most."

"I'm a hard worker and trustworthy. I've had an account here for years—"

"I'm afraid it's out of my hands, Miss Danwood. I would like to help you, and if you wanted the money to buy land or something of substance here in Austin, I might be able to see my way. Or if it was a matter of a couple hundred dollars, I would overlook the fact that there is no way to ensure that the bank could recoup its investment. But as it is, I cannot in good conscience send a thousand dollars overseas with a single lady who has no relations here in town. No matter how trustworthy and reliable I know her to be." He bowed his head a bit to catch her eye. "And I do know you to be trustworthy, miss. But what if your boat were to sink, or you were to be robbed? All sorts of unexpected things can happen."

"Don't I know it," Eva said under her breath. The worst of it was that she could see his point, and felt foolish for having come at all. She stood and extended her hand to Mr. Edmonds. "Thank you anyway, sir. I appreciate you taking the time to meet with me."

"I do wish I could help you, Miss Danwood. If there's something else I could do, you've only to name it."

"You're very kind."

She passed once more through the pretentious lobby. There had to be some way. She just hadn't hit upon the right thing yet.

At the threshold she almost ran into a figure dressed in sober black. "Good evening, Mr. Ferris. I hope you're well."

James's father nodded. "Well enough."

"Has the board made any decision about the missing money?"

He sniffed and really looked at her for the first time. "I fail to see what decision is required. I am certain the money will turn up soon."

Eva had never been brave enough to disagree with him before, but at that she shook her head. "I'm not so sure. James and I have searched every inch of those offices and it is not there. Nor has Mrs. Collins received it, and she would have by now if the envelope had been put in the post."

"What are you suggesting?"

"It may have been taken on purpose. It ought to be reported to the police."

"No one at the mission society offices would ever steal." He looked past her now, pointedly hinting for her to move out of his way.

"I agree that it is a difficult and painful thing to believe, but the money can't have simply vanished."

His nostrils flared. "Perhaps it didn't. Perhaps someone has taken it in a Machiavellian plot to get close to my James by prying his attention away from his fiancée and their wedding preparations."

Eva's jaw dropped.

"I would be highly disappointed in any such person. It is not the sort of behavior we would encourage in our missionaries, for example. The missionaries we send into the field are required to conduct themselves with sense and with dignity."

Eva tilted her chin up. "That certainly would be appalling behavior. Sir, I couldn't help but notice that you failed to mention to James that you were there that evening."

The tips of his ears tinged red. "That's because I don't answer to James. Nor do I answer to you, Miss Danwood." He moved forward, forcing her to step aside. "Good day."

Eva wanted nothing so much as a place to sit down. Her knees felt wobbly, and she was a little sick to her stomach. She had never heard such a wicked insinuation. She wouldn't put it past Mr. Ferris to spread his abominable story around either. It wouldn't be direct—an implication here, a regretful sigh there. Soon everyone would think she'd taken the money herself.

I give up, she thought. The whole mess had become such a tangle she didn't know what side was up anymore.

She walked home slowly, breathing deep of the evening-cooled air to steady her nerves. By the time she had reached the third block, she straightened.

Mr. Ferris may have done her a favor. Her decision was made. She would go to San Francisco. It was at least a step in the right direction, and she had enough in savings to tide her over until she could find a job. If she couldn't find work as a teacher, she could wash dirty laundry or work in a factory—whatever was required. She'd get by somehow.

Flush with resolve, Eva sought out Frank Mallory, the school handyman, when she arrived back at the school.

She found him working in the potting shed at the back of the school property. The loamy smell was soothing and invigorating at once. "Evening, Miss Danwood."

"Good evening, Frank. How are you?"

"I've got no complaints." And indeed he looked in remarkably good spirits. His eyes were alight with some sort of inner glow.

Eva glanced from him to the innumerable seedling and potted plants cramming every inch of available space in the shed, and even climbing the walls along a series of narrow shelves. "What are you up to?" she asked smilingly.

He glanced around as if to make sure there was no one behind her in the doorway. Then leaned in and lowered his voice. "It's a surprise."

"A surprise?"

He nodded and his usual quiet reserve melted away. "For Mrs. Collins. Her birthday is coming up, and I wanted to do something special for her."

"So—shrubbery?"

"She misses the gardens back home in England. There was a feller named Capability Brown that used to design gardens for all the lords and ladies. She's talked about him and his fine gardens for years. So I studied up and I designed a real English garden for her."

Eva stared at him, taking in the weathered features and grizzled hair in a new light. He was always polite, but normally so quiet and unassuming as to be taciturn. She knew little about him beyond the fact that he had been a soldier in the Confederate army. At her silence he colored a deep red.

"I don't know if it's a good idea or not. I just—"

"Oh, Mr. Mallory." Eva touched his arm. "It's a brilliant idea and so very kind. She will adore it."

"Do you think so?" A hopeful glimmer returned to his expression. "I've got a full dozen men lined up to come and help me with the work come time. We'll have it all done before the graduation, so she can enjoy it all summer while things are quiet here."

"If I didn't think it would embarrass us both, I'd give you a hug, Mr. Mallory. It's the sweetest idea I've ever heard. I promise not to ruin the surprise."

Again, he colored brick red, but this time he ducked his head and hid a smile too. "Now miss, I'm sure you didn't come out here to ask me about my plans. What can I do for you?"

For a moment Eva had completely forgotten her errand. Now she regretted having disturbed his labors. "When you have a moment I need my trunk brought up from the basement."

"Course I will. I'm at a good stopping place. I'll come now." He wiped his hands on a rag and moved as if to hold the door open for her. "You packing for your mission already, huh?"

"In a way."

He threw a sideways glance at her but didn't ask any prying

questions. Mr. Mallory could be surprisingly restful company.

In her room she found Mrs. Collins's letter of recommendation had been slid under the door. She took it as a confirmation of her plan. All her playacting at detection hadn't turned up anything but additional heartache. She would have to make her plans without the missing money. She tried hard to get excited about the opportunity for God to work a miracle with the whole situation, but mostly she felt tired. She would take only essentials with her to San Francisco in order to keep the weight down. She didn't require much anyway. When she'd arrived in Austin she'd had little more than the clothes on her back. She was alone then, and God had seen her through. She would be alone once again, except for God, but she did not have to fear.

Seven

Guiltily aware that she had been neglecting them in the last couple of days, Eva focused intently on her students the next morning. At last she set them all to writing an essay and she sat down to mark papers. She had made it through most of the stack before she shifted a page to reveal an open atlas beneath. The small island of Ceylon was represented in a wash of pale green surrounded by delicate blue watercolors. Details were picked out in fine ink tracery so delicate it almost looked like scroll work. She traced the outline of the island lightly with her finger.

"Miss Danwood?"

She looked up. "Yes, Jenny?"

"You promised we might finish class outside if we all finished our essays. May we, Miss Danwood?"

"I believe I did promise that, didn't I." She made a grave show of going through the small stack of essays on the corner of her desk while the class waited in breathless anticipation. "It appears that I shall have to be true to my word."

The girls gave a muted squeal. Eva held up a hand. "That doesn't mean we will fritter the afternoon away. We must still get some work done. For that you will need your notebooks and pens."

Desks and chairs immediately began clattering. Eva had the girls line up at the door to the class. Obediently they followed her out into the

287

gardens until once again she held up her hand and turned to face them. "I need you each to find six different plant species. Name them, classify them, and draw them. Bring me your pages when you are finished."

Eva smiled as she watched the girls scatter in delighted little bunches. Of late, her certainty on a number of things had been shaken. But she still knew without a doubt that the girls she taught had been placed in her charge for a reason, and she would not waste the opportunity to impact their lives.

Without meaning to, her thoughts flew back to the day when a kind lady had found her on the streets of New York City and led her gently to a home for children. She had been so little her memory was vague though the impressions were indelible. Tender hands washing her face. Someone combing through her hair and removing the vermin. A reassuring voice soothing her as she shied away.

She knew with a certainty that she longed to be the kind voice and make a difference for other children as someone had made a difference for her. There, sitting in the shade and feeling the breeze upon her face, she sighed and began to pray. Did she really need to travel the world over to find children in need? Somewhere deep in her spirit she felt a nudge, and it seemed that she was on the brink of something.

She believed in a big God. It was possible that a blunder on Megan's part wasn't enough to thwart God's plans. What if God had allowed it all so that she could be redirected in a different path? What if the loss of the money was His plan...?

Before she could examine this novel idea too closely, a half-dozen girls bounded up to her brandishing their completed projects in the hopes of being released from class early.

The clanging of the city's fire truck woke Eva from a sound sleep that night. She bolted upright and flung back the covers. From the vantage point of her window she caught a glimpse of the long vehicle swinging around the corner. Her gaze followed it, and she realized that the smoke-smudged and hazy light of the fire was only a few blocks away. Quickly she drew on the shirtwaist and skirt she'd laid out for the next day.

In the hallway Eva shooed a few curious girls back to bed. Mrs. Collins stood in the corridor below. She looked as if she too had dressed hastily.

"I can go." Eva assured her.

"We'll both go." The headmistress threw a shawl about her shoulders, and they headed out into the night to see what they could learn. With all the wood buildings in Austin and the hot, dry winds, it wouldn't take much to send the flames hop, skip, jumping toward the school. They couldn't afford to wait. If there was any chance the girls would have to be evacuated, they needed as much notice as possible.

They were not the only ones following the fire truck. A trickle of other hushed, tense neighbors joined them, as if they had all been called out by the music of some dreadful pied piper.

It wasn't difficult to determine the correct route. The lurid blaze acted as a beacon while the acrid smoke drifted thicker in the air as they drew closer. It scratched the throat and irritated Eva's eyes. As they drew closer they had to watch for bits of hot ash fluttering in the air like malevolent snowflakes. Most people hung back, clogging the street as they milled about watching the firemen at their work and asking one another questions to which no one had reliable answers. Eva followed in Mrs. Collins's wake as she pushed to the front of the crowd, and into the opening beyond.

The Harris House, a small inn that catered mostly to traveling salesmen and other patrons with strict budgets, was ablaze. It had been a respectable sort of place three stories high and clad in clapboard with a brick stoop and starched curtains at the wide windows. Firefighters were shouting to one another and scrambling about. But as Eva got a better look at what they were doing, she realized that the activity wasn't focused on the inn. They must have written it off as a loss because they were focused on damping down the nearby buildings to ensure the flames didn't spread.

On the opposite side of the street a cluster of people huddled well behind the firefighters. Most of them were still in nightclothes—nightclothes marred by soot and smoke. Eva saw James standing among them. He seemed to be trying to offer comfort. With a gesture to Mrs. Collins, Eva made her way toward him.

In his arms he held a mite of about four years old. The poor thing was crying piteously, her tears making tracks down soot-stained cheeks. An older girl, perhaps eight, clung to his pants leg. As Eva approached, a breeze caught the flames and sent a malicious shower of sparks and smoke to choke them.

James tucked the girls closer against him, trying to shield their faces. He had never felt so helpless in all his life. He ought to have bundled them away immediately but Abbie, the elder girl, had refused to move any farther away. Her mother was still in the building. God help him, he'd never felt so useless in his life.

Eva appeared next to him, dabbing a handkerchief at her watering eyes. Wheezing and coughing, she could not immediately speak. But the girls both perked up, looking past her and back to the building. James followed their gazes to see a fireman emerging from the inferno. He was shaking his head and coughing so harshly it could be heard above the roar of the flames. Another fireman ran up to him. The first man shook his head and then allowed himself to be pulled away from the door.

The girls slumped back against him. Their sooty figures left streaks against his gray suit. He patted Lucy, the younger girl, on the tangled mop of hair, urging her to rest against his shoulder.

"What happened?" Eva asked.

James kept his voice low. "They think someone fell asleep while smoking."

Lucy refused to relax, lip quivering and eyes brimming with more tears.

Eva offered her gentlest smile. "Hello, sweetheart."

As if the kindness were simply too much to bear, the child began sobbing again as she had been when James had found the two wandering together just outside the reach of the flames.

"May I take her?"

James nodded gratefully and passed the little girl over. Eva had always had a talent with children. They responded to her. "They're sisters: Lucy and Abbie."

Lucy buried her head in Eva's neck. Eva stroked her hair and murmured soft soothing nothings into her ear. A moment later James felt a whisper of movement and saw that Abbie had also switched allegiances and now clung to Eva's skirt.

James leaned close and whispered into her free ear. "Their mother is still in there."

Eva jerked to look at him. He nodded.

Tears welled in her eyes, but she blinked them away furiously.

He knew how she felt. He'd have liked to cry to at the unfairness of it. The grief these little ones would endure because of someone else's carelessness. But they could not wallow in sorrow. Not right now.

Eva tried to persuade them to move away from the fire, but they were just as recalcitrant as they had been with him and could not be budged. They watched with hungry eyes every time there was a flicker of movement at the door.

James squeezed Eva's arm, and she nodded. No words needed to be exchanged. She would know that he needed to be doing something to alleviate the suffering around them. He managed to organize some of the onlookers. They seemed grateful to be given tasks and soon he had a stack of blankets to wrap around the shoulders of those from the hotel and a steady stream of coffee which he distributed with a liberal hand.

Mrs. Collins came to take over the coffee pouring. The light of the flames etched deep lines of worry into her face, making her appear drawn and gaunt. "A single cigarette." She shook her head at the devastation wrought.

No matter how many times he urged them away, Eva and the girls remained in vigil. A low-pitched rumble began to reverberate, and James dropped the blankets in his hands and dove for the little trio. He tried to shield them with his body as the rumble grew to a roar and a great cloud of smoke and cinders spiraled upward. The children pressed their faces into Eva, their little bodies trembling. The crash of falling timbers and brickwork mixed with the sound of shattering glass tearing the night apart.

"Down. Down. Keep your heads down." He and Eva were on their knees now, forming a cocoon around the girls. Bits of debris pelted him, and the smoke and dust from the buildings collapse was so thick he could barely breathe.

When he could raise his head again, the building was little more than a pile of rubble with three of the walls collapsed inward. James looked from Eva to the little girls to Mrs. Collins. The headmistress shook her head very slowly.

Lump high and tight in his throat, James nodded. She was right. There was no way their mother could have survived that.

Eva spoke, her voice sounding raw and constricted. "I'd like to bring them back to the Abbey."

Mrs. Collins nodded. "I think that's a good idea. We'll need to find someone to speak to, to make the arrangements. I have no idea how these situations are handled."

"I know a bit about the process. I've been working on some plans—well never mind." It was no time to go into his plans, he was just grateful to have another task to focus on. "I'll make the arrangements and clear it with the appropriate authorities."

Eva gave him a grateful look, and her voice was steadier as she addressed the children. "Come along, pets, we need to get you cleaned up and in bed. It is far too late for little girls to be out."

"I want mama." The elder girl's voice could hardly be heard above the chaos around them.

James waited to see what Eva would do. She had a choice. She could fob the girl off with excuses and false promises. Instead she crouched awkwardly, still holding the girl's sister. "Abbie, I'm afraid your mama didn't survive the fire. She's not here to take care of you, but I know she'd want someone to tuck you in tonight and make sure you're taken care of. Will you let me do that for her?" Her free hand cupped the girl's cheek with infinite tenderness.

The little girl swallowed hard, her eyes brimming with tears. "You're wrong. She's coming out of there. I know she is." She pushed at Eva's shoulder.

In her wobbly, crouched position, Eva would have toppled but for James steadying her.

Abbie ran toward the fire, but it had grown so intense that even the compulsion of her need for her mother could not fight it, and she staggered back again. Before she could fall, James scooped her up. He brought her back and set her down. All her defiance and anger had been singed away. She fell into Eva's arms, wracked with sobs.

Eva held both girls tight and let them cry. James didn't think little Lucy fully appreciated why she was crying other than her fright and tiredness. The understanding of losing her mother would come later. Curious bystanders crowded close, but Mrs. Collins kept them all moving with helpful instructions on where their aid was most needed.

James slipped away to speak to the fire chief and the police chief who were standing together in serious conference. A few inquiries about the nearest phone. A call to a friend in the mayor's office.

By the time the girls were cried out, he was back. He reached to help Eva to her feet. "I've spoken to the authorities, and they'll allow the girls to go home with you. In truth, I think they're grateful. There's nowhere else they might be taken tonight. In their infinite wisdom, the state legislators established the state orphan asylum in Corsicana, a hundred and sixty miles from here."

The girls were swaying with exhaustion, and Eva took Lucy in her arms again, while James took up Abbie. "Let me help you home."

"Thank you, James." Eva was heartsick, and if it weren't for the little girls depending upon them for help she'd have broken down in tears. As it was she breathed in deeply a couple of times and promised herself that she could cry later. As much as she wanted.

Lucy was small, but Eva had been holding her for so long that her arms had grown numb and her shoulders and back were screaming in protest. She was more than happy to let Mrs. Collins lead the way. The headmistress threaded through the crowd that continued to watch the firemen as they worked desperately to contain the blaze. As they turned the corner, a bit of a breeze caught at her and she only then realized how starved for oxygen her lungs had been. Her lips felt parched and cracked, her face like she had been turned on a spit. As they came in sight of the school, the front door was thrown open to them by a couple of anxiously waiting teachers.

James handed off Abbie, but Lucy clung to Eva, not wanting to be separated. Given what had happened, Eva could hardly blame her for clinging to someone even slightly familiar over a stranger.

With Mrs. Collins directing them all as if they were actors in a play, the little girls were hustled upstairs. They were quickly bathed to rid them of the smell of smoke and dressed in clean, white nightgowns. Their long blond hair was brushed free of tangles, and they were given mugs of hot, creamy cocoa. Then they were tucked into bed in an empty student room.

Eva kissed them both on the forehead and turned to go. Abbie grabbed for her hand. "Don't go."

Eva met the child's gaze, which was at once exhausted and anxious.

"How about I stay in the other bed here?"

Abbie nodded.

Eva stripped down to her shift and climbed under the coverlet. She fell asleep almost before her head touched the pillow.

Eva woke the next morning stiff and with a crick in her neck. She moaned softly and would have sat up but realized that she was sandwiched between two small, warm figures. Gingerly she shifted to ease the ache in her neck, careful not to wake them. It was going to be a long and painful day for them. She would let them sleep as long as possible.

It was well past nine o'clock when a gentle knock at the door roused them. Eva found she had drifted off again and she rubbed her eyes sleepily. Likewise drowsy, the girls sat up with yawns and stretches.

The door opened to reveal Mrs. Collins and a tray laden with breakfast. "Good morning, ladies. I hope you're hungry."

Lucy ate, but Abbie only picked at the food. While they ate, Eva and Mrs. Collins were able to glean that the girls had come with their mother from back East. They had been in town only a day and a half and were waiting for their father to ride in from their ranch and pick them up.

"Mama's at the ranch?" Lucy asked with her mouth full.

Abbie flared suddenly. "You're so stupid." She dropped the spoon she held and jumped off the bed, fleeing down the hall. Where she meant to go since she was unfamiliar with the Abbey, Eva had no idea. She shared a glance with Mrs. Collins, and the headmistress went after the child.

Eva gave Lucy a smile and handed her another piece of toast. "No, honey, your mama's not at the ranch." Eva could not bring herself to explain further.

Lucy seemed to have forgotten her own question in the wake of her sister's tantrum. "Is Abbie mad?"

"Yes, baby. But not at you. She's so sad, she's mad."

"I want Abbie happy."

"Me too."

While a colleague covered her classes, Eva tended the little girls throughout the day, lavishing all the care and understanding she could muster. She understood all too well the pained confusion that was twisting Abbie's emotions as well as Lucy's bewilderment. Their reactions wrung out memories of her own mother's death. Not her adoptive mother, her birth mother. Memories that she had suppressed for years began to percolate. There was no way to remove all their pain, but she did her best to minimize their fear and make sure they were cared for.

When she handed the girls over to their grieving father the following afternoon, she was both relieved and bereft. They needed to be with their family, but she would miss them, and she longed to fix everything for them. She sighed as she waved after them. She could still pray for them. God could do more for them than she ever could.

It boggled her mind that there was no home for children in Austin. No refuge for babies such as this when they were facing their most desperate need. Someone needed to do something about the situation. She would talk to Mrs. Collins.

Eight

Eva was caught in a flurry of activity as the school year wrapped up over the next week. But she couldn't forget her little charges or the other victims of the fire. To benefit all of them she recruited the support of Mrs. Collins, the mission society board, and the other teachers to put together an auction which would be held during the Abbey's graduation ball. Donations came in from all over the city, and when she wasn't frantically grading year-end papers and tests, she was busy each afternoon cataloging and organizing the items.

James stopped by a few times to update her on his progress in the investigation. He interviewed Mr. Norton, the state senator, and Mr. Kettle, the greengrocer. He left no stone unturned in his pursuit of the lost funds, but she found her attention was elsewhere. She appreciated his efforts, but the money no longer seemed to be of paramount interest. Not when she knew of people who had nothing—no home, no finances, nowhere to stay. In contrast she had all her needs met. It certainly made a girl realize that she had not been as thankful for her blessings as she might have been.

When at last the big night arrived, Mrs. Collins had to shoo her away from the long line of tables containing auction items.

Eva hurried upstairs, determined to dress for the ball quickly. It really didn't matter what she wore. No one paid her much attention, and it wasn't as if anyone would care. Besides, she had exactly one party dress to choose from. She wasn't going to be dancing, just making sure the auction ran smoothly.

Within a trice she dressed in her serviceable dark wine colored moiré gown edged in black lace. She glanced in the mirror, patted her hair and shrugged. It might be a bit matronly, but it would do.

She stepped out into the hall and stopped short as she almost ran into Mrs. Collins carrying a large box of striped pink and white.

"My dear, this was delivered for you."

"Me?" Eva accepted the box hesitantly. "What?"

"Open it," Mrs. Collins urged.

Eva blinked, her sense of duty warring with desire to see what the package contained.

"You can take a few more minutes. Everything is as ready as it will be."

"All right." Eva drew back into her room, Mrs. Collins following close behind her.

She set the box on her bed and removed the lid with gentle hands. A card lay atop the tissue paper, and she drew it out.

Megan's familiar handwriting.

> Dear E,
>   I can't bear it when you're mad at me. I will find a way to make things right, I promise.
>   ~M

Beneath the tissue paper lay the most beautiful ball gown Eva had ever seen.

Delicate mint green silk was edged with dainty ecru lace along the neckline. Almost in spite of herself she drew the gown from its wrappings. The skirt was adorned with intricate embroidered butterflies in flight, more at the bottom and tapering away as they climbed up the skirt.

Mrs. Collins gasped and stepped fully into the room. "Oh my dear, it's beautiful."

"I can't accept this."

"Why not?"

"Megan only sent it because she feels guilty and she doesn't want me to be mad at her."

"So?"

"She's trying to buy my affection."

"My dear, she already has your affection. You've been best friends since you were little bitty things."

"But what she's done—"

"It doesn't matter. You love her and she loves you. You'll find your way back. And she's trying to create a bridge. Don't throw her gesture back in her face. She likes pretty things and she wanted you to have something pretty. Don't overthink it. I assure you, she did not."

Eva smiled ruefully. "You have a point."

"Good. You will look lovely in that dress, but we must do something with your hair." She shut the bedroom door decidedly.

When Eva emerged again she felt like an entirely different young woman, and Mrs. Collins was beaming like a fairy godmother.

"I'm not overdone?"

"Not in the least. I wouldn't let you go down in anything but the best taste."

"I'm sorry, I know. I'm suddenly nervous."

"You needn't be. You know all these people, and they know you."

Eva nodded and pressed her hands against her waist. She was still the same girl she'd always been. The ever practical, ever sensible Evangeline Danwood. Just because she was dressed in something Megan might wear didn't mean that she would begin acting like her.

The guests and patrons of the school were arriving, and Mrs. Collins took her place at the head of the receiving line. Eva was immediately caught up in a whirl with teachers and students as they exclaimed over the new gown. By the time the music started she found that her dance card was full—or rather, as full as she would allow it to become. She had marked off several of the dances. There was too much to do to fritter the whole evening away. Although she had to admit that the dancing was enjoyable while it lasted.

She kept watching for James to arrive. She couldn't help wanting him to see her in the dress. Not that he would notice or care, she warned herself. But still...

When he did arrive she was so busy with the auction that she almost missed him. He caught her attention in the swirl of activity only because he was standing stock-still. Their gazes met and held as if magnetized, until someone with a question approached her. He nodded to her then, sketching a bow across the room. She reciprocated with the barest hint of a curtsey before turning away to tend her would-be customer.

James had debated long and hard about coming to the ball. His father had at last insisted that if his fiancée were present, he needed to be here as well or people might start to talk. At last he had gone up to his room to put on evening clothes though the only person he was interested in stopping from talking was his father.

Arriving late had done little to soothe his frayed temper. He loved and respected his father, but there were certain topics that he feared they would never see eye to eye about. James was starting to believe that his duty to the "success" of their family was going to be one of those areas. Despite his own misgivings he had accepted his father's judgment in that area and there had not been a single day that had passed that he had not regretted it. More and more he felt as if the Lord were telling him that the world's definition of success had nothing to do with God's definition of success. Success wasn't simply wealth, prestige, and a large congregation.

As he strode in the school's door and was swept into the crush of partygoers, he looked about for Eva. When he thought of success she was the image that came to his mind. Her teaching salary wasn't large, but that made no difference. She was a success because she was willing to follow God's leading unhesitatingly. She had enough faith to leave the results up to Him. It was a rare gift.

When he finally spotted her moving gracefully through a display of goods for auction, he stopped in his tracks. Her color was high, her eyes sparkling. She was speaking with someone over her shoulder and she smiled broadly. The dark hair which she usually kept under tight rein was piled loosely on her head with just a few tendrils brushing the nape of her neck. The breath in his throat forgot if it was coming or going.

She seemed to sense his eyes upon her, and her gaze met his. She raised her hand in a small greeting, but someone else stepped between them to speak to her and she cocked her head as she listened to whatever it was they had to say.

Mouth dry, James turned away. He needed to find Megan. They were long overdue for a serious discussion.

As busy as Eva had been, the evening had rushed by at the pace of a polka, leaving her slightly breathless and her head spinning. The bubbly, fizzing giddiness was there too. The auction raised more than five-hundred dollars for the victims of the fire. It was money that would go a long way toward replacing lost clothing and providing temporary shelter. Eva wished she could tell Abbie and Lucy about it. It wouldn't touch the deeper scars of grief and loss. But perhaps an outpouring of love and concern like this from an entire community might begin to soothe a wounded heart. Eva had some experience with that herself.

Oddly content, Eva wandered out into the cool of the gardens. Despite the lateness of the hour, the ball was still in full swing and only a handful of guests had taken their leave. So many bodies made a ballroom seem too close after awhile. In contrast, even the sultry evening breeze was refreshing.

All around, couples paraded arm in arm. Hopefully none of them students. Eva's teacher instincts kicked in, and she examined the forms she passed carefully. Not that anyone was being improper, but one couldn't be too careful when it came to protecting the reputation of a young lady, or a young ladies' academy.

Eva was about to turn back from her walk and return to the school when she heard a soft, sighing susurration from behind the nearest shrubbery. There was no mistaking the intimacy in the tone. Most definitely not something she could overlook.

She rounded the hedge with her sternest schoolmarm frown fixed firmly in place, but she stopped short as the moon illumined a pile of red curls and a perfectly scandalous embrace.

Feeling suddenly cold and fragile as ice, Eva could not seem to make herself move or even to turn away. She must have made some noise because the indiscreet couple stiffened, and Megan turned to look at her.

"Eva!"

"How could you?" The constriction of her throat shredded the words and they came out ragged.

"I love Deveraux, Eva. I've been trying to tell you that." There was no anger or challenge in Megan's voice.

"And what of James?" Everything Eva had felt over the past months seemed to boil over. She was trembling, and she could hear her voice growing louder over the ringing in her ears. "I didn't begrudge you James because I knew you. I loved you. I thought you would come to love and appreciate him as he deserves. But this disregard for him—it's too cruel. I could forgive you for breaking my heart when you accepted his suit. I can't forgive you for betraying him and breaking his heart."

"I ended it." Instead of shying away or bursting into tears, Megan reached to put a hand on Eva's arm. Eva jerked free of her touch and spun to go, but Megan's next words stopped her. "Believe me, Eva, he was even more relieved than I was when we spoke. He was never mine. He had eyes and thoughts only for you."

"What?"

Megan gave a little half shrug. "You were right all along. I couldn't go on as I was. I didn't like what I was becoming, and it was time to set things right."

"You ended the engagement?"

"James never would have, but we're all wrong for each other."

"What do you mean? You're perfect for one another. Everyone said so."

Megan shook her head. "It only seemed so on paper. Our wealth and position complemented one another, but not our personalities. Not our dreams."

Eva was having a difficult time taking in what Megan was saying.

"I do love James, but like he is my brother. Not with the kind of love I should have for a husband."

"You prefer—" Eva waved a hand at Mr. Williston, who had a smirk as long as a Texas cattle drive on his face.

"I can't help it, Eva. He's—he's like a part of myself. You wouldn't understand."

"You're probably right—"

Before she could say any more James's voice brought her up short. "There you are, Eva. I've been looking everywhere. I was hoping you'd come with me to verify that the money has been securely deposited in the safe at the mission society offices. Oh." He stopped short as he came around the corner and saw Megan and Williston. "Good evening."

"Evening," Williston drawled.

"I've just been explaining to Eva about our change in circumstances." Megan said, reaching for diplomacy for the first time in her life.

Eva wanted to box her ears, but James merely smiled. "I've been well and truly jilted."

Try as she might she couldn't find much sorrow in his countenance. And she well knew that he wasn't much of a dissembler. Could it be that he really hadn't been attached to Megan? At least not romantically?

He held his arm out to her. "Are you willing to escort me to the mission offices?" He raised a satchel in his other hand. "We ought to get this safely stowed away."

"Oh, yes." She roused herself from a brown study. "Certainly." In a fog, she turned to follow him.

"Eva?"

She looked back at Megan to find her smiling.

"I'm glad you wore the dress. It's perfect on you."

Managing only a tight smile in response, she mutely allowed James to lead her from the garden. Good manners finely loosened her tongue as they stepped onto the sidewalk. "I'm so sorry for—"

He waved away her attempted condolences. "Megan and I would never have suited. The whole idea was more an arrangement between our parents than a love affair."

"Does your father know?"

James nodded ruefully. "And he's none too pleased about it, I can tell you."

"Will he come around?"

"He'll have to, won't he?" He glanced down at her face, and the flippancy left his tone. "He doesn't like seeing everything he's worked for torn apart, but once he gets over that, he will be fine."

"I do hope so. For all his gruffness, I think he loves you very much and wants the best for you."

"You're rather perceptive, Miss Danwood."

"I pay attention."

The soft glow of the gas lamps leant a misty sort of enchantment to the tree-lined street. It was a lovely evening full of moonlight and the freshening scent of spring, with young and budding plants poking their heads from the soil. Eva was content to simply stroll by James's side and enjoy the beauty of the evening.

At last they turned onto the street that held the mission society office. Was it her imagination, or did James slow his pace even more?

"I ought to have told you sooner how nice you look in that dress. It's very pretty."

"Thank you."

"I mean, nice isn't really the word I want. I—the words always get hung up—" He stopped and turned her toward him. "What I mean is, you look beautiful."

His gray eyes were intent upon her face as if he were trying to read something in her soul. Her heart was pounding in her ears and it was difficult to breathe. She felt a bit as if she were being hypnotized. The world around them seemed to recede, leaving just her and James.

With an almost physical pain she pulled away. She couldn't do this again. Once had been bad enough. But to allow herself to plunge headlong into infatuation with him again might crush her completely.

"That's very kind of you. The dress was a gift from Megan."

He caught up with her in a single stride. "The dress is nice enough, but it's you that's beautiful."

Uncomfortable with the praise, she glanced away from him. As she did, Eva caught a glimpse of a dark blur springing forward from behind a large shrub. Gasping, she shied away, which made James stop in mid-stride. The figure plowed into James who staggered sideways and sprawled on the ground.

Having been holding James's arm, she lurched with him and almost fell as well. The man, for Eva had realized that it was definitely not some sort of wild beast, grabbed for the satchel in which James carried the auction money. James snatched it back before the fellow could get a good grip on it. He pulled it in under his arm and close to his chest.

Eva jumped out of the way of the struggling figures.

Grunting, James struggled to rise while still clutching the satchel. The attacker administered a vicious kick to his head and then to his ribs.

James gave a sharp bark of pain but did not fall again. The assailant scrabbled at him, trying to take the bag. Head tucked in turtle-like, and arm still protecting the bag for all he was worth, James's other hand clenched in a fist. It connected solidly with the man's ear. The man swore.

Eva cast about for a way to help. There must be something. The men were wrestling now, each with a fierce grip on the bag.

Eva snatched up the nearest heavy object to hand and brought a flower pot down on the attacker's head. It made a horrible thudding sound and fell to the ground where it smashed.

The man fell with it, crumpling in a heap.

Nausea threatened to choke her, but hand to her throat she swallowed it back. "Are you all right?"

Breathless, James merely nodded. He thrust the bag at her and bent over the fallen man. "Can you call the police?"

"Of course." She knew the situation could be urgent, but she lingered for a second as he removed the fellow's hat and probed the man's head with gentle fingers. She had to know the worst. "Will he be all right?"

"No blood and the skull's not broken." James looked up and met her gaze. "I think his hat softened the blow. Other than a monstrous headache, he's going to be fine."

As if to confirm what James said, the fellow groaned.

Relief washed through her as welcome as a cool drink on a hot day. She pressed her hand hard against her abdomen and breathed deeply. "Thank goodness." Then she turned and hurried to unlock the mission offices and make the call.

When the call had been made, she hurried back outside. James was helping the man on the ground to sit up. As the light from the door spilled over them, familiar features assaulted her. Deveraux Williston.

Eva couldn't claim surprise, but a wave of pity for Megan welled up within her. She hoped that her friend's infatuation was not so deep seated that it would lead her any further astray. This man would bring her nothing but misery.

A mounted patrolman arrived a moment later. He dismounted and, holding his reins loosely in one hand, strode toward them, pulling a notebook and pencil from his pocket as he did so. "Evening, folks. What seems to be the problem?"

Williston was still blinking and looking about groggily. He had one hand pressed to the back of his head. James explained what had happened.

When he was done, the officer looked to Williston. "You have anything to say to this?"

"A joke." Williston picked up his battered hat and replaced it on his head, wincing as he did so. "It was just a joke." He cast Eva a wounded look. "I thought we were friends."

"Sir, some other money recently went missing from the mission offices." James stood straight, looking more severe than Eva had ever seen him. "There was some suspicion of Mr. Williston. In light of this event, I'd like to request that his home be searched for evidence."

"That's slander." Williston managed to gain his feet, but standing there wobbly-legged and wearing his crushed hat he only managed to look ridiculous.

"Not if it's true," James pointed out.

"It's not." Williston's jaw was set at a pugnacious angle.

A police sergeant arrived on his bike, and they went through the tale again. Both officers wore identical expressions of skepticism—but toward who or what was unclear. They looked so similar that Eva wondered if they received some sort of special training upon joining the police force.

"And where is the money that was almost stolen, now?"

"I put it in the safe," Eva said. She'd added nothing to the conversation before this. "Would you like me to fetch it?"

"Yes, ma'am, I'd sure appreciate that."

The sergeant accompanied her inside as she retrieved the money, which remained nestled securely in the satchel.

While she looked on, the sergeant counted out the entire amount with steady deliberation. "Looks like it's all here."

Eva bit her tongue, reminding herself that he was trying to do his job. He led the way back outside. "I'd appreciate it if you folks would come on down to the station to make formal statements."

Sulky and defensive, Williston shook his head. "I told you this was all just a misunderstanding. Why won't you people listen to me?"

"The judge will listen, believe me." The officer gave him a little push to get him moving in the right direction.

Eva gave a little sigh, feeling distinctly overdressed for a visit to the police station. She wanted to run to Megan's side and give her a hug. As infuriated as she had been with her friend, she knew this was a wound that would bite deep. On the other hand, leaving Megan to her illusions for a few more hours could be an act of kindness. The pain would start soon enough.

When at last Eva had given her statement, she was ready to drop. It had been an exceedingly long day. And tomorrow all the graduation ceremonies were taking place. She groaned. There were so many tasks yet to be completed.

Feeling as wilted as three-day-old lettuce, Eva stood in the hall waiting for James. She had a sinking sensation that Williston was going to get away with his theft, and his attempted theft. He stuck adamantly to his story that he had been playing an ill-conceived prank. She was certain that he had been behind the earlier theft too, but they had no proof, and since Megan had been adamant that he hadn't taken the money while they were there, it was entirely possible that officials would decide that the money could have been lost and there wasn't enough evidence to prosecute Williston for either crime.

A sudden thought struck her. Eva stiffened and turned around, marching back into the sergeant's office without knocking. "The money, when it was taken, was in an envelope addressed to Mrs. Augusta Collins and there were a number of bills related to the fair with it as well. If you were to find that envelope in Megan Conroy's handwriting, or those bills, then you would have your proof."

The sergeant's eyebrows went up. "Thank you, Miss Danwood. That may indeed be helpful information."

Smiling for the first time in what seemed an age, she gave him a small nod and withdrew.

She'd done all she could. The rest would be up to providence.

James arrived even before breakfast the next morning.

Eva practically ran to the parlor. "What news?"

"Believe it or not, my silly fingerprints came in handy. It seems that the set I was able to recover from the mission society safe belonged to Williston. Since he had no business being in the safe, a judge found that suspicious enough that he signed a search warrant. Police were out at Williston's ranch at dawn. They found about fifty dollars still in the envelope with Mrs. Collins's name on it."

"Then he will be charged with theft?"

"And with the attack on us." James gave a grim little smile. "And probably anything else they can think of. Mr. Williston hasn't been making himself any friends down at headquarters."

"That's a relief. It was awful to feel that someone we knew could be stealing from the mission."

"I'm just sorry for your sake that we didn't recover more of the money."

"Ah, well. God knows what He's doing, and He was never dependant on that money to make His will come to pass."

"Eva...I wanted to—"

The door burst open, and a half-dozen red-faced young would-be graduates barreled into the room. "Miss Danwood, it's a disaster.

Someone has gotten red and blue chalk dust all over our white graduation gowns." There was a significant pause as they all turned to stare at a cringing girl at the back of the pack.

"I was only trying to make the bunting look more festive."

The other girls turned their back on what they obviously felt was a feeble excuse indeed. "Mrs. Collins thought you might be able to help."

"You all sound like a Greek chorus." Eva accepted one of the proffered gowns and examined it closely. "Yes, I think we can get this out in a trice. Do excuse me, James."

He nodded, and she led the girls away.

"Girls, I need you to each bring your dresses down to the laundry immediately. I have to find some rubbing alcohol."

The girls scattered, and Eva quickly took care of the issue. She was just leaving the laundry again when she caught a glimpse of a suit-clad Frank Mallory leading Mrs. Collins gently by the hand out onto the back porch. She couldn't resist following. She dearly wanted to see Mrs. Collins's reaction to his surprise.

When she had come home the night before, the grounds had been a positive hive of activity, with some three-dozen or so men and boys laboring to bring Frank's vision to life.

As she stepped outside, she had to admit Frank had achieved something bordering on the miraculous.

The tennis court and croquet green were pristine in the morning sun. Beyond these the broad vista of empty yard had been transformed into a fairytale glade. Flowers blossomed in profusion among tall trees and little saplings. Springy grass paths wandered lazily among the trees and wrought iron benches dotting the grounds at intervals. It all looked like it had been in place for a hundred years and yet it was utterly new and so very beautiful. Not just the outcome, but the thought that had inspired it.

Eva maneuvered so that she could see Mrs. Collins's face.

"Oh, Frank, this is—I don't know what to say." Tears filled her eyes.

Eva had never seen Mrs. Collins moved to tears before. Frank looked decidedly worried. "If it ain't to your liking, I can get all the fellows here again tonight to put things back."

"Don't you dare. This is the most beautiful—the most wonderful thing anyone has ever done for me. I don't know how you managed. Walk me through it."

He held out his arm, and Eva thought for sure that she saw a small velvet ring box that he was fiddling with in his other hand. A Texas-sized smile lit her face, and she withdrew. They were going to want privacy for this next bit.

On top of the usual graduation frenzy, the whole school was buzzing with word of the transformation of the grounds. Eva and the other teachers practically had to barricade the doors to keep the girls from tumbling out into the magical new garden as girl after girl noticed that something exciting had taken place overnight.

And somehow the school grapevine, always notable for its efficiency, had picked up on Eva's nighttime adventure as well. She could hardly go a dozen steps in any direction before she was stopped and asked for the details. She finally sought refuge in her room on the pretext that she needed to dress for the graduation ceremony.

Her solitude was short lived. She had been in her room less than a quarter of an hour before a knock sounded at her door. A teary-eyed Megan stood on the other side.

Without a word, Eva enfolded her friend in a hug. Megan began sobbing in earnest then. Ever practical, Eva led her inside, closed the door on any prying eyes, and produced a handkerchief.

Megan gulped. "Deveraux has been arrested."

"I know. Are you going to be okay?"

"How could I have been so deceived?"

Eva soothed damp hair away from her face. "Meg, you always seek to see the best in everyone. Of course you wished to think well of him."

Megan raised her face to Eva's piteously. "I shouted at my father when he told me what Deve—Mr. Williston had done. Oh, Eva, I'm so ashamed."

Eva gave her another hug. "Have you apologized to your father?"

"Yes."

"Then I'm sure all is forgiven."

"But I don't know if I can forgive myself. How can I ever trust my own judgment again?"

Eva drew her over to the desk and had her sit in the chair. She took her mirror down and handed it to Megan. "Hold this." Then she began taking down the girl's disarranged hair. "I think God has been teaching me something about this too, Meg. We can't always trust our own judgment. It is often flawed. That's why we need to seek His guidance rather than consulting our own desires when we plan our futures."

"But you're always so good—and I'm not. I make a hash of things."

"God didn't call me to Ceylon."

Meg spun around in her chair, causing Eva to pull her hair cruelly. "What!"

"Sit still." Eva took her by the shoulders and turned her firmly back around. She met her eyes in the mirror. "I was so intent on my plan that God was forced to desperate measures to get my attention."

"But you've wanted to go for years."

"Yes. I've wanted to go."

"So you think Deveraux—Mr. Williston was arrested to keep me from marrying him?"

"Mr. Williston was arrested because he was a thief. You have to decide whether that will keep you from marrying him."

"He's not at all the man I thought he was. He used me and he stole from my friends. I would never marry him."

"Then you have had a very lucky escape." Eva patted the last roll of curls into place and secured it with a hairpin. "There. Good as new."

"Can you imagine if I had married him and found out what he was really like later?" Megan shivered. "That would have been awful." She stood and gave Eva a hug. "Thank you, and I'm sorry. You could have socked me in the nose when you saw me just now, but you hugged me instead. I don't know what I'd ever do without you. Is it okay to say that I'm happy you're not going to Ceylon?"

Eva snorted a laugh. "Yes, but not too loudly. My pride is still smarting a little."

Together they hurried down the stairs, and Megan took her seat among the guests while Eva hurried to the cloakroom where the other teachers had assembled. Several moments later the processional music sounded and the teachers all trooped out with a glowing Mrs. Collins at the head of the column.

The graduation ceremony was as elegant as all of the Austen Abbey events. White roses and lilies abounded. The graduates wore white dresses, and they all looked so grown-up as they glided in and took their places in the front row. It was all over in a flash, and Eva found herself at the post-graduation tea with a cup and saucer in hand. Frank was in attendance looking tall and distinguished in a broadcloth suit. He kept smiling, but was that simply politeness to the graduates, or something else? She had been trying to sneak a peek at Mrs. Collins's ring finger. She was just so sure—

"Eva?" James stood at her elbow, smiling.

"Hello, James." She craned her neck trying to see as Mrs. Collins moved behind James and out of her line of sight.

"Can I talk to you for a moment?"

Returned to the ground with a solid thud, Eva's heart gave a great lurch and the contents of her teacup began to shiver ever so slightly. There was no polite way to refuse. She nodded instead and allowed him to lead her out of the parlor and onto the verandah.

"I've talked to all the board members and they've agreed that we can start a new campaign for your mission to Ceylon. I'm confident that we will be able to raise just as much, if not more. I have some plans—"

"Oh no."

He lowered his voice. "Are you all right? You don't look—I thought you'd be pleased."

"James, it's so good of you, but I can't accept. This may sound flighty and inconstant of me. But I'm not going to Ceylon. That was only ever my dream. Not God's calling."

"Not going?"

Biting her lip, she shook her head. "I feel as if God is telling me to be useful where He has put me."

He seemed not to have heard. "You're not going."

She tried to explain, hoping that he wouldn't be too disappointed. "We need a home for children in Austin. Somewhere they can go when there is a desperate need, as there was after the fire. And someone who will care for them."

Without saying a word James drew her off the verandah and out into the newly minted garden.

"Please don't be angry, James. It's not that I've abandoned what God would ask me to do. It's the opposite. I realized that all my plans for Ceylon were of my own manufacture. I was running away."

He stopped abruptly and turned to face her. "From what?"

Her face felt as if it were on fire. But the compulsion of his gaze could not be denied. "From you. From your engagement to Megan."

He groaned and clasped her hand. "Oh my sweet Eva. I'm so sorry to have caused you even a moment's pain. My engagement to Megan was a mistake. I bowed to the pressure of our families rather than following the inclinations of my heart."

Speech was impossible.

He led her to one of the discreetly placed benches. "I have a great deal to account for. I should have called the police into the investigation of the lost money immediately. I didn't in part because of pride. But in truth it was because I wanted a reason to stay near you. To continue to see you."

Eva began to cry. It seemed like a cruel twist of the knife to hear his declaration—the very thing she had so ardently desired—but know that it could not be. "Your father would never allow it. James, there are things you don't know about me."

"I know everything I need to know."

"No you don't." She sucked in a deep breath. "I was brought west on an orphan train when I was four or five. I'm not even sure when exactly I was born. The people you knew as my parents, the Danwoods, they adopted me and raised me as their daughter. It was the best thing that could have happened to me. They were wonderful people, and if they had been my real parents then I'm sure your father might have no objection even if they were not as rich as he'd have liked."

He gave a little huff. "It's all right. I've always known you were adopted."

She carried on. "I was born in New York City. I have no idea who my father was. But my mother was addicted to opium. We both worked in a sweatshop all day and into the evening, but we barely had enough to keep body and soul together. My mother would go out at nights when there was no money for opium. Sometimes she would bring men back to our apartment and I would hide."

James said nothing, but she could see the tightness in his jaw and she wasn't sure if his silence was anger or condemnation.

She took a deep breath and plunged on. "One night the man she brought home—he got angry. He strangled her to death while I was hiding not ten feet away."

James squeezed her hand. Eva refused to look him in the eye or she would have given way to tears. She rushed on, "I spent some time, several weeks, on the streets. I ate food from garbage cans or I stole it. My memories are of cold, and hunger, and degradation. Until this beautiful lady in a fine gown saw me. And she stopped in the street and knelt down and spoke to me. To my shame I can't even really recall what she looked like. I have only impressions of clean gentle hands smoothing my lice-infested hair. A soothing voice. She operated a children's home, and she took me home with her and cleaned me up, and found me a place on the orphan train.

"I'm going to do the same thing for other children. I am uniquely able to understand what they might be suffering and offer help. I have to help." She had run out of words, unable to adequately explain the fire of conviction that seemed to come from her very bones.

Wordlessly, James pulled a letter from the inner pocket of his jacket and handed it to her.

Still unsure of how he had responded to her admissions, she set down the cup and saucer she still held and accepted the letter. What she read made her heart seem to stop in her chest. He had used his influence with the mission office and local churches to propose a children's home.

He took her hands in his, crushing the letter between them. "I can't help but see this as a confirmation that we belong to each other. I've not shown myself to best advantage in my relationship with you. But if you'll step out on faith, I will prove my constancy. Despite my past, Eva, will you marry me?"

"James, I don't think you've heard what I said."

He shook his head. "None of that matters to me. I love you. I want to marry you."

"But you surely don't understand—my mother was drunken and lewd. She entertained men and she stole things. And I loved her and I miss her, even though my earliest memories are of violence and filth. I understand that she may have felt she had no choice. She was trying to survive, and she was in the grip of a terrible addiction, but I can't easily forgive her. I have no idea who my family beyond my mother might have been. I—"

He grasped her hand. "It's me. I'm your family."

Tears stung her eyes. "Your father will never accept me. I can't put you in that position."

He took her shoulders and made her look at him. "You are not responsible for the things your mother did."

"No but I am a product of them."

"You are a product of your own choices and behavior. You are not your mother."

"It's easy for you to say that now. But the only thing that separates me from her is my choices each day."

He reached for her, taking her upper arms and drawing her nearer to him. "That's exactly what I'm saying. Your choices have made you into a strong woman of deep faith. And I am willing to take you on faith. Just as I hope you will take me on faith." He grimaced. "I could turn out to act just like my father."

This was so preposterous it gave her pause. "No you couldn't."

"I could as easily as you could turn out like your mother."

A weight somewhere around her chest seemed to shift and slide away. She looked deep into James's eyes to find them brimming with sincerity and longing. He didn't see her as anything but desirable. "All right." Her words sounded almost husky. "We'll take one another on faith."

He drew her into an embrace and kissed the top of her head. "Eva, I love you. I've been foolish. You may have a broken past, but I almost broke our future. Thank God I've come to my senses at last. My heart is and always will be yours. Please marry me."

"You're certain?"

"More than I've ever been about anything."

He kissed her then. She felt like she was sliding, sinking into a space that was at once thrilling and deeply familiar. This was right. He was right for her. And she for him. Broken though they might be, they were going to let God use them to do a new work in Austin.

She could hardly wait.

Don't Miss Volume 1 of *Austen in Austin*

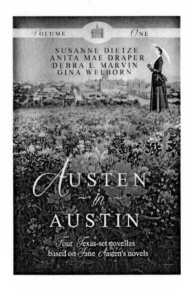

If I Loved You Less by Gina Welborn
based on *Emma*

A prideful matchmaker examines her own heart when her protégé falls for the wrong suitor.

Romantic Refinements by Anita Mae Draper
based on *Sense and Sensibility*

A misguided academy graduate spends the summer falling in love . . . twice.

One Word from You by Susanne Dietze
based on *Pride and Prejudice*

A down-on-her-luck journalist finds the story of her dreams, but her prejudice may cost her true love . . . and her career.

Alarmingly Charming by Debra E. Marvin
based on *Northanger Abbey*

A timid gothic dime-novel enthusiast tries to solve the mystery of a haunted cemetery and, even more shocking, why two equally charming suitors compete for her attentions.

CPSIA information can be obtained
at www.ICGtesting.com
Printed in the USA
FFOW04n2210200117
31497FF